Further Praise for

THE NECKLACE AND OTHER STORIES

"It is a great relief to lovers of literature (including, I should imagine, the ghost of Guy de Maupassant) to read Sandra Smith's superb translation of thirty of the three hundred Maupassant stories in an arrangement suggesting a culture of relation, of structure, of completion. It is my hope that this sensitive selection of Maupassant's stories will move readers on to Maupassant's novels, a literary form with not only the tyronic connection of shorter to longer, but the attributes of range, development, and consummation."

—RICHARD HOWARD

"Sandra Smith has a sterling reputation for shaking the dust off previous translations while leaving the meaning and the feeling of a classic work of literature intact. She has succeeded again with this beloved collection of stories by Maupassant and delivered in English the vitality and excitement his first nineteenth-century French readers appreciated."

—ALICE KAPLAN,
John M. Musser Professor of French at Yale University
and author of *Dreaming in French*

"Maupassant may have known more about venality and lust than any writer of his age, and yet he remains an artist of surprising delicacy and extraordinary range. The nightmares of war and of one's own obsessions, the sorrows of marriage and love, the delusions of pride: Sandra Smith's masterful new translations show it all to us, in a language as supple and brisk as the French original itself, and her selection includes many little-known masterpieces alongside some of his most famous tales."

—MICHAEL GORRA,
author of *Portrait of a Novel:
Henry James and the Making of an American Masterpiece*

LIVERIGHT PUBLISHING
CORPORATION

A DIVISION OF W. W. NORTON & COMPANY

Independent Publishers Since 1923

NEW YORK • LONDON

The
NECKLACE
and
OTHER STORIES

......

MAUPASSANT
for Modern Times

GUY DE
MAUPASSANT

......

Translated by

SANDRA SMITH

THIS BOOK IS DEDICATED

TO MY FORMER STUDENTS

at the University of Cambridge

who enjoyed many of these stories

and encouraged me to translate them.

Copyright © 2015 by Sandra Smith

First published as a Liveright paperback 2016

For information about permission to reproduce selections from this book,
write to Permissions, Liveright Publishing Corporation,
a division of W. W. Norton & Company, Inc.,
500 Fifth Avenue, New York, NY 10110

For information about special discounts for bulk purchases, please contact
W. W. Norton Special Sales at specialsales@wwnorton.com or 800-233-4830

Manufacturing by RR Donnelley, Harrisonburg
Book design by Barbara Bachman
Production manager: Louise Mattarelliano

Library of Congress Cataloging-in-Publication Data

Maupassant, Guy de, 1850–1893
[Short stories. Selections English]
The necklace and other stories : Maupassant for modern times / Guy de
Maupassant ; translated by Sandra Smith. — First edition.
pages cm
ISBN 978-0-87140-368-1 (hardcover)
I. Smith, Sandra, 1949– translator. II. Title.
PQ2349.A4E5 2015
843'.8—dc23
2015013246

ISBN 978-1-63149-189-4 pbk.

Liveright Publishing Corporation
500 Fifth Avenue, New York, N.Y. 10110
www.wwnorton.com

W. W. Norton & Company Ltd.
Castle House, 75/76 Wells Street, London W1T 3QT

1 2 3 4 5 6 7 8 9 0

CONTENTS

TALES OF THE SUPERNATURAL   227

GUY DE MAUPASSANT: A Chronology   317

TRANSLATOR'S
INTRODUCTION

G UY DE MAUPASSANT (1850–1893) IS ONE OF THE MOST WELL-respected writers of French literature, as well as one of the most prolific. In his short lifetime, he wrote some three hundred short stories and six novels. Along with his mentor, Gustave Flaubert, Maupassant is considered one of the progenitors of the modern short story, having influenced the likes of Chekhov and Maugham, Babel and O'Henry. Studied and appreciated by every French-speaking student and scholar, Maupassant has not, however, been fully acknowledged for his genius by modern English readers, as the majority of the existing translations of his stories are extremely dated.

The translation of any classic work automatically results in a debate that fascinates translators and critics alike: do we respect the established language, structure, and punctuation of the original text or do we update these elements to lessen the perceived distance between the work and a modern audience? Is it a requirement of a "good" translation to respect the original punctuation, even if punctuation is used differently in the two languages involved? Is it "permissible" to modernize the language of earlier centuries when we translate, or is that "sacrilege"?

In this collection, I decided along with my Liveright editor, Robert Weil, to update Maupassant's nineteenth-century style so that modern readers could fully appreciate him as a master of the short story genre. Modernizing language does not mean that certain elements from the original are necessarily lost. It does, however, pose very particular challenges to the translator. It is necessary to be sensitive to the poetic elements employed by an author—assonance, alliteration, lyricism, imagery, etc.—yet at the same time explore parallels in a modern idiom.

As Ollie Brock, the acclaimed British translator, wrote:

> Our standards for translations usually conceal an impossible demand. We want a clone of the original, only made of different stuff. . . .
>
> Imagine trying to cook the same meal twice with different ingredients. You wouldn't manage it . . . If we could get away from our reverence for the holy "original," we might be freer to enjoy the work of translators. In music, it is perfectly acceptable to arrange a previously written piece for a new instrument or ensemble. When Franz Liszt transcribed a Beethoven concerto for solo piano, no one was about to complain that they couldn't hear the violins. He was writing for the piano. In the days before recording, new arrangements of orchestral works had a practical purpose, too: to make them manageable for a salon quartet or accessible to those who lived far from the concert halls. Rather like translators, arrangers were adapting works in order to widen their audiences.[1]

Literal word-for-word translations rarely work. It is essential to find *emotional* equivalents to create the atmosphere of a text so that the reader is transported to a different time and place. I have chosen to do this partly by keeping the titles, names of characters, place names, and so on in French, adding brief explanatory footnotes when necessary. But a reader must also be able to savor being immersed in that other time and place without feeling bewildered, a stranger in a foreign land. Translation is so important because it allows us to discover and understand other worlds, cultures divided both by time and geography that we might never have access to otherwise.

---

1   "Translators Shouldn't Be Slaves to the Holy 'Original,'" *The New Statesman*, September 5, 2012.

The stories in this collection were chosen to represent three of Maupassant's predominant interests: nineteenth-century French life; the Franco-Prussian War of 1870–71 and its devastating indelible effects on French society; and the supernatural, a realm that fascinated Maupassant greatly. Each story within these three parts functions as both a historical document and an embodiment of universal, timeless emotions. Each section—*Tales of French Life*, *Tales of War*, and *Tales of the Supernatural*—is preceded by a brief commentary to provide background information to help the reader appreciate the context, while also furnishing details of Maupassant's life and how his experiences are reflected in his writing.

It was, of course, extremely difficult to decide which tales to include in *The Necklace and Other Tales*, given that Maupassant wrote over three hundred during his all-too-brief lifetime. I have therefore tried to include some of his most famous stories as well as some that are not as well known, but illustrate his mastery of the genre. While each story is obviously different, stylistic elements recur like *leitmotifs* in all of them—elements that contributed not only to Maupassant's reputation as a master of the short story but also to the very definition of what a modern short story is.

A younger protégé of Gustave Flaubert,[2] who had risen to international prominence if not notoriety in the 1850s, Maupassant adopted much of his mentor's modernistic style. Flaubert, who is mainly famous for his novels, was among the first to incorporate so many innovative elements in his writing that James Joyce acknowledged him as an influence, a precursor to "stream of consciousness." In fact, it is almost impossible to read some stories in *Dubliners* without sensing a certain stylistic kinship between early Joyce and Maupassant. Readers of *The Necklace and Other Stories* will also note an unusual use of punctuation, the contrast between very long, flowing sentences and paragraphs and very short factual ones, and the technique known as "free indirect speech," where we feel we are hearing a character's thoughts. In post-twentieth-century literature these

---

2   Gustave Flaubert (1821–1880) is best known for his novel *Madame Bovary*, but he also wrote a collection of three tales, *Trois Contes*, experimenting with various approaches to the short story genre.

elements are very common, but in the twilight of the nineteenth century they were very new indeed.

Maupassant's narrative structure also challenged the conventional forms of his day. He treats us, for example, to many twists in plot and surprise endings. His stories frequently leave us with a moral lesson, often achieved by brief aphorisms, in *The Necklace*, for example: "How little it takes to make us or break us!"

Maupassant displays great skill and humor in replicating some of his characters' varying accents and dialects, which is another great challenge to a translator. Stylistically, this is extremely important, for the contrast between satirical, humorous language and a serious theme provides a delicate balance that is often the basis for empathy and irony.

The most challenging element of translation, however, is how to deal with puns and plays on words. In fact, it is sometimes totally impossible. In such cases, I have provided brief footnotes to explain the meaning and context for anyone who does not read French. In *Boule de suif*, one of Maupassant's most famous novellas, the title character's name literally translates as "Ball of Fat" or "Ball of Suet"; but she is described as voluptuous, and food plays an important part in the tale, so I have chosen to call her "Butterball." There again, Maupassant's play on words and his choice of names provide humor and create empathy.

Yet another significant stylistic element is the author's use of a framework in which many of the stories are told by one person to another, or else directly, in the first person, to the reader. His most famous supernatural tale, *Le Horla*, is written in the form of a diary. In this way, Maupassant reinforces the idea that the genre originates from an oral tradition in which people told each other stories long before any were written down to be read.

It is my hope that the stories in *The Necklace and Other Stories* will reintroduce Maupassant's great talent to a modern audience: he is an author who deserves to be rediscovered.

—Sandra Smith
New York, 2014

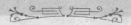

TALES OF
FRENCH LIFE

I N *TALES OF FRENCH LIFE,* MAUPASSANT EXPLORES THE BROAD swath of nineteenth-century existence among the lower, middle, and upper classes, depicting life in both the urban sophistication of Paris and the agrarian countryside. Whether rich or poor, urban or rural, the people in these stories share common concerns: the importance of family life, survival in the face of poverty, maintaining status and social approval, and how love affects us all. The title story, *The Necklace,* undoubtedly his most famous, is a perfect example of several recurrent themes: a loveless marriage made out of necessity, the plight of the working classes and how a desire for luxury and social status can have devastating effects.

Maupassant's own life and experiences obviously influenced his work. Born into a wealthy family, he spent most of his childhood in Normandy, close to a rural farming region. Several of the stories in this section—for example, *A Day in the Country* and *The Baptism*—are set in this area and provide an insight into the rural world of his time.

Some of these stories—*The Journey* and *Mademoiselle Pearl* in particular—center on the theme of unrequited love, and are both serious and touching. Others, such as *My Uncle Jules* and *The Umbrella*, take a more humorous approach to the kind of arguments and bitterness that occur in certain marriages. As Maupassant's own parents separated when he was only eleven years old, it is likely he experienced the consequences of marital strife firsthand.

THE NECKLACE

S HE WAS ONE OF THOSE PRETTY, CHARMING YOUNG WOMEN
born into a working-class family, as if by some error of fate. She had
no dowry, no hopes, no way of ever becoming famous, understood, loved
or the wife of a rich, distinguished man; she agreed to be married off to a
low-ranking clerk in the Ministry of Public Education.

She dressed simply, as she couldn't afford any jewelry, and was
unhappy, feeling she had lowered herself; for women belong to neither a
caste nor a race: their beauty, grace and charm are their heritage and family background. Their innate sensitivity, instinct for elegance and adaptable minds are their only hierarchy, and these qualities can transform an
ordinary young woman into the equal of any high society lady.

She suffered continually, feeling she had been born to enjoy every
possible delicacy and all sorts of luxury. She suffered from the shabbiness of her home, the cheapness of the walls, the worn-out armchairs,
the ugly upholstery. All of these things—things that any other woman of
her class would not have even noticed—tortured and infuriated her. The
sight of the young Breton girl who did the housework in her humble home
aroused in her a sense of despairing regret and lost hope. She dreamed
of silent antechambers hung with Oriental tapestries, lit by high, bronze
candelabra, and two tall valets in breeches who fell asleep in wide armchairs, drowsy from the heavy heat of the stove. She dreamed of great
reception rooms decorated in antique silk, expensive furniture displaying
priceless curios, and intimate, charming sitting rooms filled with the lin-

gering scent of perfume, perfect for long conversations in the late afternoon with her closest friends, famous, sought-after men whose attention
was envied and desired by every woman.

When she sat down to supper at their round table with its tablecloth
that hadn't been changed in three days, opposite her husband who opened
the tureen and said, absolutely delighted, "Ah! Beef stew! I can't think of
anything better than that . . . ," she would be dreaming of elegant din-
ners, sparkling silverware, tapestries on the walls with ancient figures and
extraordinary birds in a fairy-tale forest. She would dream of exquisite
dishes served on wonderful china, of compliments whispered to her that
she would return with the smile of a sphinx while savoring the delicate
pink flesh of a trout or the wings of a grouse.

She had no expensive dresses, no jewelry, nothing. And those were
the only things she liked; she felt she had been born for such things. She
would have so desired to be attractive, envied, seductive and elegant.

She had one wealthy friend, a former school friend from the convent;
but she didn't want to visit her any more because she suffered so much
when she had to go home. And she would cry for days at a time, from sadness, regret, despair and distress.

ONE DAY, HER HUSBAND came home holding a large envelope and
looking triumphant.

"Here," he said, "this is for you."

She eagerly tore open the envelope and took out an engraved invitation:

"The Minister of Public Education and Madame Georges Rampon-
neau request the pleasure of the company of Monsieur and Madame Loisel
at the Ministry on the evening of Monday, January 18."

Instead of being delighted, as her husband had hoped, she angrily
threw the invitation down on the table.

"And what do you expect me to do with that?"

"But, my dear, I thought you'd be happy. You never go out and this is an opportunity, and a fine one, at that! It was incredibly difficult to get the invitation. Everyone wants one; it's very sought after and they don't give out many to the clerks. Everyone important will be there."

She looked at him, annoyed and impatient, and asked:

"And what am I supposed to wear to go to something like that?"

He hadn't thought of that.

"What about the dress you wear to go to the theater?" he stammered. "I think it looks very nice . . ."

He fell silent, stunned when he realized his wife was crying. Two large tears flowed slowly down her face, from the corners of her eyes to the corners of her mouth.

"What's wrong?" he muttered. "What's wrong?"

Through an intense effort, she managed to get control of herself; she wiped her damp cheeks and calmly replied:

"Nothing. It's just that I have nothing to wear and so I can't go to the ball. Give your invitation to a colleague whose wife has fancier clothes than me."

He felt sorry for her.

"Come now, Mathilde," he said, "how much would a suitable outfit cost, something you might wear again for other occasions, something very nice but simple?"

She thought for a few seconds, working out the figures in her mind and thinking of how much she could ask for without getting a horrified response and immediate refusal from her thrifty clerk.

She hesitated, then finally replied:

"I'm not exactly sure, but I think I could manage with four hundred francs."

He went a little pale, for he had put aside exactly that amount to buy a rifle and treat himself to some hunting parties on Sundays the following summer, in the Nanterre region, with a few friends who were going down there to shoot larks.

"Fine," he said, nonetheless, "I'll give you four hundred francs. But make sure you get a beautiful dress."

....

THE DAY OF THE BALL was approaching and Madame Loisel seemed sad, anxious, nervous. But she had her dress.

"What's wrong?" her husband asked one evening. "You've been acting very strangely for three days now."

"I'm upset because I have no jewelry," she replied. "Not a single thing to wear. I'll look as poor as anything. I would almost rather not go to the reception."

"You can wear some fresh flowers," he replied. "That's very chic at this time of year. For ten francs you can have two or three magnificent roses."

She was not convinced.

"No . . . there's nothing more humiliating than looking poor in the company of wealthy women."

"You're so silly!" her husband exclaimed. "Go and see your friend Madame Forestier and ask her to lend you some jewelry. You're close enough to her to do that."

She cried out in joy.

"That's true. It hadn't even occurred to me."

The next day, she went to her friend's house and explained why she was so upset.

Madame Forestier went over to her armoire, took out a large jewelry box, brought it over and opened it.

"Take anything you like, my dear," she said to Madame Loisel.

First she looked at some bracelets, then a string of pearls, then a Venetian cross, beautifully crafted with gold and gemstones. She tried on the necklaces in front of the mirror, hesitated, unable to bring herself to take them off and give them back.

"Do you have anything else?" she kept asking.

"Of course. Keep looking. I don't know what kind of thing you like."

Suddenly, she found a superb diamond necklace in a black satin box. And her heart began to beat faster with unbridled desire. Her hands shook as she held it. She put it around her neck, over her high-collared dress, and stood entranced by her image in the mirror.

"Could you lend me this," she finally asked, hesitantly, full of anguish. "Just this?"

"Certainly; of course."

She threw her arms around her friend's neck, gave her a big kiss, then ran off with her treasure.

THE DAY OF THE BALL CAME. Madame Loisel was a great success. She was prettier than anyone else, elegant, gracious, smiling and mad with joy. All the men were watching her, asking her name, trying to get introduced. All the attachés from the Ministry wanted to waltz with her. The Minister himself noticed her.

She danced as if exhilarated, carried away, intoxicated with pleasure, lost in a dream, in the triumph of her beauty, the glory of her success, in a sort of cloud of happiness created by all the compliments, the admiration, the great desire she aroused, created by the complete and utter victory that felt so sweet to a woman's heart.

She left about four o'clock in the morning. Her husband had been sleeping in an empty little sitting room with three other men whose wives were having a wonderful time.

He threw her coat over her shoulders, the one he'd brought with him for going home, an inexpensive coat she wore every day, whose shabbiness clashed with the elegance of her ball gown. She felt this and wanted to rush away so she wouldn't be noticed by the other women who were wrapping themselves up in expensive furs.

Loisel stopped her:

"Wait here. You'll catch cold outside. I'll go and get us a carriage."

But she refused to listen to him and quickly rushed down the stairs. When they were in the street, there were no carriages, so they tried to find one, calling out after any driver they saw going by in the distance.

They walked down toward the Seine, shivering and feeling hopeless.

On the quayside, they finally found one of those old cabs you only see in Paris after dark, as if they were too ashamed of their scruffiness to be out during the day.

It took them back to their door on the Rue des Martyrs, and they sadly went upstairs to their apartment. To her, it was all over. And all he could think about was that he had to be back at the Ministry at ten o'clock.

She took her coat off in front of the mirror, so she could see herself in all her glory one last time. Suddenly, she let out a cry. The diamond necklace was gone!

"What's wrong?" her husband asked; he was already half undressed.

She turned toward him, terrified:

"I . . . I . . . I've lost Madame Forestier's necklace."

He stood up, panic-stricken:

"What! . . . But how! . . . That's impossible!"

And they looked in the folds of her dress, in her coat, in the pockets, everywhere. They couldn't find it.

"Are you sure you still had it when we left the ball?" he asked.

"Yes. I remember touching it in the lobby of the Ministry."

"But if you'd lost it in the street, we would have heard it fall on the ground. It must be in the cab."

"Yes, probably. Did you get its number?"

"No. Did you see what it was?"

"No."

They stared at each other, devastated. Then Loisel got dressed.

"I'll go back to where we started and retrace our steps to see if I can find it," he said.

Then he left. She sat there in her evening gown, without the strength to go to bed, collapsed in a chair, depressed, with no fire lit, her mind a blank.

Her husband came back at about seven o'clock. He hadn't found it.

He went to the police station, to the newspapers to offer a reward, then to the cab companies, everywhere, in fact, where there was even a glimmer of hope.

She waited all day long, in the same state of fear in the face of this horrible disaster.

Loisel came back that evening; his face was gaunt and pale; he had found out nothing.

"You must write to your friend," he said, "and say you broke the clasp of the necklace and that you're getting it fixed. That will buy us some time."

She wrote as he suggested.

BY THE END OF the week, they had lost all hope.

And Loisel, who had aged by five years, said:

"We must find out how we can replace the necklace."

The next day, they went to the jewelry shop whose name was inside the case. The jeweler looked through his books:

"I did not sell this necklace, Madame; I must have only sold the case."

So they went from one jeweler to another, looking for a necklace that was just like the one they had lost, trying to remember it in detail, both of them in a terrible state, miserable and distressed.

In a boutique near the Palais-Royal, they found a diamond necklace that was exactly what they were looking for. It cost forty thousand francs. They could have it for thirty-six thousand.

They asked the jeweler not to sell it for three days. And they made it a condition that he would take it back, for thirty-four thousand francs, if they found the one they'd lost before the end of February.

Loisel had eighteen thousand francs that his father had left him. He would have to borrow the rest.

And borrow he did, asking a thousand francs from one person, five hundred from another, five louis[1] here, three louis there. He signed for loans, accepted ruinous conditions, dealt with moneylenders and every kind of loan shark. He committed himself for the rest of his life, risked signing for loans without even knowing whether he could pay them back.

---

1   A gold coin worth about 20 francs.

And terrified by the suffering to come, by the horrible poverty he was about to face, by the prospect of all the physical deprivation and moral torment he was going to suffer, he went to the jeweler's, put thirty-six thousand francs on the counter, and bought the new necklace.

When Madame Loisel brought the necklace back to Madame Forestier, she said coldly:

"You should have returned it sooner; I might have needed it."

She didn't open the case, as her friend had feared she might. What if she noticed the substitution, what would she have thought? What would she have said? Wouldn't she have thought Madame Loisel was a thief?

MADAME LOISEL CAME TO know the horrible life of the poor. She accepted her fate at once, however, and bravely. That terrible debt must be paid. And she would pay. They let their maid go; they moved; they rented an attic.

She did all the heavy housework and the disgusting chores in the kitchen. She washed the dishes, breaking her pink nails scouring greasy pots and the bottoms of saucepans. She washed the dirty linen, the shirts and the dishcloths, and dried them on a clothesline; she carried the garbage down to the street every morning and brought back the water, stopping at every floor, out of breath. And dressed like a working-class woman, carrying a basket, she went to the fruit stall, the grocer's, the butcher's, bargaining, being sworn at, trying to hold on to every single penny of what little money she had.

Every month, they had to pay off certain debts, renew others, ask for more time.

Her husband worked evenings, doing a merchant's accounts, and late at night, he often made handwritten copies of documents for five cents a page.

And this life lasted ten years.

By the end of ten years, they had paid everything off, everything, at outrageous repayment rates and with compound interest.

Madame Loisel looked old now. She had become heavy, hard and harsh, like every other poor woman. With unkempt hair, ragged clothes and raw hands, she talked in a loud voice while throwing buckets of water on the floor to wash it. But sometimes, when her husband was at the office, she would sit beside the window and think of that wonderful evening so long ago, of the ball where she had been so beautiful and so popular.

What would have happened if she hadn't lost that necklace? Who knows? Who can know? How strange and unpredictable life is!

How little it takes to make us or break us!

ONE SUNDAY, SHE WENT for a walk along the Champs-Elysées, to relax after working so hard all week; she suddenly noticed a woman who was taking a child for a walk. It was Madame Forestier, still young, still beautiful, still attractive.

Madame Loisel was filled with emotion. Should she speak to her? Yes, of course. And now that she had paid, she would tell her everything. Why not?

She went over to her.

"Hello, Jeanne."

The other woman did not recognize her, and was surprised to be spoken to in such a familiar way by this working-class woman.

"But . . . Madame! . . . I don't . . . You must be mistaken," she stammered.

"No. It's me, Mathilde Loisel."

Her friend let out a cry.

"Oh! . . . my poor Mathilde, but you've changed so much!"

"Yes, I've had a very hard life since I saw you last; and I've been very poor, and miserable . . . and all because of you!"

"Because of me! But how?"

"Do you remember that diamond necklace you lent me to go to the ball at the Ministry?"

"Yes. What about it?"

"Well, I lost it."

"No! You gave it back to me."

"I gave you back a necklace that was exactly like it. And it's taken us ten years to pay it off. You know that wasn't easy for us, for we had nothing . . . It's finally over, and I'm really glad."

Madame Forestier stopped.

"Are you saying that you bought a diamond necklace to replace mine?"

"Yes. So you never noticed! They were virtually identical."

And she smiled with proud, naive joy.

Madame Forestier, deeply moved, took her hands.

"Oh, my poor Mathilde! But my necklace was a fake. It was worth no more than five hundred francs!"

MY UNCLE JULES

A POOR OLD MAN WITH A WHITE BEARD ASKED US FOR SOME money. My friend, Joseph Davranche, gave him one hundred sous.[1] I was surprised.

"This poor old beggar reminds me of a story," he said. "I'll tell it to you; I'm haunted by the memory of it. This is what happened."

MY FAMILY WAS ORIGINALLY from Le Havre; we weren't rich. We got by, that's all you could say. My father had a job; he came home late from the office and didn't earn much. I had two sisters.

My mother suffered a lot because they were always worried about money, and she said many bitter things to her husband—thinly disguised, sly reproaches. The poor man would then make a gesture that truly distressed me. He would wipe his forehead with his open hand as if wiping away sweat that wasn't there. I could feel his helpless pain. We spent as little as possible on everything; we never accepted an invitation to dinner because we couldn't return it; we bought food at reduced prices, the leftover stock from the shops. My sisters made their own dresses and had long discussions about the price of a piece of braid that cost fifteen centimes a yard. Our normal meals consisted of greasy soup and beef cooked

---

1   One sou was equal to 5 centimes and there were 100 centimes to a franc, so he gave the beggar 5 francs.

in many different ways. Apparently, this is a healthy and comforting kind of food; I would have preferred anything else.

Whenever I lost a button or tore my pants, there was a terrible argument.

But every Sunday, we all got dressed up in our best clothes and went for a walk along the pier. My father, in a frock coat, a large hat and gloves, offered his arm to my mother, who was decked out like a ship on a special holiday. My sisters, always the first ones ready, waited anxiously until it was time to go; but at the last moment, someone always discovered a stain my father forgot to remove from his coat, and it had to be quickly taken out with a rag soaked in benzine.

My father waited in his shirtsleeves, still wearing his big hat, until the task was done, while my mother rushed to finish the job, having adjusted the glasses she wore for close work and taken off her gloves so she didn't get them dirty.

We set out with great ceremony. My sisters walked in front, arm-in-arm. They were of marriageable age, and my parents showed them off around the town. I walked to the left of my mother, and my father to her right. And I can still remember the ostentatious demeanor of my poor parents during these Sunday walks, their serious faces, their stern appearance. They walked solemnly, standing tall, their legs straight, as if their attitude reflected a matter of extreme importance.

And every Sunday, when they saw the great ships returning from unknown, foreign lands, my father invariably said the very same words:

"Ah! What a surprise it would be if Uncle Jules were on that ship!"

My Uncle Jules was my father's brother, and after being the black sheep of the family, he became their only hope. I'd heard them talk about him ever since I was a child, and the thought of him had become so familiar to me that I believed that if I saw him, I would recognize him instantly. I knew all the details of his existence right up until the day he left for America, even though everyone spoke about that earlier part of his life in whispers.

He had, so it seemed, behaved very badly, that is to say, he frittered away some money, which is the greatest of all crimes in a poor family. In rich families, if a man who has money spends it on having a good time, he is "being silly." They just smile and say he likes to live it up. In needy families, a boy who forces his parents to make a dent in their savings is a good-for-nothing, a rascal, a scoundrel!

And this difference is fair, even if the behavior is the same, for it is only the consequences of an action that determine its seriousness.

In brief, Uncle Jules had reduced the inheritance my father had been counting on, after having spent every single penny of his own.

He had been sent to America, as was done in those days, on a merchant ship going from Le Havre to New York.

Once he arrived, my Uncle Jules set himself up as some sort of salesman, and he soon wrote to say he was earning a bit of money and that he hoped to make up for the wrong he had done to my father. That letter had a great impact on the family. Jules, whom they said was not worth a damn, suddenly became an honest, sensitive young man, a true Davranche, with as much integrity as any Davranche.

Moreover, one of the captains told us he had rented a large shop and was making a lot of money.

A second letter, two years later, read: "My dear Philippe, I am writing so that you don't worry about my heath, which is good. Business is going well. I am leaving tomorrow for a long trip to South America. You may not hear from me for several years. Don't worry if I don't write to you. I will return to Le Havre once I have made my fortune. I hope that it will not take too long, and that we will one day be happily living close to each other again . . ."

That letter became the family's Gospel. Any excuse to read it, to show it to everyone.

And, in fact, it had been ten years since we'd heard from Uncle Jules; but my father's hopes grew with each passing day; and my mother often said:

"When that kind Jules comes back, our situation will be different. Now there's someone who knew how to make his way!"

And every Sunday, as he watched the large black steamers approaching from the distance, belching out streams of smoke into the sky, my father would always say the exact same thing:

"Ah! What a surprise it would be if Uncle Jules were on that ship!"

And we almost expected to see him waving a handkerchief, shouting: "Ahoy there! Philippe."

They had fabricated a thousand plans around this guaranteed return; we were even going to use our uncle's money to buy a little house in the country, near Ingouville. I believe that my father might have actually started negotiations about it.

My eldest sister was then twenty-eight; the other was twenty-six. They couldn't find husbands, which was very sad to everyone in the family.

A suitor finally asked to marry the younger one. He wasn't rich but he had a job and was an honorable man. I've always believed that showing him Uncle Jules's letter one evening was what ended his hesitations and convinced the young man to make the decision.

His proposal was eagerly accepted, and it was agreed that after the wedding, the whole family would go on a little trip together to Jersey.[2]

Jersey is the ideal vacation spot for poor people. It isn't far; you cross the sea on a steamship and you're in a foreign country, as this little island belongs to the English. So a Frenchman only has to spend two hours on a boat to treat himself to the experience of a neighboring race of people and to study the customs, quite deplorable actually, of this island under the protection of the British flag, as ordinary people would describe it.

This trip to Jersey became the focus of all our attention, the only thing we looked forward to, our perpetual dream.

We finally set off. I can picture it as if it were yesterday: the steamer heating up at the Granville dock; my father, amazed, supervising the loading of our three bags; my anxious mother taking the arm of my unmarried sister, who seemed lost after the departure of the other one, like a chick who's the only one left in the brood; and behind us the newlyweds, who always kept well back, which made me turn my head around quite often.

The steamer whistled. Here we were, on board, and the ship left the pier, sailing along a sea as flat as a green marble table. We watched the

---

2   The largest of the Channel Islands, British Crown dependencies off the French coast.

coastline disappear into the distance, as happy and proud as anyone who does not travel often.

My father held his stomach in under his frock coat, which, that very morning, had carefully had all its stains removed, and he gave off the odor of benzine like on the days we went for our outings, which always made me think of Sundays.

Suddenly, he noticed two elegant ladies being offered some oysters by two gentlemen. An old sailor in tattered clothes opened each shell with a quick flick of a knife and handed them to the gentlemen, who in turn passed them to the ladies. The ladies ate them in a very refined way, holding the shell with a delicate handkerchief and bringing their lips forward so as not to stain their dresses. Then they drank the water with a quick little movement and threw the shell into the sea.

My father, without a doubt, was enthralled by this sophisticated act of eating oysters on a moving ship. He found it respectable, refined, superior, and he walked over to my mother and sisters and asked:

"Would you like me to get you some oysters?"

My mother hesitated, because of the expense; but my two sisters accepted at once. "I'm afraid I'll get an upset stomach," my mother said, sounding annoyed. "Just get some for the children, but not too many, you'll make them sick."

Then she turned toward me and added:

"As for Joseph, there's no need; boys shouldn't be spoiled."

And so I stayed with my mother, finding this disparity unfair. I watched my father ostentatiously lead his two daughters and his son-in-law toward the old sailor in tattered clothes.

The two ladies had just left, and my father told my sisters how to eat the oysters without spilling the water; he even wanted to show them how it was done and took hold of an oyster. Trying to imitate the ladies, he immediately spilled the liquid all over his coat, and I could hear my mother murmur:

"Can't he stop being so childish."

Suddenly, my father seemed upset; he took a few steps back, stared at his family huddled around the sailor shelling the oysters, then quickly came over to us. He looked very pale, with a peculiar expression in his eyes.

"It's extraordinary," he said quietly to my mother, "extraordinary how much that man opening the oysters looks like Jules."

"Which Jules?" my mother asked, shocked.

"Well . . . my brother . . . ," my father continued. "If I didn't know he was well set up in America, I'd really think it was him."

"You're mad!" my mother muttered, aghast. "Since you know it can't be him, why say such a stupid thing?"

But my father was insistent:

"You go and look at him, Clarisse; I'd rather you judge with your own eyes."

She stood up and went over to join her daughters. I also looked at the man. He was old, dirty, full of wrinkles and never looked up from his task.

My mother came back. I could see she was shaking.

"I think it *is* him," she said very quickly. "Go and try to get some information from the Captain. But make sure you're careful; we don't want that scoundrel to end up our problem!"

My father walked away, and I followed him. I felt strangely moved.

The Captain was a tall, thin gentleman with long sideburns who walked up and down the gangway looking important, as if he were in charge of the mail ship to the Indies.

My father approached him with great formality, asking him questions about his profession, accompanied by many compliments.

"What is Jersey known for? Its products? Its population? Customs? What kind of soil?" etc. etc.

You would have thought they were talking about the United States at the very least.

Then they talked about the ship we were on, the *Express*, then he finally got to the crew.

"You have someone here who shells the oysters," my father finally said, at last, sounding anxious. "Do you know anything about the old man?"

The captain, who was getting irritated by this conversation, replied dryly:

"He's an old French tramp I found in America last year, and I brought him home. It seems he has relatives in Le Havre, but he doesn't want to go back to them because he owes them money. His name is Jules. Jules Darmanche or Darvanche, something like that. Apparently, he was rich for a while over there, but you can see what he's reduced to now."

My father turned white.

"Ah! Ah! I see . . . , very good . . . ," he managed, looking distraught. "I'm not surprised . . . Thank you very much, Captain."

And he left, while the sailor watched him walk away in surprise.

He went over to my mother looking so upset that she said:

"Sit down; everyone will notice that something's wrong."

He fell onto the bench.

"It's him," he stammered, "it's really him!"

Then he asked: "What are we going to do?"

"We have to keep the children away from him," she replied quickly. "Since Joseph knows everything, he can go and get them. We must be particularly careful that our son-in-law suspects nothing."

My father looked completely dismayed. "What a catastrophe!" he murmured.

"I've always thought that thief would come to nothing and end up a burden on us!" my mother continued, suddenly furious. "As if you'd expect anything else from a Davranche!"

And my father wiped his forehead with his open hand as he always did when his wife criticized him.

"Give Joseph some money right now, so he can go and pay for the oysters. All we need is to be recognized by that beggar. Just imagine what people would think. Let's get over to the other end of the ship and make sure that man doesn't come near us!"

She stood up, and they walked away after giving me a hundred-sous coin.

My sisters were surprised, as they were waiting for my father. I said that Mama had felt a little seasick.

"How much do we owe you, Monsieur?" I asked the man shelling the oysters. What I wanted to say was "Uncle."

"Two francs and fifty centimes," he replied.

I handed him the hundred sous and he gave me my change.

I looked at his hand, the poor, wrinkled hand of a sailor, and I looked at his face, an old, unhappy face, sad, overworked, and I said to myself:

"That's my uncle, Papa's brother, my uncle!"

I gave him ten sous as a tip. He thanked me:

"God bless you, young man!"

He sounded like a poor man accepting charity. I thought he must have been a beggar over in America!

My sisters stared at me, astounded by my generosity.

When I gave the two francs back to my father, my mother was surprised and asked:

"They bought three francs worth? . . . That isn't possible."

"I gave him ten sous as a tip," I said in a firm voice.

My mother started and looked me straight in the eyes:

"You're mad! Giving that person, that scoundrel ten sous!"

She stopped herself after my father gave her a look, gesturing toward their son-in-law.

Then no one said anything.

In front of us, on the horizon, a purplish shape seemed to emerge from the sea. It was Jersey.

As we were approaching the dock, I felt an intense longing in my heart to see my Uncle Jules one more time, to go over to him, to say something consoling, something kind.

But no one was eating oysters any more, so he had disappeared, undoubtedly down into the squalid hold where this poor wretch lived.

And we returned home on the Saint-Malo boat, so we wouldn't run into him again. My mother was worried sick.

I never saw my father's brother again!

And that is why you will sometimes see me give one hundred sous to beggars.

THE PROTECTOR

HE NEVER WOULD HAVE DREAMED OF COMING SO FAR! THE son of a bailiff in the provinces, Jean Marin, like so many others, had come to study law in the Latin Quarter. In the various cafés where he'd become a regular customer, he made friends with several loud-mouthed students who went on and on about politics while drinking beer. He became smitten with them and obstinately followed them from café to café, even paying for their drinks when he had any money.

He became a lawyer and took on cases that he lost. Then one morning, he read in the papers that one of his former friends from the Latin Quarter had just been appointed a Député.[1]

He became his faithful dog again, the friend who does the unpleasant chores, gets things going, the person you send for when you need him without doing any favors in return. Then, because of some incident in Parliament, the Député became a Minister; six months later, Jean Marin was appointed a Conseiller d'Etat.[2]

AT FIRST, HE WAS so full of pride that he nearly went crazy. He would walk down the streets so everyone could see him, as if they could guess how important he was just by looking at him. He found a way to say who

---

1   The approximate equivalent of a U.S. Congressman in the French Parliament.
2   A senior member of the Conseil d'Etat–Council of State.

he was to the shopkeepers whose stores he frequented, the newspaper salesman, even the carriage drivers, managing to bring it up for the slightest reason:

"I'm a Conseiller d'Etat, you know . . ."

Then, quite naturally, because of his innate dignity, out of professional necessity, given his duty as an influential and generous man, he felt an imperious need to become a protector, a patron.

He offered his support to everyone, whenever the occasion presented itself, and with boundless generosity.

Whenever he met anyone he knew while walking along on the boulevards, he would go up to them, looking delighted, shake hands, ask how they were, then, without waiting for them to question him, he would say:

"I'm a Conseiller d'Etat, you know, and completely at your service. If I can help you in any way, please do not hesitate to ask. In my position, one has great influence."

Then he would go into the café with the friend he'd just run into and ask for a pen, some ink and a piece of paper—"Just one, waiter, it's to write a letter of recommendation."

And he wrote ten, twenty, fifty letters of recommendation a day. He wrote them at the Café Américain, Bignon's, Tortoni's, the Maison Dorée, the Café Riche, the Helder, the Café Anglais, the Napolitain, everywhere, absolutely everywhere. He wrote them to all the government officials, from the Justices of the Peace right up to the Ministers. And he was happy, utterly happy.

ONE MORNING WHEN HE was leaving his house to go to the Council Chambers, it began to rain. He thought about taking a cab, but decided against it, and started walking down the street.

The rain was coming down in torrents, flooding the sidewalks and the streets. Monsieur Marin had to take shelter in a doorway. An old priest was already there, an old priest with white hair. Before he became a Conseiller d'Etat, Monsieur Marin did not like the clergy at all. But ever since a cardinal had politely consulted him on a complicated matter, he treated them with respect. The rain continued to pour down, forcing the two men further inside, to take shelter in front of the concierge's lodge and avoid getting splashed. Monsieur Marin, who was always itching to talk to show off, said:

"This is horrible weather, Father."

The old priest nodded:

"Oh! Yes, Monsieur, it's very unpleasant when you only have a few days in Paris."

"Ah! Have you come from the provinces?"

"Yes, Monsieur. I'm just passing through."

"It really is very unpleasant to have it rain when you only have a few days in the capital. We officials who live here all year round, we think nothing of it."

The priest didn't reply. He looked at the street; the rain seemed to have eased up a bit. Then, suddenly making a decision, he lifted up his cassock to step over the streams of water, the way women raise their skirts.

Seeing he was about to leave, Monsieur Marin cried out:

"You'll get drenched, Father. Stay a few minutes; it will stop."

The priest hesitated, waited, then said:

"It's just that I'm in a rush. I have an urgent meeting."

Monsieur Marin felt sorry for him.

"But you'll get absolutely drenched. May I ask where you're going?"

The priest seemed to hesitate, then replied:

"I'm going in the direction of the Palais-Royal."

"In that case, if you will allow it, Father, let me share my umbrella with you. I'm going to the Council Chambers. I'm a Conseiller d'Etat, you know."

The old priest raised his head and looked at the man beside him.

"Thank you, Monsieur," he said. "With pleasure."

So Monsieur Marin took his arm and they started walking. He directed him, watched over him, gave him advice.

"Be careful of that stream, Father. And be especially careful of the carriage wheels; they can sometimes cover you in mud from head to foot. Watch out for the umbrellas of the people passing by; there's nothing more dangerous for the eyes than the tips of them. The women are particularly insufferable; they pay no attention to where they're going and always jab you in the face with their parasols or umbrellas. And they never have any consideration for anyone else. You'd think they owned the city. They take over the streets and the sidewalks. I think they've been very badly brought up, I do."

And Monsieur Marin started to laugh.

The priest didn't reply. He kept walking, slightly bent over, stepping over the puddles with care so he wouldn't get his boots or cassock muddy.

"So you've come to Paris for a little break, have you?" Monsieur Marin asked.

"No," the priest replied, "I've come on business."

"Ah! Is it anything important? Would you mind if I asked what it's about? If I can help you in any way, I am at your disposition."

The priest appeared embarrassed.

"Oh! It's just a small personal matter. A little problem with . . . with my Bishop. You wouldn't find it interesting. It's a . . . a Church matter . . . an . . . ecclesiastical issue."

Monsieur Marin pressed him.

"But that's exactly the kind of thing that the Council deals with. So do let me help."

"Yes, I'm going to the Council Chambers too, Monsieur. You really are very, very kind. I have to see Monsieur Lerepère and Monsieur Savon and Monsieur Petitpas as well, perhaps."

Monsieur Marin stopped in his tracks.

"But they're my friends, Father, my best friends, excellent colleagues, delightful men. I'll give you a letter of recommendation for all three of them, a very good one at that. You can count on me."

The priest thanked him, apologized profusely, and stammered endless words of thanks.

Monsieur Marin was delighted.

"Ah, you can boast of having some very good luck, Father. You'll see, you'll see; thanks to me, your matter will go like clockwork."

They reached the Council Chambers. Monsieur Marin took the priest up to his office, offered him a chair in front of the fire, then sat down at his desk and started to write:

"My dear colleague,

Allow me to recommend to you most highly a venerable and particularly worthy and deserving priest, Father . . ."

He stopped:

"What is your name, please?"

"Father Ceinture."

Monsieur Marin continued writing:

". . . Father Ceinture, who requires your services regarding a little matter that he will explain to you. I am pleased to have this opportunity, my dear colleague . . ."

And he ended with the customary compliments.

When he'd finished writing the three letters, he handed them to his protégé, who left after endless declarations of gratitude.

MONSIEUR MARIN DID SOME WORK, went home, spent a quiet day, slept peacefully, woke up in a good mood and had the newspapers brought to him.

The first one he opened was very left wing. This is what he read:

OUR CLERGY AND OUR GOVERNMENT OFFICIALS

We could never finish listing the damaging acts of the clergy. A certain priest, Father Ceinture, convicted of conspiracy against the present government, accused of such disgraceful acts that we cannot even mention them, suspected, moreover, of being a former Jesuit who has become a simple priest, suspended by a Bishop for reasons confirmed to be unmentionable, and summoned to Paris to give an explanation of his conduct, has found an ardent defender in one Marin, a Conseiller d'Etat, who was not afraid to provide this ecclesiastical criminal with the most glowing letters of recommendation to his colleagues, all the Republican officials.

We would call the Minister's attention to the unspeakable attitude of this Conseiller d'État ...

Monsieur Marin leaped up, got dressed and rushed to see his colleague, Petitpas.

"Well really; you must have been mad to recommend that old conspirator to me!" he said.

Monsieur Marin was beside himself.

"But no ... you see ... I was deceived," he stammered. "He looked like such an honest man. He played me ... he played me shamefully! Please, convict him; give him a harsh sentence, a very harsh sentence. I'll write a letter. Tell me who I should write to about convicting him. I'll go and see the Public Prosecutor and the Archbishop of Paris, yes, the Archbishop ..."

And he rushed over to Monsieur Petitpas's desk, sat down and started writing:

"Monseigneur, it is my honor to bring to Your Grace's attention the fact that I have recently been the victim of the intrigues and lies of a certain Father Ceinture, who took advantage of my trusting nature.

"Misled by the statements of this clergyman, I was ..." etc., etc.

Then he signed the letter, sealed it, and turned to his colleague.

"You see, my dear friend, let this be a lesson to you," he said. "Never give a letter of recommendation to anyone."

THE JOURNEY

I

WHEN THEY LEFT CANNES, THE TRAIN COMPARTMENT WAS FULL; everyone was chatting; they all knew each other. When they passed Tarascon, someone said: "This is where people get murdered." And they started talking about the mysterious, elusive killer who had been giving himself the occasional thrill for the past two years by murdering a passenger on a train. Everyone made assumptions, offered an opinion; the women shuddered and looked out at the pitch-black night, frightened they might suddenly see a man's face appear at the compartment door. And they began telling terrifying stories of horrible events, of coming face to face with madmen on an express train, of hours spent sitting opposite a suspicious person.

Each of the men knew a story that made him look like a hero; each of them had intimidated, beaten to the ground and strangled some evildoer in amazing circumstances, with exemplary coolness and daring. A doctor, who spent every winter in the Midi, also wanted to tell a story:

"I'VE NEVER HAD THE chance to test my courage in such situations," he said, "but I knew a woman, one of my patients who is now dead, who had the most extraordinary thing in the world happen to her, and it was also the most mysterious and the saddest imaginable.

"She was Russian, the Countess Maria Baranova, a very great lady and exquisitely beautiful. You know how very stunning Russian women are, at least, how stunning they seem to us with their delicate noses, fine mouths, close-set eyes—eyes of an indefinable color, a grayish-blue—and their detached gracefulness that seems almost harsh! They have something wicked and seductive about them, haughty yet sweet, tender but severe, altogether charming to a Frenchman. Perhaps, in the end, it is only the differences between our cultures and natures that make me see so many things in her."

For several years, her doctor had tried to convince her to go to the South of France, as she was in danger of dying from a chest condition. But she stubbornly refused to leave St. Petersburg. Finally, last autumn, thinking there was nothing more he could do for her, the doctor warned her husband, who immediately ordered his wife to leave for Menton.

She took the train and was alone in a compartment; her servants were in a different one. She sat next to the window, rather sad, watching the countryside and villages go by, feeling very isolated, very abandoned in this life, with no children, virtually no family, a husband whose love for her had died, and who had forced her to leave for the other end of the world without going with her, just as he would send a sick valet to the hospital.

At every station, her servant Ivan came to see if his mistress needed anything. He was an old man who had been with the family for many years; he was blindly devoted to her, prepared to carry out any order she gave him.

Night fell; the train raced along at top speed. She couldn't sleep; she was excessively upset. Suddenly, the thought occurred to her to count the money her husband had given her when she'd left: French gold coins. She opened her small bag and poured all the shining money out onto her lap.

But a cold rush of air suddenly whipped across her face. Surprised, she looked up. The door to her compartment had just opened. The Countess Maria, flustered, quickly threw a shawl over the money spread out across her dress and waited. A few seconds passed, then a man appeared;

he was wearing a tuxedo but no hat: he was panting, and he was injured. He closed the door, sat down, looked over at his neighbor with a gleam in his eyes, then wrapped his bleeding hand up in a handkerchief.

The young woman thought she would faint from fear. This man had surely seen her counting her gold coins and had come to rob and kill her.

He never stopped staring at her, out of breath, his face contorted, no doubt ready to pounce on her.

"Madame," he suddenly said, "don't be afraid!"

She could not reply, unable to open her mouth, listening to her pounding heart and the buzzing in her ears.

"I am not a criminal, Madame," he continued.

Still she said nothing, but she made a sudden movement and as her knees came closer together, her money began to fall onto the carpet like water flowing down a drainpipe.

The man, surprised, looked at the stream of coins and immediately bent down to pick them up.

Terrified, she stood up, spilling her entire fortune onto the ground, and ran toward the carriage door to hurry out onto the platform. But he understood what she intended to do, rushed forward, grabbed her, put his arms around her and forced her to sit down. Holding her by her wrists, he said: "Hear me out, Madame, I am not a criminal, and I will prove it by picking up all of your money and giving it back to you. But I am doomed, condemned to death, if you do not help me cross the border. I can't tell you anything else. We're going to pass the Russian border in an hour and twenty minutes. If you refuse to help me, I am lost, even though, Madame, I have never killed anyone, never robbed anyone, never done anything that could be considered dishonorable. I swear this to you. I can't tell you anything else."

He got down on his knees and collected all the gold coins that had fallen underneath the seats, even finding the money that had rolled furthest away into the corners. Then, when the little leather bag was full once more, he gave it to his neighbor without saying another word, and went to sit down on the other side of the compartment.

Neither of them moved. She sat motionless, said nothing, weak with terror but calming down little by little. The man remained absolutely still; he sat very tall, staring straight ahead; he was extremely pale, as pale as a corpse. Every now and again, she glanced quickly toward him, then very quickly away. He was about thirty years old, very handsome, and looked like a true gentleman.

The train sped through the darkness, its heartrending cries tearing through the night, sometimes slowing down, then rushing ahead at great speed. Then, suddenly, it whistled several times and stopped completely.

Ivan came to the door to see if she needed anything.

Countess Maria, her voice trembling, looked at her strange companion one last time, then spoke to her servant brusquely: "Ivan, you're to go back home to the Count; I won't be needing you any more."

Taken aback, the man looked very surprised.

"But . . . Barine . . ."[1] he muttered.

"No," she continued, "you won't be going with me; I've changed my mind. Here, take this money to pay for your return journey. Now give me your hat and coat."

The old servant was frightened but took off his hat and coat, silently obeying, as always, accustomed to the sudden desires and unpredictable whims of his masters. Then he left, tears in his eyes.

The train started to move again, speeding toward the border.

Then the Countess Maria said to her neighbor:

"These things are for you, Monsieur, you are Ivan, my servant. I have only one condition: you must never speak to me, never say a single word to me, not to thank me, not for any reason whatsoever."

The stranger bowed without saying a word.

Soon they stopped again and official inspectors in uniform got on the train. The Countess handed them her papers.

"That is my servant, Ivan," she said, pointing to the man sitting opposite, at the other end of the compartment. "Here is his passport."

The train set off again.

All night long, they were alone together, and said not a single word.

---

1   Alternate Russian title for Countess.

When it was morning, they stopped at a German station and the stranger got up to go out onto the platform.

"Forgive me for breaking my promise, Madame," he said, standing at the doorway, "but I have deprived you of your servant and it is only fair that I replace him. Do you need anything?"

"Go and get my maid," she replied coolly.

He went to get her. Then disappeared.

When she went to get some refreshments, she saw him watching her from a distance. They arrived at Menton.

II

THE DOCTOR FELL SILENT FOR A MOMENT, THEN CONTINUED:

One day, when I was seeing clients in my office, a tall young man came in.

"Doctor," he said, "I have come to ask you for news of the Countess Maria. Even though she does not know me at all, I am a friend of her husband."

"She is dying. She will not return to Russia."

And this man suddenly began to sob, then stood up and staggered out as if he were drunk.

That very evening, I told the Countess that a stranger had come to ask me about her health. She seemed moved and told me the story I have just told you.

"This man whom I do not know at all," she added, "is like my shadow, following me everywhere; I see him every time I go out. He looks at me so strangely, but he has never spoken to me."

She thought for a moment, then continued:

"In fact, I would bet that he is outside my window right now."

She got up from her chaise longue, went over to the window, pulled back the curtain and pointed to the very man who had come to see me; he was sitting on a bench along the promenade, his eyes raised upward toward the villa. He saw us, stood up and walked away without once turning to look back.

And so, I was witness to a sad and surprising thing: the silent love between these two people who did not know each other at all.

He loved her, yes, he did, and with the devotion of a wild animal she had rescued, grateful and loyal until death. Every day, he came to see me and asked: "How is she?", understanding I had guessed everything. And he cried horribly when he saw her grow weaker and paler each day.

"I have only spoken to this remarkable man once," she told me, "yet I feel as if I've known him for twenty years."

Whenever they met, she returned his greeting with a charming, serious smile. I felt she was happy—she was so alone and knew she was dying—I felt she was happy to be loved this way, with respect and loyalty, so extremely romantically, with such unlimited devotion. And yet she was faithful to her dignified determination and so obstinately refused to allow him to visit her, to know his name, to speak to him. "No, no," she would say, "that would ruin our strange friendship. We must never meet."

As for him, he too was surely a kind of Don Quixote, for he did absolutely nothing to try to get closer to her. He wished to keep the absurd promise he had made on the train to never speak to her, right until the bitter end.

During the long hours of her illness, she often got up from her chaise longue and opened the curtain to see if he was there, opposite her window. And when she had seen him, sitting motionless on the bench, she would go back to bed with a smile on her face.

She died one morning, at about ten o'clock. As I was leaving her villa, he came over to me, his face distraught; he already knew.

"I would like to see her for a moment, with you present," he said.

I led him by the arm back into the house.

When he reached the dead woman's bedside, he took her hand and held it to his lips in an endless kiss, then ran out like a madman.

THE DOCTOR FELL SILENT for a moment before continuing:

"And there you have, I am certain, the most unusual story of a train journey that I know. I must say that men are very strange when they are madly in love."

One of the women murmured softly:

"Those two people were not as mad as you might think . . . They were . . . they were . . ."

But she couldn't say any more; she was crying too much. We changed the conversation to calm her down, so we never found out what she wanted to say.

MADEMOISELLE PEARL

I

WHAT A STRANGE IDEA I HAD, TRULY, TO CHOOSE MADEMOISELLE Pearl as Queen that evening.

Every year, I go to my old friend Chantal's house on January 6, to celebrate.[1] My father, who was his closest friend, used to take me there when I was a child. I continued the tradition, and will certainly continue it for the rest of my life, as long as there is still a Chantal in this world.

The Chantals, moreover, have a very unusual lifestyle: they live in Paris as if they were living in Grasse, Yvetot or Pont-à-Mousson.[2]

They own a house set in a little garden near the Paris Observatory. They live there as if they were in the provinces. They know nothing about Paris; the real Paris, they have no idea what it's really like. They are far away, so very far away! Sometimes, however, they go on a journey, a long journey. Madame Chantal goes out on a "shopping spree," as it's called in the family. This is how the shopping spree works:

Mademoiselle Pearl, who holds the keys to the kitchen cabinets (for the linen closets are overseen by the lady of the house herself), Mademoiselle Pearl alerts Madame Chantal to the fact that they are nearly out of sugar,

---

1 The tradition in France is to celebrate Epiphany (January 6) by eating a special cake called the *Galette des Rois*, the cake of kings. A little charm is hidden in the cake and whoever gets it is considered to have good luck; the "King" then chooses a "Queen," or vice versa.

2 Places that are all considered very provincial.

or there are no more canned goods, or there is hardly anything left at the bottom of the coffee bag.

Thus forewarned and able to prevent a full-scale famine, Madame Chantal inspects what remains, writing everything down in a notebook. Then, after adding many numbers, she begins some long calculations followed by lengthy discussions with Mademoiselle Pearl. They do, however, end up agreeing on the quantities of everything they will need for three months: sugar, rice, prunes, coffee, jam, cans of peas, beans, lobster, salt and smoked fish, etc., etc.

After that, they decide on the day they will go shopping; they set out, in a horse-drawn carriage, a carriage with a roof rack, and go to a sizable shop owned by a grocer who lives on the other side of the bridges, in the new part of the city.

Madame Chantal and Mademoiselle Pearl go on this journey together, in secret, and come back at suppertime, exhausted but still excited, having being jolted about in the carriage, whose roof is piled high with packages and bags, as if someone were moving into a new house.

To the Chantals, the entire section of Paris located on the other side of the Seine makes up the new part of the city, an area inhabited by strange, noisy, barely respectable people who throw their money out the window, spending their days indulging in extravagances and their nights at parties. From time to time, however, the family takes their young ladies to the theater, to the Opéra-Comique or the Comédie française,[3] as long as Monsieur Chantal's newspaper recommends the play.

The young women are now nineteen and seventeen years old; they are both beautiful girls, tall and cheerful, very well brought up—too well brought up—so well brought up that they go unnoticed, as if they were two pretty dolls. Never would it occur to me to pay attention to them, or to court the Chantals' daughters; they are so unsullied that you barely

---

3   Today the Opéra-Comique is called the Théâtre national de l'Opéra-Comique; both this theater and the Comédie française are known for putting on serious operas and literary works.

dare speak to them. You're almost afraid to say hello in case it is deemed inappropriate.

As for their father, he is a charming man, highly educated, very open, very cordial, but someone who loves peace, calm, tranquility above all else; he has greatly contributed to mummifying his family in order to live as he wishes: in stagnant immobility. He reads a lot, enjoys chatting and is very sensitive. The absence of contact with others, of mixing with people and dealing with conflict has given him a very delicate skin, a moral skin. The slightest thing sets him off, upsets him and causes him anguish.

The Chantals do have relationships with others, though, but very limited relationships, chosen with care from within their area. They also exchange visits with relatives who live far away two or three times a year.

I always have dinner at their house on August 15 and January 6.

I consider this my duty, just as taking Communion at Easter is obligatory for Catholics.

On August 15, a few friends are invited, but on January 6, I'm the only stranger.

II

AND SO, THIS YEAR, LIKE EVERY OTHER YEAR, I WENT TO HAVE dinner at the Chantals' house to celebrate Epiphany.

According to the custom, I embraced Monsieur Chantal, Madame Chantal and Mademoiselle Pearl, and gave a long bow to Mademoiselle Louise and Mademoiselle Pauline. They asked me a thousand things about what was happening in town, politics, what people thought about the Tonkin Affair[4] and our representatives. Madame Chantal, a heavy woman whose every idea gives me the impression of being squared off like a freestone, has the habit of ending every political discussion by saying: "All that is a bad omen for the future." Why have I always imagined

---

4   The assassination of a French colonial official in 1883 led to troops being sent to Hanoi to reassert the French protectorate threatened by China. Until this was resolved in 1885, the ongoing conflict was a source of intense political debate.

that Madame Chantal's thoughts are square? I have no idea; but everything she says takes that shape in my mind: a square, a large square with four equal angles. There are other people whose ideas always seem round to me, and moving as fast as a hoop. As soon as one of those people start saying something about any subject, it starts rolling, it takes off, coming through in ten, twenty, fifty round ideas, big ones and little ones that I can picture running one after the other, as far as the eye can see. Other people have pointed ideas . . . But none of that really matters.

We sat down to dinner as always, and the meal ended without anyone saying a thing worth remembering.

When it was time for dessert, they brought in the Galette des Rois. Now, every year, Monsieur Chantal was King. Whether that was due to endless good luck or a family tradition, I have no idea, but he inevitably got the charm in his piece of cake and named Madame Chantal as Queen. And so I was astonished to feel something very hard in a piece of pastry that nearly broke my tooth. I carefully removed the object from my mouth and saw a small, porcelain doll, no bigger than a bean.

I was so surprised that I cried out: "Ah!" Everyone looked at me and Chantal clapped his hands and shouted: "It's Gaston. It's Gaston. Long live the King! Long live the King!"

Everyone continued the chant: "Long live the King!" And I turned completely red, the way people often blush, for no reason, in rather silly situations. I sat there with my eyes lowered, holding this little piece of china between two fingers, forcing myself to laugh, not knowing what to do or say, when Chantal added: "Now you must choose a Queen."

I was utterly dismayed. In the space of a second, a thousand thoughts, a thousand assumptions flashed through my mind. Did they want me to choose one of the Chantal daughters? Was it a way to make me say which one I preferred? Was it a soft, gentle, subtle push by their parents toward a possible marriage? The idea of marriage lurks incessantly around every home with grown-up daughters and takes all sorts of shapes, forms, disguises. A horrid fear of compromising myself rushed through me, as well as a feeling of extreme shyness in the face of the obstinately correct and expressionless demeanor of both Mademoiselle Louise and Mademoiselle

Pauline. To choose one of them over the other seemed as difficult as choosing between two drops of water; and the fear of getting myself involved in a situation that would lead me into marriage in spite of myself, little by little, by means that were as discrete, subtle and serene as this insignificant royalty, also troubled me horribly.

But suddenly, I had a flash of inspiration, and I handed the symbolic doll to Mademoiselle Pearl. Everyone was surprised at first, then they undoubtedly understood my sensitivity and discretion, for they all clapped loudly, shouting: "Long live the Queen! Long live the Queen!"

As for her, the poor spinster, she had gone completely to pieces; she was shaking and alarmed. "No . . . no . . . ," she stammered, "no . . . not me . . . please . . . not me . . . please . . ."

Then, for the first time in my life, I looked at Mademoiselle Pearl, and wondered who she really was.

I was used to seeing her in this house, the way you see the old armchairs upholstered in tapestry that you've been sitting on since you were a child without ever thinking about them. One day, you don't know why, perhaps because a ray of sunlight has fallen onto the chair, you suddenly say to yourself: "This piece of furniture is really odd, you know." And you realize that an artist carved the wood, and that the fabric is remarkable. I had never really given any thought to Mademoiselle Pearl.

She was part of the Chantal family, that's all there was to it; but how? What was her role? She was a tall, thin woman who did her best to go unnoticed, but who was not insignificant. She was treated amicably, better than a housekeeper, but not as well as a relative. I suddenly became aware, just then, of a great number of nuances I had been unaware of up until now! Madame Chantal called her "Pearl." The daughters "Mademoiselle Pearl," and Chantal only ever called her "Mademoiselle," to be more respectful, perhaps.

I began watching her—How old was she? Forty? Yes, forty—She wasn't old, but this woman, she made herself look old. I was suddenly struck by having noticed that. The way she did her hair, dressed and wore jewelry was ridiculous, yet Madamoiselle Pearl was in no way ridiculous, for in spite of everything, she had a simple, natural, inner grace, grace that was hidden, and carefully. What an odd creature she was! How was it that I had never really looked at her closely? She wore her hair in a truly grotesque style, with little old-fashioned ringlets that were completely farcical; and beneath this hairstyle befitting the Virgin Mary was her wide, calm forehead, cut across by two deep wrinkles, two wrinkles of long-suffering sadness, then blue eyes, soft and wide, so timid, so fearful, so humble, beautiful eyes that had remained innocent, full of childlike surprise, the feelings of a young girl and the sadness she had known, all these things showed in her tender eyes but without detracting from them.

Her whole face was delicate and discreet, one of those faces that had lost its light without ever having been burned out, or faded due to weariness or the intense emotions of life.

What a lovely mouth! And such pretty teeth! You would have thought she didn't dare smile!

And suddenly, I started comparing her to Madame Chantal. Mademoiselle Pearl was certainly more attractive, a hundred times better, more refined, more dignified, prouder.

I was stunned by what I was seeing. They poured the champagne. I stretched my glass out toward the Queen, toasting her good health with a well-phrased compliment. I noticed that she looked as if she wanted to hide her face in her napkin; then, as she brought her lips to her glass and sipped some of the sparkling wine, everyone cried out: "The Queen is drinking! The Queen is drinking!" She turned bright red, and nearly choked. They all laughed; but I could tell that everyone in that household loved her a great deal.

III

AS SOON AS DINNER WAS OVER, CHANTAL LED ME AWAY. IT WAS time for his cigar, a sacred moment. When he was alone, he went out into the street to smoke it; when he had a dinner guest, they went into the billiard room and had a game as they smoked. That evening, they had even lit a fire in the room, because it was Epiphany; and my old friend picked up his cue, a very slim cue that he chalked with great care.

"Your turn, my boy," he said.

He still spoke to me as if I were a young boy, even though I was twenty-five, because he had known me ever since I was child.

So I started the game. I struck a few balls, missed a few others. But as the thought of Mademoiselle Pearl was still present in my mind, I suddenly asked:

"Tell me, Monsieur Chantal, is Mademoiselle Pearl related to you?"

He stopped playing, very surprised, then looked at me.

"What? You don't know? You don't know about Mademoiselle Pearl?"

"No, I don't."

"Your father never told you?"

"No."

"Well, well, that's very strange! Ah! Now that's very strange indeed! Oh! But it's quite a story!"

He stopped for a moment, then continued:

"And if you only knew how odd it is that you should ask me about it today, on Epiphany!"

"Why?"

AH! WHY! LISTEN. It's been forty-one years, forty-one years to the day, January 6. We were living in Roüy-le-Tors then, on the ramparts; but I have to explain what the house was like, so you'll understand. Roüy was built on a slope, or rather on a knoll that overlooks a vast plain. We had a house there with a beautiful hanging garden, supported by the old battlement walls. And so the house was in the city, on the street, while the garden overlooked the plain. There was also a door at the end of a secret passageway cut through the thick stone wall—the kind you read about in novels—that led from the garden to the countryside. There was a road in front of this door, and the door had a heavy bell, for the farmers brought their provisions that way to avoid a long detour.

You can picture the place, right? Well, that year on January 6, it had been snowing for a week. It felt like the world was coming to an end. When we went over to the ramparts to look at the plain, the immense white landscape chilled our souls: it was totally white, frozen and as shiny as gloss. It made you wonder if the good Lord had wrapped up the earth to store it away in the attic of old worlds. I can assure you it was a very sad sight.

We were with our whole family then, and there were many of us, a great many of us: my father, my mother, my aunt and uncle, my two brothers and my four cousins, all girls; they were very pretty; I married the youngest. Out of everyone who was there, only three of us are left: my wife, myself and my sister-in-law, who lives in Marseille. Good Lord, how a family dwindles away! It makes me shudder just to think of it! I'm now fifty-six, so I was fifteen then.

So we were going to celebrate Epiphany and we were very cheerful, very cheerful indeed! Everyone was in the reception room waiting to be called for dinner when my eldest brother, Jacques, started to say: "There's a dog that's been howling on the plain for the last ten minutes; he must be lost, the poor little thing."

He had barely finished his sentence when the bell from the garden chimed. It sounded like one of those great church bells that make you think of the dead. It made everyone shudder. My father called the servant and told him to go and see who it was. We all waited in absolute silence; we were thinking about the snow completely blanketing the ground. When the man came back, he said he'd seen nothing. The dog was still howling, continuously, and from the very same spot.

We sat down to dinner; but we were all rather upset, especially the children.

Everything was fine until we got to the meat course; then the bell started ringing again, three times in a row, three loud, long tolls that we could feel vibrating to the tips of our fingers; it took our breath clean away. We sat there, looking at each other, forks suspended in midair, straining to hear and gripped by a kind of supernatural fear.

My mother finally spoke: "It's surprising that someone has waited so long before coming back; don't go alone, Baptiste; one of these gentlemen will go with you."

My Uncle François stood up. He was a kind of Hercules, very proud of his strength and afraid of nothing in the world. "Take a shotgun," my father said, "we don't know what we might find."

But my uncle just took a cane and immediately went out with the servant.

The rest of us sat there, trembling with terror and anguish, without eating, without speaking. My father tried to reassure us: "You'll see," he said, "it will just be some beggar or some passerby who got lost in the snow. After ringing the bell the first time, and seeing that no one answered right away, he probably tried to find his own way; but when he couldn't manage it, he came back to our house."

It felt like my uncle had been gone for an hour. He finally returned, furious and swearing: "Nothing, for goodness sake, someone playing a joke! Nothing but that damned dog howling, a hundred yards from the walls. If I'd taken a shotgun with me, I'd have killed him to shut him up."

We went back to our meal, but everyone was still nervous; we sensed that it wasn't over, that something was going to happen, that the bell would ring again, and very soon.

And it did ring, just as we were cutting the Galette des Rois. All the men stood up at the same time. My Uncle François, who had drunk some champagne, announced that he was going to kill *IT*, in such a rage that my mother and my aunt rushed over to stop him. My father, who was slightly disabled (he was limping after falling off a horse and breaking his leg), remained very calm and said that he too wanted to know what was happening and that he would go. My brothers, aged eighteen and twenty, ran to get their shotguns; and since no one was paying any attention to me, I grabbed a small hunting rifle and headed out with the expedition.

We left at once. My father and uncle walked in front, with Baptiste, who carried a lantern. My brothers, Jacques and Paul, came next, and I was at the back, despite my mother's pleas; she stood at the doorstep with my sister and cousins.

It had started snowing again an hour before, and the trees were weighed down with it. The firs bent beneath this heavy, pale covering, like white pyramids, or enormous sugar loafs. And through the grayish curtain of tightly packed, dainty snowflakes, you could hardly make out the slimmer bushes, very pale in the darkness. The snow fell so thick and fast that you could barely see ten feet ahead of you. But the lantern shed a strong light in front of us. When we started to go down the winding staircase dug out of the wall, I was truly afraid. I felt as if someone was walking behind me, someone who would grab me by the shoulders and carry me away; and I wanted to turn back; but I would have had to cross the entire garden, so I didn't dare.

I heard someone opening the door onto the plain; then my uncle started to swear: "For goodness sake, that dog's started up again! If I see even his shadow, I won't miss my chance this time, that stupid b . . ."

The sight of that plain was sinister, or rather sensing the plain in front of us, for we couldn't actually see it; all we saw was an endless veil of snow, above, below, in front, to the right, to the left, everywhere.

"Well, now that dog's started howling again," my uncle said. "I'll show him what a good shot I am. That will be something, at least."

But my father, who was a good man, said: "It would be better to go and find him; that poor animal must be howling out of hunger. He's crying for help, the poor, wretched thing; he's crying out like a man in distress. Come on, let's go."

And we set off through the curtain of thick, endless, falling snow, through the frothy mist that filled the night and the sky, whirled, floated, fell and chilled your body as it melted, freezing you as if you were burning, with a sudden, sharp stinging on your skin, every time the little white snowflakes touched you.

We were up to our knees in this limp, cold slush, and we had to raise our knees very high to walk through it. The dog's howls became louder and clearer the further we went. "There he is!" my uncle shouted. We stopped to watch him, the way you must when you come across an enemy in the dark.

I couldn't see a thing, so I joined the others and then I spotted him; that dog was terrifying and mysterious to behold; he was large and black, a sheepdog, with long shaggy hair and the head of a wolf; he was standing on all fours, at the very end of the light cast by the lantern onto the snow. He stood dead still. He had stopped howling. He was watching us.

"That's odd," my uncle said, "he's not coming toward us and he's not moving away. I'd really like to shoot him dead."

"No," my father said, decisively. "We should get hold of him."

Then my brother Jacques added: "But he's not alone. There's something near him."

There was, in fact, something behind him, something gray, but impossible to make out. We continued walking toward him with great care.

When he saw us coming nearer, he sat down. He didn't seem unfriendly. He seemed more satisfied to have succeeded in attracting someone's attention.

My father walked straight over to him and petted him. The dog licked his hands; then we realized that he was tied to the wheel of a small cart, a kind of miniature carriage entirely covered in three or four woolen blankets. They carefully removed the covers, and when Baptiste held the lantern over the cart that looked like a little house on wheels, we found a baby who was fast asleep.

We were so stunned that we couldn't say a word. My father was the first to recover, and since he had a warm heart and a rather noble soul, he reached out and placed his hand on the roof of the carriage, saying, "Poor abandoned child! You will become one of the family!" And he ordered my brother Jacques to wheel our discovery home.

My father, thinking out loud, continued: "Some love child whose poor mother came to ring at my door on this night of Epiphany, in memory of the Son of God."

He stopped again, and shouted four times, with all his might, through the night, into the four corners of the heavens: "We have taken her in!" Then, placing his hand on his brother's shoulder, he whispered: "Just think, François, what would have happened if you had shot the dog? . . ."

My uncle did not reply but he made a large sign of the cross, there in the darkness, for he was a religious man, despite his blustering.

We had untied the dog and he was following us.

Ah! Our return to the house was so very moving. At first, it was quite difficult to get the little carriage up the stairs in the ramparts; we managed it, though, and pushed it into the entrance hall.

Mama was so funny, happy but aghast! And my four little cousins—the youngest was six years old—looked like four hens around a nest. We finally took the child out of the carriage; she was still asleep. The little girl was about six weeks old. And inside her swaddling clothes, we found ten thousand francs in gold, yes, ten thousand francs! And Papa invested the money so she would have a dowry. So she wasn't the daughter of poor people . . . perhaps the child of some nobleman and a middle-class woman from the town . . . or even . . . we imagined a thousand things but never really knew . . . never knew anything . . . ever . . . No one even recognized the dog. No one in the area knew him. In any case, the man or woman who rang the bell three times at our house must have known my parents well to have chosen them that way.

So that is how Mademoiselle Pearl became part of the Chantal household when she was only six weeks old.

However, she was only named Mademoiselle Pearl later on. At first, she was baptized Marie Simonne Claire, and Claire was meant to be her last name.

I can assure you that we were a funny sight as we went back into the dining room with this tiny little thing; she had woken up and was looking all around her at the people and the lights, her blue eyes all misty and gazing vacantly into space.

We sat back down at the table and cut up the cake. I was the King; and I took Mademoiselle Pearl as my Queen, as you did, just before. But that day, she understood nothing of the honor being bestowed upon her.

And so the child was adopted and brought up as part of the family. The years passed; she grew up. She was kind, sweet and obedient. Everyone loved her and would have spoiled her terribly if my mother had not prevented it.

My mother was a woman who believed in order and hierarchy. She agreed to treat little Claire like her own children, but she insisted on a clear distance between us, and the distinction was firmly established.

Moreover, as soon as the child was old enough to understand, my

mother made her aware of her background, and very gently, even ten-
derly, instilled in the little girl's mind that to the Chantals, she was an
adopted child, taken in and welcomed by the family, but in the end, a
stranger.

Claire understood the situation with remarkable intelligence and surprising intuition and knew how to occupy and maintain the place she had
been given with so much tact, grace and kindness that she touched my
father to the point of tears.

Even my mother was so moved by the passionate gratitude and somewhat fearful devotion of this adorable, loving creature that she started
calling her "My daughter." Sometimes, when the little girl had done
something good, or sensitive, my mother would raise her glasses onto her
forehead, which always indicated she was touched, and say: "But she's a
pearl, this child is a real pearl!"—That name stuck with the little Claire,
who, to us, became and will always be Mademoiselle Pearl.

I V

MONSIEUR CHANTAL FELL SILENT. HE WAS SITTING ON THE BILLIARD TABLE,
his legs swinging, holding a billiard ball in his left hand while fiddling
with a cloth in his right hand; it was the one we called the "chalk cloth,"
used to erase the score from the slate board. Blushing somewhat, his
voice quieter, he was talking for himself now, lost in thought, moving
slowly through memories of things past and former events now awakened in his mind, the way you stroll through the old family gardens
where you were brought up—where every tree, every path, every plant,
the pointy holly, the laurels that smell so good, the yews whose thick, red
berries can be crushed between your fingers—with every step you take,
all these things bring back a brief moment from your past life, one of
those little, insignificant but delightful moments that form the very foundation of existence.

As for me, I stood opposite him, my back against the wall, my hands
holding my billiard cue.

After a moment, he started speaking again: "Goodness, she was so

pretty at eighteen . . . and graceful . . . and perfect . . . ah! Such a pretty
. . . pretty . . . and good . . . and decent . . . and charming young woman!
. . . And her eyes . . . blue . . . and clear . . . bright . . . eyes like I'd never
seen before, or since . . . never!"

He fell silent again.

"Why did she never marry?" I asked.

He reacted, but not to me: he reacted to the word "marry":

"Why? Why? She didn't want to . . . didn't want to. And yet, she had
thirty thousand francs as a dowry, and she was asked several times . . .
but she didn't want to! She seemed sad back then. It was the time when I
married my cousin, little Charlotte, my wife, to whom I'd been engaged
for six years."

I looked over at Monsieur Chantal and felt as if I'd seen into his soul, as
if I'd suddenly entered into one of those obscure, cruel tragedies of honest
hearts, moral, irreproachable hearts, one of those secret tragedies that had
been left buried, that no one had ever known about, not even the silent,
resigned victims who carried those tragedies within them.

Then, bold curiosity suddenly pushed me to ask:

"You're the one who should have married Mademoiselle Pearl, aren't
you, Monsieur Chantal?"

He shuddered, looked at me and replied:

"Me? Marry who?"

"Mademoiselle Pearl."

"Why are you saying that?"

"Because you loved her more than your cousin."

He looked at me with a strange expression, his eyes wide with apprehension.

"Me . . . loved her? . . . What?" he stammered. "Who told you that?
. . ."

"It's obvious, for goodness sake . . . and it's even because of her that
you put off marrying your cousin for so long, your cousin who waited six
years for you."

He dropped the billiard ball he'd been holding in his left hand,
grabbed the chalk cloth in both hands and, covering his face with it, he

started sobbing. He cried in a distressing, ridiculous way, tears pouring out of his eyes, nose and mouth all at the same time, the way a sponge releases water when you squeeze it. And he coughed, spluttered, blew his nose with the chalk cloth, wiped his eyes and sneezed, tears pouring down every wrinkle on his face, while making the kind of gurgling sound you make when you gargle.

I was alarmed, ashamed, and wanted to run away; I had no idea what to say or do or suggest.

Then, suddenly, Madame Chantal's voice called up the staircase: "Will you soon be finished smoking?"

I opened the door and called out: "Yes, Madame, we're just coming down."

Then I rushed over to her husband and grabbed him by the shoulders: "Monsieur Chantal, my dear friend, listen to me. Your wife is calling you, pull yourself together, and quickly, we have to go downstairs; pull yourself together."

"Yes . . . yes . . ." he stammered, "I'm coming . . . the poor woman! . . . I'm coming . . . Tell her I'm coming."

And he began carefully wiping his face with the cloth that had been used to clean off the marks on the slate board for two or three years, so he looked partly white and partly red, his forehead, nose, cheeks and chin dotted with chalk, his eyes swollen and still full of tears.

I grabbed his hands and led him into his bedroom. "Please forgive me," I whispered. "I really hope you will forgive me for having caused you such pain, Monsieur Chantal . . . but . . . I didn't know . . . you . . . you do understand . . . ?"

He squeezed my hand. "Yes . . . yes . . . some moments are difficult . . ."

Then he dipped his face into his washbowl. When he raised his head, he still didn't look any more presentable; but I had a clever idea. Since he was worried when he saw himself in the mirror, I said: "All you have to do is say that you got a bit of dust in your eye, then you can cry in front of everyone as much as you like."

So he did, in fact, go downstairs, dabbing his eyes with his handkerchief. Everyone was concerned; they all wanted to look in his eye for the bit of dust that no one could find, and everyone told stories of similar cases when it had been necessary to go and get a doctor.

As for me, I had gone over to Mademoiselle Pearl and was looking at her, tormented by intense curiosity, curiosity that became unbearable. She must have been very pretty, with her soft eyes, so big, so calm, so wide that she looked as if she never closed them, unlike everyone else. Her outfit was a little ridiculous, truly something an old maid would wear; it detracted from her but without making her look awkward.

It seemed that I could see her thoughts, the way I had just seen into Monsieur Chantal's soul, and I could completely understand her devoted, simple, humble life. But I had the urge to say something, an irresistible urge to question her, to know if she too had loved him, if she too had suffered the way he had from the same intense, secret, enduring anguish that no one sees, no one knows, no one guesses, but which escapes at night, in the loneliness of a dark bedroom. I looked at her, I could see her heart beating beneath the chiffon wrap over the top of her dress, and I wondered whether she with her sweet, honest face had moaned every night into her thick, damp pillow, sobbing, her body shaking with intense frustration.

So I spoke to her very quietly, the way children shatter a gem to see what is inside: "If you could have seen the way Monsieur Chantal was weeping just a while ago, you would have felt sorry for him."

She shuddered: "What do you mean? Was he crying?"

"Oh! Yes, he was!"

"But why?"

She seemed very moved.

"Because of you," I replied.

"Because of me?"

"Yes. He was telling me how much he loved you in the past, and how hard it was to marry his wife instead of you . . ."

Her pale face seemed to contort. Her calm, wide eyes suddenly closed, so quickly that it seemed as if they would never open again. She slipped off her chair onto the floor and collapsed, slowly, very slowly, like a scarf floating to the ground.

"Help! Help!" I shouted. "Mademoiselle Pearl has fainted."

Madame Chantal and her daughters rushed over, and while they were getting some water, a towel and some vinegar, I grabbed my hat and ran out.

I was practically leaping away, my heart pounding, my mind full of remorse and regrets. Yet at certain moments, I was happy; I felt as if I had done something admirable and necessary.

"Was I wrong?" I wondered. "Was I right?" They had both carried that weight in their hearts the way some people carry fragments of a bullet in a wound that has healed. Would they not be happier now? It was too late for their torture to begin again but early enough for them to remember it lovingly.

And perhaps one day next spring, touched by a moonbeam shedding its light through the branches onto the grass at their feet, they will hold each other and clasp each other's hands and remember all their repressed, cruel suffering. And perhaps, as well, that brief embrace will send a quiver of joy through their veins, the kind of joy they will have never before experienced, rejuvenating in a moment their dead hearts through the power of the rapid, divine sensation of the intoxication, the madness that gives two people in love more happiness in that brief moment of pleasure than other people may experience throughout their entire lives!

THE UMBRELLA

MADAME OREILLE WAS THRIFTY. SHE KNEW HOW TO COUNT her pennies and possessed an arsenal of strict principles on how to make money. Her maid had great difficulty indeed in keeping anything for herself out of the shopping money. And Monsieur Oreille only got his allowance with extreme difficulty. They were comfortably off, however, and had no children, but Madame Oreille found it really painful to spend even the slightest amount of money. She felt as if her heart would break; and every time she had to spend a large sum of money, even if it was completely unavoidable, she slept very badly indeed the following night.

"You really must be more generous," her husband constantly said to his wife. "We never spend what we earn."

"You never know what could happen," she would reply. "It's better to have too much than too little."

She was a small woman of about forty; she had a wrinkled face, was energetic, very neat and often irritable.

Her husband constantly complained about the hardships she forced him to endure. Some of these things had become particularly unpleasant, as they wounded his pride.

He was the head clerk at the Ministry of War, a post he kept solely to obey his wife, so he could increase the income they never spent.

For two years, he had been going to the office with the same patched-up umbrella that was the butt of jokes amongst his colleagues. Tired of their jeers, he finally demanded that Madame Oreille buy him a new umbrella. She bought one that was on sale at one of the larger department stores for eight and a half francs. When the other employees saw he had one of those umbrellas that were a dime a dozen all over town, they started making jokes again, and Monsieur Oreille suffered horribly. The umbrella was cheap. In three months, he couldn't use it any more, and everyone in the Ministry joined in the laughter. They even made up a song about it that you could hear everywhere in the enormous building from morning till night.

Oreille, exasperated, ordered his wife to get him a new umbrella covered in good silk that cost twenty francs, and to bring him the receipt as proof.

She bought one for eighteen francs and gave it to her husband.

"This should last you five years, at least," she said, her face bright red with irritation.

Monsieur Oreille, triumphant, was a big hit at the office.

One evening, when he got home from work, his wife looked anxiously at the umbrella and said:

"You shouldn't leave it closed; the elastic band will cut the silk. You have to be careful with it; I won't be buying you another one in a hurry."

She took the umbrella, unfastened it and shook it out. Then she stood dead still, stunned. There was a round hole, as large as a penny, in the middle. It had been burned by a cigar!

"What's that?" she stammered.

"What's wrong? What do you mean?" her husband replied calmly, without looking at it.

She was choking with rage now, barely able to speak:

"You . . . you burned . . . your . . . your . . . umbrella. But you . . . you must be mad! You want to bankrupt us!"

He turned around and felt the color drain from his face:

"What do you mean?"

"I mean you burned a hole in your umbrella. Look!"

She rushed at him as if she were going to hit him, then thrust the little circular hole under his nose.

He stood there, distraught, looking at the hole.

"What . . . what is that?" he stammered. "I have no idea! I didn't do anything, I swear to you, I didn't do anything. How should I know what happened to the umbrella?"

She was shouting now:

"I bet you were joking around with it in your office, doing tricks and opening it to show it off."

"I only opened it once," he replied, "to show everyone how beautiful it was. That's all. I swear."

But she was shaking with fury, and she started one of those fights between married couples that, to a peaceful man, make the home more dangerous than being caught in the crossfire on a battlefield.

She mended it with a piece of silk cut from the old umbrella, which was a different color; and the next morning, Monsieur Oreille left, looking sheepish, with the patched-up umbrella. He put it away in the closet and tried not to think about it, the way you try to forget some bad memory.

The moment he walked through the door that evening, his wife grabbed the umbrella, opened it to examine it and stood dumbfounded when she saw it: it was a disaster, irreparable. It was covered in tiny holes, which were obviously little burns, as if someone had emptied the ashes from a lit pipe onto it. It was ruined, beyond repair.

She stared at it without saying a word, too indignant to utter a single sound. He too looked at the damage and stood dumbfounded, terrified, filled with dismay.

Then they looked at each other. Then he lowered his eyes. Then she threw the damaged umbrella in his face. Then she recovered her voice and shouted, full of rage:

"Ah! You bastard! You did this on purpose, you bastard! I'll make you pay for this! You can forget about ever getting another umbrella . . ."

And they started fighting again. After she had ranted and raved for an hour, he was finally able to explain. He swore he knew nothing about it, that it could only be the work of some malicious person or a petty act of revenge.

He was saved when the doorbell rang. It was a friend who had come to have dinner with them.

Madame Oreille told him all about it. As for buying a new umbrella, out of the question, her husband would have to do without.

The friend argued logically:

"Well, Madame, then he'll ruin his clothes, which surely cost more than an umbrella."

The little woman, still furious, replied:

"Well, he can take one from the kitchen, then; I'm not paying for another silk umbrella."

The very idea appalled Monsieur Oreille.

"Fine, then I'll resign from my job. I will! I'm not going to the Ministry with a shabby umbrella."

"Have the silk replaced on this one," their friend suggested. "That shouldn't cost very much."

"That would cost at least eight francs!" Madame Oreille stammered, exasperated. "Eight francs plus the eighteen we paid, that makes twenty-six francs! Twenty-six francs for an umbrella, why that's madness! It's insane!"

The friend, who was a middle-class man without much money, had an idea:

"Why not get your insurance company to pay for it? They pay for anything that gets burned, as long as it happens in the house."

The little woman immediately calmed down at this thought; then, after thinking for a minute, she turned to her husband:

"Tomorrow, before going to the Ministry, go to the Maternelle Insurance Company and show them what happened to your umbrella and demand they pay for it."

Monsieur Oreille recoiled.

"Never in my life would I do such a thing! It's eighteen francs down the drain, that's all. It won't kill us."

He went to work the next day with a walking stick. Fortunately, it was a nice day.

Alone in the house, Madame Oreille could not get over losing those eighteen francs. She had put the umbrella on the dining room table and paced back and forth, up and down, unable to make up her mind.

She couldn't stop thinking about the insurance company, but she could never stand up to the scornful looks of the gentlemen who would deal with her, for she was shy with strangers, blushing for the slightest reason, embarrassed whenever she had to talk to anyone she didn't know.

But losing those eighteen francs tormented her as if she had been physically wounded. She didn't want to think about it any more, yet the idea of how much she had lost kept painfully hammering at her. What should she do? Hours passed; she couldn't make up her mind. Then, suddenly, like all cowards who are stubborn, she made her decision.

"*I'll* go, and we'll just see!"

But first she had to make sure that the damage to the umbrella was complete, and the reason for it obvious enough to make her case. She took a match from the mantelpiece and burned a hole as big as her hand inside the umbrella. Then she carefully rolled up what remained of the silk, put the elastic around it, got her hat and shawl and walked quickly toward the insurance company's offices on the Rue de Rivoli.

But the closer she got, the slower she walked. What would she say? What would *they* say?

She looked at the numbers on the houses. There were still twenty-eight buildings to go. Good! She would have time to think. She walked slower and slower. Suddenly she shuddered. There was the door: it had a large plate with the words "Maternelle Fire Insurance Company" engraved in gold. Already! She waited a moment—nervous, anxious, ashamed— walked away, came back, walked away again, then came back again.

"I really must go in," she told herself. "It's now or never."

But as she entered the building, she could feel her heart beating faster.

She went inside; it was an enormous room with counters all around. Each window had a little opening where only a man's head could be seen; their bodies were hidden.

A man walked by, carrying some documents. She stopped. "Excuse me, Monsieur," she asked shyly, "can you tell me where to go to make a claim for something that has been accidentally burned?"

He replied in a booming voice:

"Second floor, door on the left. Claims Department."

The word frightened her even more; she wanted to run away, say nothing, sacrifice her eighteen francs. But when she thought about the money, she felt a little more courageous again, and she went upstairs, stopping at every step to catch her breath.

When she got to the second floor, she saw the door and knocked.

"Come in!" someone shouted out.

She went inside and saw a large room where three stern men, all wearing military medals, were standing and talking.

"How can we help you, Madame?" one of them asked.

She could barely speak.

"I've come . . . I've come . . . to . . . to make a claim," she stammered.

He very politely pointed to a chair.

"Please take a seat, I'll be with you in just a moment."

And, turning back to the two other men, he picked up their conversation.

"The company, gentlemen, considers our obligation in your matter to come to no more than four hundred thousand francs. We cannot accept your claim for the additional hundred thousand francs you wish us to pay. Moreover, the appraisal . . ."

One of the others cut in:

"That will do, Monsieur, the courts will decide. This meeting is over." And they left after many courteous exchanges.

Oh! if she had dared leave with them, she would have; she would have run away, given up! But how could she? The gentleman came back, and bowed.

"And how can I help you, Madame?" he asked.

"I've come about . . . about this," she said with difficulty.

The manager looked down at the object she held out to him in bemused surprise.

Her hands trembling, she was trying to undo the elastic band. After several attempts, she finally managed it and quickly opened the tattered remains of the umbrella.

"It looks in very bad condition," he said sympathetically.

"It cost me twenty francs," she said, haltingly.

He was astonished: "Really! As much as that?"

"Yes, it was superb. I wanted you to see the state it's in now."

"Of course; I do see. But I really don't understand how it concerns me."

Anxiety ran through her. Perhaps this company didn't pay for small items.

"But . . . it's all burned . . . ," she said.

The gentleman couldn't deny it.

"Yes, I can see that," he replied.

She stood there, dumbstruck, not knowing what else to say; then, suddenly realizing what she had forgotten to mention, she quickly said:

"My name is Madame Oreille; we have insurance with the company; and I have come to be reimbursed for this damage."

And fearing an outright refusal, she quickly added:

"I'm only asking to have the silk replaced."

"But . . . Madame . . ." the manager said, looking uncomfortable, "we do not sell umbrellas. We cannot take responsibility for these kinds of repairs."

The little woman felt her self-assurance return. She had to fight. And fight she would! She wasn't afraid any more.

"I'm only asking you to pay for the repair, "she said. "I can arrange to have it done myself."

The manager seemed embarrassed.

"Really, Madame, it is a very small claim! We are never asked to offer compensation for such minor accidents. You must understand that we cannot reimburse people for handkerchiefs, gloves, brooms, slippers, all types of small items that are liable to get burned every day."

She blushed, feeling her anger rise.

"But, Monsieur, last December, one of our chimneys caught fire and caused at least five hundred francs worth of damages. Monsieur Oreille made no claim then, so it is only fair that you pay for my umbrella now."

The manager guessed she was lying.

"You must admit, Madame," he said, smiling, "it is very surprising that Monsieur Oreille would make no claim for damages amounting to five hundred francs but would now ask for five or six francs to repair an umbrella."

She was not in the least intimidated.

"Excuse me, Monsieur," she replied, "but the five hundred francs came out of Monsieur Oreille's money, while this eighteen francs is coming out of Madame Oreille's money, which is a very different matter."

He could see he had no chance of getting rid of her and that he would only be wasting his whole day.

"Would you be so kind as to tell me how the damage was done?" he asked, resigned.

She could sense victory, and began telling her story:

"This is what happened, Monsieur: I have a kind of bronze stand in our entrance hall where we put walking sticks and umbrellas. Well, the other day, I put my umbrella in it when I got home. There is a shelf where I keep my candlesticks and matches just above it, you see. I reached up to get four matches. I struck one, but it wouldn't light. So I tried another, which did light, but then went right out. The same thing happened with the third."

The manager cut in to make a joke.

"So they were government matches?"

She didn't understand.

"I suppose so, probably. Anyway, the fourth match worked and I lit my candle; then I went up to my room to go to bed. But a quarter of an hour later, I thought I smelled something burning. I'm always afraid there might be a fire. Oh! If we ever have a fire it will not be my fault! I'm a nervous wreck since the fire I told you about. So I get up, go out, look around, sniffing everywhere, like a hunting dog, and finally I see that my umbrella is on fire. A match had probably fallen into it. You can see the state it's in . . ."

The manager had made up his mind.

"How much do you think it will cost to repair the damage?" he asked.

She didn't know what to say; she was afraid to ask for a specific amount.

"You should get it repaired," she replied, wishing to appear accommodating. "I'll leave it in your hands."

He refused: "No, Madame, I could not do that. Just tell me how much you wish to claim."

"Well . . . I think . . . that . . . Monsieur, I don't want to take advantage of you, you know . . . So why don't I take my umbrella to a professional who will re-cover it in good, hard-wearing silk, and I will bring you the bill. Would that be all right with you, Monsieur?"

"Absolutely, Madame, agreed. Here is a note for the cashier, who will reimburse you for whatever it costs."

He gave Madame Oreille a piece of paper; she quickly took it, got up and went out, thanking him, anxious to get away in case he changed his mind.

She walked cheerfully down the street now, looking for a fashionable umbrella maker. When she found a boutique that looked expensive, she went inside.

"I'd like the silk on this umbrella replaced; use very good silk," she said, confidently. "The very best you have. Money is no object."

ON HORSEBACK

THE POOR COUPLE STRUGGLED TO GET BY ON THE HUSBAND'S meager salary. Two children had been born since they were married, and after that, their initial financial problems had turned into one of those humiliating kinds of poverty, hidden and shameful, the poverty of a noble family still hoping to maintain its place in society.

Hector de Gribelin had been educated in his father's manor house in the provinces by an elderly priest. They were not rich, but they managed to get by and keep up appearances.

Then, when he was twenty, they looked for a position for him, and he entered the Ministry of the Navy as a clerk, earning fifteen hundred francs a year. He ran aground on this reef as anyone would who hadn't been prepared for life's harsh struggles from an early age, anyone who looks at life through a cloud, who is at a loss and doesn't know how to defend himself, people in whom unique aptitudes, specific abilities, a keen desire to fight have not been developed from childhood, anyone who never held a tool or a weapon in his hand.

His first three years in the office were horrible.

He met a few family acquaintances again, elderly, old-fashioned people who were also poor but who lived in upper-class neighborhoods, on the gloomy streets of the Faubourg Saint-Germain; and he made a group of friends.

Strangers to modern life, modest and proud, these poor aristocrats lived in the upper stories of quiet houses. From the top to the bottom of these buildings, the tenants had titles; but money was just as scarce on the ground floor as on the sixth.

Their eternal prejudices, obsession with status, fear of losing their rank, haunted these families that were once so accomplished but had been ruined by lazy men.

In this social circle, Hector de Gribelin met a young girl as noble and as poor as he was, and married her.

They had two children in four years.

FOR THE NEXT FOUR YEARS, the family was plagued by poverty; their only entertainment was walking down the Champs-Elysées on Sundays and going to the theater once or twice in the winter, thanks to complimentary tickets given to them by a colleague.

But it happened that around springtime, Hector de Gribelin's employer offered him some extra work, and he received a one-off bonus of three hundred francs.

When he brought the money home, he said to his wife:

"My dear Henriette, we must treat ourselves to something, a day out for the children, for example."

And after a long discussion they decided to have a day out and lunch in the country.

"Well," exclaimed Hector, "just the once won't hurt; we'll rent a carriage for you, the children and the maid, and I'll hire a horse from the riding school. It will do me good."

And for the entire week, all they talked about was the day out they were planning.

Every evening when he got back from the work, Hector picked up his oldest son, sat him astride on his leg and bounced him up and down as hard as he could, saying:

"That's how Daddy will ride his horse when we go to the country next Sunday."

And all day long, the little boy straddled chairs, dragging them around the room, shouting:

"It's Daddy on horsey."

Even the maid looked at Monsieur in awe, thinking of him riding alongside the carriage on horseback; and at every meal she listened to him talk about riding, telling stories of his former adventures, when he lived with his father. Oh! He'd been to a good school, and once his legs were around a horse, he feared nothing, nothing at all!

"If they give me an animal that's a bit difficult, I'll be really happy," he said over and over again to his wife, rubbing his hands together. "You'll see how good I am; and we can come back along the Champs-Elysées, if you like, just when everyone is coming back from the Bois de Boulogne.[1] We'll look so impressive that I hope we run into someone from the Ministry. That's all it would take to gain the respect of my employers."

The day came, and both the carriage and the horse arrived at their house at the same time. Hector went down immediately to examine his mount. He'd had straps sewn onto the legs of his pants and was waving a riding crop he'd bought the day before.

He lifted each of the horse's legs and felt them one after the other, patted the animal's neck, flank and hocks, felt the small of his back, opened his mouth, examined his teeth and said how old he was. And while the whole family was coming downstairs, he gave a little lecture on the theory and sport of riding in general, and this horse in particular, declaring him an excellent mount.

When they were all settled in the carriage, he checked the straps on the saddle. Then, raising himself up in the stirrup, he got onto the horse, who started rearing under his weight and nearly threw off his cavalier.

Hector was alarmed and tried to calm him down:

"There, there, that's a good horse, you're a very good horse!"

Then, when the horse had calmed down and the rider had steadied his nerves, Hector asked:

"Ready to go?"

---

1   A fashionable park on the outskirts of Paris, famous for its landscaping and long walks.

"Yes," they all replied together.

"Away!" he ordered.

And the cavalcade set off.

Everyone was watching him. He trotted in the English style, exaggerating the rise and fall. Just as he touched the saddle, he bounced up again, as if he were launching himself into space. He often looked as if he might crash down onto the horse's mane; and he stared straight ahead of him, his face tense and his cheeks pale.

His wife held one of the children on her lap, and the maid the other one.

"Look at Papa!" they said over and over again. "Look at Papa!"

And the two children, overexcited by the movement of the carriage, their utter joy and the fresh air, screamed and screamed. The horse, frightened by the noise, started to gallop, and as Hector was trying to control him, his hat fell off and rolled onto the ground. The coach driver had to get down from the carriage to pick it up, and after he'd handed it to Hector, he called out to his wife from a distance:

"Don't let the children shout like that; the horse might bolt!"

They had the lunch they'd brought with them on the grass in the Vésinet woods.

Even though the carriage driver was taking care of the three horses, Hector continually got up to see if his own needed anything; he patted him on the neck, and fed him bread, cakes and sugar.

"He's a fine trotter," he said. "He shook me up a little at first; but you saw that I got control pretty quickly. He knows who's in charge now and won't rear any more."

They came back along the Champs-Elysées, as they'd decided to do.

That enormous boulevard was swarming with carriages. And on the sidewalks, so many people were walking along that they looked like two endless black ribbons unwinding from the Arc de Triomphe to the Place de la Concorde. Sunlight flooded down on everyone, reflecting off the polished horse-drawn carriages, the steel of the harnesses and the handles of the carriage doors, making them sparkle.

The mad hustle and bustle combined with an intense feeling of *joie de vivre* seemed to excite this crowd of people, carriages and animals. And in the distance, the Obelisk rose in a golden mist.

As soon as Hector's horse had passed the Arc de Triomphe, he suddenly recovered his fieriness and started trotting fast through the rows of carriage wheels, toward his stable, in spite of all his rider's efforts to calm him down.

The carriage was far away now, a long way behind them; and when the horse reached the Palais de l'Industrie, he saw an empty road, so he turned to the right and started to gallop.

An old woman wearing an apron was calmly crossing the street. She happened to be right in Hector's way; he was heading for her at top speed. Unable to control his horse, he shouted as loudly as he could:

"Hey! Look out! Watch out!"

Perhaps she was deaf, for she continued calmly on her way until she was hit by the horse, who came at her as fast as a train. She landed ten feet away, her dress flying up around her, after hitting her head and rolling on the ground three times.

Voices shouted:

"Stop him!"

Hector, terrified, grabbed the horse's mane and shouted:

"Help!"

One terrible jolt launched him over his horse's ears and into the arms of a policeman who had just come toward him.

In seconds, an angry, gesticulating, noisy crowd had surrounded him. One gentleman in particular seemed exasperated; he was an elderly man with a full white moustache, wearing a large round medal.

"Good Lord," he said over and over again, "if you're that clumsy, you should stay at home. You shouldn't come out and kill people in the street when you don't know how to handle a horse."

Then four men appeared, carrying the old woman. She looked almost dead, with her yellowish complexion and her hat askew, covered in dust.

"Take this woman to the pharmacy," the elderly man ordered, "and we'll go to the police station."

Hector set off, between the two men. A third policeman led his horse. A crowd followed; and suddenly, the carriage arrived. His wife leapt out, the maid was beside herself, the children were whining. Hector explained that he would be home soon and that he'd knocked a woman down, but it was nothing to worry about. So his terrified family left.

At the police station, his explanation was brief. He gave his name, Hector de Gribelin, employee at the Ministry of the Navy. And they waited for news of the injured woman. A policeman who'd been sent to find out how she was came back. She had regained consciousness but had terrible pains inside, she said. She was a housekeeper, sixty-five years old, named Madame Simon.

As soon as he learned she wasn't dead, Hector was filled with hope once more; he promised to pay her medical bills. Then he rushed over to the pharmacy.

A crowd of people stood in front of the door; the good woman sat slumped in a chair, moaning, her hands motionless, a dazed expression on her face. Two doctors were still examining her. Nothing was broken but they were concerned there might be some internal injuries.

"Are you in a lot of pain?" Hector asked her.

"Oh! Yes."

"Where does it hurt?"

"It's like I got a fire inside me."

A doctor walked over to him:

"Are you the gentleman responsible for the accident?"

"Yes, Monsieur."

"This woman must be sent to a nursing home; I know one where they can take care of her for six francs a day. Would you like me to arrange it?"

Hector was delighted, thanked him, and went home feeling relieved.

His wife was waiting for him, in tears.

"It's nothing," he said to calm her down. "Madame Simon is already feeling better; she'll be fully recovered in three days; I sent her to a nursing home; it's nothing to worry about."

Nothing to worry about!

The next day, after leaving the office, he went to ask how Madame

Simon was doing. He found her eating a bowl of thick soup and looking contented. "So how are you?" he asked.

"Oh! my poor Monsieur," she replied, "nothing's changed. I feel real worn out. It ain't any better."

The doctor said they'd have to wait and see, in case there were any complications.

He waited three days, then went back. The old woman looked very well; her eyes were bright; but as soon as she saw him, she started moaning. "I can't seem to move, my poor Monsieur; I just can't. It's gonna be like this till the end of my days."

A shudder ran through Hector, right down to his bones. He asked to see the doctor. "What can I say, Monsieur," the doctor said. "I just don't know. She screams every time we try to stand her up. We can't even move her chair without her letting out heartrending screams. I have to believe what she tells me, Monsieur; I can't see what's going on inside her. Until I've seen her walking, I don't have the right to conclude she's lying."

The old lady was listening, a sly look in her eyes. A week passed; then two weeks, then a month.

Madame Simon never got out of her chair. She ate from morning till night, got fat, chatted cheerfully with the other patients, seemed to have grown accustomed to remaining motionless as if it were the well-deserved rest she had earned after fifty years of going up and down the stairs, turning over mattresses, carrying coal from floor or floor, sweeping and cleaning.

A distraught Hector went to see her every day, and every day he found her calm and peaceful.

"I can't seem to move, my poor Monsieur; I just can't," she said every time.

And every evening, Madame Gribelin, worried sick, would ask:

"So how is Madame Simon?"

And he would always reply in abject despair: "Nothing's changed, absolutely nothing!"

They had to let their maid go: they couldn't afford to pay her any more. They made other economies as well; his entire bonus was used up.

Then Hector got four specialists to see the old woman. She let them examine her, test her, feel her injuries, as she maliciously watched them.

"We have to get her to walk," one of them said.

"I can't, doctor," she cried, "I just can't!"

So they all got hold of her, lifted her up and dragged her along a few steps; but she got free of them and collapsed onto the floor, making such horrific noises that they put her back into her armchair with infinite care.

They discreetly expressed their opinion but concluded there was nothing to be done.

And when Hector brought the news to his wife, she fell into a chair, muttering:

"We'd be better off taking care of her here; it would be less expensive."

He started:

"Here? In our house? Really?"

Resigned to her fate now, tears in her eyes, she replied:

"What can we do, my darling. It's not my fault!"

THE BAPTISM

⌐═╾╾╼═⌐

ALL OF THE MEN STOOD IN FRONT OF THE FARMHOUSE DOOR dressed in their Sunday finery. The May sun shed its bright light onto the apple trees in bloom, as round and sweet-smelling as immense pink and white bouquets. They formed a canopy of flowers that covered the entire courtyard. All around them, the trees continually shed a flurry of delicate petals that swayed and floated as they fell onto the tall grass where dandelions shone like flames and poppies like drops of blood.

A sow was dozing beside the dunghill; her teats were swollen and her stomach enormous; a group of little piglets swarmed around her, their little tails coiled up like a rope.

Suddenly, beyond the trees on the farms, a church bell tolled in the distance. Its steely sound rose through the joyful sky with a faint, faraway call. Swallows swooped like rows of arrows through the blue skies surrounded by tall, rigid beech trees. Every now and then, the rank odor from the stables mixed with the sweet, gentle scent of apple trees.

One of the men standing in front of the door turned toward the house and shouted:

"Come on, Mélina, come on, it's ringin' now!"

He was about thirty years old. He was tall, a farmer, but not yet deformed or bent over through long hours spent working in the fields. His father, an old man as gnarled as the trunk of an oak tree, with bulbous wrists and bowlegs, said:

"Women, you know, they ain't never ready."

The old man's other two sons started to laugh, and one of them, turning toward their older brother, said:

"Go find 'em, Polyte. Or they won't be ready before noon."

So the young man went into his house.

A group of ducks had stopped near the farmers and started quacking and flapping their wings; then they slowly waddled off toward the pond.

A stout woman came out of the door carrying a two-month-old baby. The white strings of her tall bonnet hung down her back, falling over a red shawl, as bright as fire, and the babe, wrapped up all in white, rested against the wet nurse's bulging stomach.

Then his mother, a tall, strong woman, came outside on her husband's arm; she was barely eighteen, young and cheerful. Then the two grandmothers followed, as wrinkled as old apples, their backs obviously deformed, damaged over time by difficult, painstaking work. One of them was a widow; she took the grandfather's arm; he had waited in front of the door, and they walked at the head of the party, behind the child and the midwife. And the rest of the family followed behind. The youngest ones carried paper bags full of sugared almonds.

The little church bell rang continuously, calling to the frail little baby with all its might. The young children climbed back up from the ditches; people came out to their gates; farm girls stood between two pails of milk they had put down on the ground to watch the Christening party go by.

And the wet nurse, triumphant, carried her living burden, avoiding the puddles of water in the hollow paths between the embankments lined with trees. And the old people walked ceremoniously, tottering along because of their age, and feeling their pain; and the young men wanted to dance, watching the girls who looked back as they passed by; and the mother and father walked solemnly, looking more serious, following this child who one day, in the future, would take their place in life and carry on their name here, the name of Dentu, known throughout the county.

They came out onto the flat open country and walked toward the fields, as it was quicker than following the winding road.

They could see the church now with its pointed steeple. There was an opening just below the slate roof; and something was moving inside, quickly swaying from side to side behind the narrow window. It was the church bell, still ringing, calling for the newborn baby to come inside the good Lord's house for the first time.

A dog had started following them. They threw him some candy and he leapt around all the people.

The church door was open. Father Dentu, the priest, a tall young man with red hair, thin but strong, was waiting in front of the altar. He was the baby's uncle, one of the father's brothers. And following the rites of the Church, he baptized his nephew Prosper-César, who started to cry when he tasted the salty water.

Once the ceremony was over, the family waited at the church door while the priest took off his surplice; then they all headed back. They walked quickly now, for they were thinking about the meal. All the little kids from the area followed, and every time they were thrown a handful of candy, there was a wild rush, pushing and shoving, and hair-pulling; and even the dog charged into the fray to get at the sweets, though they pulled his tail, his ears and his paws; but he was more determined than the children.

The wet nurse walked alongside the priest; she was rather tired and said:

"Tell me, Father, if you don't mind, do you think you could carry your nephew a bit to give me a break. I've got a pain or something in my stomach."

He took the child; the baby's white Christening robe made a large, bright mark against the priest's black cassock, and he kissed the boy, embarrassed by this light bundle, not knowing how to hold him, where to put him. Everyone started to laugh.

"Tell me, Father," one of the grandmothers called from behind, "don't it make you sad that you won't ever have one of those?"

The priest did not reply. He took great strides as he walked, staring at the little baby with his blue eyes and feeling the urge to kiss his chubby cheeks. He could restrain himself no longer and raising the child toward his face, gave him a long kiss.

"Hey, Father," his father shouted. "If you want one, all you have to do is say the word."

And they started teasing him, the way countryfolk do.

As soon as they sat down to eat, the unbridled cheerfulness of these country people burst out like a storm. The two other brothers were also going to get married; their fiancées were there; they had just come to the meal; and the guests continually made remarks that alluded to all the future generations promised by these unions.

They used rude words, very dirty words that made the blushing young women giggle and the young men double up. They banged the table with their fists, roaring with laughter. Neither the father nor the grandfather held back, making risqué remarks. The mother smiled; the old women also joined in the fun, shouting out bawdy remarks.

The priest was used to this kind of coarse behavior from the countryfolk; he sat calmly beside the wet nurse, wiggling his finger in his nephew's mouth to make him laugh. He seemed surprised by the sight of this child, as if he'd never seen one before. He studied him with thoughtful attention, pensive seriousness and a feeling of affection for this fragile little person who was his brother's son, a feeling that was awakened within him, the kind of affection that was strange to him, unique, intense and somewhat sad.

He heard nothing, saw nothing: he was watching the child. He wanted to hold him in his lap again, for he could still feel, against his chest and in his heart, the sweet sensation of having just carried him back from the church. He was moved by this embryo of a man as if confronted with an ineffable mystery he had never thought about, a noble and holy mystery, the incarnation of a new soul, the great mystery of life renewed, of love awakened, of a race continuing, of humanity moving ever forward.

The wet nurse was eating, her face red, eyes shining, irritated by the little one who kept her away from the table.

"Give him to me," the priest said. "I'm not hungry."

And he held the child once more. Then everything around him disappeared, vanished; and he sat there, staring at the baby's pink, chubby face; and little by little, the warmth of that little body flowed through his blanket and the cassock and into the priest's legs, like a very soft, very chaste, very gentle caress, a wonderful caress that brought tears to his eyes.

The noise the guests made grew louder and louder, frightening. Upset by the din, the child began to cry.

Someone shouted out:

"Hey, Father, give him some of yer milk."

Everyone laughed so loud that the room shook. But the mother stood up, took her son and carried him into the next room. She came back a few minutes later and said he was sleeping peacefully in his cradle.

So the meal continued. Every now and then, some men and women went outside into the courtyard, then came back and sat down at the table. Meat, vegetables, cider and wine filled them up, made their stomachs swell, lit up their eyes and made them feel intensely happy.

It was nightfall by the time they had their coffee. The priest had disappeared a long time before, but no one was surprised he'd gone.

The young mother got up to go and see if her little one was still asleep. It was dark now. She felt her way into the bedroom and stretched her arms out in front of her so she wouldn't bump into any of the furniture. But a strange noise made her stop in her tracks; she ran out, terrified, sure she had heard someone moving in the room. Very pale and trembling, she went back to where everyone was eating and told them what she'd heard. All the men jumped up, slightly drunk and threatening; the baby's father rushed ahead, carrying a lamp.

The priest was on his knees beside the cradle, sobbing, his head on the pillow next to the child.

IN THE COUNTRYSIDE

※

THE TWO COTTAGES STOOD SIDE BY SIDE, AT THE FOOT OF A
hill, not far from a small seaside town. The two farmers worked
hard on the barren land to provide for their children. Each family had four
little ones. The whole gang of kids gathered to play outside their front
doors from morning till night. The two eldest boys were six, and the two
youngest about fifteen months old; the weddings and then the births had
happened almost simultaneously in both households.

When they were all together in a heap, the two mothers could barely
tell whose children were whose; and the fathers were at a complete loss.
The eight names went round and round in their heads, constantly getting
confused; and when they wanted to call one of them, the men often had to
try three times before getting the right name.

The first of the two cottages, as you came up from the seaside town of
Rolleport, belonged to the Tuvaches, who had three girls and a boy; the
other hovel belonged to the Vallins, who had one girl and three boys.

They all got by with great difficulty on soup, potatoes and fresh air.
At seven in the morning, then at noon, then at six o'clock in the evening,
the housewives got their kids together to feed them, just as gooseherds
round up their flock. The children were seated, according to age, around
the wooden table, polished by fifty years of use. The youngest kid's mouth
barely came up to the top. They got a bowl full of soggy bread mixed
with the water they'd used to cook the potatoes, half a cabbage and three

onions; and the whole row of them ate until they were full. The mother fed the youngest one herself.

A small piece of meat in the stew on Sunday was considered a feast; and on those days, the father took longer over the meal, saying over and over again: "I'd love to have this every day."

One August afternoon, a small carriage suddenly stopped in front of the cottages, and a young woman, who was driving the horses herself, said to the man sitting next to her:

"Oh! Look at all those children, Henri! See how lovely they are, so many of them rolling around together in the dirt like that!"

The man did not answer: he was used to such tender remarks, remarks that were painful and almost a reproach to him.

"I must give them a hug!" the young woman said. "Oh, how I would love to have one of them, that one there, that tiny little boy!"

She jumped down from the carriage and ran over to the children, picked up one of the two youngest, the Tuvache boy, and lifting him up in her arms, gave him lots of big kisses on his dirty cheeks, on his curly blond hair caked with dirt, and on his little hands, which he waved about trying to escape her unwanted affection.

Then she got back into the carriage and they galloped away. But she came back the next week, sat down on the ground with them, took the little kid in her arms, stuffed him with cake and gave candy to all the others; and she played with them as if she were a young girl, while her husband waited patiently in the little carriage.

She came back again; got to know the parents, and appeared every day, her pockets full of treats and money.

Her name was Madame Henri d'Hubières.

One morning, as soon as they got there, her husband got out of the carriage with her, and without stopping to talk to the kids, who knew her very well by now, she went into the farmer's cottage.

They were chopping wood for the fire to make their soup. They stood up, completely surprised, offered the couple a seat and waited.

Then the woman, in a broken, trembling voice, started to speak:

"My dear people, I have come to see you because I would love . . . I would love to take . . . your . . . your little boy home with me . . ."

Astonished and confused, they said nothing.

She took a deep breath and continued: "We have no children, my husband and I. We are alone . . . We would take care of him, keep him . . . Would you agree to that?"

The woman began to understand.

"You wanna take our Charlot?" she asked. "Huh! no, no for sure!"

Then Monsieur d'Hubières spoke up:

"My wife hasn't explained herself very well. We would like to adopt him, but he would come back to see you. If everything turns out well, as it should, he will be our heir. If we happen to have children, he will share everything equally with them. But if he does not respond well to our care, we will give him the sum of twenty thousand francs when he comes of age, which will be immediately deposited in his name through a lawyer. And since we also wish to be considerate of you, we will pay you an allowance of one hundred francs a month, for life. Do you understand?"

The woman had stood up, furious.

"You want me to sell you our Charlot? Ah! No, that ain't the kinda thing you ask a mother! Ah! No! That would be horrible!"

The man said nothing, thinking and looking serious; but he showed he agreed with his wife by continually nodding his head.

Madame d'Hubières was distraught and began to cry; turning to her husband, sobbing, sounding like a child used to having her own way, she stammered:

"They won't do it, Henri, they won't do it."

So he tried one last time: "But, my dear friends, think of the child's future, of his happiness, of . . ."

The farmer's wife, exasperated, cut in:

"We got it, we understand, there ain't nothing to think about . . . Now get outa here, and don't let me see you round here again, or else. Like it's okay to take away a kid like that!"

Then, as she was leaving, Madame d'Hubières remembered that there were two very young children, and she asked, through her tears, with the tenacity of a willful, spoiled woman who never wants to wait for anything:

"Is the other little one yours too?"

"No, he's our neighbors' kid," Tuvache replied. "You can go 'n see them if you want."

And he went back inside his house, where they could hear his wife shouting with indignation.

The Vallins were sitting around the table, slowly eating; on a plate between them were two slices of bread spread with a tiny amount of butter.

Monsieur d'Hubières began making them offers, but more cleverly, with more innuendos, choosing his words with great care.

The two countryfolk shook their heads, a sign of refusal, but when they learned they would get a hundred francs a month, they looked at each other, glanced over at each other, very shaken up.

They said nothing for a long time, tormented, hesitant.

"What do you think, husband?" the woman finally asked.

"I say it ain't such a bad thing," he said, sounding serious.

Then Madame d'Hubières, trembling with anguish, talked to them about their child's future, his happiness, and all the money he could give them later in life.

"This allowance of twelve hundred francs," the farmer asked, "you'll swear to it in front of a lawyer?"

"But of course," replied Monsieur d'Hubières. "We can do it tomorrow."

The woman thought for a moment.

"A hundred francs a month ain't enough for us to give up the kid," she said. "He'd be workin' in a few years; we'd need a hundred and twenty."

Madame d'Hubières, who was impatiently stamping her feet, agreed at once; and since she wanted to take the child away with her then and there, she gave them a hundred francs extra, as a gift, while her husband wrote down the details. The village mayor and a neighbor were immediately called over to act as obliging witnesses.

And the young woman, radiant, carried off the howling kid, the way you come away with some priceless curio in a boutique that you've always longed for.

Standing outside their door, the Tuvaches watched in silence as the child was taken away; they looked serious, regretting perhaps their own refusal.

Nothing more was ever heard of little Jean Vallin. His parents went to the lawyer's office every month to collect their hundred and twenty francs. They had fallen out with their neighbors because Tuvache's wife continually tormented them with insults, saying over and over again in every household how it was unnatural to sell your child, how it was horrible, disgusting, corrupt.

And sometimes she would hold her Charlot in her arms, showing off, shouting to him, as if he could understand:

"I didn't sell you, not me! I didn't sell you, me little one! I ain't rich, but I don't sell my children!"

And this went on every day for years and years; every day, crass allusions were shouted outside the front door so they would be heard inside the neighbors' house. Tavuche's wife ended up believing she was better than anyone else in the entire area because she hadn't sold Charlot. And everyone who talked about her said:

"I know it sure was tempting, but all the same, she did what a good mother would."

Everyone used her as an example; and Charlot, who was nearly eighteen and had been brought up with that idea, which he heard continually, believed he was better than his friends, because his parents hadn't sold him.

THANKS TO THE ALLOWANCE, the Vallins had a rather comfortable life, which was the cause of the relentless fury of the Tuvaches, who were still very poor.

Their oldest son left to go into the army; the second oldest boy died; Charlot alone was left to work with his old father to provide for his mother and two younger sisters.

He had just turned twenty-one when, one morning, an elegant carriage stopped in front of the two cottages. A young man, wearing a gold watch chain, got down, then offered his hand to help an elderly woman with white hair.

"That one, my child, the second house," the woman said to him.

And he went into the Vallins' house as if he was going home.

His old mother was washing her aprons; his father, disabled now, was dozing near the hearth. Both of them looked up.

"Hello, Papa; hello, Mama!" the young man said.

They both stood up, frightened. The farmer's wife was so stunned that she dropped her soap into the water.

"Is it you, my boy?" she stammered. "Is it really you?"

He took her in his arms, hugged and kissed her, saying over and over again: "Hello, Mama." Meanwhile, the old man was trembling all over. "So you've come back, Jean," he said in the calm tone of voice he never lost, as if he had just seen him a month ago.

After they had got acquainted again, his parents wanted to take their son out right away, to show him off all over the neighborhood. They took him to see the mayor, the deputy mayor, the priest and the schoolteacher.

Charlot stood outside the front door of his cottage and watched him go by.

That evening, during supper, he said to his elderly parents:

"You must've been real stupid to let 'em take the Vallins' boy."

"I wouldn't've sold my child," his mother stubbornly replied.

His father said nothing.

"Ain't it a shame, being sacrificed like that," his son added.

Then Tuvache got angry:

"You ain't gonna blame us for keeping you now, are you?" he said.

"Yeah, I do blame you, 'cause you're such fools," the young man said cruelly. "Parents like you two make your kids' life a misery. I should get outta here, that's what you deserve."

The old woman was crying into her plate. She groaned while swallowing the spoonfuls of soup, spilling half of them:

"And you kill yourself to bring up kids!"

"I wish I hadn't been born instead of bein' what I am," her son said harshly. "When I saw him, that other one, my heart near stopped. I says to myself, 'See what I could've been now!'"

He stood up.

"Listen, I can tell I'd be better off not stayin' here, 'cause I'd be throwin' it up to you from morning till night, and I'd make your life a misery. I won't never forgive you for it, you know!"

The two old people said nothing, distraught and in tears.

"No, that would be too much," he continued. "I'd sooner look for a place to live my life somewhere else."

He opened the door. They heard the sound of voices. The Vallins were celebrating their child's return.

Charlot stamped his foot on the ground and turned toward his parents, shouting:

"Peasants!"

Then he disappeared into the night.

ADIEU[1]

T HE TWO FRIENDS WERE JUST FINISHING DINNER. FROM THE café window, they could see the wide avenue, crowded with people. They felt the gentle breeze that wafts through Paris on warm summer evenings and makes passersby look up, giving everyone the urge to leave, to go somewhere far, far away, where there are trees, creating dreams of moonlit rivers, glowworms and nightingales.

One of the two men, Henri Simon, gave a deep sigh:

"Ah! I'm getting old. It's sad. On evenings like this in the past, I felt a fire in my blood. Now, I only feel regret. Life goes by so quickly!"

He was already somewhat heavy, about forty-five years old and very bald.

His friend, Pierre Carnier, was slightly older, but thinner and more dynamic.

"Well, as for me, I've hardly noticed growing old. I've always been cheerful, strong and energetic, you know. Now, because we look at ourselves in the mirror every day, we don't notice how we age, for it happens slowly, steadily, and it changes our faces so gradually that the transformation is barely obvious. That's the only reason we don't die of sadness after only two or three years of time's devastating effects. It's because we don't

---

1   The French make a distinction between *Adieu*—farewell, which has a sense of finality, and *au revoir*—goodbye, or until we see each other again.

notice them. To really see them, we'd have to not look at ourselves in a mirror for six months—Oh! Wouldn't that be a shock?

And as for women, I do feel sorry for the poor things! All their happiness, their power, their lives depend on their beauty, which only lasts ten years.

As for me, I grew older without noticing it; I thought I was almost an adolescent, even when I was almost fifty. I didn't feel frail in any way, so I lived my life, happy and peaceful.

I realized I was aging in a simple and terrible way, and it overwhelmed me for nearly six months . . . then I accepted my fate.

I had often fallen in love, as all men do, but one time in particular stands out."

I MET HER AT THE SEASIDE IN ETRETAT, about twelve years ago, shortly after the war.2 Nothing is nicer than the beach there in the early morning, when people go out for a swim. It's small, in the shape of a horseshoe, framed by high white cliffs that are full of unusual holes called the "Portes." One enormous stretch of stone extends a giantlike leg into the ocean; the one on the other side is low and circular. A crowd of women gather on the narrow strip of this pebbly beach, transforming it into a dazzling garden of bright clothing, set against the high rocks. The sun beats down on the shores, on the multicolored parasols, on the bluishgreen sea; and everything is cheerful, charming, a delight to the eyes. You sit down right at the water's edge and you watch the women swim. They come down, wrapped in thick flannel bathrobes; then they take them off with a lovely gesture when they reach the frothy top of the low waves; and they walk into the water, taking quick little steps, stopping from time to time to gasp and shiver a little when they feel the lovely, cool water.

Very few can pass the test of the water. It is there that they are

---

2   This story was written in 1885, so the reference is to the Franco-Prussian War of 1870–71.

judged, from head to foot. When they come out of the water, their defects are particularly revealed, although seawater tightens flabby skin wonderfully.

The first time I saw this young woman coming out of the water, I was thrilled, infatuated. She passed the test well, very well indeed. And then, there are some bewitching faces that suddenly strike you and take hold of you. You sense you have found the woman you were born to love. I felt that feeling and that shock.

I found a way to be introduced, and was soon more in love than ever before. She devastated my heart. It's a frightening yet wonderful thing to be under a woman's spell.

It is almost torture, but at the same time, endless joy. Her look, her smile, her hair fluttering in the wind, even the tiniest lines on her face, the slightest movement of her features, delighted me, overwhelmed me, drove me wild. Everything about her enthralled me, her gestures, her bearing, even the clothes she wore, which seemed to cast a spell on me. I melted at the sight of her hat with its veil on some piece of furniture, her gloves thrown onto a chair. The way she dressed seemed unique. Nobody had hats like hers.

She was married, but her husband only came to join her every Saturday and left again on Monday. He didn't matter to me. I wasn't jealous of him at all, I don't know why; never in all my life did anyone seem less important or warrant my concern less than that man.

But her! I loved her so much! She was so beautiful, graceful and young! She was youth, elegance, brightness itself! Never before had I realized what pretty, refined, delicate creatures women are, full of charm and grace. Never before had I appreciated the seductive beauty of a curve of a cheek, the movement of a lip, the circular folds of an ear, the shape of the silly feature called the nose.

It lasted for three months, then I left for America, my heart crushed, in despair. But the thought of her stayed with me, persistent, dominant. Even at such a distance, she possessed me, just as she had owned me when I was near her. Years passed. I could not forget her. Her bewitching face remained in my heart and mind. And my love for her never died. But it was a peaceful feeling now, like the treasured memory of the most beautiful and enchanting moment in my life.

TWELVE YEARS ARE SO little in the life of a man! You don't feel them slipping away. The years go by, one after the other, steadily but quickly, slowly yet pressing, each one long yet over so soon! And they add up so fast, leaving so few traces behind, disappearing so completely, that when you try to look back at the years gone by, you can no longer recapture them, and you can't understand how you got to be old.

I really felt that only a few months had passed since that wonderful time on the pebbly beach of Etretat.

Last spring, I was on my way to have dinner with some friends who live in Maisons-Laffitte.

Just as the train was leaving, a stout lady with four little girls climbed onto the train and into my carriage. I barely noticed the mother hen; she was very big, very round and wore a hat with ribbons that framed a face like a full moon.

She was breathing heavily, out of breath from having walked so quickly. The children started chattering. I opened my newspaper and began to read.

We had just passed Asnières when my neighbor suddenly asked:

"Excuse me, but are you Monsieur Garnier?"

"Yes, I am, Madame."

Then she started to laugh, the happy laugh of a good woman, yet tinged with sadness.

"You don't recognize me, do you?"

I hesitated. I thought I'd seen her face somewhere before, but where? And when?

"Yes . . . and no . . . ," I replied. "I certainly know you, but I can't remember your name."

She blushed a little.

"Madame Julie Lefèvre."

Never had I been so shocked. In a split second, it seemed as if my life had ended! I felt as if a veil had been ripped from my eyes and I was about to witness terrifying, distressing things.

It was her! Could that fat, ordinary woman really be her? And she'd produced those four girls since I'd last seen her. And those four children astounded me as much as their mother did. She'd given birth to them; they were already big girls; they were an important part of her life. She, however, no longer counted, she, that miracle of coquettish, elegant grace. I felt it was only yesterday that I'd seen her, and this is how she looked now! Was it possible? An intense feeling of grief rushed through my heart, as well as a sense of revolt against nature itself, an illogical surge of indignation against nature's brutal, infamous acts of destruction.

I looked at her, aghast. Then I took her hand; tears filled my eyes. I cried over her lost youth. I cried for the woman who had died. For I no longer knew this fat lady at all.

She too was overcome with emotion.

"I've changed a lot, haven't I?" she stammered. "What can you do, everything changes. I'm a mother now, you see, nothing but a mother, a good mother. *Adieu* to the rest, that's all over. Oh! I thought you'd never recognize me if we ever saw each other again. You've changed as well, though; it took me a while to be sure it was really you. You've gone all gray! Imagine. It's been twelve years! Twelve years! My oldest daughter is already ten."

I looked at the child. And I recognized some of her mother's former charm in her, but not yet fully formed, a promise to be fulfilled, something yet to come. And I felt as if life moved by as swiftly as a passing train.

We were approaching Maisons-Laffitte. I kissed my former love's hand. All I'd been able to say to her were terribly trite words. I was too overwhelmed to talk.

That night, alone, at home, I looked at myself in the mirror for a long time, a very long time. And I finally managed to conjure up the man I had once been, picturing my brown moustache, my dark hair, and my youthful face. Now, I was old. *Adieu!*

A DAY IN THE COUNTRY[1]

⌦⌫

FOR FIVE MONTHS, THEY HAD BEEN PLANNING A TRIP TO HAVE lunch in the outskirts of Paris to celebrate Madame Pétronille Dufour's Saint's Day.[2] Since they had been looking forward to the outing with great impatience, they got up very early that day.

Monsieur Dufour drove a horse-drawn cart he'd borrowed from the milkman. It had two wheels and was very clean; it had a covered top supported by four iron poles with curtains attached. The curtains had been raised so they could see the countryside; only the one at the back fluttered in the wind, like a flag. Madame Dufont sat next to her husband, looking striking in an extraordinary cherry red silk dress. Behind them, on two chairs, sat their elderly grandmother and a young woman. You could just make out the head of a young man with blond hair who was stretched out at the back of the cart because there wasn't another seat.

After driving down the Champs-Elysées, they passed the fortifications at the Porte Maillot and began looking at the countryside.

When they arrived at the Neuilly bridge, Monsieur Dufour said: "Here we are in the countryside, at last!" and his wife, taking his lead, began making sentimental comments about nature.

At the Rond-Point de Courbevoie, they were filled with admiration

---

1   This story—*Une Partie de campagne*—was made into a movie by a friend of Maupassant, Jean Renoir, son of the artist Auguste Renoir. It was released in the United States in 1950.

2   Saint Pétronille is celebrated on May 31.

at the sight of the horizon in the distance. To the right was Argenteuil, with its tall belltower; above it were the Sannois hills and the mill at Orgemont. To the left, the Marly Aqueduct was outlined against the bright morning sky, and far away in the distance, they could see the wide avenue leading to Saint-Germain, while opposite them, at the end of a series of hills, the freshly dug earth was evidence of the work being done to construct a new fort at Cormeilles. Far away, very far away in the distance, beyond the plains and the villages, they could just make out the dark green forests.

The sun was starting to burn their faces; dust constantly got in their eyes, and on both sides of the road stretched the countryside, dirty and reeking, barren as far as the eye could see. It looked as if a plague had ravaged it, eaten away at the houses, for the skeletons of dilapidated, abandoned buildings and small cabins, unfinished because their owners couldn't pay the workmen, stood empty with four walls and no roof.

Every now and then, tall factory chimneys rose up from the barren earth, the only vegetation on those putrid fields where the spring breeze carried the smell of gasoline and shale, mixed with another odor that was even worse.

Finally, they crossed the Seine a second time, and the view from the bridge was wonderful. The river sparkled in the light; a mist rose up from it, filtered by the sun, and they felt a sweet sense of pleasure, a cooling mist that made them feel delightful as they drank in the cleaner air, air that had never been filled with black smoke from the factories or the disgusting fumes from the sewage works.

A passerby told them the name of the area: Bezons.

The cart stopped and Monsieur Dufour began to read the attractive sign outside a cheap restaurant: *Restaurant Poulin, fried fish in wine sauce, private dining rooms, orchards and swings*. Well, Madame Dufour! Will this do? What do you think?"

Then his wife read the sign: *Restaurant Poulin, fried fish in wine sauce, private dining rooms, orchards and swings*. She studied the restaurant for a long time.

It was a country inn, painted white, set by the roadside. Through the open door, you could see the shiny counter of the bar where two workmen sat in their Sunday best.

At last, Madame Dufour made a decision: "Yes," she said, "this is fine; and it also has nice views." The cart entered a huge field behind the inn; it was planted with tall trees and was only separated from the Seine by a towpath.

They got out of the wagon. The husband jumped down first, then held out his arms to help his wife. The running board was supported by two pieces of iron; it was low down, so in order to reach her husband, Madame Dufour had to reveal the lower part of her leg, whose former slenderness had now disappeared into the rolls of fat on her thigh.

Monsieur Dufour, who was already getting frisky by being in the countryside, pinched her calf hard, then, taking her in his arms, heaved her onto the ground, as if she were some enormous package. She shook the dust from her silk dress, then looked around to see what kind of place it was.

She was a heavy woman, about thirty-six, radiant and attractive. She was squeezed so tightly into her corset that she breathed with difficulty; and the pressure of the corset forced her overabundant, jiggling bosom right up to meet her double chin.

Next, the young woman put her hand on her father's shoulder and jumped lightly down, by herself. The young man with the blond hair had got down by stepping on the wheel, and he helped Monsieur Dufour lift his grandmother out.

Then they unharnessed the horse and tied it to a tree; the cart dropped straight down, both shafts resting on the ground. The men took off their jackets, washed their hands in a bucket of water, then went to join the ladies, who were on the swings.

Mademoiselle Dufour was trying to swing standing up, but she couldn't get a good push off. She was a pretty girl of about eighteen or twenty, one of those young women who suddenly arouse intense desire when you come across them on the street, leaving you with heightened senses and a vague feeling of restlessness well into the night. Tall, with a small waist and broad hips, she had very dusky skin, very big eyes, very black hair.

Her dress clearly outlined her curvaceous, firm body, accentuated even further by the way she used her hips in an effort to swing higher. She stretched her arms up to hold onto the ropes above her head, which made her bosom rise smoothly with every push she gave. Her hat was blown off by a gust of wind and hung down her back; and after the swing rose higher and higher, you could see her shapely legs up to the knee every time the swing came down again, and a puff of air from her skirt, more intoxicating than the scent of wine, blew right into the faces of the two men who were watching her and laughing.

Sitting on the other swing, Madame Dufour moaned in a continual, monotonous way: "Cyprien, come and push me; come and give me a push, Cyprien!" In the end, he went over to her, and after rolling up his sleeves, the way you do before getting down to some hard work, he got his wife swinging, but with very great difficulty.

Clutching the ropes, her legs straight out in front of her so they wouldn't touch the ground, she was enjoying the heady feeling of the swing going up and down. Her body was shaking, trembling continually, like jelly on a plate. But as she swung higher and higher, she got very dizzy and was afraid. Every time she came down, she let out a piercing cry that made all the local kids come running; and further away, beyond the hedge in the garden, she could vaguely make out a line of naughty little children, laughing and making silly faces.

A servant girl came out and they ordered lunch.

"Fried fish, sautéed rabbit, salad and dessert," Madame Dufour said proudly. "And bring us two quarts of beer and a bottle of Bordeaux," her husband said. "We'll have lunch on the grass," the young woman added.

The grandmother got emotional when she saw the owners' cat and ran after it for ten minutes, trying to coax it to come to her by calling it by the sweetest names. In vain. The animal, doubtless secretly flattered by her attentions, came close to the good woman's hand, but stayed just out of reach and slowly circled the trees, rubbing itself against them, tail in the air and purring softly with pleasure.

The blond young man was wandering around when he suddenly shouted, "Look! There are some really great boats!" They all went to

have a look. In a wooden shed hung two superb skiffs; they were as beautiful and finely worked as expensive furniture. They stood side by side,
as narrow and bright as two tall, slender young women, and they filled
you with a desire to drift along the riverbanks covered in flowers on
bright summer mornings and warm summer evenings, down the river
where the trees dip their branches into the water, where the rushes are
continually rustling, where the swift kingfishers fly off like flashes of
blue lightning.

The whole family looked at them respectfully. "Oh yes, they really
are nice!" Monsieur Dufour said solemnly. And he examined them as if
he were an expert. He had often gone rowing when he was younger, he
said; and when he had those things in his hands—he mimed pulling on
the oars—the rest of the world disappeared. He had thrashed more than
one Englishman in the past, at the Joinville regattas; and he made a joke
about the word "ladies" because the two mountings where the oars rested
were called "the ladies," and he said that rowers could never go out without their "ladies." And he got very excited while he was showing off and
stubbornly bet that in a boat like that he could easily row eighteen miles
an hour.

"Lunch is ready," said the waitress, who appeared at the entrance to
the boathouse; they all hurried off. But two young men had taken the best
spots that Madame Dufour had chosen in her mind, and they were eating lunch there. They were surely the owners of the skiffs, for they were
wearing boating clothes.

They were stretched out, almost lying on the chairs; their faces were
tanned by the sun and their thin, short-sleeved white cotton shirts showed
their bare arms, which looked as strong as a blacksmith's. They were two
strapping young men, showing off their muscles, but whose every movement displayed an elasticity and gracefulness in their arms and legs that is
only achieved by exercise, and is so different to the deformity that monotonous, hard work stamps on ordinary workmen.

They exchanged a quick smile when they saw the mother, then another
look when they spotted the daughter. "Let's give them our spot," one of
them said. "It will give us a chance to meet them." The other one imme-

diately stood up, and holding his black and red boating cap in his hand, offered the ladies the only shady place in the garden with great chivalry. After apologizing profusely, they finally accepted, and to make the experience more befitting the countryside, they sat down on the grass, with no tables or chairs.

The two young men took their dishes and silverware a little further away and started eating again. They showed off their bare arms at every opportunity, which embarrassed the young woman a little. She even deliberately looked away, but Madame Dufour, who was rather bolder, and drawn by a woman's curiosity that might have even been desire, looked at them constantly, comparing them, with regret, no doubt, to her husband, whose naked body she found ugly.

She had rolled down onto the ground, her legs crossed in front of her, and she kept wriggling around, on the pretext that ants were crawling on her somewhere. Monsieur Dufour, in a bad mood due to the presence of the polite, friendly strangers, was trying to get into a comfortable position, but he couldn't, and the young man with the blond hair was silently stuffing himself.

"It's a really lovely day, Monsieur," the fat woman said to one of the rowers. She wanted to be friendly because they had given them their spot. "Yes, Madame," he replied. "Do you often come out to the country?"

"Oh! Just once or twice a year, to take in some fresh air. And you, Monsieur?"

"I come and sleep here every night."

"Ah! That must be very nice."

"It certainly is, Madame."

And he spoke poetically about his everyday life, so poetically that it aroused a foolish love of nature in the hearts of these middle-class people who stood all year long behind the counter of their shop, deprived of the sight of grass and thirsting for long walks in the country.

The young woman was moved and looked up at the rower. Monsieur Dufour spoke for the first time: "Now that's what I call the good life," he said. "A bit more rabbit, my dear?" he asked his wife. "No thank you, dear."

She turned toward the young men again, and pointing to their arms, asked: "Don't you ever get cold like that?"

They both began to laugh, and astounded the family with stories about the extreme exhaustion they had endured, swimming while sweating profusely and rowing in the fog at night; then they banged their chests hard to show how they sounded. "Ah! You look very strong," said the husband, who had stopped talking about the time he had thrashed more than one Englishman.

The young woman was now secretly studying them, and the blond young man had a coughing fit—his drink had gone down the wrong way—spluttering all over Madame Dufour's cherry red silk dress. She got angry and had some water brought over so she could get out the stains.

Meanwhile, it had become terribly hot. The sparkling river looked on fire, and the wine was going to their heads.

Monsieur Dufour, who gave a violent hiccough, had opened his vest and the top button of his pants, while his wife, who was suffocating, unfastened her dress one button at a time. The apprentice was happily shaking his shaggy blond hair and kept pouring himself one glass of wine after the other. The old grandmother realized she was drunk and sat up very tall and dignified. The young woman gave nothing away; only her eyes looked somewhat brighter, and her swarthy cheeks turned more rosy.

By the time they'd finished their coffee, they were done for. They suggested singing and each of them sang a verse, which the others applauded enthusiastically. Then they stood up, with difficulty, and while the two women, who were rather dizzy, were trying to get a breath of air, Dufour and the blond young man, who were completely drunk, started doing gymnastics. Heavy, limp, their faces bright red, they hung awkwardly from the iron rings but couldn't hoist themselves up; and their shirts were continually on the verge of flying out of their pants to flutter in the wind like flags.

Meanwhile, the two rowers had put their boats in the water and came back to politely offer to take the ladies for a ride down the river.

"Would that be all right, Monsieur Dufour?" his wife cried. "Please say yes!" He gave her a drunken look, without understanding. Then one of the rowers handed the two men fishing rods. And the hope of catching a gudgeon, a city shopkeeper's dream, made the man's dull eyes light up; and he let the ladies do whatever they wanted while he sat in the shade, under the bridge, his feet dangling over the river, next to the blond young man who fell asleep beside him.

One of the rowers made the sacrifice: he took the mother. "Let's go to the little wood on the Ile aux Anglais!" he shouted as he rowed away. The other boat went more slowly. The rower was looking at his female companion so intently that he could think of nothing else, and a feeling had seized hold of him that left him weak.

The young woman, who was sitting in the cox's seat, relaxed, enjoying the sweet sensation of gliding on the water. She felt overcome by a need not to think, a sense of tranquility in her arms and legs, a feeling of complete luxury, as if she had been simultaneously overcome by several forms of intoxication. She had turned bright red and was breathing fast. The exhilaration of the wine, increased by the torrid heat, made all the trees along the bank seem to bow to her as she passed. A vague need for sensual pleasure and the blood she could feel flowing in her veins rushed through her whole body, aroused by the heat of the day; and she was flustered by being alone with a young man on the water, in a place that was deserted because of the blazing heat, a young man who thought she was beautiful and whose passionate eyes seemed to kiss her flesh, and whose desire for her was as penetrating as the sun.

Their inability to speak heightened their emotion, so they looked around at the scenery. Then he made an effort and asked her name. "Henriette," she said. "Really!" he replied. "My name is Henri."

The sound of their voices had calmed them; they looked out at the riverbanks. The other boat had stopped and seemed to be waiting for them. The rower shouted: "We'll meet you in the wood; we're going to Robinson's, because Madame Dufour is thirsty." Then he leaned over his oars and took off so fast that he was soon out of sight.

Meanwhile a continual rumbling that they had vaguely heard for some time was coming closer, fast. The river itself seemed to shudder, as if the muted sound were rising from its depths.

"What's that noise?" she asked. It was the sound of the lock closing that cut the river in two at the island. He was in the middle of explaining it to her when they heard a bird singing from very far away, through the noise of the waterfall. "Listen!" he said. "The nightingales are singing during the day: that means the female birds must be brooding."

A nightingale! She had never heard one before, and the idea of listening to one aroused a vision of poetic tenderness in her heart. A nightingale! The hidden witness of Juliet's meetings with her lover on the balcony; the celestial music that accompanies man's kisses, the eternal inspiration for all the languorous love stories that offer an idyllic blue sky to the poor, tender little heart of every sensitive young woman!

She was going to hear a nightingale sing.

"Don't make a sound," her companion said. "We can get off at the woods and sit down near him."

The boat seemed to glide. They could just see the trees on the island; its banks were so low that they could look deep into the thickets. They stopped. He tied up the boat. Henri helped Henriette out and they made their way through the branches of the trees. "Bend down," he said. She leaned down, and they entered a tangled web of creepers, leaves and reeds that led to a secret shelter. The young man laughed and called it "my private hideaway."

Just above their heads, perched in one of the trees that hid them from sight, the bird was still singing as loudly as he could. He trilled and warbled, then made loud, echoing sounds that filled the air before fading in the distance, floating along the river and disappearing above the plains, through the fiery silence that descended upon the countryside.

They didn't speak in case they frightened it away. They were sitting close together; slowly, Henri put his arm around the young woman's waist and gently squeezed it. She wasn't angry, but she pushed his bold hand away, and continued moving it every time he put it around her, without, however, feeling any embarrassment from his caress, as if it were something quite natural that she was pushing away just as naturally.

She was listening to the bird, enraptured. An endless longing for happiness, a sharp desire for affection rushed through her, an overwhelming desire for poetic declarations of love, and she felt her tension subsiding and her heart melting so fast that she began to cry, without knowing why. The young man was now holding her close; she no longer resisted; it didn't even occur to her.

Suddenly the nightingale stopped singing. A voice called out in the distance:

"Henriette!"

"Don't answer," he whispered. "You'll frighten the bird away."

She had no desire to reply.

They remained as they were for quite some time. Madame Dufour had sat down somewhere, for every now and then they could vaguely hear the fat woman letting out little shrieks when the other rower, no doubt, tried to fondle her.

The young woman was still crying, filled with very sweet sensations; her flesh was hot and aroused in a way she had never experienced before. Henri's head rested on her shoulder; suddenly, he kissed her on the lips. She pushed him away angrily, and fell backwards, trying to avoid him. But he threw himself on top of her, covering her entire body with his. For a long time, he tried to kiss her, but she kept turning away; finally, he pressed his lips against hers. Then, overcome by intense desire, she returned his kiss, clutching him to her breast, and all her resistance crumbled, as if crushed by a very heavy weight.

Everything was still. The bird started singing again. He let out three piercing notes that sounded like a call to love, then, after a moment's silence, he continued warbling very slowly, very softly.

A gentle breeze drifted in, rustling the leaves, and deep beneath the branches, passionate sighs mingled with the nightingale's song and the soft sound of the wind in the woods.

The bird was filled with ecstasy, and his song gradually grew faster, like a fire that is lit or passion that grows stronger, a musical accompaniment to the sound of kisses beneath the tree. Then he started singing at the top of his voice, lost in frenzy. He let out long, swooning notes, great melodious tremors.

Sometimes, he rested for a while, drawing out two or three soft sounds that suddenly ended on a shrill note. At other times, he sang madly, going through all the scales, trilling, starting and stopping, like a song of wild love, ending in triumphant cries.

Then he fell silent, hearing beneath him such a deep moan that you would have thought a soul was leaving a body. The sound lasted for a time, then ended in a sob.

They were both very pale when they left their grassy bed. The blue sky looked clouded over; the burning sun had lost its glimmer; all they felt was solitude and silence. They walked quickly, side by side, without speaking, without touching each other, for they seemed to have become irreconcilable enemies, as if a feeling of disgust had taken over their bodies and hatred filled their minds.

Every now and then Henriette called out: "Mama!"

They heard a lot of commotion coming from under a bush. Henri thought he saw a white petticoat quickly being pulled down over a fat calf muscle; and the enormous woman appeared, rather flustered and even redder, her eyes shining brightly and her chest heaving, standing a little too close, perhaps, to her companion. The young man must have seen something very amusing, for his face was contorted with laughter; he was doing his best to control himself, but without much success.

Madame Dufour took his arm affectionately and they headed back to the boats. Henri, still silent, was walking ahead, alongside the young woman; he suddenly thought he heard them give each other a long kiss, which they tried to do quietly.

They finally got back to Bezons.

Monsieur Dufour, now sober, was waiting impatiently. The young man with the blond hair was having something to eat before leaving the inn. The cart was harnessed in the courtyard and the grandmother had already got in; she was upset because she was afraid to be out on the plains in the dark; the outskirts of Paris were not very safe.

Everyone shook hands, and the Dufour family set off. "Goodbye!" shouted the rowers. They were answered by a sigh and a tear.

....

TWO MONTHS LATER, when Henri was walking along the Rue des Martyrs, he saw a sign over a door: *Dufour's Hardware Store*.

He went in.

The fat woman was even larger behind the counter. They recognized each other immediately, and after endless polite remarks, he asked what they had been doing lately. "And Mademoiselle Henriette, how is she?"

"Very well, thank you; she got married."

"Ah!"

He felt moved.

"But . . . who did she marry?" he asked.

"That young man who was with us, you know who I mean; he'll be joining the business."

"Oh! I see."

He started to leave, feeling very sad, but without really knowing why. Madame Dufour called him back.

"And how is your friend?" she asked, shyly.

"Oh, he's fine."

"Do send him our regards; and tell him to come and see us if he happens to be in the neighborhood . . ."

She turned bright red and added: "Tell him I would be very happy to see him again."

"Of course, I will. Well, this is goodbye then!"

"Not at all . . . see you soon, I hope."

THE FOLLOWING YEAR, ONE very hot Sunday, all the details of that moment of love, which Henri had never forgotten, suddenly came back to him so clearly and made him feel such desire that he went back to their love nest in the woods all alone.

He was astonished when he went inside. She was there, sitting on the grass, looking sad, while next to her, his shirtsleeves still rolled up, the young man with the blond hair looked like some animal, fast asleep.

She turned so pale when she saw Henri that he thought she might faint. But then they began to chat quite naturally, as if nothing had ever happened between them.

But when he told her that he liked this place very much and often came on Sundays to relax, thinking about many past memories, she looked into his eyes for a long time.

"I think about it every night," she said.

Her husband yawned. "Come on, girl," he said. "I think it's time for us to get going."

THE QUESTION OF LATIN

⌒═⟩⟨═⌒

THE QUESTION OF LATIN, WHICH HAS BEEN THE SUBJECT OF endless discussions for some time now, reminds me of a story, a story from my youth.

I was finishing my studies in one of the large cities in central France, enrolled in a private school, the Robineau Institute, run by a money-grubbing principal; it was famous throughout the area for the excellent Latin courses it offered.

For ten years, the Robineau Institute had beaten the city's top lycée and all the middle schools in the suburbs in all the national competitions in Latin, and its success was due to a tutor, an ordinary tutor—or so they said—named Monsieur Piquedent,[1] or rather Old Man Piquedent.

He was one of those middle-aged men whose age is impossible to guess but whose life story you understand the minute you see them. He'd started as a tutor in some educational establishment or other when he was twenty, so he could continue his own studies, to get his college degree, then even a doctorate. But he'd become so caught up in that miserable world that he'd remained a simple tutor all his life. Yet he'd never lost his love for Latin, and it plagued him like an unhealthy passion. He continued reading the poets, prose writers and historians, interpreting them, examining them closely, writing critiques of them with the kind of perseverance that bordered on obsession.

---

1   The name translates loosely as "Monsieur Toothache."

One day, he got the idea of making all his students speak to him only in Latin and he persisted in that resolution until they were able to hold an entire conversation with him as if they were speaking their native language.

He listened to them the way a maestro rehearses the musicians in an orchestra, continually banging his ruler on the edge of his desk:

"Monsieur Lefrère, Monsieur Lefrère, you're making a grammatical mistake! Can you really not remember the rule . . . ?

"Monsieur Plantel, your sentence structure is completely French and in no way Latin. You must understand the spirit of a language. Listen, listen to me. . . ."

And this is why the students at the Robineau Institute won all the prizes at the end of the school year, all the prizes for writing, translating and speaking in Latin.

The following year, the owner of the school, a little man as cunning as a monkey—he even resembled one with his grotesque, fixed grin—the owner had printed on his brochures and advertisements, and painted on the school's main entrance:

Specialists in Latin. Five First Prizes won in all Five Classes of the Lycée. Two Top Prizes in the National Competition of all the Lycées and Middle Schools of France.

For ten years, the Robineau Institute triumphed in the same way. Now my father, enticed by such success, sent me as a day student to this Robineau, which we called Robinetto or Robinettino, and had me take extra private lessons with Old Man Piquedent, at five francs an hour, out of which the tutor got two francs and the owner three. I was eighteen years old and in my final year.

These lessons took place in a little room that looked out onto the street. Now instead of making me speak Latin, as he did in class, Old Man Piquedent told me all about his problems in French. With no family, no friends, the poor man took a liking to me, and poured his heart out.

It had been ten or fifteen years since he'd spoken to anyone alone.

"I am like an oak tree in the wilderness." he said, "*Sicut quercus in solitudine*."

The other tutors repelled him; he knew no one in the city because he had no free time to form relationships.

"Not even at night, my boy, and that's the hardest for me. I dream of having a room with my own furniture, my books, all the little knick-knacks that belong to me and that no one else could touch.

"And I have nothing, nothing but my pants and frock coat, nothing, not even my own pillow and mattress! I don't have four walls where I can shut myself away, except when I come here to give you your lessons. Can you understand that, can you, a man who spends his entire life without ever having the right or the time to shut himself away, all alone, anywhere, to think, to reflect, to work, to dream? My dear boy, a key, a key to a door that you can lock, that's happiness, that and that alone would be true happiness!

"I'm here at the school during the day, in the classroom with all the little rascals running around, and at night, in the dormitory with the same rascals, who snore. And I sleep in a bed in the same room, at the bottom of two rows of those naughty boys I have to watch over. I can never be alone, never! If I go out, the street is crowded with people, and when I'm tired of walking, I go into a café and that too is full of people smoking and playing billiards. I'm telling you, it's hell."

"Why didn't you do something else, Monsieur Piquedent?" I asked.

"What could I have done, my dear boy?" he cried. "I'm not a shoe-maker, or a carpenter, or a hat maker or a baker or a hairdresser. All I know is Latin, that's all, and I don't even have any degrees that would allow me to make any real money from it. If I had my doctorate, I'd make one hundred francs for the twenty cents I get now; and I'd most likely not do as good a job because my title would be enough to maintain my reputation."

Sometimes he said:

"The only peaceful moments I have in life are the times I spend with you. But don't worry; you won't lose out. I'll make up for it by having you speak twice as much as the others during lessons."

One day, I decided to be bold and offered him a cigarette. At first, he stared at me in astonishment, then he glanced over at the door:

"But what if someone came in, my boy?"

"Well then, let's smoke over by the window," I said.

And we went and leaned over the window that looked out over the street, hiding the thin, hand-rolled cigarettes in our cupped hands.

Opposite us was a laundry: four women wearing flowing white blouses pressed the clothes that were laid out in front of them with a hot, heavy iron that gave off steam.

Suddenly, another young woman, a fifth, came outside, carrying a basket on her arm that was so heavy she bent under its weight; she started giving the clients their shirts, handkerchiefs and sheets. She stopped at the door, as if she were already tired, then she looked up, smiled when she saw us smoking, and with her free hand, blew us a kiss—the mischievous kiss of a carefree working girl; then she walked slowly away, dragging her feet.

She was about twenty, petite, rather thin, pale, pretty with a girlish expression, smiling eyes and messy blond hair.

Old Man Piquedent was moved.

"What a terrible job for a woman!" he murmured. "Real donkey's work."

He was touched by the poverty of the working classes. His heart was full of sentimental, democratic ideas, and he spoke of the exhaustion of the poor, quoting Jean-Jacques Rousseau in a voice choked with emotion.

The next day, we were leaning out of the same window when the same young woman saw us. "Hello there, schoolboys!" she said in a funny little voice, thumbing her nose at us.

I threw her a cigarette and she started to smoke it right away. Then the four other laundresses rushed out to the door, stretching out their hands, so they could each have one as well.

And every day, the friendship grew between the women workers on the sidewalk and the lazybones in the school.

Old Man Piquedent was really funny to watch. He was terrified of being caught, for he could have lost his job, and he made shy, laughable gestures, an entire sign language of lovers on the stage, to which the women replied with a hail of kisses.

A perfidious idea was growing in my mind. One day, as we were going into the study room, I whispered to the old tutor:

"You won't believe this, Monsieur Piquedent, but I met the little laundress! You know who I mean, the one with the basket, and I spoke to her!"

He was quite worried by my tone of voice and asked:

"What did she say to you?"

"She told me . . . good Lord . . . she told me . . . that she thought you were really nice . . . Actually, I think . . . I think . . . that she's a little in love with you . . ."

I watched the color drain from his face. "She's making fun of me, no doubt. That kind of thing doesn't happen to a man my age."

"Why not?" I said, sounding serious. "You're very attractive!"

When I realized he was moved by my ruse, I didn't insist.

But every day, I pretended to have run into the young woman and to have talked to her about him; I was so convincing that he ended up believing me, and he started blowing passionate kisses to her.

Then, one morning, on my way to school, I actually did run into her. I went straight up to her as if I'd known her for ten years.

"Hello, Mademoiselle. How are you?"

"Very well, Monsieur, thank you."

"Would you like a cigarette?"

"Oh! Not out in the street."

"Well, you can smoke it at home."

"In that case, thanks very much."

"Tell me, Mademoiselle, do you realize that . . ."

"What, Monsieur?"

"The old man, my teacher . . ."

"Old Man Piquedent?"

"Yes, Old Man Piquedent. So you know his name?"

"Well, really! What about him?"

"He's in love with you, that's what!"

She started laughing like a madwoman and cried: "You're joking, right?"

"No, it's no joke. He talks to me about you during our lessons. I bet he wants to marry you."

She stopped laughing. The idea of marriage makes all young women become serious. "You're joking, right?" she said again, incredulous.

"I swear it's the truth."

She picked up the basket she'd put down at her feet. "We'll see about that!" she said.

Then she walked away.

As soon as I got inside the school, I took Old Man Piquedent to one side: "You must write to her; she's crazy about you."

So he wrote a long letter, sweet and tender, full of loving words and innuendos, metaphors and comparisons, academic ideas and compliments, a true masterpiece of ludicrous elegance. And he gave me the letter to deliver to the young woman.

She read it with the utmost seriousness, with emotion, then whispered:

"He writes so well! You can tell he's very educated! Is it true he wants to marry me?"

"Good Lord!" I replied boldly. "He's crazy about you."

"Well then, he must invite me to dinner on Sunday on the Ile des Fleurs."

I promised she would be invited.

Old Man Piquedent was very moved by everything I told him about her.

"She loves you, Monsieur Piquedent," I added, "and I think she's a decent young woman. You mustn't seduce her and then abandon her!"

"I too am a decent person, my boy," he replied firmly.

I didn't have any particular plan, I admit that. I was playing a practical joke, a schoolboy's prank, nothing more. I had guessed the old tutor's naïveté, his innocence and his weakness. I was having fun without ever wondering how it would all turn out. I was eighteen, and I'd had the reputation at school of being a sly joker for some time.

And so it was agreed that Old Man Piquedent and I would get a carriage to the dock at Queue-de-Vache where we would meet Angèle, and I would take them out in my boat, for I was a rower back then. I would take them to the Ile des Fleurs, where all three of us would have dinner. I had imposed my presence on them so I could really enjoy my triumph, and the old man, accepting my offer, proved he actually was crazy about her by risking his job that way.

When we arrived at the dock, where my boat had been tied up since morning, I noticed an enormous red parasol through the tall grass, or rather above the reeds on the riverbank; it looked like some monstrous poppy. Beneath the parasol, the little laundress was waiting for us, in her Sunday best. I was surprised; she was really very nice, despite being rather pale, and she was gracious, even though she looked rather common.

Old Man Piquedent took off his hat and bowed to her. She reached out her hand and they looked at each other, without saying a word. Then they got into my boat and I took the oars.

They sat side by side in the back of the boat.

The old man spoke first:

"Now this is lovely weather for a boat ride."

"Oh, it is!" she said softly.

She put her hand into the water, letting her fingers trail along its surface, which brought up a little trickle of clear water, like a shard of glass. It made a soft sound, a gentle lapping, all along the boat.

When we were in the restaurant, she found her voice again and ordered her meal: some fried fish, chicken and some salad; then she showed us around the island, which she knew extremely well.

She was cheerful, coquettish and even rather mocking.

Until dessert, no one brought up the subject of love. I had treated them to some champagne and Old Man Piquedent was drunk. She was a little tipsy too and called him "Monsieur Piquenez."[2]

Suddenly, he said: "Mademoiselle, Monsieur Raoul has told you how I feel."

She became as sober as a judge. "Yes, Monsieur!"

"Do you feel the same way?"

---

2   Translates as "Hurts your nose."

"You never answer questions like that!"

He was choking with emotion and continued: "Well then, do you think that the day might come when you could like me?"

She smiled: "Silly thing! You're very nice."

"Well then, Mademoiselle, do you think that at some later date we could . . . ?"

She hesitated, just for a second; then she asked, her voice trembling: "Are you asking to marry me? Because I'd never any other way, you know?"

"Yes, Mademoiselle!"

"Well then, that's fine, Monsieur Piquenez!"

And that is how these two scatterbrains promised to marry each other, thanks to a naughty schoolboy. But I didn't believe it was serious; neither did they, perhaps.

She thought of something and hesitated:

"You know I have nothing, not a penny."

He stammered, for he was as drunk as Silenus:[3]

"But I've got five thousand francs saved up."

"Then we can buy a business," she cried triumphantly.

"What kind of business?"

"How would I know? We'll have to see. With five thousand francs, you can do a lot. You don't want me to come and live with you at the school, do you?"

He hadn't thought that far ahead and he became very perplexed: "Buy some kind of business?" he stammered. "That wouldn't do at all! All I know is Latin!"

She thought about it as well, going over in her mind all the professions she aspired to.

"Couldn't you be a doctor?"

"No, I haven't got the qualifications."

"A pharmacist?"

"Not that either."

---

3   In Greek mythology, Silenua was tutor to Dionysus, the god of wine.

She let out a cry of joy. She'd found it. "Well, then we'll buy a grocer's shop! Oh, what a stroke of luck! We'll buy a grocer's shop! Not a big one, you know; five thousand francs won't go that far."

He rebelled: "No, I can't be a grocer . . . I'm . . . I'm too well known . . . All I know is . . . is . . . Latin, just Latin . . ."

But she thrust a glass of champagne to his lips. He drank it and fell silent.

We got back into the boat. It was dark out, very dark. I could see, however, that they had their arms around each other and kissed several times.

It was a catastrophe. Our little escapade was discovered and Old Man Piquedent was fired. And my father, furious, sent me to finish my final year at the Ribaudet boarding school.

I took my baccalaureate six weeks later. Then I went to Paris to study law. I didn't go back to my hometown for two years.

At the bend of the Rue du Serpent, a shop caught my eye. The sign said *Piquedent: Exotic Products.* Then underneath, to explain to the less well educated: *Grocery.*

"*Quantum mutatus ab illo!*"[4] I cried.

And he looked up, walked away from his client and rushed toward me with outstretched arms.

"Ah! My good friend, so you're here, my good friend! What a stroke of luck! Real luck!"

A beautiful but ample woman quickly came out from behind the counter and threw her arms around me. I barely recognized her, she had grown so fat.

"So, things are going well?"

Piquedent had gone back to weighing something:

"Oh! Very well, very well, very well indeed. I had three thousand francs profit this year!"

"What about your Latin, Monsieur Piquedent?"

"Oh! Good Lord. Latin, Latin, Latin. A man can't live on Latin alone!"

---

4 "How he's changed since then!"

TALES OF
WAR

OF THE MANY WARS FRANCE FOUGHT IN THE NINETEENTH century, the Franco-Prussian War bears the distinction of being the only one in which France was invaded and occupied. Otto von Bismarck's powerful Prussian army defeated Napoleon III at the Battle of Sedan in September 1870, and in January 1871, Paris finally fell, after being reduced to virtual starvation. While France was occupied for only a relatively short time (the Treaty of Frankfurt ended the war on May 10, 1871), the devastating effects of this war and the humiliation of losing to the hated Prussians carved a deep groove in French culture of the era. It is the experience of the Prussian occupation of France and his own experience in the war that forms the basis for most of Maupassant's stories about this conflict.

Maupassant was drafted into the army in July 1870 and took part in the retreat after the defeat at Sedan. He experienced many of the horrors of war firsthand, and details them with a black humor that highlights the bleak absurdity of war as seen from the ground level. For both the French and Prussian soldiers, the outcome of the war makes almost no difference, as we see in *Two Friends*, where one protagonist says to the other, "How stupid do you have to be to kill each other this way!"

The themes of frustration and impotence (*A Duel*), courage and patriotism (*Mademoiselle Fifi*), and a desire for revenge against the sadistic Prussian soldiers (*Père Milon*) permeate the stories in this section. Yet Maupassant does not lose sight of the fact that many of the Prussian soldiers are ordinary men who have no desire to fight: *The Adventure of Walter Schnaffs* and the depiction of the young Prussian soldiers in *La Mère Sauvage* are perfect examples of this.

Boule de suif, one of Maupassant's most famous novellas, and deservedly, expertly combines many of the recurring themes here, serving as an important document of the political events and social mores of the time.

In the majority of these stories, Maupassant parodies the Prussians, who speak French with incorrect grammar and a heavy accent. The contrast between the satirical, humorous language and the serious themes provides biting irony. I have done my best to replicate this technique by transcribing a Germanic accent into the English.

MADEMOISELLE FIFI

THE MAJOR, THE PRUSSIAN COMMANDANT, COUNT VON FARLS-berg, was finishing reading his mail; settled back in a large tapestry-covered armchair, his boots were propped up against the elegant marble fireplace where his spurs, during the three months he had occupied the Château d'Uville, had made two holes that got deeper with every passing day.

A cup of steaming coffee sat on a small marquetry pedestal table that was stained with liquor, burnt by cigars, scratched by the conqueror's penknife; every now and again, he would stop sharpening a pencil and carve some numbers or drawings on the beautiful piece of furniture, according to his whims.

When he had finished the letters and looked through the German newspapers his orderly brought him, he stood up and threw three or four enormous pieces of green wood onto the fire, for these gentlemen were gradually cutting down all the trees in the estate in order to keep warm. He walked over to the window.

The rain flooded down, the kind you typically have in Normandy, rain that looked as if it were being unleashed by some furious hand; it came down in great diagonal sheets that formed a kind of wall with slanted stripes, the driving, splashing rain that floods everything, the true downpour you get in the outskirts of Rouen, that chamberpot of France.

For a long time, the officer stared at the flooded lawns and the Andelle River in the distance that was overflowing its banks. He was tapping out a

German waltz on the window pane when a noise made him turn around: it was his second in command, Baron von Kelweingstein, who held the rank of Captain.

The Major was an enormous man with broad shoulders and a long beard that spread out and covered his chest like a fan; his solemn, noble bearing made him look like a peacock in uniform, a peacock who carried his tail spread out over his chin. He had blue eyes that were pale and cold, and a scar on one cheek made by a sword in the war with Austria. And he had the reputation of being a decent man as well as a brave officer.

The Captain was a short, fat, red-faced man who looked as if he'd been poured into his tight uniform; his fiery beard was cut so short it was almost like stubble, and in a certain kind of light, his face looked as if he were covered in phosphorous. He'd lost two teeth one night at someone's wedding party—he couldn't exactly remember how—and because of this, he spat out his words, so you couldn't always understand what he was saying. He had no hair at the very top of his head; the bald spot was surrounded by golden, shiny, curly hair, so that he looked like a monk.

The Major shook his hand and drank his cup of coffee in one gulp (his sixth of the morning), while listening to his subordinate's report on the various incidents that had occurred; then the two of them walked over to the window, remarking on how gloomy it looked. The Major, a calm man who had a wife back home, adjusted well to everything; but the Captain, a tenacious pleasure-seeker who frequented seedy dives, and an obsessive womanizer, was furious at having been forced into celibacy in the middle of nowhere for the past three months.

Someone tapped at the door and the Captain shouted for him to come in; one of his orderlies appeared at the door; the fact that he was there meant that lunch was ready.

In the dining room, they found three lower-ranking officers: a lieutenant, Otto von Grossling, and two second lieutenants, Fritz Scheunaubourg[1] and the Marquis Wilhem d'Eyrik, a very short dandy who was

---

[1]   The name "Fritz" was used in French slang to mean any German.

proud, brutal toward men, harsh to the people they'd beaten and as dangerous as gunpowder.

Ever since he'd arrived in France, his comrades refused to call him anything but "Mademoiselle Fifi." The nickname was a result of his coquettish manner, his slim waist that looked as if he was wearing a corset, his pale face on which you could barely see any moustache growing, and the habit he had adopted of expressing his supreme disdain for people and things by constantly using the French phrase "*fi, fi donc*,"[2] which he pronounced with a slight whistle.

THE DINING ROOM IN the Château d'Uville was long and majestic; its antique crystal mirrors were cracked by bullets, and its long Flemish tapestries were cut to ribbons, slashed with a sword and falling down in places: both evidence of how Mademoiselle Fifi amused himself when he had nothing better to do.

Three family portraits hung on the walls: a knight in a suit of armor, a cardinal and a judge; all three had long porcelain pipes sticking out of their mouths, so it looked like they were smoking. And in an antique frame whose gilding was worn with age, the painting of a noblewoman in a tightly corseted dress proudly displayed an enormous moustache added in charcoal.

The officers ate their lunch in virtual silence in this mutilated room that looked even gloomier in the rain, sadder in its vanquished appearance, the old oak parquet as grimy as the floor in a tavern.

After the meal, when they started smoking and drinking, they began talking about their boredom, as they did every day. Bottles of cognac and liquors were passed around, and all of them, leaning back in their chairs, kept taking sips of alcohol, never removing the long, curved stem of the pipes whose faience bowls were gaudily painted as if to attract some Hottentot.[3]

---

2 Translates roughly as "To hell with that!"
3 Contemptuous reference to a nomadic tribe from Africa.

As soon as their glasses were empty, they would refill them with a gesture of resigned weariness. But since Mademoiselle Fifi constantly smashed his, a soldier always immediately brought him another.

A cloud of bitter smoke shrouded them, and they seemed to slump into a sad, drowsy state of drunkenness, the kind of gloomy intoxication of men with nothing to do.

Then the Baron suddenly sat up. He was shaken awake by a feeling of revolt. "For God's sake," he swore, "we have to think of something to do; we can't go on like this."

Lieutenant Otto and Second Lieutenant Fritz, both eminently endowed with the heavy, serious traits of the German race, replied at the same time: "But what, Captain?"

He thought for a few seconds. "What? Well, we should organize a party," he continued, "that is, if the Commandant will allow it."

The Major took the pipe out of his mouth: "What kind of party, Captain?"

The Baron walked over to him: "I'll take care of everything, Major. I'll send *Le Devoir* [4] to Rouen to bring us back some women; I know where to get them. We can have dinner here; we have everything we need, and at least we'll have a good time."

Count von Farlsberg smiled and shrugged his shoulders.

"You must be mad."

But all the officers had stood up, surrounding their leader: "Oh, please let the Captain arrange it, Major," they begged. "It's so depressing here."

In the end, the Major gave in. "Fine," he said; and the Baron immediately called for *Le Devoir*. He was an old, non-commissioned officer whom no one had ever seen smile, but he fanatically carried out all the officers' orders to the letter, whatever they were.

He stood there, impassively, taking the Baron's instructions, then left; five minutes later, a large military wagon covered in tight canvas was hitched to four horses and galloped off in the driving rain.

---

4   Another name that is a play on words: it means "duty" or "obligation."

The officers all suddenly felt lively; their languid bodies stood tall, their faces lit up and they started chatting.

Even though it was raining as hard as ever, the Major said it didn't look so dark, and Lieutenant Otto declared with great conviction that it was going to clear up. Even Mademoiselle Fifi didn't seem to be able to sit still. He got up, sat down again. His harsh, pale eyes looked around for something to break. Suddenly, staring at the Noblewoman with the Moustache, the blond young man pulled out his revolver.

"*You* will not see it," he said, and from his chair, took aim. He fired twice, and two bullets pierced the eyes of the portrait.

Then he shouted: "Let's make a *mine*!" which is what he called his bomb![5] And the conversations suddenly stopped, as if some powerful, new amusing idea had taken hold of everyone.

The bomb was his invention, the way he destroyed things, his favorite pastime.

When he left the château, the rightful owner, Count Fernand d'Amoys d'Uville, didn't have time to take anything with him; the only thing he managed to hide was the silver, which he hurriedly stashed in a crevice in the wall. The dining room adjoined the large reception room, which was richly and magnificently decorated; before its owner fled, it had resembled a gallery in a museum.

Expensive paintings, drawings and watercolors hung on the walls, while the furniture, shelves and elegant display cabinets held hundreds of antiques: ornamental vases, statuettes, Dresden figurines, Chinese pagoda figures, old ivory pieces and Venetian glass, strange, precious objects that filled the enormous room.

Hardly anything was left now. Not that they had been pillaged; the Major would never have allowed that, but Mademoiselle Fifi made a bomb every now and again, and, on those days, all the officers had five minutes of good fun.

The little Marquis went into the reception room to get what he needed.

---

5   The expression in French is *faire une mine*, which can mean either "let's make a face" or "let's make a bomb."

He came back with a really lovely *famille rose* china teapot that he filled with gunpowder. Then he carefully pushed a long piece of tinder down its spout, lit it, and rushed to put his deadly toy in the adjoining room.

Then he ran quickly out, closing the door behind him. All the Germans were standing there, waiting, smiling with childish curiosity; and as soon as the explosion shook the château, they all ran in together.

Mademoiselle Fifi got there first; he clapped his hands in delight when he saw the terra-cotta Venus whose head had blown off; then they all picked up bits of porcelain, surprised and delighted by their odd, jagged shapes and examined them again, declaring that some of the damage had been done by a previous bomb, and the Major looked with a fatherly expression at the enormous reception room destroyed by these explosions in a manner worthy of Nero and strewn everywhere with fragments of fine works of art. He was the first to leave, after saying, in quite a friendly way: "It worked very well this time."

An enormous cloud of smoke in the dining room had merged with the tobacco smoke from before, so they couldn't breathe. The Commandant opened the window, and all the officers, who had come back to have another glass of cognac, walked over to it. The damp air rushed into the room, bringing with it the smell of floodwater and a kind of powdery mist that settled in their beards. They looked at the tall trees weighed down by the heavy flood, the wide valley covered in fog by the water unleashed from the low, dark clouds, and the church's belltower, in the distance, rising up like a gray spike in the driving rain.

The bells had stopped ringing when they arrived. In fact, the only resistance the invaders had encountered in the region was the refusal to ring the bells. The country priest had not refused to take in or feed the Prussian soldiers, not at all; on several occasions, he had even agreed to drink a bottle of wine or beer with the enemy Commandant, who often used him as a benevolent intermediary. But there was no point in asking him to ring a single bell; he would have sooner offered to be shot. This was his own way of protesting against the invasion, by peaceful resistance, by remaining silent, the only form of resistance, he claimed, that was suitable to a priest, a man of kindness, not a bloodthirsty man; and everyone, for thirty miles around, praised the strength and heroism of Father Chantavoine, who dared proclaim the mourning of the French, who shouted it out by the stubborn silence of his church bells.

The entire village, fired up by his resistance, was prepared to support their priest to the very end, to risk anything at all, considering his tacit resistance the safeguard of their national honor. And because of this, the people of the region thought they deserved to be considered more patriotic than Belfort or Strasbourg,[6] believing they had set just as good an example, and that the name of their village would become immortalized. Apart from this one thing, however, they offered no resistance at all to the Prussian conquerors.

The Commandant and his officers laughed among themselves at such harmless bravery, and since everyone in the area was adaptable and obliging toward them, they gladly tolerated their silent patriotism.

Only the little Marquis Wilhem wanted to force them to ring the bells. He was furious about his superior's political concession to the priest, and every day he begged the Commandant to let him ring "ding-dong" once, just once, as a joke. And he made his request with the charm of a little kitten, the cajoling voice of a woman, the sweet tones of a mistress mad with desire; but the Commandant did not give in, so to console himself, Mademoiselle Fifi set off a bomb in the Château d'Uville.

The five men crowded around for a few minutes, breathing in the damp air. Then Lieutenant Fritz gave a hoarse laugh and said: "These ladies vill definitely not have a good ride in such bad weather."

Then everyone left, as they each had to get back to their official assignments, and the Captain had a great deal to do to prepare for the dinner party.

When they met up again toward evening, they laughed at seeing how they had all spruced themselves up to look attractive, like the days on formal inspections: squeaky clean, hair slicked back, wearing cologne. The Commandant's hair looked less gray than it had in the morning; and the

---

6   Belfort and Strasbourg, besieged by the Prussians, had resisted for several months.

Captain had shaved, keeping only his moustache, which made him look as if his upper lip was on fire.

In spite of the rain, they left the window open; and every now and then, one of them went over to see if they could hear anything. At ten past six, the Baron said he heard a wagon rumbling in the distance. Everyone rushed over; and soon the large truck arrived, its four galloping horses caked in mud, panting and foaming at the mouth.

And five women came out onto the steps, five beautiful women, carefully chosen by the Captain's friend to whom *Le Devoir* had delivered the officer's calling card.

The women hadn't hesitated at all, certain of being well paid; they knew the Prussians, after all, as they'd been servicing them, and they had resigned themselves to the men as they did to all things. "That's how it is in this job," they told each other during the journey, no doubt to stifle a secret resentment in their hearts.

They all went into the dining room at once. It seemed even more dismal in its pitiful, dilapidated condition when the lights were on; and the table covered in food, on fine, silver plates they'd found in the wall where their owner had hidden them, made the scene look like a tavern where bandits would go to eat after a pillage. The Captain, absolutely delighted, grabbed hold of the women as if he knew them, complimenting them, kissing them, sniffing them, determining their worth as ladies of the night; and when the three young men wanted to take one each, he firmly refused, reserving to himself the right of handing them out fairly, according to the soldiers' rank, in order to respect the hierarchy.

So, to avoid any discussion, objection or suspicion of partiality, he lined them up in size order, then spoke to the tallest:

"Name," he said, making it sound like an order.

"Pamela," she replied in a loud voice.

"Number one, the aforementioned Pamela, assigned to the Commandant," he stated.

He immediately kissed Blondine, the second one, to indicate he was having her, then offered the chubby Amanda to Otto; Eva, the Tomato, to Second Lieutenant Fritz; and the smallest one of all, Rachel, a very young brunette with eyes as black as ink—a Jewess whose snub nose was the exception to the rule attributing hooked noses to everyone of her race—Rachel was given to the youngest officer, the frail Marquis Wilhem d'Eyrik.[7]

All of them, though, were pretty and plump, with no distinctive features, their looks and the way they held themselves very similar as a result of having sex every day and living in a brothel together.

The three youngest men immediately tried to get their women upstairs, using the pretext of offering them some soap and hairbrushes to freshen up; but the Captain wisely opposed this, stating that they were quite clean enough to sit down to dinner and that the men who wanted to go upstairs would want to change partners when they came back down, which would cause a problem for the other couples. His experience won out. They settled for many kisses, many kisses of anticipation.

Suddenly, Rachel started choking, coughing until her eyes watered, and smoke flowed out of her nostrils. The Marquis, pretending he wanted to kiss her, had blown tobacco smoke into her mouth. She didn't get angry, didn't say a word, but she stared at her owner with rage simmering deep in her dark eyes.

They sat down. Even the Commandant seemed delighted; he placed Pamela to his right, Blondine to his left, unfolded his napkin and said: "This was a charming idea of yours, Captain."

Lieutenants Otto and Fritz, as polite as if they had been in the company of socialites, intimidated the women a little; but Baron von Kelweingstein felt right at home: he beamed, made risqué remarks and looked as if he were on fire with his crop of red hair. He flattered the women in the French of the Rhine; and his gross compliments, spluttered through the hole left by his two missing teeth, covered the young women in a spray of saliva.

---

7   After the French Revolution (1789), France was the first European country to recognize Jews as equal citizens under the law. Nevertheless, in some parts of France anti-Jewish hatred was severe by the late nineteenth century. The Ligue Nationale Antisémitique de France was formed in 1889 and organized propaganda, riots and violent pogroms against local Jews. It was extremely rare for a Jewish woman to be a prostitute, and the remark about Rachel's nose reflects the stereotyping of the time. This story, however, portrays Rachel as brave and patriotic.

In fact, they didn't understand a word; and they did not seem to wake up until he started spitting out obscene words, crude expressions, distorted by his accent. Then all of them started laughing at the same time, laughing like mad things, falling over onto the men beside them, repeating the words the Baron had said; then he started saying them all wrong again, on purpose this time, just to hear the women say the dirty words. They gladly spewed them out, for they were drunk after the first few bottles of wine; then they got control of themselves and fell back into their usual behavior, kissing the moustaches of the men on either side of them, pinching their arms, shouting loudly, drinking from all the glasses, and singing French verses and bits of German songs they'd picked up from their daily contact with the enemy.

Soon even the men went wild, howled, smashed dishes, intoxicated by the women's flesh they could smell and touch, while impassive soldiers stood behind to serve them.

Only the Commandant showed restraint.

Mademoiselle Fifi had Rachel on his lap, and, getting very aroused, he would sometimes passionately kiss the little dark curls that fell onto her neck, breathing in the sweet warmth of her skin and the scent of her flesh through the slight gap between her dress and her body, and sometimes pinch her brutally through the cloth, making her scream, for he was overwhelmed by ferocious rage, a vicious desire to ravage her. He often held her with both arms, pressing down on her as if to join her body to his, placing his lips on the young Jewess's cool mouth, kissing her for so long she could hardly breathe; then, suddenly, he bit her so hard that a trickle of blood flowed down the young woman's chin onto her bodice.

She looked hard at him again, and, dabbing water on her wound, she murmured: "I'll make you pay for that." But all he did was give a merciless laugh and say: "Yes, I will."

Dessert was being served; they poured some champagne. The Commandant stood up and in the same tone of voice he might use to drink to the health of the Empress Augusta,[8] he made a toast: "To our ladies!"

---

8   The wife of the emperor William of Prussia.

And a round of toasts started, toasts full of the kind of compliments paid by roughnecks and drunkards, toasts filled with obscene jokes that sounded even more brutish because of the soldiers' inability to speak the language.

They stood up, one after the other, trying to be witty, forcing themselves to be funny; and the women, who were so drunk they could barely stand up, with slurred speech and vacant expressions, applauded wildly at each one.

The Captain, wishing no doubt to give the orgy the appearance of gallantry, raised his glass again and said: "To our triumph over your hearts."

Then Lieutenant Otto, a kind of bear from the Black Forest, stood up, drunk as a skunk, and suddenly overwhelmed by alcoholic patriotism passionately cried: "To our triumph over the French!"

As drunk as they were, all the women fell silent, but Rachel was trembling. "I know certain Frenchmen you wouldn't dare say that to, you know," she retorted.

But the little Marquis, who still had her sitting on his lap, started to laugh, for the wine had made him very giddy. "Ha! Ha! Ha! Well, *I've* never met any. As soon as we show up, they run away!"

The young woman, furious, shouted straight at him: "You're lying, you bastard!"

For a moment, he stared at her with his pale eyes, the way he stared at the paintings he destroyed with his gun, then he started to laugh. "Ah! Yes, Let's talk about those Frenchmen, my pretty! Would we even be here at all if they were really brave!" Then, getting even more worked up, he shouted: "We are the masters here! France belongs to us!"

She jumped off his lap and fell into a chair. He stood up, raised his glass toward the center of the table and said once more: "France and the French belong to us—we own their woods, their fields and all the houses in France!"

The others, completely drunk, were suddenly overwhelmed by military enthusiasm, the enthusiasm of brutes; they grabbed their glasses while shouting: "Long live Prussia!" then emptied them in a single gulp.

The young women did not protest; they were reduced to silence and overcome with fear. Even Rachel felt helpless and could find nothing to reply.

Then the little Marquis refilled his champagne glass and balanced it on the head of the Jewess, shouting: "And all the women in France belong to us as well!"

She got up so quickly that the glass tipped over, spilling the golden wine over her black hair, as if she were being baptized, before it dropped to the floor and shattered. Her lips quivering, she glowered at the officer, who was still laughing, then stammered in a voice choked with rage: "That . . . that's not true; you won't have all the women of France, you know."

He sat down again so he could laugh more comfortably, and putting on a Parisian accent said: "Zat is very funny, very funny, so what are you doing here, ma chère?"

She was so stunned that she said nothing at first, so upset that she didn't really understand him; then, once she realized what he was saying, she grew indignant and shouted vehemently: "Me! I'm not a woman; I'm a whore, and that is all you Prussians deserve."

She had barely finished speaking when he slapped her hard across the face; when she saw him raise his arm again, she flew into a rage, grabbed a small silver dessert knife from the table and quickly—so quickly that no one saw what had happened at first—she stabbed him right in the neck, right in the hollow of his neck, just above his chest.

Something he was about to say stuck in his throat, and he sat there with his mouth gaping open and a horrible look in his eyes.

All the men let out a roar and leaped up in a panic, but she threw her chair at Lieutenant Otto's legs, knocking him to the ground, rushed over to the window, opening it before they got to her, and ran out into the night, where the rain was still pouring down.

In two minutes, Mademoiselle Fifi was dead. Then Fritz and Otto drew their swords and wanted to kill the women, who threw themselves at their feet and clutched their legs. The Major prevented the massacre, but not without difficulty, and sent the four terrified women to be locked in a room with two guards at the door. Then he organized a party to hunt down the fugitive, as if he were ordering soldiers into combat, quite certain she would be caught.

Fifty men, fired up by threats, were sent running into the grounds. Two hundred others searched the woods and every house in the valley.

The table was cleared in a flash and used as a bed on which to lay the dead man, and the four officers, now standing upright and sober, with the harsh expression of men of war carrying out their duties, remained at the windows, trying to see whatever they could in the dark.

The torrential rain continued. An endless lapping sound filled the darkness, the murmur of flowing water that rises and falls, water that drips and then splashes up again.

Suddenly, they heard a gunshot, then another, quite far away; and for the next four hours, they could hear shots fired, some close by, some in the distance, along with calls to regroup, foreign words shouted as a rallying call in guttural voices.

Everyone returned the next morning. Two soldiers had been killed and three others wounded by their own soldiers in the heat of the chase and the confusion of their search through the darkness.

Rachel had not been found.

Then the people in the area were terrorized, their houses turned upside down, the entire region searched, the countryside scoured; they looked everywhere. The Jewess seemed not to have left a single trace of where she had gone.

The General was informed and ordered that the business be hushed up, so as not to set a bad example to the army, but he severely reprimanded the Commandant, who punished his inferiors. "We didn't go to war for a good time and to have fun with prostitutes," the General had said. And the frustrated Count Farlsberg swore to avenge his country.

Since he needed a pretext to act ruthlessly, he called for the country priest and ordered him to ring the bells at the funeral of the Marquis d'Eyrik.

Much to his surprise, the priest was docile, humble, considerate. And when Mademoiselle Fifi's body left the Château d'Uville to be taken to the cemetery, carried by soldiers, followed by soldiers, surrounded by soldiers, all with loaded rifles, the church bells pealed the funeral toll for the first time, but cheerfully, at a lively pace, as if a friendly hand were caressing them.

The church bells rang again that night, and the next day, and every day; they rang as often as anyone could have wished. Sometimes, they even started ringing in the middle of the night, all by themselves, gently releasing two or three notes into the darkness, full of a strange kind of cheerfulness, awakened for some unknown reason. The townspeople believed the belltower was bewitched, and no one except the priest and the sexton dared go near it.

All this happened because a poor young woman was living up there, alone and frightened, and only the priest and the sexton secretly brought her food.

She remained there until the German troops were gone. Then, one evening, the priest borrowed the baker's horse-drawn wagon and drove the woman he'd been hiding to the edge of Rouen. When they got there, he gave her a peck on the cheek; she got out and quickly ran back to the brothel, whose Madame thought she was dead.

A little while later, a patriotic gentleman took her away from the brothel; he held nothing against her and admired her for her good deed. Then he fell in love with her in her own right, married her and made a lady of her, as worthy as any other.

THE MADWOMAN

"YOU KNOW," SAID MONSIEUR MATHIEU D'ENDOLIN, "THESE woodcocks remind me of a very appalling story about the war.

You know my property on the outskirts of Cormeil. I was living there when the Prussians arrived.

I had a neighbor at the time who was mad; she had lost her mind after some terrible misfortunes. A long time ago, when she was twenty-five, her father, her husband and her newborn baby all died within the space of a month.

Whenever death enters a household, it returns there almost immediately, as if it recognizes the door.

The poor young woman, overwhelmed by grief, grew gravely ill, and was delirious for six weeks. Then, a kind of calm weariness followed that violent attack and she became paralyzed, hardly ate and only moved her eyes. Every time someone tried to get her to stand up, she would scream as if she were being murdered. And so they left her in her bed, only pulling her from under the sheets to wash her and turn over the mattress.

An old maid stayed with her, making her drink something from time to time, or take a few mouthfuls of cold meat. What was going through her hopeless heart? No one ever knew, for she never spoke again. Was she thinking about the dead? Was she lost in sad daydreams about nothing in particular? Or was her vacant mind as stagnant as still waters?

For fifteen years, she remained withdrawn and indifferent.

War broke out; and during the early part of December, the Prussians pushed through to Cormeil.

I remember it as if it were yesterday. It was freezing cold outside and I was stretched out in an armchair, laid up with gout, when I heard the sound of their heavy, regular marching. I could see them going by from my window.

They filed past in an endless line, in unison as always, like puppets on strings. Then their leaders sent their men to lodge with various townspeople. I had seventeen of them. My neighbor, the madwoman, had twelve, including a major, a real roughneck, violent and surly.

The first few days, everything went on as usual. They told the officer who lived next door that the woman was not well, and he barely gave it a second thought. But he soon became annoyed by this woman he never saw. He asked about her illness; they said that the woman who owned the house hadn't left her bed for fifteen years after a severe bout of grief. He didn't believe a word of it, no doubt, and thought that the poor madwoman refused to get out of bed so she didn't have to see the Prussians, didn't have to speak to them or be near them.

He demanded that she see him; he was taken into her room.

"I ask you, Madame, you vill get out from bed und come down so vee can see you," he said sharply.

She turned her blank, vacant eyes toward him and said nothing.

"I vill not tolerate such insolence," he continued. "If you do not get out from bed by yourself, I vill find some vay to make you."

She remained dead still, as if she hadn't even seen him.

He became furious, taking her calm silence as a sign of utter scorn.

"You better come down tomorrow . . ." he added.

Then he walked out.

The next day, the old maid, panic-stricken, wanted to get her dressed, but the madwoman started to scream and fight her. The officer rushed upstairs, and the servant threw herself at his knees, crying:

"She won't, Monsieur, she won't. Please forgive her; she is so unhappy."

The soldier didn't know what to do, not daring to tell his men to force her out of bed, in spite of his anger. Then suddenly, he started to laugh, and shouted out some orders in German.

Soon after, a group of soldiers was seen carrying a mattress, the way they would carry a wounded man on a stretcher. On the mattress, still with its bedding intact, was the madwoman, ever silent, ever calm, indifferent to whatever was happening, as long as she could stay in her bed. One man followed behind, carrying a bundle of women's clothing.

And the officer rubbed his hands together and said:

"I vill make sure you get yourself dressed und go for a little valk."

Then we saw the cortège heading for the Imauville forest.

Two hours later, the soldiers returned, alone.

No one ever saw the madwoman again. What had they done with her? Where had they taken her! No one ever knew.

SNOW FELL NOW, all day and all night, burying the plains and the woods with a shroud of icy frost. The wolves howled, coming right up to our doors.

The thought of this doomed woman haunted me; and I made several requests to the Prussian authorities to try to get some information. I nearly got myself executed.

Spring returned. The occupying forces were leaving. My neighbor's house remained locked up; thick grass grew in the paths.

The old maid had died during the winter. No one was concerned about what had happened any more; I was the only one who thought about it constantly.

What had they done with that woman? Had she escaped through the woods? Had she been taken in somewhere, put into a hospital where they could learn nothing from her? Nothing happened to lessen my concerns, but gradually, time calmed my troubled heart.

The following autumn, the woodcocks flew by in a large group; and as my gout was not very painful at the time, I hobbled into the forest. I had already killed four or five long-billed birds when I hit one that disappeared into a ditch full of branches. I had to climb down into it to retrieve it. I found it lying next to someone's skull.

The memory of the madwoman hit me at once, as if I' been punched in the chest. Many others had surely died in these woods during that terrible year, yet I don't know why I was sure, completely sure, I'm telling you, that I had found the head of that poor, miserable madwoman.

And suddenly, I understood, I could picture it all. They had left her here on her mattress, in the cold, deserted forest, and, in keeping with her obsession, she had simply let herself die beneath the thick, light blanket of snow, without moving at all.

Then the wolves had eaten her.

And the birds had made their nests with the stuffing from her torn bed.

I kept that sad skull. And I prayed that our sons would never have to experience war again."

LIEUTENANT LARÉ'S
MARRIAGE

T THE VERY BEGINNING OF THE WAR, LIEUTENANT LARÉ had captured two cannons from the Prussians. His general said: "Thank you, Lieutenant," and awarded him the *Croix d'honneur*.

Since he was as modest as he was brave, skillful, creative, clever and resourceful, he was put in charge of a hundred men; he organized a group of reconnaissance scouts who saved the army on several occasions during their retreat.

But the invasion flooded in from all sides, like an ocean crashing onto the beach. Great waves of men arrived one after the other, casting marauders from their crests onto the shore. General Carrel's brigade, separated from its division, continually had to retreat, fighting every day but suffering very few losses, thanks to the vigilance and swiftness of Lieutenant Laré, who seemed to be everywhere at once, avoided all the enemy's traps, outwitted them, led their Uhlans' on a wild goose chase and killed their scouts.

One morning, the General asked to see him.

"Lieutenant," he said, "here is a dispatch from General Lacère, who will be in grave danger if we do not come to his aid by dawn. He is in Blainville, twenty-four miles from here. You will leave as soon as it is dark with three hundred men whom you will position all along the roads. I will wait

---

1   Prussian Lancers (light cavalry) who often accompanied reconnaissance parties.

two hours and then follow you. Study the route carefully; I'm afraid we might run into an enemy division."

It had been freezing cold for a week. At two o'clock, it started snowing; by evening, the ground was covered in it, and thick, white swirls of snow hid even the objects closest to hand.

At six o'clock, the detachment set off.

Two men were sent out first, alone, as scouts, about three hundred yards ahead. Then came a platoon of ten men whom the Lieutenant commanded himself. The rest of the men followed in two long columns. Three hundred yards to each side of the small troop, to the right and to the left, a few soldiers walked in pairs.

The snow kept falling, covering the men in white powder; it didn't melt on their clothes, and because it was dark, they blended in with the endless whiteness of the countryside.

Every now and again, they stopped. All they could hear was the faint rustling of falling snow, more a feeling than a sound, a distant whisper, sinister and difficult to make out. An order was passed along, very quietly, and when the troop started walking again, it left some men behind, ghostly, white shapes in the snow who gradually grew fainter and finally disappeared. These living signposts had to guide the army that followed.

The reconnaissance team slowed down. There was something up ahead.

"Go around to the right," said the Lieutenant, "toward the de Ronfé woods. The château is over to the left."

Soon the order to "Halt!" spread. The detachment stopped and waited for the Lieutenant; he went up to the château with only ten other men.

They advanced, crawling beneath the trees. Suddenly, they all stopped dead. A terrifying stillness hovered above them. Then, close by, a young woman's voice—clear and lyrical—floated through the silent woods:

"We're going to get lost in the snow, Father, we'll never make it to Blainville."

"Don't worry, my girl," a stronger voice replied. "I know this countryside like the back of my hand."

The Lieutenant said a few words and four men set out, as quiet as shadows.

Suddenly, a woman's piercing cry rose in the night. Two prisoners were led in: an old man and a very young woman. The Lieutenant questioned them, still speaking very softly.

"Name?"

"Pierre Bernard."

"Profession?"

"Head butler to Count de Ronfé."

"Is this your daughter?"

"Yes."

"What does she do?"

"She's a laundress at the château."

"Where are you going?"

"We're running away."

"Why?"

"Twelve Uhlans were there tonight. They shot three guards and hung the gardener; I was afraid for my daughter."

"Where are you going?"

"To Blainville."

"Why?"

"Because the French army is there."

"Do you know how to get there?"

"Absolutely."

"Very well, come with us."

They returned to the rest of the troop and continued walking through the fields. The old man was silent; he walked alongside the Lieutenant. His daughter walked next to him. She suddenly stopped.

"Father," she said, "I'm so tired that I don't think I can go on much longer."

Then she sat down. She was shivering from the cold and looked as if she were about to die. Her father wanted to carry her, but he was too old and too weak.

"Lieutenant," he said, sobbing, "we're going to get in your way and slow you down. France comes first. Go on without us."

The officer had already given an order. A few men had left. They returned with some cut-off tree branches. In a minute, they had made a stretcher. The entire detachment had joined them.

"There is a woman here dying of the cold," said the Lieutenant. "Will anyone offer to give up his coat for her?"

Two hundred coats were offered.

"Now who wants to carry her?"

They all stretched out their arms. The young woman was wrapped up in the soldiers' warm greatcoats and gently placed on the stretcher; then four strong arms lifted her up. And like an Oriental queen carried by slaves, she was taken to the middle of the detachment. They walked more briskly now, more courageously, more cheerfully, moved by the presence of a woman, the supreme inspiration that allowed so many prodigious events to be accomplished in the long-standing tradition of France.

After an hour, they stopped again and everyone lay down in the snow. In the distance, in the middle of the field, they could see a large, dark shape. It was like some surreal monster that grew longer, like a snake, then suddenly coiled back into a mass, darted quickly forward, stopped, and continuously changed shape. Orders were whispered and circulated among the men, and every now and then they heard the sharp, short click of metal. The moving mass was fast approaching, and they could see twelve Uhlans, one behind the other, lost in the dark, galloping quickly toward them. A bright flash of light suddenly revealed two hundred men on the ground in front of them. The sound of rapid gunfire faded away into the silent, snowy night, and all twelve of them, along with their horses, fell down dead.

The French detachment waited a long time. Then they started walking again. The old man they'd met served as their guide.

At long last, a distant voice cried out: "Who's there!"

Someone closer by replied with the watchword.

They waited some more; discussions took place. It had stopped snowing. A cold wind swept the clouds away, and behind them, high in the night sky, countless stars were shining. They grew fainter as the sky turned pink in the east.

A staff officer arrived to welcome the detachment. When he asked who the person was being carried on the stretcher, it moved; two small hands threw off the heavy blue greatcoats, and an adorable little face appeared. It was as rosy as dawn, with eyes as bright as the stars that had now disappeared, and a smile as bright as the rising sun.

"It's me, Monsieur," she said.

The soldiers, wild with delight, broke out into applause and carried the young woman triumphantly back to camp, where the soldiers were taking up arms. Soon after, General Carrel arrived. At nine o'clock, the Prussians attacked. They were forced to retreat at noon.

That evening, Lieutenant Laré, utterly exhausted, was sleeping on a bale of hay when the General called to see him in his tent. He was chatting with the elderly man the Lieutenant had met during the night. As soon as Lieutenant Laré came in, the General shook his hand.

"My dear Count," he said to the man, "here is the young man you were just telling me about. He's one of my best officers."

He smiled, lowered his voice and added:

"Actually, *the* best."

Then, turning toward the stunned Lieutenant, he said:

"Allow me to introduce Count de Ronfé-Quédissac."

The old man took both the Lieutenant's hands in his.

"My dear Lieutenant," he said, "you saved my daughter's life and I know of only one way to thank you . . . come and see me in a few months to let me know if . . . if you find her pleasing . . ."

One year later, to the day, Captain Laré married Mademoiselle Louise-Hortense-Geneviève de Ronfé-Quédissac in the Church of Saint Thomas Aquinas.

She brought him a dowry of six hundred thousand francs, and everyone said she was the prettiest bride they had seen all year.

TWO FRIENDS

PARIS WAS BESIEGED;[1] STARVING, ON THE VERGE OF DEATH. There were hardly any sparrows on the rooftops and even the rats had deserted the sewers. People ate anything they could find.

One bright morning in January, Monsieur Morissot was walking sadly along a street on the outskirts of the city, his hands in the trouser pockets of his uniform;[2] he was hungry. He was a watchmaker by profession and a homebody by nature. He stopped in his tracks when he suddenly ran into someone he knew. It was Monsieur Sauvage,[3] a friend he had made at the riverbank while out fishing.

Every Sunday, before the war, Morissot would set out before dawn with a bamboo fishing rod in his hand and a tin box slung over his shoulder. He would take the train to Argenteuil, get out at Colombes, and then walk to the Ile Marante, the place of his dreams. As soon as he arrived, he would start to fish, and he would fish all day long, until night fell.

Every Sunday, they met there. Monsieur Sauvage was a short, stout, jovial man, a notions seller from the Rue Notre-Dame-de-Lorette, and another enthusiastic fisherman. They would often spend half a day

---

1 Paris was besieged by the invading Prussians in the last week of September 1870, and finally surrendered in January 1871.

2 National Guard uniform.

3 *Sauvage* can mean two things in French: "savage," or "someone who is shy and doesn't socialize much." In this case, we must assume the latter, though Maupassant later plays on the other meaning ironically to point out the savagery of the Prussians.

together, sitting side by side, holding their fishing rods and swinging their legs above the flowing water. And they became good friends.

On certain days, they didn't even speak. Sometimes they would chat a little, but they got along extremely well without saying a word because they shared the exact same tastes and feelings.

In the springtime, around ten o'clock, when the morning sun cast a fine mist over the water and warmed the backs of the two keen fishermen, Monsieur Morissot would sometimes say to his companion: "Isn't it wonderful here!"

And Monsieur Sauvage would reply: "I can think of nothing better." And those simple words were enough to prove that they understood and respected each other.

In the fall, near dusk, when the setting sun blazed on the horizon, turning the sky blood red, when the water reflected scarlet clouds from above, made the entire river crimson, burned the faces of the two friends as if they were on fire and cast a golden glow on the russet trees that already shimmered in a wintry haze, Monsieur Sauvage would smile and look over at Monsieur Morissot and say: "What a wonderful sight!" And Morissot, entranced, would continue staring at his floater and reply: "This is so much better than the city, don't you think?"

Now, as soon as they recognized each other, they shook hands enthusiastically, both men poignantly moved at having met again under such different circumstances. Monsieur Sauvage sighed and murmured: "What terrible times we're going through!" Monsieur Morissot groaned gloomily: "And the weather's been so awful! Today is the first nice day this year."

The sky was, indeed, a cloudless bright blue.

They started walking along together, side by side, sad and lost in thought. Monsieur Morissot added: "And remember when we went fishing? Oh, it's so good to think back to those times!"

"When do you think we'll be able to go back there?" asked Monsieur Sauvage.

They went into a small café and drank some absinthe; then they went back outside and continued walking.

Monsieur Morissot suddenly stopped. "How about another, what do you think?" Monsieur Sauvage agreed. "Your wish is my command." And they went into another bar.

They were extremely drunk when they came outside again, like people who have been fasting and then find their stomachs full of alcohol. It was warm out. A gentle breeze tickled their faces.

Monsieur Sauvage, totally drunk now because of the warm weather, stopped walking: "What if we went?"

"Went where?"

"Went fishing."

"But where?"

"To our little island. The French outposts are near Colombes. I know Colonel Dumoulin; we can easily get through."

Monsieur Morissot trembled with desire: "Right. I'm in." And they went their separate ways to pick up their fishing gear.

An hour later, they were walking side by side on the main road. Then they reached the house where the Colonel lived. He smiled at their request and agreed to their whim. They continued on their way, armed with their travel pass.

Soon they crossed the outposts, walked through the deserted region of Colombes and followed a little vineyard that led down to the Seine. It was about eleven o'clock in the morning.

On the other side of the river, the village of Argenteuil looked dead. The Orgemont and Sannois hills towered above the entire region. The vast plain that stretched to Nanterre was deserted, completely deserted, with nothing but bare cherry trees and gray earth.

Monsieur Sauvage pointed to the tops of the hills and whispered: "The Prussians are up there!" And the two friends stood dead still, terrified, in this isolated spot.

"The Prussians!" They had never seen any, but for months now, they could sense they were there, all around Paris, destroying France, pillaging, massacring, causing everyone to starve, invisible and all-powerful. A kind of superstitious terror mingled with the hatred they felt toward these victorious foreigners.

"Hey! What if we ran into some of them?" Monsieur Morissot stammered.

Monsieur Sauvage's Parisian cockiness returned to him, in spite of everything.

"We'll offer them some fish to fry," he replied.

But they hesitated when it came to venturing into the countryside, intimidated by the silence that stretched across the horizon.

Finally, Monsieur Sauvage made a decision: "Come on, let's go! But let's be careful." And they went down into the vineyard, hunched over, crawling, using the bushes as cover, fearfully on the lookout and straining to hear any noise.

One strip of bare land remained to be crossed before they could get to the river. They started running, and as soon as they reached the riverbank, they huddled in the dry reeds.

Monsieur Morissot pressed his ear to the ground, trying to hear if anyone was marching in the area. He heard nothing. They were alone, completely alone.

They felt reassured and began to fish.

Opposite them, the deserted Ile Marante hid them from view from the other side of the river.

The little restaurant was closed and seemed as if it had been neglected for many years.

Monsieur Sauvage caught the first fish, a gudgeon. Monsieur Morissot caught the second one, and every minute or so, they would reel in their lines with a wriggling, silvery fish attached; it was a truly miraculous catch.

They very carefully slipped the fish into a fine mesh fishing net that dripped water down onto their feet. And a wonderful sense of joy ran through them, the kind of joy that takes hold of you when you once again experience a pleasure you love, and that you have been deprived of for so long.

The delightful sun spread its warmth down their backs; they no longer listened out for anything, no longer thought about anything; the rest of the world just didn't exist: they were fishing.

But suddenly, a muffled sound that seemed to come from underground made the earth shake. A cannon had started firing again.

Monsieur Morissot looked around and, beyond the bank, to the left, he saw the high outline of Mont-Valérien; there was a wispy white feather at its summit, a cloud of smoke it had just spit out.

Immediately, a second spurt of smoke shot from the top of the fortress; and a few seconds later, a new explosion roared out.

Then others followed, and every few minutes the mountain spewed its deadly breath, its milky mist billowing then rising slowly into the calm sky, forming a cloud above the summit.

Monsieur Sauvage shrugged his shoulders. "Here they go again," he said.

Monsieur Morissot, who was anxiously watching the feather of his floater sink with every roar of the cannon, was suddenly overwhelmed with the kind of anger a peaceable man feels toward the madmen who fought like this. "How stupid do you have to be to kill each other this way!" he grumbled.

"They're worse than animals," replied Monsieur Sauvage.

And Monsieur Morissot, who had just caught a fish, said: "And to think it will always be like this as long as there are governments."

Monsieur Sauvage cut in: "The French Republic wouldn't have declared war . . ."

But Monsieur Morissot interrupted him: "With kings we have wars in other countries; with the Republic, we have wars in our own."

And they calmly began a discussion, trying to untangle the great political problems of the day with the clear logic of kind, ordinary men of average intelligence, agreeing on this one point: that people would never be free. And Mont-Valérien thundered tirelessly, firing cannonballs that demolished French homes, crushed lives, destroyed people, put an end to dreams and to so many anticipated joys, to so much hope and happiness, filling the hearts of women, the hearts of daughters, the hearts of mothers, far away, in other lands, filling their hearts with endless suffering.

"That's life," said Monsieur Sauvage.

Monsieur Morissot laughed and added: "You mean, that's death."

But they shuddered in fear, sensing that someone was walking behind them, and they were right. They looked around and saw four men standing there, four big, bearded men with guns, dressed like livery servants and wearing flat caps, four men who were pointing their rifles at them.

They dropped the two lines they were holding, which slowly sank down into the river.

In a few seconds, the two friends had been grabbed, tied up, carried off, thrown into a small boat and taken to the island.

And behind the house they had thought was deserted, they saw about twenty German soldiers.

A kind of hairy giant sat straddling his chair and smoking a long porcelain pipe. "Now then, gentlemen," he said in excellent French. "Have you caught a lot of fish?"

A soldier had made sure to bring the fish with them and he placed the full net at the officer's feet. The Prussian smiled.

"Well! Well! I can see that you didn't do badly at all. But that's not what I want to discuss. Listen to me and don't worry.

As far as I am concerned, you are two spies sent to find me. I catch you and shoot you. You were pretending to be fishing in order to best hide your real plan. You fell into my hands, too bad. That's war for you.

But since you got past the outposts, you surely have a password to get you back. Tell me the password and I'll let you live."

The two friends, pale as ghosts, stood side by side, their hands trembling slightly from anxiety. They said nothing.

The officer continued: "No one will ever know and you can go safely back home. The secret will go with you to your grave. If you refuse, you will die, and right now. Choose."

They stood dead still without saying a word.

The Prussian remained calm and pointed toward the river. "In just five minutes, you will be at the bottom of that water," he continued. "Just think about it: in five minutes! You must have families, don't you?"

Cannon fire from Mont-Valérien continued to thunder.

The two fishermen stood in silence. The German gave orders in his own language. Then he moved his chair away so he wouldn't be too close to the prisoners, and twelve men came and stood at twenty paces from them, rifles at their sides.

"You have one minute," the officer added, "not a second more."

Suddenly, he stood up, went over to the two Frenchmen, took Monsieur Morissot by the arm and dragged him further away. "Quickly," he said very quietly, "tell me the password, all right? Your friend will never know; it will just look as if I've calmed down a bit."

Monsieur Morissot said nothing.

The Prussian then dragged Monsieur Sauvage to the side and asked him the same question.

Monsieur Sauvage said nothing.

The two friends stood side by side once more.

The officer started shouting out orders. The soldiers raised their weapons.

Then Monsieur Morissot happened to glance over at the fishing net full of gudgeon that sat on the grass a few feet away.

A ray of sunlight reflected off the heap of fish that were still moving, making them shine brightly. And a feeling of weakness swept through him. He just couldn't help himself, his eyes filled with tears.

"Goodbye, Monsieur Sauvage," he stammered.

"Goodbye, Monsieur Morissot," his friend replied.

They shook hands, trembling uncontrollably from head to foot.

"Fire!" shouted the officer.

The twelve bullets hit them all at once.

Monsieur Sauvage fell straight down, face-first. Monsieur Morissot, who was a bigger man, swayed, pivoted around and fell diagonally across his friend, his face raised to the heavens as blood gushed from his chest beneath his jacket.

The German shouted more orders.

His men scattered, came back with ropes and stones and tied them to the dead men's feet, then carried them to the riverbank.

Mont-Valérien, now shrouded in smoke, never stopped thundering.

Two soldiers took Monsieur Morissot by the head and feet; two others got hold of Monsieur Sauvage in the same way. They swung the bodies with great effort and heaved them far into the river; their bodies flew up, arched, then fell straight down into the water, the stones pulling them in feet-first.

The water splashed, bubbled up, rippled, then was calm, while tiny little waves hit the riverbanks.

A small pool of blood floated on the surface.

The officer, still very calm, said quietly: "Now the fish can get even."

Then he headed back to the house.

Suddenly, he noticed the net full of gudgeon in the grass. He picked it up, examined it, smiled and shouted: "Wilhelm!"

A soldier wearing a white apron came running out. And the Prussian, throwing him the dead men's catch, ordered:

"Throw these little fish into a frying pan for me right away, while they're still alive. They'll be delicious!"

Then he picked up his pipe and continued to smoke.

PÈRE MILON[1]

For a month now, the sun's scorching rays have been raining fire down onto the fields. All life is blossoming radiantly beneath this torrent of fire; the land is green as far as the eye can see. The blue sky stretches out over the horizon. From a distance, the farms scattered over the flat, open countryside of Normandy look like clusters of small woods, surrounded as they are by circles of tall beech trees. From close up, after you open the worm-eaten gate, you think you have entered an enormous garden, for all the old apple trees, as knobbly as the farmers, are in bloom. Their old dark trunks, gnarled, bent, set in rows in the courtyard, reach upward toward the sky, showing off their dazzling canopy of pink and white blossom. The sweet scent of their flowers mingles with the thick smells from the open stables and the steaming dung as it ferments, pecked at by the hens.

It is noon. The family is eating in the shade of a pear tree planted in front of the door: the father, the mother, their four children and five servants—two women and three men. They hardly speak. They eat their soup, then dish out the meat stew with plenty of potatoes and bacon.

Every now and again, one of the servants gets up and goes down to the cellar to refill the cider jug.

The man, a tall fellow, about forty years old, is staring at a grapevine

---

1 The French often use *Père* (Father) to describe someone older or to distinguish the person from his son.

growing up toward the shutters over one wall of the house; it has no fruit yet; it is as long and twisted as a snake.

"Father's vine is budding early this year," he says at last. "Maybe it'll have some fruit."

The woman turns around and looks at it as well, without saying a word.

The vine was planted at the very spot where his father had been shot and killed.

IT HAPPENED DURING THE 1870 war. The Prussians were occupying the whole country. France's General Faidherbe and the Northern army were fighting them.

The Prussians had set up their headquarters at this farm. The old farmer who owned it, Père Milon, Pierre, had accepted them and made them as comfortable as possible.

For a month, the German vanguard had kept watch in the village. The French soldiers held their position, about thirty-five miles away. And yet, every night, some Uhlans disappeared.

None of the small groups of scouts, the ones that had only two or three men sent out on patrol, ever came back.

Their dead bodies were found the next morning, in a field, or outside a courtyard or in a ditch. Even their horses were found dead along the roadside, their throats cut by a sword.

These murders seemed to be carried out by the same men, who were never found.

The whole region was terrorized. Farmers were shot if anyone simply pointed a finger at them; women were put in prison. Children were threatened to try to get information out of them. They learned nothing.

Now it happened that one morning, Père Milon was found in his stable with a gash on his face.

Two Uhlans had been found dead, their stomachs cut open, about three miles from the farm. One of them still had his bloody sword in his hand. He had fought back, trying to defend himself.

A military tribunal was set up right in front of the farm, and the old man was brought out.

He was sixty-eight years old. He was short, thin, a little bent over, with large hands that looked like the claws on a crab. His drab hair was as soft and downy as a duckling's, so you could see patches of his scalp here and there. The suntanned, wrinkled skin on his neck had thick veins that ran down into his jaws and reemerged at his temples. He was known in the area as stingy and hard to do business with.

They stood him between four soldiers, in front of the kitchen table they'd brought outside. Five officers and the Colonel sat opposite him.

The Colonel began speaking in French:

"Père Milon, ever since we have been here, we have had only praise for you. You have always been considerate and even attentive toward us. But today, a terrible accusation is hanging over you, and we must clear things up. How did you get that wound on your face?"

The farmer did not reply.

"Your silence tells us you are guilty, Père Milon," the Colonel continued. "I want you to answer me, do you understand? Do you know who killed the two Uhlans that were found this morning near the cross at the roadside?"

"I did," the old man said clearly.

The Colonel, surprised, fell silent for a moment, staring at the prisoner. Père Milon remained impassive; he looked like an old, confused farmer, his eyes lowered as if he were speaking to his priest. Only one thing gave away what he was feeling inside: he continually swallowed his saliva, with visible difficulty, as if his throat had completely closed up.

Père Milon's family, his son Jean, daughter-in-law and two grandchildren, stood a few feet behind him, terrified and filled with dismay.

"Do you also know who killed all the scouts from our army we've been finding in the countryside every morning for a month?" the Colonel continued.

The old man replied with the same brutish passivity:

"Me."

"You're the one who killed all of them?"

"Each and every one of 'em, yes, me."

"You, just you?"

"Only me."

"Tell me how you did it."

This time, the old man seemed upset; it was clear he was uncomfortable at having to talk at length.

"Don't know, just did it, however it happened," he muttered.

"I'm warning you," the Colonel said, "that you have to tell me everything. You would be better off to resign yourself to that right now. How did it start?"

The man looked anxiously over at his family who were listening attentively behind him. He hesitated again for a moment, then suddenly, made a decision.

"I was coming back one night, must've been around ten o'clock, the day after you got here. You and your soldiers had robbed me of more than fifty écus² worth of fodder and a cow and two sheep. So I says to myself: whatever they're takin' from me, fifty écus or whatever, that's what I'll take back from them. And I also had other things I was feeling that I'll tell you about. I seen one of your cavalrymen smoking his pipe near the ditch behind my barn. I went and got my scythe and come back real quiet like from behind so he didn't hear a thing. And I cut off his head in one go, just one, like it was an ear of corn, before he could even say 'Ouch!' You just look in the bottom of the pond: you'll find him in a coal sack, with a stone from the wall.

Then I got an idea. I took all his stuff, from his hat right down to his boots, and hid 'em in the vaulted tunnel leading to the lime kiln in the Martin woods, behind the farm."

The old man fell silent. The officers, stunned, looked at each other.

The interrogation continued, and this is what they were told:

ONCE HE'D CARRIED OUT this murder, the man had been obsessed by one thought: "Kill the Prussians!" He hated them with the sly, fierce

---

2   An old form of money.

hatred of a greedy farmer, and a patriotic one. He knew his mind, as he put it. He waited a few days.

He had displayed such humility, submission and compliance toward the conquerors that he was allowed to come and go as he pleased. He saw the dispatch riders leaving every evening, so he went out one night, after overhearing the name of the village where they were headed, having learned the few words of German he needed from living with the soldiers.

He left by the courtyard, slipped into the woods, reached the tunnel leading to the lime kiln, went to the very end of it where he found the dead man's clothes he'd left on the floor and put them on.

Then he started prowling through the fields, crawling on all fours, following the embankment so he wouldn't be seen, listening out for the slightest noise, as anxious as a poacher.

When he felt the time was right, he got closer to the road and hid behind a bush. He waited a while. Finally, around midnight, he heard the sound of a horse galloping along the solid earth on the road. He put his ear to the ground to make sure that only one horseman was coming, then got ready.

The Uhlan was galloping fast, bringing back the dispatches. He listened carefully, kept his eyes open. When he was no more than ten feet away, Père Milon crawled out onto the road, groaning: "*Hilfe! Hilfe!*— Help, help!" The horseman stopped, thinking there was a wounded German on the ground; he got off his horse, went up to him, suspecting nothing, and leaned over the stranger. The long, curved blade of a sword sliced through his middle. He fell down dead at once, without realizing what had happened, his body quivering in the final throes of death.

The old Norman farmer beamed with silent joy; he stood up and cut the dead man's throat, just for fun. Then he dragged the body to the ditch and threw it in.

The horse was calmly waiting for his master. Père Milon mounted him and took off at a gallop across the flat, open country.

About an hour later, he spotted two more Uhlans riding side by side, on their way back home. He headed straight at them, again shouting: "*Hilfe! Hilfe!*" The Prussians, recognizing the uniform, made way for him, utterly trusting. And the old man charged through them like a cannonball, killing one with his sword, then shooting the other.

Then he slit the horses' throats, German horses! He calmly returned to the tunnel leading to the lime kiln and hid his horse at the back. He took off the uniform, put on his old, tattered clothes, went home to bed and slept until morning.

He didn't go out again for four days, waiting for the inquest that had been ordered to finish; but on the fifth day, he went out again and killed two more soldiers using the same technique. After that, he never stopped. Every night, he wandered around, prowled about wherever his fancy led him, killing Prussians wherever he found them, galloping through the empty fields in the moonlight, a lost Uhlan, on a manhunt. Once he had completed his task, leaving dead bodies lying beside the road, the old rider went back to the tunnel where he hid his horse and his uniform.

Every day around noon, he calmly took oats and water to his horse in his underground hiding place; he gave him a lot to eat, as he demanded a great deal of work from him.

The night before, however, one of the men he'd attacked had been suspicious, and had slashed the old farmer's face with his sword.

He'd still managed to kill them though, both of them! He'd gone back to the woods again, hidden his horse and put on his tattered clothes; but as he was coming home, he felt very weak and had dragged himself to the stable, unable to make it to the house.

He'd been found there, bleeding, stretched out in the hay . . .

WHEN HE'D FINISHED HIS STORY, he suddenly raised his head and looked proudly at the Prussian officers.

The Colonel, who was pulling at his moustache, asked: "Do you have anything else to say?"

"No, nothing, the debt is paid. I killed sixteen of 'em, not one more, not one less."

"You know that you are going to die?"

"I don't want no mercy."

"Were you ever a soldier?"

"Yes. I was in the service, in the past. And back then, you were the ones who killed my father, he was a soldier under the first Emperor.[3] And don't forget you killed my youngest son, François, last month, near Evreux. You had it comin' and I give it to you. We're even."

The officers looked at each other.

"Eight for my father," the old farmer continued, "eight for my son, so we're even. I didn't go lookin' for a fight, not me! I don't even know you! I don't even know where you come from! Here you are, in my house, givin' orders like you owned the place. I got back at you through the others. And I ain't sorry."

Then, pulling his stiff old body straight, he crossed his arms, striking the pose of a humble hero.

The Prussians talked amongst themselves for a long time. One of the captains, who had also lost his son the month before, defended the high-minded villain.

Then the Colonel stood up and went over to Père Milon.

"Listen to me old man," he said quietly, "there is perhaps a way to save your life, if you . . ."

But Père Milon was not listening; staring straight at the conquering officer, as the wind rustled through the downy hairs on his head, he grimaced terribly, tensing his thin face with the gash on it, and puffing out his chest, he spit, as hard as he could, right into the Prussian's face.

The Colonel, furious, raised his hand, and for the second time, the man spit at him, right in the face.

All the officers had stood up and were shouting orders at once.

In less than a minute, the old man, still impassive, was pushed against the wall and, smiling at Jean, his older son, his daughter-in-law and his two grandchildren, he was shot dead, as they all looked on in horror.

---

3 Napoleon I.

THE ADVENTURE OF
WALTER SCHNAFFS

E VER SINCE HE HAD ENTERED FRANCE WITH THE INVADING army, Walter Schnaffs considered himself the unhappiest of men. He was very round, walked with difficulty, was often out of breath and suffered terribly from painful feet that were very thick and very flat. And he was a kindly, peaceful man, neither bloodthirsty nor overly generous, the father of four children he adored and married to a young blond woman whose kisses, attention and affection he missed desperately every night. He liked getting up late and going to bed early, savoring good food and drinking beer in restaurants. He also believed that everything sweet in life eventually disappears; and in his heart, he held a horrific, instinctive and logical hatred for cannons, rifles, guns and sabers, but most especially for bayonets, as he felt incapable of maneuvering that particular weapon quickly enough to defend his fat belly.

When night fell and he was wrapped up in his coat and stretched out on the ground next to his snoring comrades, he thought for a long time about the family he'd left back home, about the dangers he might encounter along the way. What would happen to his little ones if he were killed? Who would provide for them and bring them up? They weren't rich, in spite of the debt he'd gotten himself into so he could give them a bit of money before he left. And so Walter Schnaffs sometimes cried.

At the start of the fighting, he felt his legs were so weak that he would have let himself fall to the ground if he hadn't believed that the entire army would trample his body. The sound of bullets whizzing past made his hair stand on end.

For many long months he had lived in terror and anguish.

His platoon was advancing toward Normandy; one day he and a small reconnaissance party were sent on ahead simply to explore a section of the area and then withdraw. Everything seemed calm in the country-side; nothing led them to believe they would meet with any organized resistance.

The Prussians were calmly going down a little valley cut through by deep ravines when heavy rounds of gunfire stopped them in their tracks, killing about twenty of their men; and a group of snipers suddenly rushed out from a tiny wood, running forward, bayonets on their rifles.

At first, Walter Schnaffs stood dead still, so astonished and terrified that he didn't even think of running away. Then he was seized by a mad desire to flee; but he realized at once that he was as slow as a tortoise in comparison to the thin Frenchmen who were leaping about like a herd of goats. Then he noticed a large ditch full of brushwood covered in dry leaves a few steps in front of him, so he jumped into it feet-first, without even stopping to wonder how deep it was, just as you might jump into a river from a bridge.

As straight and sharp as an arrow, he pierced a thick layer of vines and sharp brambles that scratched his hands and face, then fell heavily on his bottom onto a bed of stones.

He immediately looked up at the sky through the hole he'd made. That gaping hole might give him away, so he carefully crawled, on all fours, to the back of the ditch, under the roof made of linked branches, going as fast as possible, to get far away from the battlefield. Then he stopped and sat down again, crouching out of sight like a hare in the tall, dry grass.

For some time, he could still hear explosions, shouting and cries. Then the clamor of the battle died down, stopped altogether. Everything became silent and calm once more.

Suddenly, something moved next to him. He jumped in terror. It was a little bird scattering dead leaves as he landed on a branch. For nearly an hour, Walter Schnaffs's heart raced and pounded wildly.

Night fell, engulfing the ravine in darkness. And the soldier began to think. What was he going to do? What would happen to him? Could he get back to his army. . . ? How? Which way? But if he went back, he would have to start living that horrible life all over again: the life of anguish, terror, exhaustion and suffering he'd led since the beginning of the war! No! He couldn't face it any more! He no longer had the strength he needed to endure the marches and face danger at every moment.

But what could he do? He couldn't hide in this ravine until the end of the hostilities. No, certainly not. If he hadn't needed to eat, this idea would not have been such a bad one; but he did need to eat, and every day.

And so he found himself all alone, in uniform, armed, on enemy territory, far from anyone who could help him. He was shaking from head to toe.

"If only I were taken prisoner!" he suddenly thought, and his heart quivered with desire, an intense, passionate desire to be captured by the French. Prisoner! He would be saved, fed, given shelter, safely away from the bullets and sabers, with nothing to feel anxious about, in a well-guarded, good prison. Prisoner! How perfect!

And he immediately made his decision:

"I'm going to be taken prisoner."

He stood up, determined to carry out his plan without wasting another minute. But he stood very still, suddenly overwhelmed by dreadful thoughts and terrifying new fears.

Where should he go to be taken prisoner? How? Which way? And horrifying images, images of death, rushed through his soul.

He would be in great danger, roaming about the countryside in his pointed helmet.[1]

What if he ran into some farmers? If any of them saw a lost Prussian, a helpless Prussian, they would kill him as if he were a stray dog! They would murder him with their pitchforks, their pickaxes, their scythes, their shovels! They would reduce him to a pulp, give him a real beating, with the fierceness of frustrated losers.

---

[1]   The Prussians wore distinctive helmets with sharp metal spikes on top.

What if he ran into any snipers? Snipers who were madmen, who obeyed no rules and had no discipline: as soon as they spotted him, they would shoot him just for fun, to help pass the time, for a laugh. And he could already picture himself crushed against a wall facing the butts of twelve rifles whose round little black eyes seemed to be staring at him.

What if he ran into the French army itself? The men in the front lines would take him for a scout, some bold, evil private who had gone on a reconnaissance mission all alone, and they'd open fire on him. And he imagined the erratic blasts of gunfire from soldiers hidden in the brush, imagined himself standing in the middle of a field, then falling to the ground, riddled with holes from the bullets he could already feel penetrating his body.

He sat down again, in despair. There seemed to be no way out of his situation.

It was completely dark now, silent and dark. He didn't move, shuddering at the slightest strange noise he heard in the shadows. A rabbit, thumping his bottom at the edge of a burrow, nearly made Walter Schnaffs run for his life. The hooting of the owls pierced his soul, cut through his heart with sharp, painful blows that terrified him. He squinted, trying to see in the dark; and he constantly imagined he could hear people walking close by.

After endless hours and suffering the terrors of the damned, he looked through the covering of branches and saw that day was breaking. Then he felt enormously relieved; he stretched out his arms and legs and suddenly relaxed; his heart felt calm; his eyes closed. He fell asleep.

When he woke up, the sun seemed to be more or less in the middle of the sky; it must have been noon. Not a single sound disturbed the gloomy silence of the fields; and Walter Schnaffs realized that he was extremely hungry.

He yawned, salivating at the idea of some sausages, the delicious sausages that soldiers eat; and his stomach hurt.

He stood up, took a few steps, felt that his legs were weak, and sat down again to think. For two or three hours more, he considered the pros and cons, changing his mind from one minute to the next, defeated, unhappy, torn between contradictory ideas.

One thought finally seemed both logical and practical to him, and that was to keep an eye out for some villager who was walking past all alone, unarmed, and without any dangerous workman's tools, to run out in front of him and put himself in his hands, making it very clear that he was surrendering.

Then he took off his helmet, as its sharp point could give him away, and taking infinite care, he poked his head outside his hiding hole.

Not a single soul was in sight. Further away, to the right, he could see the smoke rising from the rooftops of a little village, the smoke from the kitchens! Further away, to the left, he saw a wide passageway lined with trees, leading to a large château flanked by turrets.

He waited until nightfall, his hunger causing him terrible pain, seeing nothing but crows in flight, hearing nothing but the muted rumbling of his entrails.

And night descended upon him once more.

He stretched out at the back of his shelter and fell asleep: it was a feverish sleep, haunted by nightmares, the sleep of a starving man.

Dawn broke once more above his head. He started keeping watch again. But the countryside was as empty as the day before; and a new fear spread through the mind of Walter Schnaffs, the fear of starving to death! He could picture himself stretched out in the corner of his hiding place, on his back, his eyes closed. Then the animals, all sorts of small animals, went over to his corpse and started eating him, attacking him everywhere at once, sliding underneath his clothes to bite at his cold flesh. And a large black crow was pecking at his eyes with its sharp beak.

Then he nearly went mad, imagining he might faint from weakness and wouldn't be able to walk any more. And he was just about to rush toward the village, determined to brave everything, when he spotted three farmers walking through the fields, their pitchforks slung over their shoulders, and he jumped back into his hiding place.

But as soon as night fell over the plain, he slowly came out of the ditch, and started to walk toward a château he could see in the distance; bent over, frightened, his heart pounding, he preferred to go there rather than the village, which seemed as terrifying to him as a lair full of tigers.

Light shone through the downstairs windows. One of them was even open; a strong smell of roasted meat wafted out, an aroma that quickly flooded through Walter Schnaffs, from his nose right down to his stomach; it made him flinch, made him pant, irresistibly attracting him, filling his heart with desperate daring.

Then, without stopping to think, he pressed his face against the window; he was still wearing his helmet.

Eight servants were having dinner around a large table. Suddenly, one of the maids stood stock-still, stunned, eyes wide, and dropped her glass. Everyone turned to see what she was staring at!

It was the enemy!

Good Lord! The Prussians were attacking the château!

At first, there was a cry, a single cry, made up of the cries of eight different voices, a horrible cry of terror, then a chaotic jumping up, a scramble, a free-for-all, a mad rush for the back door. Chairs fell back, men knocked women down and stepped over them. In two seconds, the room was empty, deserted, the table piled high with food. Walter Schnaffs stood looking at it through the window, stunned.

After hesitating a few minutes, he climbed over the parapet and walked over to the plates of food. His extreme hunger made him tremble like a man delirious with fever: but one terrible fear held him back, nailed him to the spot. He listened. The entire house seemed to be shaking; doors slammed shut, footsteps raced through the floor above. The anxious Prussian listened to the baffling din; then he heard some muted sounds, as if bodies were falling onto the soft ground, at the foot of the walls, bodies jumping from the first floor.

Then all the movement, all the commotion stopped, and the large château became as silent as a tomb.

Walter Schnaffs sat down in front of one of the plates that had not been broken and began to eat. He gulped down great mouthfuls, as if he were afraid he might be interrupted too soon, before having wolfed enough down. He used both hands to throw pieces of food into his mouth, which was opened as wide as a trap door; and lumps of food fell into his stomach one after the other, making his throat swell as he swallowed them. Every now and again he stopped, ready to explode like a pipe about to burst. Then he took the pitcher of cider and cleared his esophagus the way you wash out a clogged pipe.

He emptied all the plates, all the dishes and all the bottles; intoxicated on food and drink, dazed, bright red, shaking from hiccups, his mind confused and his mouth greasy, he unbuttoned his uniform so he could breathe, incapable of taking a single step. His eyes closed, his mind grew sluggish; he placed his heavy head on the table, onto his crossed arms, and little by little lost all consciousness of everything around him.

THE LAST CRESCENT of the moon dimly lit up the horizon above the trees in the grounds of the château. It was the time of morning just before dawn when it was still cold.

Shadows slipped through the many silent thickets, and every now and then, a moonbeam struck a piece of steel, making it glow in the darkness.

The imposing, dark silhouette of the peaceful château stood tall. Only two windows on the ground floor still had their lights on.

SUDDENLY, a booming voice shouted:

"Forward men! Onward! Charge!"

Within seconds, the doors, the shutters and the windows crashed down under a wave of men who rushed forward, shattered everything, broke everything, and swarmed into the house. Within seconds, fifty soldiers armed to the teeth flooded into the kitchen where Walter Schnaffs was resting peacefully; they held fifty loaded rifles to his chest, knocked him down, rolled him over, held him down and tied him up from head to toe.

He was panting with shock, too stunned to understand what was happening, beaten, hit with their rifle butts and absolutely terrified.

And suddenly, a fat soldier wearing many gold medals set his foot on the stomach of Walter Schnaffs, shouting:

"I am taking you prisoner, surrender!"

The Prussian only understood the word "prisoner," so he groaned, "*Ja, ja, ja.*"

His conquerors hauled him up, tied him to a chair and examined their prisoner, who was wheezing like a whale, with keen curiosity. Several of them were so overcome with emotion and exhaustion that they had to sit down.

And Walter Schnaffs was smiling, he was smiling now, certain at last that he'd been taken prisoner!

Another officer came in.

"Colonel, the enemy has fled," he said. "Several of them seem to have been wounded. We have taken control of the château."

The fat soldier wiped his forehead and shouted: "Victory!"

Then he made some notes in a small business diary that he took out of his pocket:

"After a fierce battle, the Prussians were forced to retreat, taking their dead and their wounded with them, an estimated fifty men put out of action. Several of them were taken prisoner."

"What arrangements shall I make, Colonel?" the young officer asked.

"We are going to withdraw," the Colonel replied, "to avoid a new offensive with superior troops and artillery."

And he gave the order to leave.

Two lines of soldiers formed in the dark, beneath the walls of the château, and started to move, surrounding Walter Schnaffs on all sides; he was tied up and led along by six warriors pointing guns at him.

A reconnaissance patrol was sent on ahead to scout the road. They advanced cautiously, stopping from time to time.

As day broke, they reached the subprefecture of La Roche-Oysel, whose National Guard had brought home this military victory.

The eager, overexcited townspeople were there, waiting. When they saw the prisoner's helmet, they started shouting vehemently. Younger women raised their arms in the air; old women wept; one grandfather threw his crutch at the Prussian but hit one of the guards on the nose, wounding him.

"Stand guard over the prisoner," the Colonel shouted.

They finally reached the Town Hall. The prison door was opened and Walter Schnaffs was untied and thrown inside.

Two hundred armed men stood watch around the building.

And then, in spite of the symptoms of indigestion that had been troubling him for some time, the Prussian, mad with joy, began to dance, dance frantically, raising his arms and legs in the air, dancing and shouting frenetically, until he finally dropped down, exhausted, against a wall.

He was a prisoner! He was saved!

AND THAT IS HOW the Château de Champignet was won back from the enemy after being occupied for only six hours.

Colonel Ratier,[2] a fabric salesman, who pulled off this coup as chief of the National Guard of La Roche-Oysel, was awarded a medal.

---

2   Again, Maupassant uses his characters' names for humor: a *ratier* is "a dog who chases rats."

LA MÈRE SAUVAGE[1]

I

I HADN'T BEEN BACK TO VIRELOGNE FOR FIFTEEN YEARS. I returned in the autumn, to stay with my friend Serval and go hunting; he'd finally rebuilt his château after the Prussians destroyed it.

I loved this part of the country a great deal. It is one of those wonderful places that appeal to the eye with sensual charm. The kind of place you feel a physical love for. People like us who are seduced by the countryside remember certain streams, woods, lakes, hills with great affection, for we have seen them so often and they have touched us the way all joyful events do. Sometimes, our thoughts return to one part of a forest, to the edge of a riverbank, or to an orchard filled with flowers, perhaps seen only once, on a happy day, but they remain in our hearts like certain women you happened to meet in the street, one spring morning, women wearing light, transparent dresses who leave an unforgettable feeling of unrequited desire in our bodies and souls, the sensation of having briefly encountered happiness.

I loved all the countryside around Virelogne; it was dotted with little woods and brooks that ran through the ground like veins, carrying blood deep into the earth. You could fish there for trout, crayfish and eels. Such

---

1   Maupassant often uses names to indicate a character's nature. *Sauvage* can mean "savage," "wild," and also "antisocial." Calling someone *La Mère* indicates she is both a mother and elderly.

divine happiness! There were places to go swimming, and you often found wading birds in the tall grass that grew along the banks of these narrow streams.

I was walking along, as sprightly as a goat, watching my two dogs sniffing the ground ahead of me. Serval, who was about a hundred yards to my right, was stamping through a field of alfalfa. I turned past the bushes at the edge of the Saudres woods and noticed a cottage in ruins.

Suddenly, I remembered the way it looked the last time I'd seen it, in 1869: clean, covered in vines, with chickens outside the door. Is there anything sadder than a lifeless house, with its dilapidated, sinister skeleton still standing?

I also remembered that one day when I was very tired, a kind woman had given me a glass of wine in that house, and that Serval had told me the story of the people who lived there. The father, an old poacher, had been killed by the police. The son, whom I had seen in the past, was a tall, thin young man who was also known as an avid game hunter. People called them "the Savages."

Was that their real name or a nickname?

I called out to Serval. He took long steps, like a wading bird, and came over to me.

"What happened to the people who lived over there?" I asked.

And he told me this story.

II

WHEN WAR WAS DECLARED, THE SON, WHO WAS THEN THIRTY-three, enlisted, leaving his mother alone in her house. No one felt very sorry for the old woman because she had money, and everyone knew it.

And so she lived all by herself in this isolated house, at the edge of the woods. But she wasn't afraid; she came from the same stock as the men in her family; she was a tough old woman, tall and thin, who hardly ever laughed and the kind of person you didn't joke with. In fact, none of the women who worked in the fields in these parts hardly ever laughed. Only the men could laugh and joke around. The women have sad, poor hearts, because their lives are gloomy and dull. The farmers learn a bit of cheerfulness at the taverns, but their wives remain serious and always look stern. The muscles in their faces never learned how to laugh.

La Mère Sauvage continued her ordinary life in her cottage, which was soon covered in snow. She went to the village once a week to buy bread and a little meat; then she returned to her hovel. Because everyone talked about wolves in the woods, she always went out with a rifle on her shoulder, her son's rusty rifle with the worn-down butt; and she was a strange sight, the tall Mère Sauvage, a little bent over, walking slowly through the snow, the gun barrel sticking out above the black hat, the kind of hat everyone wore in these parts; it fit tightly on her head and kept her white hair well covered; no one had ever seen her hair.

One day, the Prussians arrived. They were sent to lodge with the townspeople, according to their wealth and resources. The old woman, who was known to be rich, got four soldiers.

They were four big young men with pale skin, blond beards and blue eyes; they were still fat in spite of the strain they'd already endured, and they were good lads, despite occupying the country they'd defeated. Alone in the home of this elderly woman, they showed great concern for her, sparing her, as much as possible, any extra work and expense. You could see all four of them around the well in the morning getting washed, in their shirtsleeves, on the cold, damp, snowy days, splashing water onto their pale, pink skin typical of all the men from the North, while La Mère Sauvage bustled about, preparing her soup. Then they cleaned the kitchen, scrubbed the floors, chopped the wood, peeled the potatoes, washed the clothes, did all the household chores, like four good boys with their mother.

But the old woman thought about her own son constantly, her tall, thin son with his hooked nose, brown eyes, the thick moustache that covered his upper lip with a strip of dark hair. Every day, she asked one of the soldiers living with her:

"Do you know where the Twenty-third French Regiment has gone? My son is with them."

"No, not know, not know anything."

And since they understood her pain and anxiety—they too had mothers back home—they were attentive to her in hundreds of little ways. And she liked them very much, her four enemies, because the country folk rarely harbor any patriotic hatred; that is common only among the well-to-do. The lower classes, the ones who pay the most because they are poor and because every new tax is more of a burden to them, the ones who are killed en masse, the ones who are the true cannon fodder because they are the majority of the population, the ones, in the end, who suffer most cruelly the atrocious miseries of war because they are the weakest and can defend themselves the least, these poor people understand little of the thirst for war, the easily aroused sense of honor and the so-called political strategies that wear down two nations in the space of six months, two nations: both the conquered and the conquerors.

Whenever they talked about La Mère Sauvage's Germans, the townspeople always said:

"Those four sure got themselves a good home."

Now, one morning when the old woman was alone in the house, she saw a man in the distance, walking across the plain toward her cottage. She soon recognized him; he was the mailman who delivered the letters on foot. He handed her a folded piece of paper; she took the glasses she used for sewing from their case and began to read:

Madame Sauvage,

I am writing to give you some very bad news. Your son Victor was killed yesterday by a cannonball, which virtually cut his body in half. I was close by, as we always walked side by side in the regiment, and he talked to me about you so I could let you know right away if anything happened to him.

I took the watch out of his pocket to bring back to you when the war is over.

Yours sincerely,
Césaire Rivot,
Private 2nd class, 23rd Regiment

The letter was dated three weeks earlier.

She didn't cry, not at all. She stood dead still, so overwhelmed, so stunned that she didn't yet feel any pain. "So now Victor is dead," she thought. Then tears slowly rose to her eyes, and pain pierced her heart. Ideas occurred to her, one by one, horrible, agonizing ideas. She would never hold him in her arms again, never kiss him again, her child, her boy, never again, never again! The police had killed her husband, the Prussians had killed her son . . . His body had virtually been cut in half by a cannonball. And she felt she could picture what happened, the horrible thing that had happened: his head slumped down, his eyes open as he chewed on the corner of his long moustache, the way he always used to when he was angry.

What had they done with his body, afterwards? If only they'd brought her child's body back to her the way they'd given her husband's body to her, with the bullet in the middle of his forehead.

She heard voices. It was the Prussians coming back from the village. She quickly hid the letter in her pocket and wiped the tears from her face; she greeted them calmly, making sure her expression gave nothing away.

All four of them were laughing, delighted because they'd brought back a nice live rabbit, stolen no doubt, and they gestured to the old woman that they would have something good to eat.

She immediately began preparing lunch; but when it came time to kill the rabbit, she didn't have the heart to do it, though it would not have been the first time. One of the soldiers smashed his fist against the back of its head and killed it.

Now that it was dead, she skinned it, pulling its red body from under the skin, but as she worked, the sight of the blood that covered her hands, the sensation of the warm blood she could feel cooling and coagulating, made her whole body tremble, and she kept seeing her son cut in half and covered in blood, just like this animal whose flesh was still quivering.

She sat down at the table with the Prussians, but she couldn't eat, couldn't eat a single mouthful. They wolfed down the rabbit without giving her a thought. She watched them, furtively, without speaking, forming an idea, and her face was so impassive that they didn't notice a thing.

Suddenly, she said: "I don't even know your names and it's been a month since we've been together." They understood, not without difficulty, what she wanted, and told her their names. But that wasn't enough; she wanted them to write them down on a piece of paper, with the addresses of their families; and placing her glasses on her large nose, she studied their strange handwriting, then folded the paper in half and put it in her pocket, along with the letter telling her that her son was dead.

When the meal was over, she told the men:

"I'm going to do something for you."

And she began carrying hay up into the loft where they slept.

They were surprised to see her do this; she explained they'd be warmer and they helped her. They piled the bales of hay right up to the thatched roof; and they made a kind of large bedroom with four walls of fodder, warm and sweet-smelling, where they would get a wonderful night's sleep.

At suppertime, one of them was concerned that La Mère Sauvage was still not eating. She said she had an upset stomach. Then she lit a nice fire to keep warm, and the four Germans climbed up into their room on the ladder they used every night.

As soon as the trap door was shut, the old woman moved the ladder away, then silently opened the front door, went out and came back with enough bales of hay to fill the kitchen. She walked barefoot in the snow, so quietly that not a sound was heard. Every now and then, she listened to the muffled, irregular snoring of the four sleeping soldiers.

When she felt she'd prepared everything well enough, she lit one of the bales of hay and threw it into the house; when it spread to the others, she went back outside and watched.

In seconds, a bright flash of light lit up the entire inside of the house, then it became a terrifying inferno, an enormous, blazing furnace whose bright light streamed through the narrow window, casting a reddish glow over the snow.

Then a great cry came from the top of the house, the roar of human voices, heartrending cries of anguish and terror. The trap door crashed down and a swirl of fire rushed through the loft, pierced the thatched roof and rose into the sky like an immense burning torch; the entire cottage was ablaze.

Nothing could be heard inside except for the crackling fire, the creaking walls, the wooden beams crashing down. Suddenly, the roof caved in, and from the glowing shell of the house, a great plume of smoke filled with sparks flew up into the air.

The countryside, white with snow, lit up by the fire, glistened like a silvery cloak tinged blood red.

In the distance, a church bell began to ring.

La Mère Sauvage remained there, standing in front of her house, armed with her rifle, her son's rifle, in case any of the men had managed to escape.

When she saw it was all over, she threw her gun into the fire. She heard it explode.

People began to arrive, farmers, Prussians.

They found the old woman sitting on a tree stump, calm and contented.

A German officer, who spoke French like a native, asked:

"Where are your soldiers?"

She stretched out her thin arm toward the red rubble of the fire that was starting to die out. "In there!" she replied in a loud voice.

Everyone rushed around her.

"How did it catch fire?" the Prussian asked.

"*I* set it on fire," she replied.

No one believed her, thinking the disaster had suddenly made her go mad. Since everyone was standing around and listening to her, she told her story from start to finish, from the arrival of the letter to the final cries of the men burning inside her house. She left out no detail about what she had felt or what she had done.

When she had finished, she took the two papers from her pocket and adjusted her glasses to see them better in the light of the dying fire, then she held one of them up and said: "This one is about Victor dying." Holding up the other one, she nodded toward the flaming ruins and added: "This one is their names so you can write to their families." She calmly handed the white sheet of paper to the officer who was holding her by the shoulders.

"You'll write and tell them what happened, and you'll tell their parents that I, Victoire Simon,[2] La Mère Sauvage, was the one who did it! Don't forget."

The officer shouted out orders in German. They grabbed her, threw her against her house, against its walls that were still warm. Then twelve men quickly lined up opposite her, about twenty yards away. She stood dead still. She had understood, she was waiting.

An order was shouted, followed by a long volley of gunfire. One shot rang out alone, after all the others.

The old woman did not fall down. She sank to the ground as if someone had cut off her legs.

The Prussian officer walked over to her. She was almost cut in half, and in her clenched hand, she held her letter, soaked in blood.

"DESTROYING MY CHÂTEAU WAS as an act of reprisal by the Germans," my friend Serval continued.

I thought about the mothers of the four kind young men who had burned to death in that cottage, and I thought of the horrific heroism of that other mother, gunned down against the wall.

Then I picked up a small stone that was still charred, black from the fire.

---

2   We now learn that the mother's real name is *Victoire*—Victory.

THE PRISONERS

NOT A SOUND IN THE FOREST APART FROM THE GENTLE FLUT-
ter of snow drifting onto the trees. It had been falling since noon, a
light, fine snow that covered the branches in an icy, frothy powder, casting
a silvery glint over the dead leaves that still clung to the trees. It spread
an immense, soft white blanket over the roads and intensified the endless
silence of this sea of trees.

In front of the cottage in the forest, a young woman with bare arms
was chopping wood over a stone with an ax. She was tall, slim but strong,
a young country woman, the daughter and wife of foresters.

"We're alone tonight, Berthine," a voice called from inside the house.
"Better come inside, it's gettin' dark and there may be some Prussians and
wolves prowlin' round."

The woodcutter split a large log with powerful blows that made her
chest expand every time she raised her arms.

"I'm done, Ma," she replied. "I'm here, it's okay, don't worry; it's still
light out."

Then she piled the logs and kindling beside the fireplace, went outside to close the enormous hard oak shutters and finally came back inside,
locking the heavy bolts on the door.

Her mother was spinning wool by the fire; she was an old woman with
wrinkles who had grown more fearful with age.

"I don't like it when your Pa ain't here," she said. "Two women alone
ain't strong enough."

"Oh!" the young woman replied, "I'd happily kill a wolf or a Prussian, you know."

And she glanced over at a large revolver hanging above the hearth.

Her husband had been taken into the army at the beginning of the Prussian invasion, and the two women had been left alone with her father, Nicolas Pichon, an old gamekeeper nicknamed "Stilts." He'd stubbornly refused to leave his house to stay in town.

The closest town was Rethel, an ancient fortified city built high on a rock. Its inhabitants were patriotic and had decided to resist the invaders, to blockade themselves in and fight, following Rethel's tradition. Twice already, under Henri IV and Louis XIV, they'd become famous for their heroic defense of the town. And they would do the same this time, you can bet your boots! Or else they'd have to burn them alive within the city walls.

And so they had bought cannons and rifles, equipped a militia, formed battalions and companies, and held drills all day long on the Place d'Armes. Everyone—bakers, grocers, butchers, notaries, lawyers, carpenters, book-sellers, even pharmacists—took their turn at military training at precise times of the day, under the command of Monsieur Lavigne, a former Second Lieutenant in the Dragoons, now a notions dealer, since he'd married the daughter of Monsieur Ravaudan[1] Senior and inherited his shop.

He'd awarded himself the rank of Major, and since all the young men had gone off to the army, he'd enlisted all the other men, and they were training to put up a fight. The fat men in town now jogged along the streets to lose weight and improve their stamina while the weaker men carried heavy bundles to build up their muscles.

And so they waited for the Prussians. But the Prussians never came. They weren't far away, though: on two occasions their scouts had already made it deep enough into the woods to reach the house of Nicolas Pichon, Stilts.

The old gamekeeper, who was as fast as a fox, had gone to warn the town. They'd prepared their cannons but no enemy had been seen.

---

1   The verb for repairing clothing is *ravauder*, quite similar to this man's name and profession.

Stilts's house was used as an outpost in the Aveline Forest. Twice a week, he went to town to buy provisions and to tell the townspeople what was happening in the countryside.

ON THIS PARTICULAR DAY, he'd gone to tell them that a small detachment of German infantrymen had stopped at his house the day before, then left again almost immediately. The Second Lieutenant in charge could speak French.

When he went on these trips, he took along his two ferocious dogs— huge hounds with jaws like a lion—and he left the two women on their own with instructions to barricade themselves inside the house as soon as it got dark.

The young woman wasn't afraid of anything, but the old woman was always trembling with fear. "This will end in disaster, it will," she said over and over again. "You'll see, disaster."

That evening, she was even more anxious than usual. "Do you know what time Pa will be gettin' home?" she asked.

"Not before eleven, for sure. Whenever he has dinner with the Major, he always gets home late."

And the young woman had just hung her cooking pot over the fire to make the soup when she heard a strange noise echoing down the chimney; she stopped stirring.

"There's people walkin' through the woods, seven or eight of 'em at least."

Her mother, terrified, stopping the spinning wheel. "Oh, my God!" she stammered. "And your Pa's not here!"

She had barely finished what she was saying when someone started banging angrily at the door, so hard that it shook.

When the women did not reply, a loud, guttural voice shouted: "Open the door!"

Then, after a silence, the same voice continued: "Open now or I break down your door!"

Berthine slipped the heavy revolver from over the fireplace into the pocket of her skirt, then put her ear against the door. "Who are you?" she asked.

"I am detachment from the other day," the voice replied.

"What do you want?" the young woman asked.

"I am lost since morning, in dese voods, mit meine men. Open now or I break down your door!"

The forester's daughter had no choice; she quickly undid the bolts, then pulling open the heavy door, she saw six men, six Prussian soldiers standing in the snow, outlined in its pale light, the same men who'd come the day before.

"What are you doing here at this time of night?" she asked in a firm tone of voice.

"I am lost," the Second Lieutenant said once more, "completely lost und I recognized your house. My men und I have not eaten anysing since dis morning."

"But I'm alone here with my mother tonight," Berthine said.

The soldier, who seemed an honest man, replied: "Does not matter. I vill not hurt you but you must to give us somesing to eat. Vee are all dying of hunger und very tired."

Berthine stepped back. "Come inside," she said.

They went in, covered in light snow, and their helmets had a kind of creamy froth on them that made them look like meringues. And they seemed weary, exhausted.

The young woman pointed to the two wooden benches, one on either side of the long table.

"Sit down," she said. "I'll make you some soup. You really do look worn out."

Then she bolted the door again.

She put more water in her cooking pot, threw in some more butter and potatoes, then took a large slab of bacon that was hanging over the fireplace, cut half of it off and added it to the pot.

The six men watched her every move, a look of intense hunger in their eyes. They'd put their rifles and helmets in the corner and were waiting, as well behaved as good little children on their benches at school.

Her mother had started spinning wool again, but constantly glanced over at the invaders in terror. The only sounds were the gentle humming of the spinning wheel, the crackling of the fire and the soup bubbling in the pot.

Then, suddenly, a strange noise made everyone jump, something like the heavy, hoarse breathing of a wild animal at the door.

The German officer leapt up and was heading toward the rifles. Berthine smiled and gestured for him to stop.

"It's only the wolves," she said. "They're just like you, hungry and prowling around."

He wasn't convinced and wanted to see with his own eyes; as soon as he opened the door, he saw two large, gray animals running away with quick, rapid strides.

"I vould never have believed it," he murmured, sitting down again.

And he waited for his food to be ready.

They wolfed down their meal, their mouths gaping open so they could swallow more, their wide eyes opening and closing in unison with their jaws, and their throats made the same noise as water gurgling down a drainpipe as they swallowed the soup.

The two women stood there, silently watching the rapid movements of their long red beards; the potatoes looked as if they were sinking into undulating sheepskins.

They were thirsty too, so Berthine went down into the cellar to get some cider. She stayed down there for a long time. It was a small vaulted cellar that had been used as both a prison and a hiding place during the Revolution, or so people claimed. You got to it by opening a trap door and going down a narrow, winding staircase at the back of the kitchen.

When Berthine returned, she was laughing, laughing slyly to herself. She gave the Germans the jug of cider.

Then she and her mother had their supper at the other end of the kitchen.

The soldiers had finished eating; all six of them were falling asleep at the table. Every now and again, someone's head dropped down with a thud, then he would quickly wake and sit up straight again.

"Why don't you all go lie down by the fire," Berthine said to the officer. "There's plenty of room for all six of you, you know. I'm going upstairs to my room with my mother."

And the two women went up to the second floor. The soldiers could hear them lock the door and walk around for a while; then they didn't make any more noise.

The Prussians stretched out on the floor, their feet toward the fire, their heads on top of their rolled-up coats, and all of them were soon snoring: a medley of six different snores, from dull to shrill, but all continuous and loud.

THEY'D BEEN SLEEPING for quite a long time when a gunshot rang out, so loudly that it sounded as if it had been fired right at the wall of the house. The soldiers sprang up. Then they heard two more gunshots, followed by three others.

The door from the second floor opened suddenly and Berthine appeared barefoot, wearing only her nightshirt and skirt. She held a candle in her hand and looked terrified.

"It's the French army," she stammered. "There must be at least two hundred of 'em. If they find you here, they'll burn down our house. Quick, get down into the cellar, and don't make a sound. If you make any noise, we're finished."

"*Ja, ja*, vill go," the terrified officer whispered. "How do vee get down?"

The young woman hurriedly opened the narrow, square trap door and the six men disappeared down the small winding staircase, backwards, one after the other, so they could feel their way down the steps.

As soon as the spike on the last helmet had disappeared, Berthine slammed shut the heavy oak door—as thick as a wall, as strong as steel—complete with hinges and a lock big enough for a dungeon; she turned the key twice and started to laugh, a silent laugh of delight, and she was filled with a mad desire to dance over the heads of her prisoners.

They made no noise, locked down there as if they were in a safe, a safe made of stone with only a small barred vent to let in some air.

Berthine immediately relit the fire, put the cooking pot back over it and made some more soup.

"Pa will be worn out tonight."

Then she sat down and waited. The only sound that broke the silence was the dull, regular *tick-tock* of the clock's pendulum.

Every now and again, the young woman glanced anxiously at the clock, with an expression that seemed to say:

"He's taking his time."

But soon she thought she could hear mumbling beneath her feet. Incomprehensible words spoken in low voices rose up through the brick-work from the cellar. The Prussians were beginning to guess she'd tricked them, and before long, the Second Lieutenant went to the top of the little staircase and started pounding on the trap door.

"You vill open it," he shouted.

She stood up, walked closer and, imitating his accent said: "Vat do you vant?"

"You vill open it."

"I von't."

"Open or I vill break down the door!" the man said angrily.

She started to laugh: "Go ahead and try, little man, just you try!"

And he began hitting the solid oak trap door above his head with the butt of his rifle. But the door would have stood firm against a battering ram.

Berthine heard him go back down the stairs. Then the soldiers each came, in turn, to inspect the door and try their strength. Realizing their efforts were pointless, no doubt, they all went back down into the cellar and started talking amongst themselves.

The young woman listened to them, then went to open the front door to see if she could hear anything in the dark.

She heard the sound of barking in the distance. She gave the kind of whistle a hunter would, and almost immediately, two enormous dogs came out of the darkness and playfully leapt around her. She grabbed them by the scruffs of their necks and held them so they wouldn't run away. Then she shouted as loudly as she could: "Hey! Pa?"

A voice replied, still quite far away: "Hey, Berthine."

She waited a few seconds, then said again: "Hey! Pa."

The voice was closer now and replied: "Hey, Berthine."

"Don't go past the cellar window," she continued: "There's Prussians down there."

And suddenly the tall silhouette of the man could be seen to her left, standing still between two tree trunks.

"Prussians down the cellar. What're they doin' there?" he asked, sounding worried.

The young woman started to laugh: "It's the ones what came yesterday. They got lost in the forest. I put them down the cellar to cool 'em off."

And she told him the whole story, how she'd frightened them by firing the gun and locked them down the cellar.

The old man looked worried: "What am I supposed to do with 'em at this time of night?"

"Go get Monsieur Lavigne and his men," she replied. "He'll take them prisoner. He'll be real happy, he will."

Old Pichon smiled: "Y'know, he will at that."

"I made some soup," his daughter continued. "Eat it real quick and then get goin'."

The old gamekeeper put two plates of food on the floor for his dogs, sat down at the table and ate his soup.

The Prussians heard people talking and went quiet.

Stilts left fifteen minutes later. And Berthine sat, her head in her hands, and waited.

THE PRISONERS STARTED getting restless. They were shouting now, calling out, angrily beating the unmovable trap door of the cellar with the butts of their rifles, over and over again.

Then they started firing shots through the cellar window, hoping, no doubt, to be heard by some German detachment that might be passing through the woods.

Berthine sat absolutely still but the noise was upsetting her, irritating her. A feeling of malicious anger ran through her; she would have gladly killed them all, the villains, just to shut them up.

Then she grew more and more impatient, and started watching the clock and counting the passing minutes.

Her father had left an hour and a half ago. He would have reached the town by now. She pictured what he would do. He'd tell his story to Monsieur Lavigne, who would turn pale with emotion and ring for his maid to bring his uniform and weapons. She felt she could actually hear the drummer rushing through the streets. Terrified faces pressed against windows. The citizens' army would rush out of their homes, out of breath, still buckling their belts, and run toward the Major's house.

Then the troop, with Stilts leading the way, would set out through the night, through the snow, toward the forest.

She looked at the clock. "They could be here in an hour."

She was overwhelmed by anxious impatience. They were taking so long!

The time she'd imagined they would arrive came at last.

She opened the door once more to see if she could hear them coming. She caught a glimpse of a shadow walking cautiously toward the house. She let out a cry of fear. It was her father.

"They sent me to see if anything's changed," he said.

"No, nothing."

Then he gave a long, shrill whistle out into the night. Soon, they could see dark shapes emerging slowly from behind the trees: ten men had been sent on ahead of the rest of the soldiers.

"Don't walk by the cellar window," Stilts said over and over again.

So the first men to arrive showed the ones behind them where the dangerous vent was.

Finally, the main body of the troop appeared, two hundred men in all, each carrying two hundred bullets.

Monsieur Lavigne, trembling and very excited, ordered them to surround the house, leaving a wide open space free in front of the little black opening at ground level where air was let into the cellar.

Then he went inside and asked how many enemies there were and their state of mind, for they'd gone so silent you might have thought they'd disappeared, vanished, flown away through the little window.

Monsieur Lavigne stamped his foot against the trap door. "I wish to speak to the Prussian officer," he said.

The German did not reply.

"I want the Prussian officer," he said again.

In vain. For twenty minutes he demanded that this silent officer surrender, along with all their arms and kit, promising that none of them would be killed and that the officer and his men would be treated with military courtesy. But he received no sign of either agreement or hostility. The situation was becoming difficult.

The citizens' army stamped their feet into the snow and slapped their shoulders with their arms to keep warm, the way coachmen do, and they watched the little window with an increasing, childish desire to walk in front of it.

One of them, a very supple man named Potdevin,[2] finally took a chance. He gathered speed and leapt in front of the window like a stag. He succeeded. The prisoners seemed to be dead.

"No one's down there," a voice cried.

And another soldier walked across the empty space in front of the dangerous vent. Then it became a game. One after the other, the men jumped past the vent, going from one side to the other, like children having a race, and they ran so fast that each one kicked up snow and sent it flying. To keep warm, they'd lit fires made with large pieces of dead wood, and the silhouettes of the running National Guard were lit up as they quickly raced from side to side.

"It's your turn, Maloison!"[3] someone shouted.

Maloison was a chubby baker whose fat stomach was the subject of many jokes among his fellow soldiers.

He hesitated. They teased him. So he made up his mind and started

2   Literally, "Jug of wine," but it actually means a "bribe" or "backhander."
3   Literally, "Naughty Little Goose."

running at an easy, jogging pace; he was breathing heavily, which made his fat belly jiggle.

The entire detachment laughed until they cried.

"Bravo, bravo, Maloison!" they shouted, to encourage him.

He'd made it about two thirds of the way across when a long, red flame suddenly shot out of the vent. They heard a gunshot and the huge baker let out a horrible scream and fell flat on his face.

NO ONE RUSHED OVER to help him. Then they saw him crawling on all fours through the snow, groaning, and as soon as he was out of danger's way, he fainted.

He'd been shot in the upper thigh.

After the initial shock and terror had worn off, they all started laughing again.

But Major Lavigne came out onto the doorstep of the cottage. He'd decided on his plan of attack.

"Planchut the plumber and his workmen, now!" he ordered in a booming voice. Three men came forward.

"Detach the drainpipes from the house."

And fifteen minutes later, twenty yards of drainpipes were brought to the commander.

Then, taking infinite care, he had a little round hole cut into the trap door and built a conduit made from the pipes that went from the water pump down into the hole.

"Now we're going to offer our German friends something to drink!" he announced, sounding delighted.

A frenzied "hurrah!" of admiration was followed by shouts of joy and hysterical laughter. And the commander organized groups of men who would work for five minutes and then hand over to the next group.

"Pump," he ordered.

And after getting the pump handle going, they heard the soft sound of water running down the pipes into the cellar, splashing over each step, like a gurgling waterfall flowing into a pool with goldfish.

They waited.

An hour passed, then two, then three.

The agitated Major paced up and down in the kitchen, stopping every now and again to press his ear against the ground to try and work out what his enemies were doing, wondering if they would soon surrender.

Their enemies were moving around now. They could hear them shifting barrels, talking, splashing about.

Then, around eight o'clock in the morning, a voice rose up from the vent:

"I vant to speak to the French officer."

Lavigne replied from near the window, taking care not to stick his head out too close to it.

"Do you surrender?"

"I surrender."

"Then hand over your rifles."

A weapon immediately appeared through the bars of the vent and fell onto the snow, then two, then three—then all their weapons.

"Vee have no more," said the same voice. "Hurry up! I am drowning."

"Stop pumping," the commander ordered.

They stopped and dropped the pump handle.

Then, having filled the kitchen with all the armed soldiers who'd been waiting, he slowly raised the oak trap door.

Four heads appeared first, four blond soaking wet heads with long, light hair, then one after the other, the six Germans emerged, shivering, drenched, and terrified.

They were taken and tied up. Then, fearing some unexpected event, the citizens' army left immediately, in two convoys, one driving off with the prisoners, the other with Maloison carried on a mattress on top of some poles.

They entered Rethel in triumph.

Monsieur Lavigne was decorated for having captured a Prussian detachment, and the fat baker received a medal for having been wounded by the enemy.

A DUEL

THE WAR WAS OVER; THE GERMANS WERE OCCUPYING FRANCE; the country was trembling like a beaten warrior beneath the foot of the conqueror.

Paris was starving, panic-stricken, in despair. The first trains left the capital, slowly crossing the countryside and villages, headed toward the newly established borders. The first passengers looked out of the windows at the devastated land and burnt-out hamlets. In front of the few houses that remained standing, Prussian soldiers wearing black helmets topped with brass points sat astride chairs, smoking their pipes. Others were working or chatting as if they were one of the family. When the trains passed through the cities, you could see entire regiments practicing maneuvers in the town squares, and despite the noise from the railway tracks, the sound of raucous orders could still be heard every now and then.

Monsieur Dubuis, who had been in the National Guard in Paris throughout the entire siege, was going to join his wife and daughter in Switzerland; he'd sent them abroad before the invasion, just in case.

Neither famine nor exhaustion had managed to diminish his big stomach, for he was a wealthy, peace-loving merchant. He had lived through the horrible events with sad resignation and bitter thoughts on the savagery of man. Now that the war was over and he was headed for the border, it was the first time he actually saw any Prussians, even though he'd been on duty on the city's ramparts and stood watch on many a cold night.

He looked with annoyed terror at these armed, bearded men who were occupying France as if they were at home, and in his soul, he felt a kind of fever of powerless patriotism along with a great need to beware, a kind of new instinct for caution that remains with us to this day.

In his compartment, two Englishmen, who had come to witness the events, viewed everything through calm and curious eyes. They were both fat and chatted in their own language, sometimes leafing through their tourist guide, which they read out loud in an effort to recognize the places it described.

Suddenly, the train stopped at a small town and a Prussian officer noisily climbed up the steps of the train, his saber clanging loudly as he entered the compartment. He was a big man, bursting out of his uniform, and had an enormous beard. His red hair seemed to be on fire and his long moustache, a bit paler in color, flew up and cut across both sides of his face.

The Englishmen immediately started staring at him, smiling with satisfied curiosity, while Monsieur Dubuis pretended to be reading a newspaper. He huddled in his corner, like a thief in the presence of a policeman.

The train started to move again. The Englishmen continued talking, trying to locate the precise place where a battle had been fought. Suddenly, when one of them pointed to a specific village on the horizon, the Prussian officer stretched out his long legs, leaned back in his seat and said in French:

"I killed tvelve Frenchmen in this village. I take more than a hundred prisoners."

The Englishmen, totally fascinated, immediately asked, also in French: "Oh! What's this village called?"

The Prussian replied, "Pharsbourg," then continued, "I took dese naughty boys und teached dem a lesson."

And he looked at Monsieur Dubuis and arrogantly roared with laughter.

The train kept on moving, passing through the occupied villages.

You could see German soldiers all along the roads, near the fields, standing next to the fences or chatting in cafés. They covered the land like a swarm of African locusts.

The officer stretched out his hands.

"If I vere in charge, I vould have taken Paris und burned everysing und killed everyvun. No more France!"

Not wishing to be impolite, the Englishmen simply replied: "Oh, yes."

"In tventy years," the soldier continued, "all Europe, all, vill belong to us. Prussia stronger dan everyvun."

The Englishmen, somewhat anxious, said nothing more. Their faces had become impassive and seemed made of wax between their long side-burns. Then the Prussian officer began to laugh. And still leaning back in his seat, he started making jokes. He made fun of defeated, crushed France, viciously insulted his enemies. He made fun of Austria, which had recently been conquered; he joked about the fierce but powerless defense encountered in the provinces; he insulted the troops and their inferior artillery. He announced that Bismarck was going to build an iron city made from the captured cannons. And suddenly, he pressed his boots against Monsieur Dubuis's thigh. His face burned red with anger, but he turned away.

The Englishmen seemed to have become indifferent to everything, as if they'd suddenly found themselves back on their isolated island, far from the maddening crowd.

The officer took out his pipe and stared at the Frenchman.

"You have some tobacco, yes?"

"No, Monsieur," replied Monsieur Dubuis.

"If you please," the German continued, "you vill go und buy me some at next stop."

And he started laughing once more.

"I vill give you a tip."

The train whistled as it slowed down. They passed the burned-out building of a station and came to a stop.

The German opened the door of the compartment, grabbed Monsieur Dubuis by the arm, saying:

"Go on, go do my errand, *und schnell*—fast!"

A detachment of Prussian troops filled the station. Other soldiers stood watch, positioned all along the wooden fences. The train was already whistling to announce it was about to leave. Monsieur Dubuis suddenly jumped out onto the platform and, ignoring the stationmaster who was waving his arms at him, rushed into the next compartment.

HE WAS ALONE! His heart was beating so hard that he was panting; he opened his jacket and wiped off his forehead. The train stopped again at a station.

And suddenly the officer appeared at the door and got into his compartment along with the two Englishmen, who followed out of curiosity. The German sat down opposite the Frenchman and, still laughing, said:

"You did not vant to do my errand."

"No, Monsieur," replied Monsieur Dubuis.

The train had just started to move again.

"Then I vill cut your moustache," the officer said, "und use it to fill my pipe."

And he extended his hand toward Monsieur Dubuis's face.

The Englishmen, ever impassive, couldn't take their eyes off them.

The German had already got hold of a bit of hair and was pulling on it when Monsieur Dubuis slapped his arm away with the back of his hand, and grabbing him by the neck, he threw the officer against his seat. Then, overwhelmed with mad rage, temples pounding, eyes blazing, he continued strangling him with one hand while punching him furiously in the face with the other. The Prussian tried to fight back, to get his sword out, to overcome this enemy who was holding him down. But Monsieur Dubuis was crushing him with the weight of his enormous stomach, and he kept hitting and hitting, relentlessly, without stopping to catch his breath, without even knowing where his blows were landing. Blood flowed. The German, choking, gurgling, spluttering, tried—in vain—to push off this fat, frustrated man who was beating him to death.

The Englishmen inched closer to get a better look. They stood there, full of joy and curiosity, ready to bet for or against each of the rivals.

Then suddenly, exhausted by such a struggle, Monsieur Dubuis got up and sat down without saying a word.

The Prussian was so aghast, so stunned, so astonished and in so much pain that he didn't pounce on him. When he'd caught his breath, he said:

"If you vill not have a duel with me because of dis insult, I vill kill you."

"Whenever you like," Monsieur Dubuis replied. "With pleasure."

"Here is Strasbourg," the German continued. "I vill take two officers as my vitnesses; I have time before the train goes."

Monsieur Dubuis, who was puffing as much as the train, said to the Englishmen:

"Would you like to be my witnesses?"

They both replied at once: "Oh, yes!"

The train stopped.

The Prussian quickly found two friends who carried the pistols, and everyone climbed up onto the ramparts.

The Englishmen constantly took out their watches to check the time, hurried everyone along and made them go through the formalities very quickly, worried that they might not make it back to the train before it left.

Monsieur Dubuis had never held a pistol in his life. He was placed twenty paces from his enemy.

"Are you ready?" he was asked.

As he was replying, "Yes, Monsieur," he noticed that one of the Englishmen had opened his umbrella to protect himself from the sun.

A voice shouted:

"Fire!"

Without hesitating, Monsieur Dubuis fired blindly and was astonished to see the Prussian opposite him sway, fling his arms in the air and fall face first onto the ground. He had killed him.

One of the Englishmen, full of joy, satisfied curiosity and cheerful impatience, shouted: "Oh!" The other one, who still had his watch in his hand, grabbed Monsieur Dubuis by the arm and started running, dragging him toward the station.

The first Englishmen marked time as he ran, elbows close to his body and fists clenched.

"One, two! One, two!"

And all three of them jogged along, in spite of their fat stomachs, like three caricatures in a satirical magazine.

The train was leaving. They jumped into their compartment.

The Englishmen then took off their hats, waved them in the air and shouted, "Hip, hip, hip, hurrah!" three times in a row.

Then, one after the other, they solemnly shook hands with Monsieur Dubuis and sat back down in their seats.

BOULE DE SUIF[1]

F OR SEVERAL DAYS IN A ROW, THE REMNANTS OF THE DEFEATED
army had been passing through the city. They were no longer a
unified regiment, just a scattered group of soldiers. The men had long,
dirty beards, uniforms in shreds, and advanced listlessly, without a flag,
without a regiment. All of them looked dejected, exhausted, incapable of
coming up with a single idea or plan. They simply kept marching through
habit, dropping with exhaustion the moment they stopped. Some were
peace-loving men who had lived a life of ease and were then called up to
serve, hunched over under the weight of their rifles. Some were eager vol-
unteers, easily frightened but full of enthusiasm, as ready to attack as to
flee. And among them were a scattering of soldiers in their red breeches,
the wreckage of a division that had been overwhelmingly defeated in a
great battle. Gloomy artillerymen marched along with these various foot
soldiers, and every now and again they were joined by the shiny helmet
of some dragoon who could barely keep up with the faster pace of the
ordinary soldiers.

Bands of snipers and guerrillas with heroic-sounding names—
"Avengers of the Defeat," "Citizens of the Tomb," "Dealers of Death"—
also passed by, looking like bandits.

---

1   The closest translation of this nickname is "Butterball." The contrast between the
main character's humorous name and what happens to her is a typical example of Maupassant's irony.

Their leaders, former fabric or grain merchants, tallow or soap sellers, soldiers by some quirk of fate, were appointed officers because of their wealth or the length of their moustaches; they were heavily armed, wore flannel uniforms with stripes indicating their rank, and spoke in booming voices, discussing campaign plans and bragging that they alone could support a dying France on their shoulders. Yet they sometimes feared their own soldiers, criminals who were often excessively brave but basically debauched looters.

People were saying that the Prussians were about to enter Rouen.

For the past two months, the National Guard had cautiously sent reconnaissance scouts into the nearby woods; they sometimes shot their own sentries and were ready for action whenever a small rabbit stirred under the brush. They had all gone back home. Their weapons, their uniforms, all the murderous gear that had formerly terrified everyone up and down the main road for miles around, all of it had mysteriously disappeared.

The last of the French soldiers had just managed to cross the Seine, making their way through Saint-Sever and Bourg-Achard to reach Pont-Audemer; and bringing up the rear, in between two orderlies, their general walked in despair, unable to do anything with such a mass of stragglers, dismayed by the great debacle of a nation used to victory yet disastrously beaten despite its legendary bravery.

Then a profound sense of calm, a silent and terrifying waiting game descended on the town. Many portly middle-class men had grown soft thanks to their easy lives; they anxiously awaited the arrival of their conquerors, quaking at the thought that their roasting spits or large kitchen knives might be considered weapons.

Life seemed to have stopped; the shops were closed, the streets silent. Sometimes, one of the people who lived there would quickly walk down the road, huddling against the buildings, frightened of the silence.

The anguish of waiting made them wish the enemy would actually arrive.

On the afternoon of the day after the French troops had left, a few lancers—who seemed to have come out of nowhere—sped through the city. Then, a little later, a dark mass of bodies came down from Saint Catherine's Hill, while two other waves of invaders appeared on the roads from Darnetal and Boisguillaume. The advance guard of these three battalions arrived at the square in front of the Town Hall at exactly the same time. Then the German army poured in from every nearby street, their battalions pounding along the sidewalks with their harsh, rhythmical steps.

Orders shouted in foreign, guttural voices rose up through the houses that appeared empty and dead; but behind closed shutters, people watched out fearfully for these victorious men, masters over their town, their destinies and their lives, determined by the "rules of war."

The townspeople sat in their darkened rooms, overwhelmed with the kind of fear brought about by such cataclysmic events, huge upheavals that destroy the land, and that neither wisdom nor strength can overpower. For the same feeling emerges every time the established order is overthrown, when no one feels safe any more, when everything that protected the laws of nature or of man is suddenly at the mercy of ferocious, reckless brutality. An earthquake that buries an entire population beneath their crumbling homes; a river that floods, sweeping away farmers and the dead bodies of their cattle alike, along with beams ripped from the roofs of houses; or the glorious army massacring anyone who fights back, taking the rest as prisoners, pillaging in the name of the Sword and thanking their God to the sound of cannon fire—all terrifying plagues that destroy any belief in eternal justice, any confidence we are taught to have in protection from Heaven and human rationality.

Small detachments of troops knocked at every door before disappearing inside the houses. Occupation followed the invasion. The conquered were obliged to be gracious to their conquerors.

After a while, once the initial terror had worn off, a new sense of calm returned. In many families, a Prussian officer sat down to share a meal with them. Sometimes he had good manners and showed pity for France out of politeness, expressed his repugnance at having participated in the war. People were grateful for such feelings; and, of course, his protection might be needed one day. By handling him properly, they would perhaps have fewer men they had to feed. And why upset someone you were completely dependent on? To behave in such a way would be more reckless than brave. And recklessness was no longer one of the faults of the good people of Rouen, as it had been during the heroic resistance in the past, which had made their city famous. In the end, people told themselves that it was quite permissible to be polite to the foreign soldiers inside their houses, as long as they did not appear friendly in public, a supremely rational idea in keeping with French manners. Outside the house, they were strangers, but inside, they happily chatted together, and the German stayed longer and longer each evening, to keep warm by the fire in the living room.

Little by little, the city started to look like itself again. The Frenchmen still hardly ever went out, but the Prussian soldiers milled about in the streets. Moreover, the officers of the Blue Hussars, who arrogantly dragged their great deadly weapons along the pavement, did not seem to be significantly more disdainful of the ordinary people than the French cavalry officers who had drunk in the very same cafés the year before.

And yet there was something in the air, something subtle and strange, an intolerable foreign atmosphere, like a bad smell that spreads: the stench of invasion. It filled the houses and public squares, changed how the food tasted, gave everyone the impression they were on a journey, very far away, a journey to the land of dangerous, barbaric tribes.

The conquerors demanded money, a lot of money. The townspeople always paid; besides, they were rich. But the richer a Norman merchant becomes, the more he suffers from having to sacrifice anything, any small part of his fortune, watching it pass into someone else's hands.

But six or seven miles south of the city, following the course of the river as it flowed toward Croisset, Dieppedalle or Biessart, sailors and fishermen often hauled out the swollen corpse of some German in uniform, beaten to death with a wooden shoe, or stabbed, or his head bashed in by a stone, or someone who had been pushed into the river from the top of a bridge. The sludge of the river buried these obscure acts of vengeance, savage but justifiable, unknown acts of heroism, silent attacks, more dangerous than battles fought in broad daylight and without any hint of glory.

For the hatred of the Foreigner always arms a few Brave Men who are prepared to die for an Idea.

In the end, even though the invaders had subjugated the city with their strict discipline, they had not carried out any of the horrific deeds they were rumored to have committed throughout their long, triumphal march, and so the inhabitants grew bolder: the need to trade arose again in these merchants' hearts. Some of these men had important commercial dealings in Le Havre, which was occupied by the French army, so they wanted to try to get there by traveling overland to Dieppe where they could get a boat to the port.

The German officers they had gotten to know used their influence with the General in charge to get them a permit to leave.

And so, a large carriage pulled by four horses was hired for the journey and ten people signed up to travel with the owner. They decided to leave one Tuesday morning, just before daybreak, to avoid attracting a crowd.

For some time now, the frost had hardened the ground, and that Monday, around three o'clock, great dark clouds descended from the north, and it snowed steadily all that evening and continued snowing throughout the night.

At four-thirty in the morning, the travelers gathered in the courtyard of the Hôtel de Normandie, where they'd been told to meet the coach.

They were still very sleepy and shivered beneath their blankets. It was difficult to see in the darkness, and the way everyone was bundled up in heavy winter clothing made them all look like fat priests in their long cloaks. But two of the men recognized each other; a third one went up to them and they started chatting: "I'm bringing my wife along," one of them said. "So am I." "Me too." "We're not going to come back to Rouen," the first one said, "and if the Prussians make it to Le Havre, we're going to head for England." They were all very much alike, so they all had the same plan.

Meanwhile, the horses were not being harnessed. A little lantern carried by a stable boy appeared every now and then from a dark doorway only to disappear at once into another. The horses' hooves stamped on the ground, muted by the dung and straw, and a man's voice talking to the animals and swearing could be heard inside the building.

The faint jingle of bells meant they were fixing the harness; the soft sound soon became a clear, continuous ringing that followed the rhythm of the horse's movement, sometimes stopping, then suddenly continuing once more, accompanied by the dull thud of a horseshoe striking the ground.

The door suddenly closed. Not a sound could be heard. Everyone was freezing and had stopped talking: they simply stood there, stiff from the cold.

An endless blanket of white snow shimmered as it spread over the ground; it made it impossible to see any shapes, covering everything in a powdery layer of frost. And in the great silence of the calm city buried beneath the winter's snow, all that could be heard was the strange rustling of the falling snow, more a feeling than a sound, the mingling of invisible particles that seemed to fill the sky and engulf all the world.

The man reappeared with his lantern, pulling a sad-looking horse along by a rope, who didn't seem eager to follow. He placed him beside the beam, secured the ties and walked slowly all around to make sure the harness was properly fitted; he could only use one hand as he was carrying the lantern in the other. As he went inside to get the next horse, he noticed all the motionless travelers, already covered in snow. "Why don't you get into the carriage?" he asked. "At least you'll be out of the snow."

They hadn't thought of that, of course, and rushed into the carriage.

The three men helped their wives inside and then got in themselves; then the other hesitant people, covered in snow, took their seats without exchanging a word.

Their feet sank into the straw that covered the floor.

The women had brought along little copper foot-warmers filled with some sort of chemical fuel; they lit them and spoke quietly for some time, explaining the advantages of having them, repeating things to each other that they already knew for quite some time.

Finally, six horses were harnessed to the carriage instead of four because of the weight of the load. A voice from outside asked: "Is every-one in?" A voice from inside replied: "Yes." And they set out on their way.

The carriage moved slowly, very slowly.

The wheels sank in the snow; the entire carriage groaned with a muted, creaking sound; the animals slipped, huffed and puffed, and the coachman's enormous whip snapped continuously, flicking in all direc-tions, curling up and unfolding like some slim serpent, sharply stinging the horses' flanks which instantly tensed and made them strain to go faster.

But day was gradually breaking. The delicate snowflakes that one of the travelers, a native of Rouen, had described as a stream of cotton wool, no longer fell. A murky light filtered through heavy, dark clouds, making the countryside look even more dazzling white; sometimes they could see a row of tall trees covered in ice, sometimes a cottage with a roof laden with snow.

Inside the carriage, in the bleak light of daybreak, everyone looked at each other with curiosity.

Right at the back, in the best seats, Monsieur and Madame Loiseau, wine distributors from the Rue Grand-Pont, sat opposite one another, dozing.

A former assistant to an employer who had lost everything, Loiseau had bought the business and made his fortune. He sold very bad wine at very low prices to retailers in small villages and was known amongst his friends and acquaintances as a sly devil, a true Norman, tricky and jovial.

His reputation as a rogue was so well established that one evening, at the city's administrative offices, Monsieur Tournel, a writer of fables and songs, a local legend thanks to his subtle, biting wit, had suggested to some of the ladies who seemed about to doze off that they play a game called "Loiseau the Thief."[2] The term immediately caught on and spread rapidly through the local area, then into the heart of the city, and had made everyone roar with laughter for an entire month.

In addition, Loiseau was well known for playing tricks of all kinds and telling jokes, sometimes funny and sometimes mean, and no one could

---

2   A play on words: L'oiseau means "bird" and *voler* means both "to fly" and "to steal."

ever mention him without immediately adding: "That Loiseau is just a scream!"

He was short and stocky, with a round belly and ruddy complexion beneath his long, graying moustache.

His wife was tall, sturdily built, confident, and had a high-pitched voice; she made snap decisions and was the one who organized and kept the accounts of the business, which her husband cheerfully ran.

Next to them was Monsieur Carré-Lamadon, a more dignified gentleman belonging to a higher social class, who was considerably wealthy and the owner of three cotton mills, an officer of the Legion of Honor and a member of the Conseil général.[3] During the entire reign of the Empire,[4] he had been the leader of the benevolent opposition party, solely in order to make himself more money by recruiting others to the cause he was fighting, using what he called "polite weapons." Madame Carré-Lamadon, who was much younger than her husband, brought solace to the officers from the best families who were garrisoned at Rouen.

Sitting opposite her husband, she looked adorable: very pretty, petite, curled up in her fur coat, as she glanced sadly at the terrible condition of the inside of the carriage.

The people next to her, the Count and Countess Hubert de Bréville, bore one of the most ancient and noble names in Normandy. The Count, an elderly gentleman of aristocratic appearance, attempted to emphasize, by artificial means, his natural resemblance to Henri IV, who, according to a proud family legend, had gotten one of the de Bréville ladies pregnant and so had made her husband a count and governor of the province.

A colleague of Monsieur Carré-Lamadon in the Conseil général, Count Hubert was head of the Orléanist Party[5] in the region. The story of his marriage to the daughter of an insignificant shipowner from Nantes had always remained a mystery. But as the Countess looked very aristocratic, was second to none as a hostess, and said even to have been loved

---

3   A regional administrative body.
4   The Second Empire (1852–70).
5   The duc d'Orléans was one of the two claimants to the French throne.

by one of the sons of Louis-Philippe, every member of the nobility invited her to their parties; and her *salon*[6] was considered the best in the country, the only one where traditional values of gallantry were still respected, and the most difficult to be accepted into.

The de Brévilles' fortune consisted entirely of property and was worth, or so it was said, five hundred thousand francs a year.

These six people sat in the back of the carriage, the place reserved for the landed gentry, confident and strong men and women, the honest members of society who were Religious and had Principles.

Through a strange coincidence, all the women were seated on the same side, and the Countess had two additional neighbors: two good nuns who wore long rosary beads and whispered their *Paters* and *Aves*. One of them was old, with a face so marked and pitted by smallpox that she looked as if she had been hit by machine gun fire. The other nun was scrawny but had a rather pretty yet sickly-looking face: her chest sounded as if she had consumption, her strength sapped by the all-devouring faith that creates martyrs and eccentric visionaries.

Everyone was looking at the man and woman who sat opposite the two nuns.

The man was famous: Cornudet, *le démoc*,[7] who inspired fear in the hearts of respectable people. He had been dipping his red beard into the beer glasses of every republican café for the past twenty years. He and his friends had already spent the rather large fortune that had been left to him by his father, a former confectioner, and he was waiting, impatiently, for the rise of the Republic so he could finally take the place he rightly deserved after consuming so many revolutionary glasses of beer. On September 4,[8] perhaps as a result of a joke, he believed he had been appointed Prefect; but when he tried to take up his post, the office workers who had taken over the place refused to recognize his authority and he was forced

---

6   The noblewomen of the time held regular, exclusive gatherings for their friends, usually to increase their influence or to support the arts. These were called *salons* because
they were held in the reception rooms of the great houses.

7   Militant of the Second Republic proclaimed in 1848.

8   September 4, 1870, when Napoleon III was forced to abdicate.

to leave. Despite all of this, he was a rather likable young man, inoffensive and helpful, and he threw himself into defending Paris with unequaled passion. He had holes dug in the plains, cut down all the young trees in the neighboring forests, scattered traps along all the roads and then, satisfied with all his preparations, as soon as the enemy was getting closer, he hightailed it back to the city. He now thought he would be more useful in Le Havre, where new entrenchments were going to be needed.

The woman, one of the variety known as "courtesans," was famous for her youthful sexuality and voluptuous figure, which had earned her the nickname "Butterball." Short, curvaceous, extremely chubby, with puffy fingers pressed in at the joints like rows of little sausages, she had smooth, glowing skin and an enormous bosom that bulged over her low-cut dress. She was quite delectable and extremely popular; her fresh youthfulness made her very attractive. Her face was like a red apple, a peony bud about to blossom; thick eyelashes cast a shadow over her magnificent dark eyes. She had shiny little baby teeth, and her enchanting mouth with its slender, moist lips was made to be kissed.

She also possessed, or so people said, other inestimable qualities.

As soon as she was recognized, the righteous women started whispering, and at once the words "prostitute" and "shameful hussy" were murmured so loudly that she looked up. She then gave each of her neighbors such a provocative, scathing look that a great silence immediately followed, and every one of them lowered their eyes, except for Loiseau, who was enthralled and salaciously watched her every move.

But soon the conversation between the three women started up again, since the presence of this young women suddenly made them bond as friends, almost intimate acquaintances. For they believed they had to create a pact, as it were, based on their dignity as honest wives, to stand together against this shameless hussy.

For legitimized love always takes the high moral ground in the face of its more licentious sister.

The three men, bound by an instinct for conservatism at the sight of Cornudet, began talking about money in a contemptuous way that was insulting about the poor. Count Hubert listed the damage the Prussians had done to him, the losses suffered due to the cattle he'd had stolen and the lost harvest, but with the smug confidence of a noble lord who was a millionaire ten times over and so would recoup these losses within a year. Monsieur Carré-Lamadon, an experienced cotton manufacturer, had had the foresight to send six hundred thousand francs to England, a nest egg for the disastrous time he anticipated he might one day face. As for Loiseau, he had made sure he'd sold all the cheap table wine left in his cellars to the French Military Supply Corps, so the state owed him a great deal of money, which he hoped to be paid in Le Havre.

All three of them looked at each other in a friendly way. Despite their different social status, they felt themselves united in the brotherhood of money whose members could always hear the sound of gold coins jingling whenever they reached into their pockets.

The carriage was traveling so slowly that by ten o'clock in the morning, they had barely gone twelve miles. The men got out three times to walk up the hills on foot.

Everyone was starting to get anxious, for they were meant to be having lunch at Tôtes, but now they feared they wouldn't even make it there by evening. They were all gazing outside in the hope of finding an inn along the road when the carriage sank in a bank of snow; it took two hours to dig it out.

They were getting hungrier and hungrier and more and more disheartened. Not a single cheap restaurant or wine shop could be found: the approach of the Prussians and the starving French troops that passed through had frightened everyone away, so they had closed all their stores.

The gentlemen rushed out to see if they could find some food in the farms along the road, but they couldn't even get any bread: the wary farmers hid all their reserves out of fear of being pillaged by the soldiers who, having nothing whatsoever to eat, grabbed anything they could find by force.

At around one o'clock in the afternoon, Loiseau announced that he definitely felt a big hollow in his empty stomach. Everyone had been suffering the same way for a long time, and the desperate need to eat continued to grow, killing all conversation.

Every now and again, someone yawned; someone else did the same almost immediately, and each one of them, in turn, according to his character, sophistication and social status, either noisily opened his mouth or modestly held a hand to cover the gaping hole, their breath escaping in a kind of mist.

Butterball bent down several times, as if she were looking for something under the folds of her dress. She hesitated for a moment, looked at her companions, then calmly sat up straight again. Everyone looked pale and tense. Loiseau said he would pay a thousand francs for a hunk of ham. His wife began to make a gesture as if to protest, then stopped herself. She always found it painful to hear talk about money being wasted and could not really understand how anyone could make jokes about such a thing. "I don't feel well at all," said the Count. "How could I have not thought of bringing along some food?" Everyone reproached himself in the same way.

Cornudet, however, had a bottle of rum; he offered it around: everyone coldly refused. Only Loiseau accepted and took a few sips, thanking him when he handed back the bottle: "That's good, it really is, it warms you up and makes you forget about being hungry." The alcohol put him in a good mood and he suggested they follow the words of a sailor's song: to eat the fattest passenger. This indirect allusion to Butterball shocked the respectable people in the carriage. No one said a word; only Cornudet was smiling. The two good nuns stopped saying their rosary and sat very still, their eyes looking stubbornly down, their hands hidden inside their wide sleeves, doubtlessly offering back the suffering Heaven had sent them as a sacrifice.

At three o'clock, they found themselves in the middle of flat, open country as far as the eye could see, without a single village in sight. Butterball quickly bent down and pulled out a large basket covered in a white cloth from under her seat.

First she took out a small earthenware plate, then a small silver cup and finally an enormous dish that contained two whole chickens cut into joints preserved in aspic, and everyone could see many other wonderful things wrapped up in the basket—pâtés, fruit, sweets—enough food to last three days without having to depend on stopping at inns.

The necks of four bottles peeked out from between the packages of food. She picked up a chicken wing and began to daintily nibble at it, along with one of the rolls known in Normandy as a "Regency."

Everyone was staring at her. Then the smell of chicken filled the carriage, causing their nostrils to flare, their mouths to water and their jaws to contract in pain. The scorn the ladies felt toward this young woman grew savage: they would have liked to kill her or throw her out of the carriage into the snow, her, her silver cup, her basket and all her food.

Loiseau's eyes devoured the dish of chicken. "Well, well! I can see that Madame thought ahead more than we did. Some people always manage to think of everything." She looked up at him: "Would you like some, Monsieur? It's difficult to go without food all day." He bowed. "Well, to tell the truth, I wouldn't say no. I'm at the end of my tether. All's fair in love and war, don't you think, Madame?" And looking all around him, he added:

"At times like this, it's very lucky to find such generous people."

He spread some newspaper over his trousers so he wouldn't stain them and using the pocketknife he always carried, helped himself to a chicken thigh covered in aspic, tore a piece off with his teeth and chewed it with such obvious satisfaction that a great sigh of distress from the others filled the carriage.

Then Butterball, in a soft, humble voice, asked the nuns if they would like to share her food. They both accepted immediately, and, without looking up at her, began eating quickly, after mumbling a few words of thanks. Cornudet did not refuse his neighbor's offer, and, along with the nuns, they made a kind of table by spreading the newspaper out over their knees.

Mouths opened and closed, chewing, swallowing, greedily devouring the food. In his corner of the carriage, Loiseau was hard at work, and quietly urged his wife to follow his example. She resisted for a long time, but after her stomach contracted painfully, she gave in. Her husband, assuming his most polite manner, asked whether their "charming companion" would mind offering a little bit to Madame Loiseau.

"But of course, Monsieur," she replied with a kind smile, as she held out the dish.

There was an awkward moment when the first bottle of Bordeaux was opened: there was only one drinking cup. It was wiped clean before being passed to the next person. Only Cornudet, undoubtedly out of gallantry, drank from the same moist spot as his neighbor.

Surrounded by people who were eating, virtually choking on the wonderful smell of food, the Count and Countess de Bréville and Monsieur and Madame Carré-Lamadon suffered the hideous form of torture that has long been associated with the name of Tantalus.[9] Suddenly, the young wife of the cotton manufacturer let out such a great sigh that everyone turned to look at her; she was as white as the snow outside; her eyes closed, her head dropped forward: she had fainted. Her husband, extremely upset, begged everyone for help. No one knew what to do until the older nun supported the sick woman's head, placed Butterball's drinking cup in between her lips and made her take a few sips of wine. The pretty young woman stirred, opened her eyes and said in a faint voice that she felt quite well again now. But to prevent her from fainting again, the nun made her drink a whole glass of wine. "She's just hungry, that's all," she said.

Butterball then blushed terribly from embarrassment. "Good Lord," she stammered, looking at the four travelers who had had nothing to eat, "if I presumed to offer these ladies and gentlemen . . ." She stopped herself, fearing their contempt. But Loiseau spoke up: "Well, in such situations we are all brothers and should help each other. Come now, ladies, don't stand on ceremony: accept her offer, for goodness sake! Are we even sure we'll find somewhere to spend the night? At the rate we're going, we won't even make it to Tôtes before noon tomorrow." They hesitated; no one wanted the responsibility of being the first to say yes. But the Count solved the problem. He turned toward the frightened, chubby girl and using his most sophisticated manner said: "We accept most gratefully, Madame."

The first step was the most difficult. Once the Rubicon was crossed, they didn't hesitate to tuck in. The basket was emptying but still had much food left: there was a pâté de foie gras, a lark pie, a piece of smoked tongue, some Crassane pears, a square Pont L'Evêque cheese, some petits

---

9   The mythical figure condemned by Zeus to a life of constant hunger and thirst.

fours and a cup full of pickles and pickled onions, because Butterball, like all women, adored raw vegetables.

It was impossible to eat this young woman's food without speaking to her. And so they began to chat, reservedly at first, then, as she seemed more well mannered and better educated than they had imagined, more openly. The de Bréville and Carré-Lamadon ladies, who were very sophisticated, became quite gracious but tactful. The Countess especially displayed the kind of amiable condescension typical of the upper-class nobility that cannot be stained by contact of any kind with lesser beings, but could not have been more charming. Only the stocky Madame Loiseau, who had the soul of a policeman, remained surly, speaking little and eating a great deal.

Naturally, they talked about the war. They told terrible stories about the Prussians, gave examples of the courageous qualities of the French; and all these people who were running away, paid homage to the bravery of the others. Soon they began talking about themselves, and Butterball, with great emotion, with that warm way of speaking that young girls sometimes use when expressing their natural passions, explained how she had left Rouen: "At first, I thought I could stay on there," she said. "I had my house, well stocked with food, and I preferred to feed a few soldiers than to run away heavens knows where. But when I saw those Prussians, I just couldn't stand it! They made my blood boil with anger and I cried with shame all day long. Oh! If only I were a man, you'd see! I watched them from my window, the fat swine with their spiked helmets, and my maid had to grab my hands to stop me throwing furniture down at them. Then some of them came and said they would be lodging with me, so I lunged at the throat of the first one I saw. It's no more difficult to strangle them than anyone else! I would have finished him off if I hadn't been pulled away by the hair. After that, I had to go into hiding. And so, when I saw the opportunity, I left, and here I am now."

Everyone congratulated her warmly. She rose in the estimation of her companions, who had not demonstrated such courage; and as Cornudet listened to her, he smiled with the kindly, approving smile of an apostle, the same smile a priest might wear when he hears a devout person praising

God, for the long-bearded democrats have the monopoly on patriotism just as priests have on religion.

When it was his turn, he spoke dogmatically, stressing his words in a way he had learned from the proclamations hung on the walls of the city every day, and he concluded with a choice morsel of oratory in which he eloquently crushed Louis-Napoleon, that "villain, Badinguet."[10]

Now Butterball got angry, for she was for Bonaparte. She blushed redder than a cherry and stammered in indignation: "I would have liked to see what you would have done in his place. Oh, yes! What a mess you would have made! *You're* the ones who betrayed him! No one would have any choice but to leave France if we were governed by scoundrels like you!" Cornudet, impassive, kept smiling in a superior, disdainful way, but they could sense that insults would soon be exchanged, so the Count intervened. He managed to calm the angry young woman down, but not without difficulty, stating firmly that all sincerely held opinions should be respected. But the Countess and the manufacturer's wife, who felt the irrational hatred of all respectable people toward the Republic, along with the instinctive tenderness that women cherish for despotic, ostentatious governments, felt drawn, in spite of themselves, to this prostitute who was full of dignity and whose feelings so closely resembled their own.

The basket was empty. Ten people had easily emptied it; their only regret was that there had not been more. The conversation continued for a while, though everyone was more distant since they had finished eating.

Night was falling; it was getting darker and darker, and the cold, which everyone felt more as they were digesting their food, made Butterball shiver, in spite of her plumpness. So Madame de Bréville offered her her foot-warmer, which had been refueled several times since the morning, and she accepted at once, for her feet were freezing cold. Madame Carré-Lamadon and Madame Loiseau gave theirs to the two nuns.

The driver had lit his lanterns. They cast a bright glow over the mist that hovered above the horses' sweating rumps, and on the snow along

10   Badinguet was the worker who lent his clothes to Louis-Napoleon so he could escape from prison in 1846. The nickname is derogatory.

both sides of the road that seemed to uncurl beneath the moving reflection of the lamps.

It was so dark inside the carriage that it was impossible to see anything. Then suddenly, something moved between Butterball and Cornudet, so Loiseau peered into the darkness and thought he saw the man with the long beard pull quickly away as if he had been hit, silently but hard.

Several small lights appeared on the road ahead. It was Tôtes. They had been traveling for eleven hours, fourteen if you counted the four times they had stopped to let the horses rest and eat some oats. They entered the town and stopped in front of the Hôtel du Commerce.

The coach door opened! A well-known sound made all the travelers shudder: it was the harsh noise of scabbards being dragged along the ground. Then someone shouted something in German.

Even though the carriage was standing still, no one got out, as if they expected to be massacred the moment they did. Then the driver appeared with one of the lanterns in his hand, lighting up the inside of the carriage with its two rows of frightened faces, their mouths gaping open and their eyes wide with surprise and terror.

In the bright light, they could see a German officer standing next to the driver. He was a tall young man, excessively thin and blond, stuffed into his uniform like a woman in a corset, wearing his flat, shiny cap tilted to one side, which made him look like a bellboy in some English hotel. His extremely long, straight moustache tapered off at both ends into a single strand of blond hair so thin that it seemed endless, and the weight of the moustache seemed to drag down the corners of his mouth, pulling at his cheeks and making his lips droop.

He spoke the French of the Alsace region; in a dry voice, he asked the passengers to come out of the carriage: "Vill you please to come out, ladies und gentlemen?"

The two nuns were the first to obey, with the compliance of religious women used to always being submissive. The Count and Countess were next, followed by the manufacturer and his wife, then Loiseau, who pushed his larger, better half in front of him. Once out of the carriage, Loiseau said: "Hello, Monsieur," more out of a feeling of prudence than politeness. The officer, as insolent as anyone in a position of power, looked at him without replying.

Butterball and Cornudet were the last to emerge, even though they were seated next to the door; they looked serious and dignified in the face of the enemy. The plump young woman tried to control herself and seem calm; the democrat twisted his long, reddish beard in anguish, his hand trembling. Both of them wanted to maintain their dignity, understanding that in such situations every individual represents his country; and, equally revolted by the servility of their companions, Butterball tried to look prouder than her neighbors, the respectable women, while Cornudet, feeling it was up to him to set an example, maintained an attitude of sabotage, which was his mission ever since he had decided to travel.

They went into the enormous kitchen at the inn and the German asked them to show him their travel passes authorized and signed by the General in command; these gave the names, description and profession of each traveler. He studied them carefully, comparing the people in front of him with their details.

Then he said briskly: "Es gut," and walked out.

They could breathe again. They were still hungry; supper was ordered. It would take half an hour to prepare, so while two servants started getting it ready, everyone went to see their rooms. They were all located along a long corridor; a glazed door with a ¢ ("cent") sign on it—the bathroom—was at the very end.[11]

They were about to sit down to eat when the owner of the inn appeared. He was a former horse trader, a heavy, asthmatic man who was always wheezing, coughing and clearing his throat. His father had given him the name Follenvie.[12]

"Mademoiselle Elisabeth Rousset?" he asked.

Butterball shuddered and turned around:

---

11   A note in the Pléiade edition of the original explains that in certain hotels, the bathroom door used to be indicated by the number 100, because in French, the word for hundred, *cent*, sounds exactly the same as the word for smell, *sent*. I have taken the liberty of transposing the pun using the (s)cent sign.—Trans.

12   "Mad Desire."

"Yes, that's me."

"Mademoiselle, the Prussian officer wishes to speak to you at once."

"To me?"

"Yes, if you are Mademoiselle Elisabeth Rousset."

She was flustered, thought for a second, then declared firmly:

"He may want to see me, but I'm not going to see him."

Everyone gesticulated all around her, talking and trying to understand why the officer had asked to see her.

"You are wrong, Madame," said the Count, going over to her. "Your refusal could cause a great deal of trouble, not just for you, but for all of us as well. You must never oppose the people who are strongest. Your agreement to this request could not be dangerous in the least: it is undoubtedly to do with some detail that's been overlooked."

Everyone agreed with him. They begged her, pressured her, lectured her and ended up convincing her, for everyone feared the complications that might result from her stubbornness.

"I will do this for your sakes," she finally said, "for you!"

The Countess took her hand:

"And we thank you for that."

She left the room. They waited for her to come back before sitting down at the table. Each of them was upset at not having been summoned instead of this impulsive, short-tempered girl and mentally prepared the platitudes they would say in case they were the next to be called.

Ten minutes later, she returned, staggering, bright red and terribly upset. "That bastard!" she stammered. "That bastard!"

Everyone pressed her to find out what had happened but she wouldn't say a word, and when the Count became insistent, she replied with great dignity: "No, it has nothing to do with any of you: I cannot tell you."

So everyone sat down at the table where a large soup tureen gave off the aroma of cabbage. In spite of the incident, the meal was enjoyable. The cider was good, so the Loiseaus and the nuns had some; they didn't want to spend a lot of money. The others ordered wine; Cornudet asked for a beer. He had an unusual way of opening the bottle and getting a head on the drink; he leaned the glass on its side and studied it, then raised it up beneath the light to take a good look at its color. As he drank, his long beard, which was about the same color as the drink he liked so much, seemed to tremble lovingly; his eyes squinted so he could keep his beer mug in sight, and he looked as if he were fulfilling the unique purpose for which he had been born. It was almost as if he had established in his mind an affinity between the two great passions in his life—Lager and the Revolution—and he obviously could not drink the one without thinking of the other.

Monsieur and Madame Follenvie were seated at the very end of the table. The gentleman, groaning like a broken-down train, wheezed too much to be able to speak while eating; his wife, however, talked incessantly. She shared, in great detail, her impressions of when the Prussians first arrived and how they behaved, what they said, and how she loathed them—in the first place because they cost her money, but also because she had two sons in the army. She spoke mainly to the Countess, flattered at being able to have a conversation with a grand lady.

Then she lowered her voice and started talking about more delicate subjects, though her husband interrupted her from time to time: "You really should be quiet, Madame Follenvie." But she paid no attention to him.

"Yes, Madame, these Germans do nothing but eat potatoes and sausages or sausages and potatoes," she continued. "And don't think they are clean. Oh, no! With all due respect, they leave garbage everywhere. And if you could see them doing maneuvers all day long for days on end: there they all are in some field, marching forward, marching backward, turning this way, turning back. If only they could plow the fields or go back home and work on fixing the roads! But no, Madame, these soldiers do nothing worthwhile. Why should we poor people have to feed them so that they can learn how to kill us! I'm just an old woman with no education, it's true, but when I see them wearing themselves out marching about from dawn to dusk, I say to myself: 'When there are people who make so many discoveries that are helpful, why should others go to so much trouble to do harm! Really, isn't it horrible to kill people, whether they are Prussian, or English or Polish or French?' If we take revenge against someone who has done us harm, it's considered wrong and we're punished for it; but when they hunt down our boys with rifles as if they're game, that's just fine, because they award medals to whoever kills the most? You see? I'll never understand that!"

Cornudet spoke up:

"War is barbarous if you attack a peaceful neighbor, but a sacred duty if it is a matter of defending your country."

The old woman lowered her head:

"Yes, when you act in self-defense, that's another matter; but wouldn't it perhaps just be better to kill all the kings who make war to amuse themselves?"

Cornudet's eyes blazed with passion as he said:

"Bravo, Madame citizen."

Monsieur Carré-Lamadon was deep in thought. Although he was an enthusiastic admirer of famous military men, the great common sense of this countrywoman made him think of the wealth that could be brought to a country by so many idle and consequently inexpensive hands, by so much unproductive strength, if only they were used to work on great industrial projects that would take centuries to complete.

Loiseau stood up, went over to the innkeeper and said something to him in a low voice. The big man laughed, coughed, spluttered; his enormous belly wobbled with joy at his neighbor's jokes, and he bought six casks of Bordeaux wine from Loiseau to be delivered in the spring, after the Prussians had gone.

Everyone was completely exhausted, so as soon as supper was over, they all went to bed.

Now Loiseau, who had noticed certain things, sent his wife to bed. He then looked through the keyhole and listened by the door to try and uncover what he called "the secrets of the corridor."

After about an hour, he heard a rustling sound and quickly had a look; there was Butterball, looking rounder than ever in a blue cashmere peignoir trimmed with white lace. She was holding a candle in her hand and walking toward the bathroom at the end of the corridor. Then one of the doors at the side opened a little, and when she came back after a few moments, Cornudet, suspenders holding up his pants, followed her. They spoke to each other quietly, then stopped. Butterball seemed to be firmly refusing to allow him into her room. Unfortunately, Loiseau couldn't hear exactly what they were saying, but toward the end, he managed to catch a few words as they were speaking more loudly. Cornudet was extremely insistent.

"Really, you're being stupid. What difference should it make to you?" he said.

She looked indignant.

"No, my dear," she replied. "There are certain times when you just don't do such things, and in this place, it would be shameful."

He did not understand at all and asked her why. Then she got really upset and spoke even louder:

"Why? You really don't understand why? When there are Prussians in this inn, perhaps even in the room next door?"

He said nothing. The patriotic modesty of this harlot who refused to allow herself to be touched because the enemy was close by must have awakened the failing dignity within his heart, for he just gave her a kiss and slipped back into his own room.

Loiseau, who was quite aroused, walked away from the keyhole, pranced around the room, tied a handkerchief around his head as a kind of sleeping cap, lifted up the sheet where the hard carcass of his wife was laying, woke her with a kiss and whispered: "Do you love me, my darling?"

The entire house fell silent. But soon a sound was heard from somewhere, perhaps the cellar or maybe the attic, the sound of someone snoring loudly, a steady, regular, muted series of snores like a kettle bubbling over. Monsieur Follenvie had fallen asleep.

They had decided to leave early in the morning, so everyone was in the kitchen by eight o'clock, but the carriage, its roof covered in snow, stood by itself in the middle of the courtyard, with no horses and no driver. They looked for the coachman in the stables, the storage houses, the sheds, all in vain. So the men decided to go out and find him, and they left. They found themselves in the town square; the church was at the far end with low houses on either side; they could see some Prussian soldiers. One of them was peeling potatoes. Another was cleaning a barbershop.

Yet another, a soldier with a very long beard, was hugging a little kid who was crying, rocking him on his lap to try to calm him down; and the fat countrywomen, whose husbands were "in the army at war," gestured to their obedient conquerors to make them understand what tasks they had to do: chop the wood, ladle soup over the bread, grind the coffee; one of them was even washing his hostess's laundry, as she was so old she could hardly move.

The Count, astonished, questioned the verger who was coming out of the presbytery. The old church mouse replied: "Oh! Those men aren't so bad: they're not Prussians, apparently. They're from far away, I don't exactly know where they come from, but all of them have left a wife and children behind; they don't like war, not at all!

"I'm sure that people are crying over them back home just as we are here, and the war is causing terrible problems for them as much as for us. It's not too bad here at the moment, because they aren't doing any harm and they're working as if they were in their own homes. You see, Monsieur, the poor have to help each other . . . It's the noblemen who make war."

Cornudet, indignant at finding such amiable relations between the conquerors and the conquered, walked away, preferring to stay inside the inn. "They are trying to repopulate the place," Loiseau joked. But Monsieur Carré-Lamadon spoke seriously: "They are repairing the damage they've done." Meanwhile, the coachman was nowhere in sight. They finally found him in the village café, having a friendly chat with the officer's orderly.

"Weren't you told to harness the horses at eight o'clock?" Carré-Lamadon asked.

"Yes, but I got another order after that."

"What other order?"

"Not to harness them at all."

"Who gave you such an order?"

"The Prussian officer."

"But why?"

"I have no idea. Go and ask him. If I'm told not to harness the horses, I don't harness the horses. That's all there is to it."

"And the officer himself gave you that order?"

"No, Monsieur: it was the innkeeper who passed the message on to me."

"When was that?"

"Last night, just as I was about to go to bed."

The three men went back to the inn, very worried.

They asked for Monsieur Follenvie, but the servant replied that because of his asthma, he never got up before ten o'clock. He had expressly forbidden them to wake him earlier unless there was a fire.

They wanted to see the officer, but this was absolutely impossible, even though he was staying at the inn. Monsieur Follenvie was the only person authorized to speak to him about matters to do with civilians. And so they waited. The women went back to their rooms and kept themselves busy with this and that.

Cornudet sat down alongside the tall fireplace in the kitchen, beside a blazing fire. He had a small table and a bottle of beer brought to him, and he smoked his pipe. The pipe was appreciated by all democrats almost as much as it was by him, as if it served the country by serving Cornudet. It was a superb meerschaum pipe, admirably seasoned, as black as its owner's teeth, but sweet-smelling, curved, shiny, fitted to his hand and complementing his appearance. He sat there, very still, sometimes staring at the flames in the fireplace, sometimes at the froth that crowned his beer; and every time he took a drink, a look of satisfaction spread across his face and he would run his long thin fingers through his long greasy hair as he sucked the foam up from his moustache.

Loiseau, pretending he wanted to stretch his legs, went out to sell some wine to the local merchants. The Count and the manufacturer started talking politics. They were imagining the future of France. One of them believed in the Orléans, the other in some unknown saviour, a hero who would emerge when everyone was on the verge of despair: a du Guesclin,[13] a Joan of Arc, perhaps? Or another Napoleon I? Ah! If only the Prince

---

13 Bernard du Guesclin (1320–1380), known as the Eagle of Brittany because of his courage, was a legendary figure of the Hundred Years' War.

Imperial Louis-Napoleon wasn't so young! Cornudet listened to them, smiling like a man who can predict the future. The smell of his pipe wafted throughout the kitchen.

At ten o'clock, Monsieur Follenvie appeared. They quickly asked him all sorts of questions, but all he could do was to repeat word for word what the officer had said to him two or three times: "Monsieur Follenvie, you will forbid them to harness these travelers' carriage tomorrow. I do not want them to leave until I give the order. You understand. Now go."

So they wanted to see the officer. The Count sent in his calling card on which Monsieur Carré-Lamadon added his name and all his titles. The Prussian replied that he would allow these men to speak to him after his lunch, which meant at about one o'clock.

The ladies came downstairs and everyone had a bit of food, in spite of their anxiety. Butterball looked sick and extremely worried.

They were just finishing their coffee when the orderly came to get the two gentlemen.

Loiseau joined the two men; when they tried to get Cornudet to come along as well, to give more weight to their interview, he proudly stated that he would never have anything to do with the Germans.

He sat back down near the fireplace and ordered another beer.

The three men went upstairs and were shown into the most beautiful room in the inn, where the officer received them; he was stretched out in an armchair, his feet resting on the mantelpiece, smoking a long porcelain pipe and wrapped in a flamboyant bathrobe that he doubtless stole from some abandoned house belonging to some bourgeois with bad taste. He did not get up, did not greet them, did not even look at them. He was a magnificent example of the rudeness that comes naturally to a victorious army.

After a few moments he finally spoke:

"Vat do you vant?"

"We wish to leave, Monsieur," said the Count.

"No."

"Might I ask the reason for your refusal?"

"Because I do not vish it."

"With all due respect, Monsieur, I must point out that your general gave us permission to travel to Dieppe, and I don't believe we have done anything to deserve your orders."

"I do not vish it . . . That is all . . . You go now."

The three men bowed and left the room.

The afternoon was awful. No one understood this German's whim, and the strangest, most upsetting thoughts filled their heads. Everyone was sitting in the kitchen, talking continuously, imagining the most bizarre things. Perhaps they wanted to keep them hostage—but why?— or take them prisoner? Or maybe demand a large ransom? This idea left them panic-stricken. The richest ones were the most terrified, picturing themselves forced to hand over sacks of gold to this arrogant soldier in order to save their own lives. They wracked their brains trying to work out believable lies, how to hide their wealth so they would seem poor, very poor. Loiseau removed the chain from his watch and hid it in his pocket. As night fell, they grew more and more apprehensive. They lit the lamp and since they wouldn't be having dinner for another two hours, Madame Loiseau suggested a game of *trente et un*.[14] It would take their mind off things. Everyone agreed.

Even Cornudet politely put out his pipe and joined the game.

The Count shuffled the cards and dealt out the hands; Butterball had 31 right away and soon everyone concentrated on the game, which lessened the fears that haunted them. Cornudet noticed that Loiseau and his wife were cheating.

Just as they were about to sit down to eat, Monsieur Follenvie returned. In his hoarse voice, he said: "The Prussian officer wished me to ask Mlle Elisabeth Rousset if she had changed her mind yet."

Butterball went very pale and stood deadly still; then she suddenly turned bright red and was so overcome with fury she couldn't speak. Finally, she shouted: "Please tell that Prussian scoundrel, that filthy pig, that bastard, that I will never change my mind. Do you hear me? Never, never, never!"

---

14   A card game in which the winner has to get the closest to thirty-one points.

The fat innkeeper went out. Then everyone swarmed around Butterball, questioning her, begging her to reveal the secret of her visit to the officer. She refused at first, but her frustration won out in the end: "What does he want? . . .What does he want? . . . He wants to sleep with me!" she cried. Everyone was so indignant that they weren't even shocked. Cornudet banged his beer mug so violently on the table that it shattered. A great outcry of protest broke out against this repulsive thug, mixed with a wave of anger; everyone was united in resistance, taking a common stand, as if the sacrifice demanded of Butterball was shared by each of them. The Count declared in disgust that those people behaved like barbarians did in the past. The women especially expressed tender and enthusiastic sympathy toward Butterball. The two nuns, who only came downstairs for meals, looked away and said nothing.

Once the initial anger had subsided, they had dinner; but they hardly spoke: they were thinking.

The ladies went to bed early; the men continued to smoke and organized a game of *écarté*,[15] which they invited Monsieur Follenvie to join, so they could subtly question him as to how to convince the officer to change his mind. But he concentrated on his cards, wouldn't listen to them, wouldn't answer them; he just said over and over again: "Let's play cards, gentlemen, cards!" He was so intent on the game that he forgot to spit out the phlegm from his lungs, which made his chest sometimes wheeze like a note held too long on a keyboard. His whistling lungs hit every note of the asthmatic scale, from the deep serious chords right up to the sharp screeches of young roosters trying to crow.

He even refused to go up to bed when his wife came looking for him. She was exhausted—she was an "early bird," always up at dawn—so she went upstairs alone; her husband, however, was a "night owl," always eager to stay up late with friends. "Put my eggnog in front of the fire," he shouted after her, then went back to his cards. When the others saw that

---

15   Another card game, similar to gin rummy, named for the French verb *écarter* ("to set aside").

they couldn't get anything out of him, they said it was time to go to bed, and everyone went to his room.

They were up fairly early the next day, feeling a vague sense of hope, an even greater desire to leave than before and great fear at having to spend another day at this horrible inn.

Alas! The horses were still in the stable; the driver was nowhere in sight. They walked round and round the coach, bored, with nothing else to do.

Lunch was depressing, and everyone seemed colder toward Butterball, for after thinking it over during the night, their opinion had changed. They now virtually held a grudge against her for not having secretly gone to the Prussian so that her companions would have a nice surprise that morning. What could be easier? Who would even have known? She could have saved face by telling the officer that she felt sorry for the others who were so upset. What difference would it make to someone like her!

But no one admitted what they were thinking, at least, not yet.

That afternoon, they were bored to death, so the Count suggested they take a walk on the outskirts of the village. Everyone dressed up warmly and the little group set off, except for Cornudet, who preferred to sit by the fire, and the nuns, who spent their days in church or with the priest.

The cold, which was getting worse and worse every day, bitterly stung their noses and ears; their feet became so painful that every step they took brought more suffering, and when they finally reached open ground, the fields looked so mournful and gloomy under an endless sheet of snow that they immediately turned back, their souls and hearts icy cold.

The four women walked in front, followed a little way behind by the men.

Loiseau, who understood the situation, suddenly asked if "that slut" was going to force them to spend much more time in such a place. The Count, who was always polite, said they could not demand such a painful sacrifice from any woman; it had to be her decision. Monsieur Carré-Lamadon pointed out that if the French were preparing a counterattack from Dieppe, as was rumored, there would most likely be a battle at Tôtes.

This thought worried the other two men. "What if we got away on foot?" asked Loiseau. The Count shrugged his shoulders: "Do you really think we could, in this snow? With our wives? We'd be hunted down and found in ten minutes and taken back as prisoners, at the mercy of the soldiers." It was true; everyone fell silent.

The ladies talked about clothes, but a certain sense of reserve seemed to come between them.

Suddenly, the officer appeared at the end of the street. Against the snowy backdrop of the horizon, he looked like a wasp in uniform; he walked with his legs apart, with that gait unique to military men who are trying not to dirty their meticulously polished boots.

He bowed as he passed the ladies, then looked scornfully at the men, who at least enjoyed the dignity of not having tipped their hats to him, though Loiseau at first had started to.

Butterball's whole face turned red, and the three married women felt a great surge of humiliation to have run into this soldier in the company of this young woman whom he had treated so cavalierly.

And so they began talking about him, his physique, his face. Madame Carré-Lamadon, who had known many officers and considered herself an expert, remarked that he was not bad at all; she even regretted he wasn't French, for he would make a very handsome Hussar, and all the women would be mad about him.

ONCE BACK AT THE INN, they did not know what to do. Bitter words were exchanged over really insignificant things. The silent dinner was soon over and everyone went up to bed, hoping to sleep longer to kill the time.

The next day, they all came downstairs looking tired and frustrated. The women barely spoke to Butterball.

A church bell rang out. It was for a baptism. The chubby young woman had a child who was being raised by countryfolk in Yvetot. She saw him barely once a year, and never thought about him, but the idea of the child about to be baptized filled her heart with a sudden, urgent wave of tenderness for her own son, and she was determined to go to the ceremony.

The moment she had gone, everyone looked at each other and brought their chairs closer together, for everyone felt they had to make some sort of decision. Loiseau had a brainwave: he suggested they propose that the officer should only keep Butterball and let the rest of them leave.

Monsieur Follenvie was given the task, but he returned almost immediately. The German, who knew something about human nature, had thrown him out. He intended to hold everybody there until his desire had been satisfied.

Then Madame Loiseau's vulgar character revealed itself: "We're not going to die of old age here," she shouted. "Since it's that tart's profession to sleep with men, I don't see why she has the right to refuse any one man in particular. Honestly, that thing had anyone and everyone in Rouen, even the coach drivers! Yes, Madame, the coachman from the police station! I know it's true, yes, I do, because he buys his wine from us. And now, when it's a question of getting us out of this bad situation, she gives herself airs and graces, the snotty little thing! . . . If you ask me, this officer has behaved properly. Perhaps he has done without it for a long time; and there were three others he would have no doubt preferred. But no, he'll make do with the woman anyone can have. He respects married women. Think about it: he's in charge here. All he had to say was: 'I want . . .' and he and his soldiers could have taken us by force."

The other two women shuddered. The pretty Madame Carré-Lamadon's eyes shone and she went a bit pale, as if she could feel herself being taken by force by the officer.

The men, who had been discussing the problem amongst themselves, joined the women. Loiseau, furious, wanted to hand "that wretched woman" over to the enemy by force. But the Count, having come from three generations of ambassadors and endowed with the physique of a diplomat, was more inclined to use subtler tactics: "We must persuade her," he said.

And so began their conspiracy.

The women huddled together, lowered their voices and a general discussion began with each person giving her opinion. They spoke, however, in the most polite terms. The ladies in particular found the most delicate turns of phrase and the most subtly charming expressions to say the most shocking things. They were so careful about their language that an outsider wouldn't have understood a thing. But since only a thin layer of modesty veils the surface of any society woman, they really began to enjoy this naughty little adventure, actually finding it a great deal of fun, feeling they were in their element, toying with love with the kind of sensuality a gourmet chef feels when he prepares dinner for someone.

In the end, the situation seemed so funny to them that their cheerfulness returned. The Count told some rather risqué jokes, but in such a clever way that they made everyone smile. Then Loiseau added some even more explicit stories, but no one was in the least offended. And the thought so brutally expressed by his wife stood out in all their minds: "Since it's that tart's profession to sleep with men, I don't see why she has the right to refuse any one man in particular." The sweet Madame Carré-Lamadon even seemed to think that if she were in Butterball's place, she would be less inclined to refuse this officer than any other man.

The plan of attack was carefully prepared, as if they were in a fortress under siege. Each of them agreed the role they would play, the arguments they would use, the maneuvers they had to carry out. They decided their campaign, their strategies, their surprise attacks, to force this human citadel to crumble and yield to the victorious enemy.

Meanwhile, Cornudet stood apart, wanting nothing to do with this business.

Their minds were so completely concentrated that they didn't even hear Butterball come in. Then the Count softly whispered "Shush," which made everyone look up. She was there. Everyone quickly fell silent and a kind of embarrassment prevented anyone from speaking to her at first. The Countess, more skillful at the duplicity practiced in high society, asked: "Did you enjoy the baptism?"

The chubby young woman, still moved, described everything, the people, what they looked like, even the church itself. Then she said: "It feels so good to pray sometimes."

Until lunchtime, the ladies were happy to be pleasant to her, in order to encourage her trust and convince her to accept their advice.

As soon as they sat down to dinner, they began maneuvers. First came a thinly veiled conversation about self-sacrifice. They gave examples from ancient times: Judith and Holofernes,[16] then, for no apparent reason, Lucretia and Sextus,[17] and Cleopatra, who slept with all the generals who opposed her in order to turn them into her slaves. Next they told a totally unbelievable story, made up by these ignorant millionaires, which detailed how the women of Rome seduced Hannibal, in Capua, along with all his lieutenants, soldiers and mercenaries. They named all the women who were victorious over their conquerors by turning their bodies into a battlefield, a means of domination, a weapon, women who conquered hideous, hateful beings through heroic caresses, sacrificing their chastity to the noble cause of vengeance and loyalty.

They even described, in veiled terms, the Englishwoman from a noble family who allowed herself to be given a horrible, contagious disease in order to infect Bonaparte; but he was miraculously saved moments before their deadly tryst by a sudden moment of weakness.

And all these things were said with moderation and politeness, interspersed with moments of forced enthusiasm designed to encourage a spirit of competition.

By the end, one would almost have believed that the unique role of a woman on this earth was to endlessly sacrifice herself, to offer up her body continually to the desires of military men.

The two nuns seemed to hear nothing at all and remained lost in thought. Butterball didn't say a word.

All afternoon, she was left to think things over. But instead of calling her "Madame" as they had up until now, they simply called her "Mademoiselle," without actually knowing why, but sensing that it would lower her a notch in their esteem, and to make her understand her shameful situation.

---

16   Escaping from the city being besieged by Holophernes, Judith is supposed to have seduced him before murdering him.

17   It is not clear why Maupassant invokes the story of Lucretias's rape by Sextus Tarquinius which, according to ancient historians like Livy, led to the fall of Rome.

Just as the soup was being served, Monsieur Follenvie returned, repeating the question he had asked the night before:

"The Prussian officer wished me to ask Mlle Elisabeth Rousset if she had changed her mind yet."

"No, Monsieur," Butterball replied curtly.

During dinner, the coalition weakened. Loiseau made three inappropriate remarks. Everyone was wracking their brains to find new illustrations, in vain, when the Countess, perhaps without malice or forethought, perhaps simply feeling a vague need to pay homage to the Church, questioned the older of the nuns about the important facts in the lives of the saints. Now, many saints had committed acts that would be considered crimes to us, but the Church gives total absolution to any acts carried out for the glory of God or for the good of their fellow man. It was a powerful argument; the Countess took advantage of it. And so, either through tacit understanding or disguised collusion—anyone wearing an ecclesiastical habit excels in such things—or simply out of simple ignorance or sheer stupidity, the old nun provided great support to the conspiracy.

They had believed she was shy, but she showed them she was bold, talkative, passionate. This nun was not concerned by the trials and errors of casuistry; her doctrine was ironclad; her faith resolute; her conscience devoid of scruples. She found the sacrifice of Abraham a simple matter, for she would have killed her mother and father at once if she had been commanded to do so from on high; and nothing, in her opinion, could displease the Lord when the intention was admirable. The Countess, taking advantage of the holy authority of her unexpected accomplice, coaxed her on to make a salutary paraphrase of the ethical axiom: "The end justifies the means."

"And so, Sister," the Countess asked, "do you think that God would accept any means and would forgive any act if the intention is pure?"

"Who could doubt it, Madame? An act that is guilty in itself often becomes praiseworthy through the thought that inspires it."

And they continued talking in this way, determining God's will, predicting His decisions, assuming Him to be interested in things that barely truly concerned Him.

Everything said was veiled, skillful, discreet. But every word of the holy sister in her cornet headpiece weakened the indignant resistance of the courtesan.

Then the conversation took a somewhat different turn and the nun wearing the long string of rosary beads spoke about the convents in her order, about her Mother Superior, about herself and her darling little companion, Sister Saint Nicephore. They had been asked to go to the hospitals in Le Havre to nurse the hundreds of soldiers who had caught smallpox. She described these poor men, giving details of their illness. And while they were being held here on their way to Le Havre, a great number of Frenchmen might be dying who could have been saved! Nursing soldiers was her particular specialty; she had been in the Crimea, in Italy, in Austria, and as she told stories about the various military campaigns she had been involved in, she suddenly revealed herself to be one of those nuns who seemed eager to follow the army from camp to camp, gathering up the wounded in the midst of battles; and she could control these great undisciplined ruffians with a single word better than any of their leaders. She was a true drum-beating nun, and her haggard face, covered in pockmarks, seemed the very incarnation of the destructive nature of war.

The effect of her words was so excellent that no one spoke after she'd finished.

As soon as the meal was over, everyone rushed up to their rooms, and only came back down again late the next morning.

They had a quiet lunch. They were giving the seed sown the night before time to grow and bear fruit.

The Countess suggested they go for a walk in the afternoon; the Count offered Butterball his arm, as arranged beforehand, and walked with her a little behind the others.

He spoke to her in that familiar, paternal and slightly condescending tone that upper-class men use with young women, calling them "my dear child," talking down to her because of his social position, his indisputable respectability. He came straight to the point:

"So you prefer to keep us here, leaving us vulnerable—along with yourself—to all the violence that would surely follow a Prussian defeat rather than consent to an act of sacrifice, as you have so often in your life?"

Butterball said nothing.

He used kindness, reasoning, sentiment to try to persuade her.

He knew how to maintain his status as "the Count," while showing himself to be gallant when necessary, complimentary, even amiable. He glorified the service she would be doing them, mentioned their gratitude; then suddenly, he spoke to her in a very familiar tone: "And you know, my darling, he would be able to brag at having had the pleasure of knowing you, because he wouldn't find many pretty girls like you in his country."

Butterball said nothing and joined the others.

As soon as they got back, she went upstairs and did not come back down again. Their anxiety was extreme. What would she do? How embarrassed they would feel if she held out!

The dinner bell rang; they waited for her, in vain. Then Monsieur Follenvie came in and stated that Mlle Rousset was not feeling well and wouldn't be having dinner. Everyone listened intently. The Count went over to the innkeeper. "So it's done?" he asked quietly. "Yes." He said nothing to his companions, out of politeness; he simply nodded slightly to them. A great sigh of relief rose up at once and everyone's face lit up with joy. "Splendid!" shouted Loiseau. "The champagne's on me, if they have any in this place!" and Madame Loiseau was very upset when the owner came back with four bottles. Everyone had suddenly become talkative and boisterous; vulgar joy filled their hearts. The Count noticed that Madame Carré-Lamadon was charming; the manufacturer paid compliments to the Countess. The conversation was lively, cheerful, witty.

Suddenly, Loiseau, looking anxious, raised his arms and shouted, "Be quiet!" Everyone fell silent, surprised and almost frightened. Then he raised his eyes toward the ceiling, strained to hear something, gestured them to be quiet, listened again and finally said: "Don't worry, it's all right," his voice sounding normal again.

At first they didn't understand, but soon they all smiled.

A quarter of an hour later, he pulled the same prank again, and repeated it often during the evening; and he pretended to question someone on the floor above, giving him advice that had double meanings drawn from his traveling salesman's sense of humor. Sometimes he looked sad and sighed: "Poor girl!" or muttered from between clenched teeth:

"Well, well! you Prussian devil!" Sometimes, just when they had forgotten all about it, he would shout, "Enough, enough!" several times, adding, as if he were talking to himself, "I hope we will see her again; I hope that contemptible man doesn't kill her!"

Even though these jokes were in the worst possible taste, everyone found them funny and no one was offended, for a feeling of indignation depends on the atmosphere, as does everything else, and the atmosphere they had gradually created was full of risqué thoughts.

During dessert, even the women made witty, funny allusions. Their eyes sparkled; they had all drunk a lot. The Count, who retained a serious demeanor even when relaxed, made a comparison that was much appreciated by everyone between their situation and the end of the icy winter at the North Pole and the joy of shipwrecked passengers who finally see a path leading south.

Loiseau, on a roll, stood up, a glass of champagne in his hand: "A toast to our freedom!" Everyone stood up and cheered. Even the two nuns, encouraged by the ladies, agreed to take a sip of the bubbly, which they had never tasted. They declared it was like sparkling lemonade, but much more subtle.

Loiseau summed up the situation.

"It's a shame there isn't a piano; we could dance a quadrille."

Cornudet hadn't said a word or made a gesture; he even looked as if he were lost in deep thought, tugging angrily at his long beard now and then, as if he were trying to make it even longer. Finally, around midnight, just as they were all about to go, Loiseau, who was staggering a little, suddenly poked Cornudet's stomach and mumbled: "You weren't much fun tonight; don't you have anything to say, man?" Cornudet quickly raised his head and gazed at the others, one by one, a cutting, horrible look in his eyes. "I say that you have all done a vile thing!" He stood up, went over to the door, said, "Vile!" once more and walked out.

At first, this had a sobering effect. Loiseau was taken aback and said nothing; but he suddenly recovered his composure and bent over with laughter, saying over and over again: "They have no idea, they just have no idea."

No one understood, so he revealed the "secret of the corridor." Everyone became extremely cheerful. The women were laughing like idiots. The Count and Monsieur Carré-Lamadon laughed so hard they cried. They couldn't believe it.

"What! Are you sure! He wanted to . . ."

"I'm telling you that I saw it with my own eyes."

"And she refused . . ."

"Because the Prussian was in the next room."

"And you're sure?"

"I give you my word."

The Count was choking with laughter. The manufacturer clutched his stomach with both hands.

"And so you see why he didn't find tonight very funny," Loiseau continued, "not funny at all."

And all three men began to laugh again, choking, spluttering, out of breath.

Then they all parted. But Madame Loiseau, who had a spiteful nature, remarked to her husband as they were going to bed that Madame Carré-Lamadon—"the little vixen"—had forced herself to laugh all evening. "You know that when a woman is attracted by a uniform, she couldn't care less if it belongs to a Frenchman or a Prussian; it's all the same to her, I'm telling you. Good Lord, it's disgusting!"

And all night long, flutters, distant sounds, barely audible, like breathing, the light touch of bare feet and faint creaking noises filled the dark corridor. And of course, they all slept very late; slivers of light slipped beneath their doors for a very long time. Champagne has that effect; it causes restless sleep, or so it's said.

The next day, a bright winter's sun made the snow sparkle. The carriage, harnessed at last, was waiting at the door, while a flock of white pigeons with pink eyes that had a small black dot in the center, heads tucked beneath their thick feathers, walked calmly between the legs of the six horses, pecking about for food in the steaming manure.

The coachman was in his place, wrapped up in a sheepskin coat, smoking a pipe, and all the delighted passengers quickly wrapped up some food for the rest of the journey.

They were waiting for Butterball. At last she appeared.

She seemed rather upset and ashamed as she walked shyly toward her companions; all of them turned away at once, as if they hadn't seen her. The Count took his wife's arm with great dignity and led her far away from this impure contact.

The chubby young woman stopped, astonished; then, gathering all her courage, she walked over to the manufacturer's wife and humbly murmured, "Good morning, Madame." The other woman merely nodded slightly in an insolent way and looked at her with an expression of offended virtue. Everyone seemed busy and kept their distance from her, as if some disease were festering under her dress. Then they hurried toward the carriage, followed by Butterball, who, all alone, was the last to climb in; she silently sat down in the same seat she had taken during the first part of the journey.

It was as if no one saw her, no one knew her; though Madame Loiseau looked at her with indignation from a distance and remarked to her husband, loud enough to be heard: "Thank goodness I'm not sitting next to *her*."

The heavy carriage started out and continued on its way.

At first, no one spoke. Butterball didn't dare look up. She felt indignant toward all her companions, and, at the same time, humiliated to have given in; she felt dirty for having allowed the Prussian to kiss her and hold her in his arms where the others had so hypocritically forced her.

But soon the Countess turned toward Madame Carré-Lamadon and broke the silence:

"I believe you know Madame d'Etrelles?"

"Yes, she's one of my friends."

"She's such a charming woman!"

"Delightful! An exceptional person, highly educated as well, and a true artist: she sings beautifully and her drawing is sheer perfection."

The manufacturer was chatting with the Count, and in between the rattling of the windows, certain words stood out now and again: "Share— maturity date—bonus—futures."

Loiseau, who had stolen the old pack of cards from the inn, covered in grease from five years of contact with badly cleaned tables, began a game of bezique with his wife.

The nuns took hold of their long rosary beads that hung down below their waists, made the sign of the cross, and suddenly began mumbling quickly, getting faster and faster, rushing their words as if they were in a race to see who could say the most prayers; and they kissed a medallion from time to time, crossing themselves again, then went on with their rapid, continual muttering.

Cornudet sat motionless, deep in thought.

After they had been traveling for three hours, Loiseau put away the cards. "Time to eat," he said.

His wife picked up a package tied with string and took out a piece of cold veal. She cut it up properly into neat, thin slices and both of them began to eat.

"Shall we eat as well?" said the Countess. Everyone agreed, and she unwrapped the provisions prepared in advance for the two couples. In one of those long earthenware dishes with a lid decorated with a hare to show that it contains a game pie, there was a succulent pâté with white streaks of lard crisscrossing on top of the mixture of finely chopped dark meats. A large wedge of Gruyère cheese that had been wrapped in newspaper had the words *News in Brief* on its creamy surface.

The two nuns took out some sausages that smelled of garlic; and Cornudet dug into both deep pockets of his thick coat to pull out four hard-boiled eggs from one and a piece of bread from the other. He peeled the eggs, threw the shells on the straw beneath his seat, and began biting into them, dropping tiny bits of yolk into his long beard; they stuck there, looking like little stars.

In the haste and confusion of the morning, Butterball had not had time to think about anything, and she watched in stifled rage and frustration as all these people ate so calmly. Her extreme anger caused her whole body to tense at first, and she started to open her mouth to shout a flood of insults at them for what they had done; but she was choked by so much exasperation that she couldn't say a single word.

No one looked at her or gave her a second thought. She felt as if she were drowning in the disdain of these virtuous villains who had first sacrificed her, then rejected her, as if she were unclean and useless. Then she thought back to her large basket full of all the delicious things they had greedily devoured, her two chickens shining in aspic, her pâtés, her pears, her four bottles of Bordeaux wine, and her fury suddenly gave way, like a rope pulled too tightly that finally snaps, and she felt herself on the verge of tears. She made a great effort to control herself, sat up taller, stifled her sobs the way children do; but her tears rose up, glistened in the corners of her eyes, and soon two heavy teardrops broke free and rolled slowly down her cheeks. Others followed more quickly, rushing down like drops of water filtering from behind a rock, falling steadily onto the rounded curve of her bosom. She continued to sit tall, staring straight ahead, her face tense and pale, hoping that no one would see her.

But the Countess noticed and warned her husband with a gesture. He shrugged his shoulders as if to say: "What can I do? It's not my fault." Madame Loiseau gave a silent laugh and whispered triumphantly: "She's crying out of shame."

The two nuns had wrapped up what was left of their sausages and gone back to their prayers.

Then Cornudet, who was digesting his eggs, stretched his long legs out under the seat opposite, leaned back, crossed his arms, smiled like a man who has just heard a good joke, and began whistling the *Marseillaise*.[18]

The faces of all his companions went dark. This song of the common

---

18   The French national anthem was composed in 1792 by Rouget de Lisle for the French Army of the Rhine. The irony here—Cornudet's "good joke" is also Maupassant's—is that this victorious military marching song, subsequently adopted by generations of revolutionaries, is sung in the context of a terrible defeat.

people did not please them in the least. They grew anxious, irritated, and looked as if they were about to howl, the way dogs do when they hear the sound of a hurdy-gurdy.

He noticed but didn't stop. At times, he even started singing the words:

> *Amour sacré de la patrie,*
> *Conduis, soutiens, nos bras vengeurs,*
> *Liberté, liberté chérie,*
> *Combats avec tes défenseurs!* [19]

They were traveling more quickly now, for the snow was packed and harder. And all the way to Dieppe, throughout the long, dreary hours of the journey, through the jolts of the carriage along the road, at dusk, then in the heavy darkness of the carriage, he continued, with ferocious determination, his vengeful, endless whistling, forcing his weary, frustrated listeners to follow the song from start to finish, to remember every word of every verse.

And Butterball continued to cry, and every now and then, a sob she could not hold back was heard between two lines of the song, in the darkness.

---

19   *Drive on sacred love of country,*
   Support our avenging arms,
   Liberty, cherished liberty,
   Join the struggle with your defenders!

TALES OF THE SUPERNATURAL

THE STORIES IN THIS SECTION WERE ALL WRITTEN AFTER 1881; they deal with the themes of terror, death, the occult, madness, and suicide, subjects common in the literature of the nineteenth century.

Several of these stories reflect an interest in the early stages of psychiatry and pseudoscientific beliefs such as Franz Anton Mesmer's theory of "animal magnetism," which posited that there was a natural transfer of energy between all animate and inanimate objects, and formed the basis of "mesmerism," a popular practice associated with hypnotism, which we see in *Le Horla*. Another contemporary advocate of hypnotism was Dr. Jean-Martin Charcot, famous for his early work on neurology and hysteria. Charcot gave lectures and demonstrations at the Salpêtrière Hospital in Paris, some of which Maupassant attended. One of the most famous doctors in Paris at the time, Dr. Emile Blanche, a specialist in mental illness, ran a clinic where he treated Maupassant and other well-known literary figures.

It has often been speculated that Maupassant's interest in such macabre and supernatural themes after 1877 coincided with his discovery that he had contracted syphilis. He was suffering from hair loss, headaches, eye problems, and stomach pains, and his diagnosis meant a steady degradation of both mind and body, to incurable madness followed by certain death. Many have seen these supernatural stories as the possible expression of an addled brain suffering the effects of the disease.

In addition, Maupassant's obsession with madness and death must have been intensified by the fact that his younger brother, Hervé, suffered from syphilis too, and by September 1887 was showing signs of the mental instability linked to the disease. Hervé was committed to an asylum near Paris for a month that year, but in January 1888 he had a nervous breakdown. The following year, Hervé was sent to another asylum near Lyon, where he died a few months later of syphilis.

By 1891, Maupassant's own physical and mental state had become quite dire. At the start of 1892, shortly after New Year's Day, he tried to commit suicide by slitting his own throat. A week later, he was taken to Paris—in a straitjacket—and interned in Dr. Blanche's clinic, having obviously gone insane. He died there on July 6, 1893, at the age of forty-two.

ON THE WATER*

I RENTED A LITTLE COUNTRY HOUSE ON THE BANKS OF THE SEINE last summer, several miles from Paris, where I would go to sleep every evening. After a few days, I made the acquaintance of one of my neighbors, a man of around thirty or forty who really was the oddest character I'd ever met. He was an old man, who was mad about boats—always near the water, always on the water, always in the water. He must have been born on a boat and he would surely be carried away on that final journey upriver.

One evening when we were strolling along the riverbank, I asked him to tell me some stories of his life on the river. All of a sudden the good man got so animated that his whole demeanor changed; he was transformed, became eloquent, almost poetic. In his heart he had one great, all-consuming, irresistible passion: the river.

"AH!" HE SAID, "I have so many memories of this river you see flowing beside us! You city dwellers, you don't really know the river, but listen to a fisherman say that word. To him, it is the most mysterious thing; deep and strange: a fairy-tale world of mirages and specters, where you see things in the darkness that aren't real, where you hear noises you cannot

---

* Translated by Sandra Smith in collaboration with Eleanor Hill of Sarah Lawrence College.

recognize, where you shake in fear without knowing why, as if you were walking through a cemetery: in fact, it is the most sinister of cemeteries: the kind with no tombstones.

Land confines the fisherman, but in the darkness on a moonless night, the river goes on forever. A sailor doesn't feel the same way about the sea. It is often malicious and cruel, that's true, but the great sea cries, it screams, it does not lie: it is trustworthy, whereas the river is silent and treacherous. It does not roar, it flows along without a sound, and it is this eternal movement of the river that is more terrifying to me than any of the highest waves created by the ocean.

Dreamers claim that the sea hides in its heart immense bluish waters where drowned men float amongst the slender fish, in the midst of strange forests and crystal caves. The river has nothing but black depths where you rot in the slime. Yet it is beautiful when it sparkles and shines in the light of the rising sun, when it softly laps against its banks covered in rustling reeds.

The poet speaks of the Ocean:

> O waves, how many mournful stories you know!
> Deep waters, feared by mothers on bended knee,
> You tell your stories as you rise with the tides
> And they become the despairing voices
> We hear at night, as you come toward us[1]

Well, I think that the stories whispered by the slender reeds with their soft little voices are far more sinister than any of the tragedies told by the howling waves.

But since you've asked me for some of my memories, I will tell you of one strange experience that happened to me, right here, about ten years ago.

I was living in the house of Madame Lafon as I am now, with one of my

---

1 Verses from Victor Hugo's poem *Oceano nox*, translated by Sandra Smith.

closest friends, Louis Bernet, who had moved into a village[2] seven miles further down the river. He doesn't go boating any more: he gave up his sloppy clothes along with the glorious pleasures of the river to get into the *Conseil d'Etat*. We had dinner together every day, sometimes at his place, sometimes at mine.

One evening, I was coming home alone, somewhat tired, in my boat—a twelve-footer that I always took out at night—I stopped for a few seconds to catch my breath beside the reed-covered point as I'd been rowing with some difficulty; see, over there, about six hundred feet in front of the railway bridge. It was a beautiful night; the moon shone magnificently, the river shimmered and sparkled in its light, the air was calm and mild. This tranquility appealed to me; I thought it would be pleasant to smoke a pipe there, so I did just that. I took my anchor and cast it into the river.

The boat floated a little downstream with the current until its chain was taut, then stopped; and I sat in the stern on my sheepskin, trying to make myself as comfortable as possible. It was silent, absolutely silent: only occasionally I thought I could make out the sound of the water lapping on its banks, although I could barely hear it; and I could just glimpse the strange shapes the group of reeds made on the higher banks; every now and again, they seemed to flutter.

The river was perfectly calm, but I found myself moved by the extraordinary silence that surrounded me. The frogs, the toads, the water creatures that sing in the marshes at night made no sound. Suddenly, a frog croaked to my right. I shuddered: it went quiet; I heard nothing more, and decided to smoke a little to take my mind off it. But although I was well known as a pipe-smoking man, my stomach turned as soon as I took the second puff and I stopped; I just couldn't. I began to sing, but the sound of my voice irritated me, so I lay down in my boat and watched the sky, and after a while, I calmed down. But soon the slight movements of the boat on the water began to worry me; it felt like it was swaying and rocking fiercely against the riverbanks, hitting each of them in turn. I thought that

2   The original French has "village de C. . . ." The village alluded to is either Chatou or Croissy.

some invisible force or creature was slowly dragging my boat to the bottom of the river, then lifting it up just to let it fall back again. I was thrown about as if I were in a storm; I heard sounds all around me; I leapt up; the water was glistening, everything was calm.

I realized I was a little shaken and decided to leave. I pulled the chain of my anchor and the boat began to move a little, but then, I could feel it was stuck; I pulled harder, but the anchor didn't move; it had caught on something at the bottom of the river and I couldn't pull it free; I tried again, but in vain.

I used my oars to turn the boat around, hoping that it would change the position of the anchor. But again, it was in vain, it held fast; I flew into a rage and furiously rattled the chain. Nothing moved.

I sat down utterly discouraged and began to think about my situation. I couldn't even consider breaking the chain or separating it from the boat because it was enormous and attached at the bows to a piece of wood larger and thicker than my arm; but as the weather was so fine, I thought that it surely couldn't be long before some fisherman would come along and help me. My failed attempt had calmed me; I sat down and could finally smoke my pipe. I also had a bottle of rum, so I drank a few glasses and soon my situation began to make me laugh. It was very warm, so warm that I could spend the night quite comfortably sleeping under the stars if I had to.

All of a sudden, something hit my boat. I jumped; chills ran down my spine, from the top of my head to the tips of my toes. The sound had probably been made by some piece of wood floating past with the current, but still, it was enough to fill me once again with strange, overwhelming anxiety; I tensed my muscles, seized the chain and pulled in desperation. The anchor held firm. I sat down again, exhausted.

Meanwhile, the thick white fog was gradually settling low down onto the river, spreading softly across the water, so that even while standing I could no longer see the water, or my feet, or my boat. All I could make out was the tops of the reeds in the distance and the flat open country, very pale in the moonlight, filled with the long dark shadows of a cluster of Italian poplars ascending toward the sky. I felt buried to the waist in a soft cotton cloud of dazzling whiteness, and I began to imagine all sorts of supernatural things. I imagined that someone was trying to climb onto the boat—that I could no longer see—and that the river, hidden in this dense fog, was filled with strange beings swimming all around me. I felt horribly frightened, my head throbbed and my heart was beating so fast I thought I would die; panic-stricken, I thought of swimming away, of saving myself, but even that idea made me shake with terror. I could picture myself lost, drifting through the thick fog, struggling through the grass and reeds, gasping with fear, unable to escape, unable to see the riverbanks, unable to find my boat again; and I felt as if I would be dragged feet-first all the way down to the bottom of this endless, black water.

And since I would have had to swim against the current for at least five hundred yards before finding the gap in the grass and rushes where I could get a foothold, there was still only a one in ten chance that I would be able to navigate through that fog and swim to shore, regardless of how good a swimmer I was.

I tried to reason with myself. I felt a strong desire not to be afraid, but something besides this desire burned within me, and this other thing was afraid. I wondered what it was that I feared; the brave *me* mocked the cowardly *me*, and never so strongly as on this day did I feel the conflict between these two beings that live within us, one desiring, the other opposing, and each in turn winning over the other.

This ridiculous, inexplicable fear grew and grew until I was completely terrified. I stood absolutely still, eyes wide open, listening and waiting. For what? I had no idea, but it must surely be something horrible. I believe that if a fish had suddenly jumped out of the water, as often happens, that's all it would have taken to make me drop down, unconscious.

Still, with extreme effort, I eventually managed to pull myself together. I grabbed my bottle of rum and took a couple of swigs. Then I had an idea, and I began to shout as loudly as possible in every direction. When my throat was absolutely dry, I listened. A dog was howling, far off in the distance.

I drank some more and stretched out at the bottom of my boat. I stayed like that for an hour or so, perhaps even two, without sleeping, eyes wide open, nightmares swirling around me. I didn't dare get up, although I desperately wanted to; I put it off again and again. I told myself: "Come on, get up!" but I was too scared to move. I finally stood up very, very cautiously, as if making the slightest noise was a matter of life and death; I looked over the side.

I was dazzled by the most marvelous, most wondrous display imaginable. It was one of those apparitions from a fairy-tale world, one of those visions recounted by voyagers returning from afar that we listen to in disbelief.

The fog, which two hours earlier had covered the surface of the river, had ebbed away and settled on the riverbanks, leaving the water absolutely clear. It had formed a dense mound on each side, eighteen or twenty feet high, which shone in the moonlight with the dazzling brilliance of snow. You could see nothing but the river gleaming in a fiery light between those two white mountains; and far above my head sailed the great full moon, bright, luminous, amid a milky blue sky.

All the water creatures were now awake; the frogs croaked loudly, and every now and then, sometimes from the right, sometimes from the left, I could hear the short, sad notes of the toads, their coppery voices echoing up to the stars. The strange thing was, I was no longer afraid; I was in the heart of such an extraordinary landscape that even the most mysterious events would not have surprised me.

I don't know how long this lasted, for I finally drifted off to sleep, and when I opened my eyes again, the moon was low on the horizon, the sky full of clouds. The water lapped mournfully, the wind sighed, it was cold: darkness reigned.

I drank what was left of the rum and listened, shivering, to the rustling of the reeds and the sinister sounds of the river. I tried to see, but I couldn't even make out my boat or my hands as I raised them toward my face.

Little by little, however, the cloud of darkness began to disperse. Suddenly, I thought I could sense a shadow gliding by me; I let out a cry, a voice replied; it was a fisherman. I called out, he came over and I told him about my terrible night. He stopped his boat next to mine and both of us pulled on the anchor. It stood firm. It was dawn, a somber, gray, rainy, icy day, one of those sad, melancholic days. I spotted another boat and we flagged it down. Then the three of us pulled at the chain together and gradually the anchor began to give way. It rose slowly, ever so slowly, loaded down by a considerable weight. Finally, we could make out a black mass, and pulled it on board:

It was the body of an old woman with a large stone around her neck."

FEAR*

After dinner, we climbed back up onto the deck. In front of us shone the Mediterranean, not a ripple anywhere; its entire surface mirrored the shimmering, full moon. The vast ship sailed, sending a great serpent of black fumes billowing up toward the sky scattered with stars; and behind us, the water, clear and white, whisked by the rapid passage of the heavy vessel and its propeller, foamed, frothed, seemed to twist and turn, shedding so much light that it seemed as if the moon was bubbling over.

There were six or eight of us, silent, admiring, eyes turned toward distant Africa, where we were headed. The Captain, who had joined us and was smoking a cigar, suddenly continued the conversation we'd started at dinner.

"Yes, I was afraid that day. The sea had battered my boat; there was damage from a rock to the hold and we stayed aboard for six hours. But luckily we were picked up by an English coal merchant who'd spotted us."

A big man with a tanned face and a serious expression spoke for the first time. He was one of those men you can tell had traveled to unknown, distant lands and faced constant danger, someone you know had seen strange, mysterious wonders that are carefully kept secret but that you can

---

* Translated by Sandra Smith in collaboration with Eleanor Hill of Sarah Lawrence College.

occasionally glimpse when you look directly into his eyes, one of those men with steely courage.

"You say, Captain, that you felt fear that day; I don't believe you. You are not using the right word, and you are mistaken about what you really felt. An active man is never afraid in the face of imminent danger. He is agitated, aroused, anxious; but fear is something else entirely."

The Captain laughed and replied:

"Ha! I swear to you, it was fear."

Then the man with the tanned complexion began speaking, in a slow steady voice:

"LET ME EXPLAIN! Fear is something truly horrifying (and the bravest of men sometimes experience it); it is a terrible feeling, like the rotting of a soul. It stops hearts and thoughts dead, and even thinking about it leaves you shivering in anguish. But when you're brave, you don't feel it when facing an attack, or inevitable death, or even the more common forms of danger; you only feel it in certain, unusual circumstances, under certain mysterious influences and in the face of some vague menace. Real fear is a recollection of fantastical terrors from long ago. A man who believes in ghosts and who thinks he sees one in the dead of night must feel this kind of fear in all its terrifying horror.

I felt that fear in broad daylight, it must be ten years ago now, and I felt it again this past winter, on a cold December night.

And yet, I have lived through many dangers, many events that seemed lethal. I have often had to fight for my life. In America, thieves left me for dead; I have been condemned as an insurgent to be hanged; and on the coast of China, I was thrown into the sea from the deck of a ship. Every time I thought I was doomed, I immediately accepted my fate, with no self-pity and even without regrets.

But true fear is entirely different.

I felt it in Africa. And yet, fear is the child of the North; the sun banishes it like the morning mist. Think about this, gentlemen. In Eastern countries, life counts for nothing; you are resigned at once; the nights are clear and devoid of legends, and souls are devoid of those dark worries that haunt the mind in colder countries. In the East, they may know panic but they have never experienced fear.

Well, then, this is what happened to me in Africa:

I was crossing the great sand dunes to the south of Ouargla,[1] one of the strangest places in the world. You've seen the long, smooth sands of the endless ocean beaches. Well! Imagine the ocean itself turning to sand in the middle of a storm; imagine a silent tempest of unmoving yellow waves of dust as high as mountains, waves as unequal and unique as the waves unleashed in floods, but even higher and striated like watered silk. And the still, silent desert sun pours its remorseless flames straight down onto this furious sea. You have to climb up and down those waves of golden ash, over and over again, without stopping, without resting and without any shade. Horses gasp, sink to their knees and slide down the slopes of those unpredictable hills.

It was just me and my friend, followed by eight Spahis[2] and four camels with their drivers. We were overwhelmed by the heat: exhausted, dehydrated, totally unable to speak any more. Suddenly one of the men let out a kind of scream; we all stopped dead in our tracks, surprised by an inexplicable phenomenon known to travelers in these lost lands.

Somewhere near us, though I couldn't tell where, a drum sounded: the mysterious beat of the dunes. It beat distinctively, sometimes loudly, sometimes quietly, then stopped, only to continue its haunting sound again.

Terrified, the Arabs looked at each other. "Death is with us," one of them said in their language. Suddenly, my companion, my closest friend, whom I thought of as almost my brother, fell straight off his horse, head-first, unconscious with sunstroke.

For two hours, while I was trying in vain to save him, the strange, sporadic, regular beating of the drums filled my ears; and fear, real fear, monstrous fear, gripped me, right down to my bones as I sat by my best

---

1   Ouargla, or Wargla, is a town and oasis in northeast Algeria.

2   Locally recruited soldiers in the Cavalry corps of the French army in North Africa.

friend's dead body, in that horrible place, scorched by the blazing sun, between four mountains of sand while the mysterious echo of the drum continued to beat furiously, two hundred miles from any French camp, plunging us all deeper into fear.

That day I understood what it felt like to be afraid, but I felt it even more on another occasion . . ."

The Captain interrupted him:

"Excuse me, Monsieur, but what was the drum?"

The traveler replied:

"I have no idea. Nobody knows. Our officers, who often hear this strange noise, generally believe it is a rising echo, intensified and heightened by the undulation of the dunes, caused by a sandstorm when grains of sand are carried along by the wind and crash into tufts of dry grass; we've noticed that the phenomenon only happens in areas with little plants that are as tough and dry as parchment, completely burnt by the sun.

This drum is perhaps a kind of sound mirage. Nothing more, nothing less. But I didn't learn that until much later.

Here is my other story about my experience with fear.

It was last winter, in a forest in northeastern France. The sky was so gray that it got dark two hours earlier than usual. A local farmer was my guide; he walked beside me on the narrow road under the canopy of fir trees, beneath a sharp, howling wind. In between the tops of the trees, I watched the clouds, frenzied, frantic, as if fleeing from something terrible. Sometimes, under a huge gust of wind, the whole forest groaned in anguish and bowed in the same direction; and the cold rushed through me, despite our quick pace and my heavy coat.

We were going to get some food and sleep in a cabin belonging to a gamekeeper; it wasn't very far away. I was going there to hunt.

Every now and then, my guide looked up and murmured: "Godawful weather!" He then told me about the people we would be staying with at the cabin. The father had killed a poacher two years before and since then he seemed tormented, as if haunted by a memory. His two sons were married and lived with him.

It was pitch-black; I couldn't see anything in front or around me, and the thick branches of the trees brushed against each other, filling the night with an endless murmur. Finally, I saw a light, and soon my companion knocked on a door. Piercing female shrieks rang out. Then a man's voice, somewhat choked, demanded: "Who's there?" My guide gave his name. We went inside; the scene we saw was unforgettable.

Waiting for us in the middle of the kitchen was an old man with white hair, a wild look in his eyes and a loaded shotgun. Two large, burly men, armed with axes, guarded the door, and I could just make out two women kneeling in the dark corners of the room, their faces hidden, pressed against the wall.

He explained. The old man put his gun back on the wall and gave an order to prepare my room; then, as the women hadn't moved, he suddenly said:

"The thing is, Monsieur, I killed a man exactly two years ago tonight. Last year, he came back to haunt me. I'm expecting him again tonight."

Then, in a tone that made me smile, he added:

"So we're a little nervous."

I reassured him as best I could, happy to have arrived that evening and to see this spectacle of terrified superstition. I told them stories to pass the time and slowly began to calm everyone's nerves.

Near the fireplace, an old dog with long whiskers, almost blind—one of those dogs that looks like someone you know—slept with his nose in his paws.

Outside, the raging storm shook the cabin, and through a small, square pane of glass, a sort of spyhole placed near the door, I suddenly saw a flash of lightning illuminate the night sky, revealing a huge mass of trees twisting, turning and thrashing in the wind.

"Despite my efforts, I could clearly see these people were deathly afraid, and every time I stopped speaking, they listened intently for the faintest sound. Weary of being in the presence of such silly superstition, I was about to ask to be shown to my bedroom when suddenly the old gamekeeper leapt off his chair, seized his shotgun and spluttered wildly: "He's come, he's come! I can hear him!" The two women fell to their knees and hid their faces in the corner; the two sons grabbed their axes again. I was going to try and calm them down again when the sleeping dog suddenly woke up, raised his head, tensed his neck, looked toward the fire with his dull eyes and let out a long, mournful howl, one of those howls that makes travelers shudder at night in vast, shadowy woodlands.

Everyone turned to stare at him; he didn't move, as still as if haunted by a vision, and then, his fur bristling with fear, he began howling at something invisible, something strange, something truly horrible. The gamekeeper, deathly pale, cried: "He can sense him! He can sense him! He was there when I killed him!" Both the women, overwhelmed with fear, went mad and began howling along with the dog.

In spite of myself, an intense shiver ran down my spine. The spectacle of that animal in that place, at that time, with these panic-stricken people, was absolutely terrifying.

For an entire hour, the dog stood dead still and howled; he howled as if tortured by a dream; and fear, that terrible, horrifying fear, rushed through me. Fear of what, though? How can I explain it? It was quite simply *fear*.

We stood there, motionless, white as sheets, our ears straining, our hearts pounding every time we heard the slightest sound, waiting for something terrible to happen. Then the dog began to walk around the room, sniffing the walls, whimpering the whole time. This beast was driving us mad! In a fit of furious terror, the man who'd brought me there grabbed the dog, opened the door and flung the animal outside, into a little courtyard.

He stopped howling at once; and we were plunged into an even more terrifying silence. Suddenly we all jumped; something glided past the outside wall on the forest side; then it came to the door, feeling it tentatively with its hand; for two minutes we didn't hear a sound—it drove us mad; then it came back, scraping against the wall, slowly scratching it like a child would with its nails; then suddenly, a face appeared at the spyhole, a white face with the gleaming eyes of a wild beast. It let out a sound: an agonized, mournful moan.

A dreadful noise exploded in the kitchen; the old gamekeeper had fired his rifle. The two sons immediately rushed over to the spyhole and covered it up with the large dining table, reinforcing it with the sideboard.

And I swear to you that at the explosion of that gun, which took me completely by surprise, my heart, my body and my soul filled with such dread that I thought I would collapse, on the point of dying of fright.

We stayed there until dawn, unable to move or to speak, completely paralyzed by an overwhelming sense of fear.

We didn't dare take the barricade down until a slim ray of sunlight appeared through a crack in the shutters.

And at the foot of the wall, against the door, the old dog lay dying, his face ripped apart by a bullet.

He'd escaped from the courtyard by digging a hole under the fence."

THE MAN WITH THE tanned face fell silent. After a moment, he added:

"Although I wasn't in any danger that night, I would prefer to relive each and every moment of terrible danger I've ever faced than that one minute when the gunshot was fired at the bearded face in the window."

THE APPARITION

PEOPLE WERE TALKING ABOUT A RECENT TRIAL, A CASE WHERE someone had been committed to an asylum illegally. It was toward the end of a small gathering of friends one evening on the Rue de Grenelle, in a very old private house, and everyone had a story to tell, a story each person affirmed was true.

Then the elderly Marquis de La Tour-Samuel, who was eighty-two years old, stood up and went to lean against the fireplace. He told his story in a trembling voice:

"I ALSO KNOW OF SOMETHING strange, something so strange that it has been the prime obsession of my life. It has been fifty-six years since it happened to me, and not a month goes by without my reliving it again in a dream. From the day that it happened, I was marked, marked by fear, do you understand what I'm saying? Yes, for ten minutes I was overcome by horrific terror, and it was so strong that ever since that moment, a kind of endless dread lingers in my soul. Unexpected sounds make me shudder deep inside; objects I can barely make out in the darkness of evening fill me with a mad desire to escape. I am actually afraid at night.

Oh! I would never have admitted this until now, having reached the age I am. Now I can tell you about it. It is acceptable to be fearful when faced with imaginary dangers when you're eighty-two years old. However, when faced with real danger, Mesdames, I have always stood my ground.

This event distressed me so deeply, spread such horrific, mysterious and extreme anxiety within me that I have never told it to anyone. I kept it hidden in the most private corner of my heart, the place where we bury our painful secrets, shameful secrets, all the moments of weakness that we have experienced and that we cannot bring ourselves to admit.

I am going to tell you what happened without any explanation. There certainly is an explanation, unless I experienced a moment of madness. No, I was not mad, and I will prove it to you. Think what you will. Here are the simple facts.

It happened in July of 1827. I was then stationed in Rouen.

One day, while I was walking along the quayside, I came across a man whom I thought I recognized, but without being able to place him. I instinctively hesitated for a moment. The stranger noticed, looked at me and threw his arms around me.

He was a childhood friend whom I had liked a great deal. In the five years since I'd last seen him, he looked as if he had aged by half a century. His hair was completely white, and he walked bent over, as if he were exhausted. He could see my surprise and he told me what had happened. A terrible misfortune had shattered his life.

He had fallen madly in love with a young woman and married her in a kind of rapture of happiness. After one year of extraordinary bliss and unabated passion, she had died suddenly of a heart condition, killed by love itself, most likely.

He left his château as soon as the funeral was over and went to live in his house in Rouen. He lived there alone, in despair, tormented by grief, so unhappy that all he could think about was suicide.

"Since I've run into you like this," he said, "I'm going to ask you to do me a great favor: to go to my château and get me some papers I need urgently; they're in the writing desk in my bedroom, in our bedroom. I can't ask a subordinate or a businessman to take care of this for I require the utmost prudence and absolute discretion. As far as I'm concerned, nothing in the world could make me return to that house."

I'll give you the key to the bedroom that I locked myself when I left, and the key to my desk. And I'll write you a note for you to give to my gardener who will open the château for you.

But come and have breakfast with me tomorrow, and we can discuss it."

I promised to do this simple favor for him.

Besides, it would just be an outing for me as his estate was located a few miles away, on the outskirts of Rouen. It would only take about an hour on horseback.

I was at his house at ten o'clock the next morning. We had breakfast alone, but he barely spoke. He asked me to forgive him. The thought that I was going to go into his bedroom, where his happiness had died, moved him deeply, he said. He did, in fact, seem unusually upset, preoccupied, as if a mysterious battle were taking place within his soul.

He finally explained exactly what I had to do. It was very simple. I had to take two packets of letters and a bundle of papers locked in the first drawer to the right of his writing desk, to which I had the key.

"I suppose I don't need to ask you not to look at any of them," he added.

I was hurt by his words and told him so, a little angrily.

"Forgive me," he muttered. "I'm in so much pain."

And he began to cry.

I left him about one o'clock to carry out my task.

The weather was beautiful, and I galloped along at a fast pace across the meadows, listening to the singing skylarks and the rhythmic sound of my saber against my boot.

Then I entered the forest and slowed my horse down to a trot. The branches from the trees caressed my face, and every now and again, I would catch a leaf with my teeth and chew on it greedily, experiencing one of those joyous moments in life that, for no particular reason, fills you with intense happiness, an almost fleeting happiness, a kind of surge of power.

As I approached the château, I took the letter I'd been given for the gardener out of my pocket and noticed, with astonishment, that it was sealed. I was so surprised and annoyed that I nearly turned back without carrying out my task. Then I thought that doing so would be to admit I was unnecessarily touchy, which was in bad taste. And besides, my friend must have sealed the note without realizing it, given the emotional state he was in.

The manor house looked as if it had been deserted for twenty years. The gate was open; it was so rotten that it was impossible to tell how it remained standing. The pathways were overrun with grass; you couldn't even see the flowerbeds on the lawns.

I banged my foot against one of the shutters and, hearing the sound, an old man came out of a side door; he was astonished to see me. I leapt off my horse and handed him the letter. He read it, reread it, turned it over, gave me a suspicious look and put the paper in his pocket.

"Well! What do you want?" he asked.

"You should know," I replied bluntly, "since you've read your master's orders in that letter. I want to go inside the château."

He seemed appalled. "So, you're going to go into . . . into his bedroom?" he asked.

I was beginning to get annoyed. "Good heavens! Are you really going to stand there and interrogate me?"

"No . . . Monsieur," he stammered. "It's just that it . . . it hasn't been opened since . . . since the . . . death. If you would wait for me for five minutes, I'll go . . . go and see if . . ."

I cut in. "Really now, do you take me for a fool?" I asked angrily. "You can't go in there because I have the key right here."

He didn't know what to say.

"Well, then, Monsieur, I'll show you the way."

"Just show me the staircase and then go. I'll find it very easily without you."

"But Monsieur . . . all the same . . ."

This time, I got very angry.

"Not another word, now, understand? Or you'll have to answer to me."

I pushed him hard, out of my way, and went inside the house.

I walked through the kitchen, then two smaller rooms where the gardener lived with his wife. Then I crossed a large entrance hall, went up the stairs and found the door my friend had described to me.

I opened it without difficulty and went inside.

The room was so dark that at first, I couldn't make out a thing. I stopped, overwhelmed by that moldy, sickly smell you find in rooms where no one has lived and that have been locked up, funereal rooms. Then, little by little, my eyes adjusted to the darkness and I could clearly see a very large bedroom in total chaos; the bed had no sheets, just a mattress and pillows. One of the pillows had the deep impression of an elbow or a head, as if someone had just lain on it.

The armchairs looked as if they'd collapsed. I noticed that one door, from the wardrobe no doubt, had been left ajar.

I went over to the window to open it, to let some light in, but the hinges on the shutter were so rusty that I couldn't get them to budge.

I even tried to break them with my sword, without success. I was getting annoyed by these fruitless attempts, and as my eyes had now completely adjusted to the dim light, I gave up hope of seeing any better and walked over to the writing desk.

I sat down in an armchair, raised the flap and opened the appropriate drawer. It was full to bursting. I needed only three bundles of papers that I knew how to recognize, so I started to look for them.

I opened my eyes wide to see better, and as I was trying to make out the addresses, I thought I heard, or rather felt, something rustling behind me. I didn't think anything was wrong: I just thought it was a draft blowing against a piece of fabric. But a minute later, another movement, almost imperceptible, caused an unpleasant shiver to run through my body. It seemed so ridiculous to be afraid, even a little afraid, that I didn't want to turn around, out of a sense of self-respect. I had just found the second bundle of papers I needed, and as soon as I found the third one, a long, painful sigh coming from right behind my shoulder made me start like a madman and jump six feet away. As I leapt, I turned around, my hand on the hilt of my sword, and if I hadn't felt it right by my side, I surely would have fled like a coward.

A tall woman dressed all in white stood watching me, behind the arm-chair where I had been sitting just a second before.

A shock ran through my arms and legs so powerfully that I nearly fell backwards and collapsed! Oh! No one can understand such terrifying and astounding horrors unless they have experienced them. Your soul fades away, you can't feel your heart beating any more, your entire body feels as limp as a sponge. It felt like everything inside me was caving in.

I do not believe in ghosts; well, I weakened in the face of the hideous fear of the dead, and I suffered, oh! in those few moments, I suffered more than in all the rest of my life, caught in the spellbinding anguish of super-natural horror.

If she hadn't spoken, I might well have died! But she did speak; she spoke in a soft, mournful voice that made me tremble. I wouldn't go so far as to say that I got control of myself again, or that I was thinking ratio-nally. No. I was so frantic that I didn't know what I was doing any more, but my innate sense of pride as well as a touch of ego that comes from my profession forced me to maintain a semblance of dignity, almost in spite of myself. I stood tall out of self-respect, and for her, of course, for her, whatever she might have been, a real woman or a ghost. I only became aware of all this later on, for I can assure you that the very moment I saw that apparition, my mind was a complete blank. I was quite simply afraid.

"Oh, Monsieur," she said, "I would be so grateful if you could help me!"

I wanted to reply but I couldn't manage to utter a single word. A kind of vague sound came from deep inside my throat.

"Will you?" she continued. "You can save me, make me better. I am suffering so terribly. Suffering . . . oh I am suffering so much!"

She gently sat down in my armchair.

"Will you?" she asked, looking at me.

I nodded, still totally unable to speak.

Then she handed me a tortoiseshell comb.

"Comb my hair, oh! comb my hair," she murmured, "that will make me all better. I need someone to comb my hair. Look at my head . . . I'm suffering so much, and my hair, my hair, it hurts so much!"

Her hair fell loose, and it was very long, very dark, and seemed to hang all the way down the back of the chair and touch the floor.

Why did I do it? Even though I was shaking, why did I let her hand me the comb, and why did I hold her long hair in my hands? It gave me the horrendous feeling I was touching cold snakes. I don't know why.

That feeling remains in my fingers still and makes me shudder every time I think of it.

I combed her hair. Somehow, I took her icy mane of hair in my hands. I twisted it, put it up, let it down again, braided it the way you set a horse's mane. She sighed, tilted her head to one side, looked happy.

Suddenly she said, "Thank you!" grabbed the comb from my hand, and ran out through the door I'd noticed was ajar.

For several minutes after I was alone again, I experienced the terror you feel just after you wake up from a nightmare. Then I finally calmed down. I rushed over to the window and angrily broke the shutter open.

A flood of light filled the room. I threw myself against the door where that creature had gone. It was locked and immovable.

Then I was filled with a desperate urge to flee, a panic, the kind of panic you feel in battle. I quickly grabbed the three bundles of letters from the open writing desk, ran through the rooms, leapt down the stairs four at a time, found myself outside, I really don't know how, and spotting my horse a few feet away, I jumped into the saddle in a single bound and galloped away.

I didn't stop until I was in front of my house in Rouen. After throwing the reins to my orderly, I ran to my room and locked myself in so I could think.

For an hour, I anxiously wondered if I hadn't been the victim of a hallucination. I surely must have had one of those incomprehensible nervous attacks, one of those panics in the mind that are the source of miracles, moments that endow the Supernatural with so much power.

And I was about to believe it had all been just a hallucination, a trick of the senses, until I walked over to the window. My eyes happened to wander down to my chest. The jacket of my uniform was covered in long hairs—a woman's long hair—that had got caught in the buttons!

I picked them off one by one, and with trembling hands, I threw them out the window.

Then I called for my orderly. I feel too overwrought, too upset, to go to see my friend the same day. And I also wanted to think about what I should tell him.

I had his letters taken to him and he gave my orderly a receipt. He asked about me in detail. He was told that I wasn't feeling well, that I was suffering from sunstroke, something like that. He had seemed concerned.

I went to see him the next day, just after dawn, determined to tell him the truth. He had gone out the night before and had not returned.

I went back that afternoon but he was still nowhere in sight. I waited a week. He never returned. So I went to the police. They looked everywhere for him but without finding a trace of where he had been or where he was.

A meticulous examination of the deserted château was carried out. Nothing suspicious was found.

There were no indications that a woman had ever been hidden there.

The investigation revealed nothing; the search was abandoned.

And fifty-six years have passed and I still have learned nothing. I still know nothing more."

THE HAND

EVERYONE GATHERED AROUND THE JUDGE, MONSIEUR BER-
mutier, who was giving his opinion about the mysterious case that
had happened in Saint-Cloud. This inexplicable crime had thrown all of
Paris into a panic for the past month. No one understood a thing about it.

Monsieur Bermutier stood, leaning against the fireplace as he talked;
he brought up evidence and discussed various opinions on the case but
came to no conclusion.

Several women got up and went to stand closer to him, concentrating
on the judge's clean-shaven face as he spoke in a serious tone of voice.
They shuddered and trembled, gripped by fear and curiosity, by a keen,
insatiable need to feel terror: it haunted their souls and tormented them
like the need for food.

One of the women, paler than the others, broke the silence:

"It's horrible. It's almost 'supernatural.' No one will ever know what
really happened."

The judge turned toward her:

"Yes, Madame, it is very likely that we'll never know what happened.
But the 'supernatural' as you call it has nothing to do with this case. We
are faced with a crime that was very cleverly conceived, very skillfully
carried out and so shrouded in mystery that we cannot disentangle it from
the enigmatic circumstances surrounding it. However, I did once, long
ago, know of a case where something truly inexplicable seemed to be

involved. The case had to be dropped, though, as there was simply no explanation for it."

"Oh! Do tell us about it," several ladies urged, all at once.

Monsieur Bermutier smiled, but still looked serious, as was befitting a judge.

"Please do not think, even for a moment, that I assumed something supernatural happened during this case," he continued. "I only believe in natural causes. However, if instead of using the word 'supernatural' to explain things we do not understand, we simply spoke of 'the inexplicable,' that would be more appropriate. In any case, in the story I am about to tell you, it was the external, preliminary circumstances that disturbed me the most. Here are the facts."

"AT THE TIME, I was a judge in Ajaccio,[1] a small white city nestled at the edge of a beautiful bay and surrounded on all sides by high mountains.

Most of my cases were to do with murderous vendettas. Some of them were extraordinary, impossibly dramatic, vicious or heroic. Ajaccio is the place where you can find the most amazing motives for revenge you could ever imagine: local feuds that die down for a while but are never forgotten, abominable cunning, assassinations that turn into massacres, acts that could almost be described as noble. For two years, all I heard people talk about was vengeance, the terrible Corsican prejudice that demands revenge for any insult on the offending party, his descendants and his family. I had seen elderly people, children and cousins have their throats slit; my mind was full of such stories.

Now one day, I learned that an Englishman had just taken a long-term lease on a small villa at the end of the bay. He had brought a French servant with him, someone he had found while passing through Marseille.

Everyone was soon talking about this unusual man who lived alone in his house and only went out to go hunting or fishing. He spoke to no one,

---

1   This story takes place in Corsica, known in the past for its vendettas.

never went into town, and, every morning, practiced shooting his pistol and rifle for an hour or two.

People started inventing stories about him. Some said he was an important person who had run away from his country for political reasons; others claimed he was in hiding after committing a horrible crime. They even gave particularly gruesome details of the circumstances.

As a judge, I wanted to see if I could get some more information about this man but it proved impossible. He called himself Sir John Rowell.

So all I could do was keep an eye on him from up close, but to tell the truth, there was nothing at all suspicious about him.

Meanwhile, rumors about him continued to spread; they became more and more exaggerated and accepted, so I decided to try to see this foreigner myself, and I started to go hunting regularly in the area near his property.

An opportunity only arose after a long wait. It happened when I shot and killed a partridge right in front of the Englishman. My dog brought it to me; but I immediately took the partridge and went to apologize for my inappropriate behavior and ask Sir John Rowell to accept the dead bird.

He was a big man with red hair and a red beard; he was very tall, very broad, a kind of polite, placid Hercules. He had none of the so-called British reserve and he thanked me warmly for my sensitivity in his broken French, with a thick British accent. By the end of the month, we had chatted together five or six times.

One evening, when I was walking past his house, I saw him in the garden, straddling a chair and smoking his pipe. I greeted him and he invited me to come and have a glass of beer. I accepted at once.

He received me with all the scrupulous courtesy of the English, and spoke in glowing terms of France and Corsica, saying how much he loved this "countryscape" and this "riveredge."

Then, taking the utmost care and under the pretext of being terribly interested, I asked him a few questions about his life and plans. He replied openly, told me he had traveled a lot, in Africa, India and America.

"Oh! Yes, I've had many adventures!" he added, laughing.

Then I started talking about hunting again and he told me the strang-

est details of the way he had hunted hippopotamus, tigers, elephants and
even gorillas.

"All those animals are dangerous," I said.

He smiled: "Oh, no! The worst is man."

Then he started to laugh, the hearty laugh of a big, contented Englishman:

"I also hunted men a lot too, I did."

Then he began to talk about weapons, and invited me to come inside
to show me all his different rifles.

His drawing room had black drapes, black silk drapes embroidered
with gold. Large yellow flowers ran across the dark material, as brilliant
as fire.

"It's Japanese fabric," he said.

But in the middle of the widest panel, something strange drew my
attention. A black object stood out on a square of red velvet. I walked over
to it: it was a hand, a man's hand. It wasn't the clean, white hand from a
skeleton, but a shriveled-up black hand with long yellow nails, its muscles
exposed and traces of old, dried-up blood on the bones, the kind of blood
you find on some piece of debris. And the bones looked as if they had been
cleanly cut off by an ax, just in the middle of the forearm.

Around the wrist, an enormous iron chain was riveted and soldered to
this filthy hand, pinning it to the wall by a ring that was strong enough to
keep an elephant in check.

"What is that?" I asked.

"That was my best enemy," the Englishman replied calmly. "It came
from America. It has been cut off with a sword and the skin peeled off
with a stone, then dried in the sun for a week. Oh . . . very good, it is."

I touched the human remains that must have belonged to a giant. The
fingers were unbelievably long and attached by enormous tendons that
still had some shredded skin attached in places. The hand was horrible to
look at, flayed the way it was, and naturally made you think of some kind
of vicious vengeance.

"The man must have been very strong," I said.

"Ah, yes, but I'm stronger than him. I put him on that chain to hold him," the Englishman replied quietly.

I thought he was making a joke.

"That chain is quite pointless now," I said; "the hand isn't going to run away."

"It always tries to escape," Sir John Rowell replied in all seriousness, "that chain is necessary."

I glanced quickly over at him to look at his face. "Is he mad?" I wondered, "or just making it up?"

But it was impossible to read his expression; he remained calm and kindly. I changed the subject, admiring his rifles.

I did, however, notice that there were three loaded revolvers sitting on several pieces of furniture, as if he lived in constant fear of being attacked.

I went back to his house several times. Then I stopped going. People had got used to him; no one cared about him any more.

A YEAR PASSED. Then one morning, toward the end of November, my valet woke me up and told me that Sir John Rowell had been murdered during the night.

Half an hour later, I went into the Englishman's house with the chief of police and the Captain. Sir John's valet, distraught and in despair, was crying in front of the house. At first I suspected him, but he was innocent. The person responsible was never found.

As soon as I walked into the reception room, I saw Sir John's body. He was stretched out on his back, in the middle of the room.

His vest was torn and one of the sleeves of his jacket ripped off; everything indicated there had been a terrible struggle.

The Englishman had been strangled! His dark, swollen face was horrible, and his contorted features meant he had seen something utterly terrifying. His neck was covered in blood and had five puncture marks that looked as if they'd been made with iron spikes. There was something between his clenched teeth.

A doctor came in.

He examined the finger marks on the neck for a long time and then said something truly strange:

"You'd think he'd been strangled by a skeleton."

A shudder ran down my spine, and I glanced over at the wall, at the spot where I'd seen the horrible flayed hand. It was gone. Its chain hung there, broken.

I leaned over the dead man and saw one of the fingers of the missing hand in his closed mouth. It had been cut, or rather bitten off just above the knuckle.

Then we began investigating. Nothing was found. Not a single door or window had been forced and no furniture had been disturbed. The two watchdogs had not woken up.

Here is a summary of the valet's statement:

"My master had seemed anxious for about a month. He'd received a lot of letters, but he burned them as soon as he'd read them.

He would often grab a riding crop and in a rage that verged on madness, he would furiously whip the dried-up hand that was chained to the wall. The hand disappeared, no one knows how, on the very night of the crime.

He went to bed very late and made sure his door was properly locked. He always had a weapon close by. He often talked out loud at night, as if he were having an argument with someone."

That night, strangely enough, he hadn't made any noise, and it was only when the valet came into the room to open the windows that he found Sir John had been murdered. He didn't suspect anyone.

I told the judges and public officials everything I knew about the dead man, and they carried out a thorough investigation throughout the island. Nothing was discovered.

Then, one night about three months after the crime, I had a terrible nightmare. I could see the hand, that horrible hand, scurrying down my curtains and over my walls, like a spider or scorpion. Three times I woke up, three times I went back to sleep, three times I saw the hideous hand hurtling around my bedroom, using its fingers as legs.

The next day, the hand was brought to me; it had been found on Sir John Rowell's grave, in the local cemetery where he had been buried, as we could not trace any of his family. The index finger on the hand was missing.

And there you have my story, Mesdames. I know nothing more."

THE WOMEN WERE ALL PALE, trembling, distraught. One of them cried out:

"But that story doesn't have an ending, or an explanation! We're not going to be able to sleep if you don't tell us what you think really happened."

The judge smiled unsympathetically.

"Well then, ladies, I will certainly prevent you from having bad dreams. Quite simply, I think that the real owner of the hand was not actually dead, and that he returned with his remaining hand to reclaim it. But I have no idea how he did it, you know. It was a kind of vendetta."

"No, it couldn't be that," one of the women whispered.

The judge kept on smiling.

"I did warn you that you wouldn't like my explanation."

LOST AT SEA[1]

I

EVERYONE IN FÉCAMP KNEW THE STORY OF POOR MADAME PATIN. She certainly had not been happy with her husband, this Madame Patin: before he died, he used to beat her. He beat her the way people thresh wheat in their barns.

He owned a fishing boat and had married her, long ago, because she was kind, even though she was poor.

Patin, who was a good sailor, but violent, was a regular customer at Auban's inn, where he normally drank four or five glasses of Marc[2] a day, eight or ten or even more when he'd had a good day at sea, depending on how he felt, or so he said.

Auban's daughter served the Marc; she was a pretty brunette who attracted people to the inn because of her good looks, for no one ever implied there was any other reason.

Whenever Patin went to the inn, he would simply look at her, at first, and speak politely and calmly to her, like a decent man. After drinking the first glass of Marc, he found he liked her even more. After the second glass, he winked at her. After the third, he said: "If you would like to, Mam'zelle Désirée . . ." without ever finishing his sentence. After the

---

1 The original title of this story is *Le Noyé*, literally *The Drowned Man*.

2 A very strong liqueur, similar to brandy.

fourth glass, he tried to grab her skirt so he could kiss her, and, when he'd had ten glasses, it was her father who served him the rest.

The old innkeeper, who knew all the tricks of the trade, had Désirée walk around the tables to make people order more drinks; and Désirée, who was not Auban's daughter for nothing, strolled amongst the drinkers, joked with them, a smile on her lips and a gleam in her eye.

Because he drank all those glasses of Marc, Patin got so used to seeing Désirée's face that he would picture it even when at sea, or when he threw his nets into the water, on the high seas, on windy nights or calm nights, on moonlit nights or in the darkness. He thought about her face when at the helm, or in the back of the boat, while his other four companions were dozing, their heads resting on their hands. He always pictured her smiling at him, pouring the golden Marc with a slight movement of her shoulder, then asking, as she walked away, "There. Satisfied now?"

And because he couldn't stop picturing her and thinking about her, he was overcome by such a desire to marry her that he couldn't hold out any longer and finally asked for her hand.

He was rich. He owned a boat, his own fishing nets and a house at the foot of the hill on the Retenue;[3] her father had nothing. His proposal was thus eagerly accepted, and the wedding took place as quickly as possible, as both parties were anxious to conclude the business, though for different reasons.

Three days after the wedding, however, Patin just couldn't understand how he might have believed that Désirée was different from any other woman. Had he truly been so stupid as to burden himself with a penniless woman who had seduced him with her Marc? For she had surely put some nasty drug in his drink.

And he swore the whole time he was out at sea, broke his pipe with his teeth, was violent to his crew, and after cursing out loud, using all the vulgar swear words possible against everyone and everything he knew, he vented the rest of his anger on the fish and lobsters caught in one of his

---

3   The basin in a port where boats can dock and float regardless of the tide.

nets, throwing them into his large wicker baskets while cursing in filthy language.

Then, once back home, where Auban's daughter, his wife, was in close range of both his foul mouth and his hands, he never failed to treat her like the lowest of the low. But as she listened to him, resigned, accustomed to her father's outbursts, he became frustrated at seeing her so calm, so one evening, he gave her a beating. And life at home then became truly terrible.

For ten years, all anyone ever talked about on the Retenue was the thrashings that Patin subjected his wife to and the way he cursed, about everything, whenever he spoke to her. He swore in a particular way, in fact, with a richness of vocabulary and a thundering voice that no other man in Fécamp could match. As soon as his boat entered the port, after his fishing trips, everyone waited for the first volley of abuse hurled from the jetty to the dock the moment he spotted his wife's white bonnet.

Standing at the back, he would steer his boat, watching the stern and the sail when the sea was rough, and in spite of having to guide the boat through a narrow, difficult passage, in spite of waves that swelled as high as mountains, he would peer through the foamy surf to find his own wife amongst the women waiting for their sailors, his wife, Auban's daughter, the wretched woman!

In spite of the noise of the wind and the waves, as soon as he spotted her, he would start bellowing at her in such a booming voice that everyone would start laughing, even though they felt very sorry for her. Then, as soon as the boat had docked at the quay, he had a way of throwing overboard any ballast of good manners, as he called it, while unloading his fish, which attracted all the vagabonds and layabouts from the port around his moorings.

The words flew out of his mouth, sometimes short and horrible, like cannonballs, sometimes like thunder that lasted for five full minutes, such a hurricane of curses that his lungs seemed to hold all the fieriness of the God of the Old Testament.

Then, after getting off his boat and standing face to face with her amid the fishwives and other curious onlookers, he would fish around his hold for an entire new cargo of insults and harsh words, and they would go back home together, she in front, he behind, she crying, him shouting.

Once he was alone with her behind closed doors, he would hit her for the slightest reason. Any excuse to raise his hand, and once he'd started, he didn't stop, spitting the true reasons for his hatred in her face. With every slap, every punch, he would shout, "Ah, you penniless creature, you tramp, you miserable wretch, I really did myself a favor the day I drank your father's rotgut, that crook!"

The poor woman now lived in constant terror, an endless, gripping fear that ran through her body and soul, in a hopeless state of waiting— waiting for his insults and her beatings.

And this life lasted ten years. She was so fearful that she grew pale whenever she spoke to anyone, and all she could think about were the beatings she was threatened with, so she became thinner, dryer and more yellow than a smoked fish.

II

ONE NIGHT, WHILE HER HUSBAND WAS OUT AT SEA, SHE WAS AWAK-ened by the horrid howling the wind makes when it swoops in like a wild dog! She was frightened and sat down on her bed; when she heard nothing more, she climbed back in, but almost immediately, a roar came down the chimney that shook the entire house, then spread across the sky, like a herd of furious snorting, bellowing beasts, stampeding through the night.

She got out of bed and ran down to the port. Women carrying lanterns arrived from all directions. Men rushed over as well, and everyone watched the frothy crests of the waves light up in the darkness above the sea.

The storm lasted fifteen hours. Eleven sailors never returned, and Patin was among them.

The remains of his boat, the *Jeune-Amélie*, were found near Dieppe. His dead crew was discovered near Saint-Valérie, but Patin's body was never found. Since the hull of his boat had been cut in two, his wife expected, and feared, his return, because if there had been a collision, it was possible that the other boat might have picked him up, just him, and taken him far away.

Then, little by little, she got used to the idea that she was a widow, though she would shudder every time a neighbor, a beggar or a traveling salesman unexpectedly came to her house.

One afternoon, about four years after her husband had disappeared, she was walking down the Rue aux Juifs when she stopped in front of the house of an old sea captain who had recently died and whose furniture was being sold.

AT THAT VERY MOMENT, they were auctioning off a parrot, a green parrot with a blue head, who was watching everyone with an anxious, mean look in his eyes.

"Three francs!" cried the auctioneer. "Here's a bird that can talk like a lawyer, three francs!"

One of Désirée's friends nudged her.

"You should buy it, you've got the money," she said. "It'll keep you company. That bird there's worth more than thirty francs. You can always resell it for twenty or twenty-five francs, you know!"

"Four francs! Ladies, four francs!" the man said again. "He sings Vespers and preaches like the parish priest. He's extraordinary . . . miraculous!"

Madame Patin bid fifty centimes more; the creature with the hooked nose was given to her in a little cage, and she took him away.

Then she got him settled at home; when she was opening the wire door of the cage to give him something to drink, he bit her finger so hard that it cut her skin and made her bleed.

"Oh!" she said. "He's very malicious."

Nevertheless, she gave him some hempseed and corn, then let him preen his feathers while staring at his new house and new mistress, a shifty look in his eyes.

The next morning, just as day was breaking, Madame Patin heard a voice, a loud, deep, booming voice, her husband's voice—there was no mistaking it—shouting:

"Well, are you going to get up, you bitch!"

She was so utterly terrified that she hid her head under the covers, for every morning in the past, as soon as he opened his eyes, her dead husband had screamed those words in her ear, those very words, words she knew only too well.

Trembling, curled up in a ball, her back tensed in anticipation of the beating she expected to get, her face hidden in the bedcovers, she whispered:

"Good God, he's here! He's here! He's come back. Good God!"

The minutes passed; not a sound broke the silence of her room. Then she lifted her head from under the covers, shaking, sure that he was there, laying in wait, ready to beat her.

She saw nothing, nothing but a ray of sunshine coming in through the window.

"He's hiding, for sure," she thought.

She waited for a long time, then, feeling somewhat calmer, she thought:

"I must've dreamt it, since he ain't here."

She closed her eyes again, feeling less worried, when a furious voice, the thunderous voice of the drowned man, shouted out, quite close by:

"Hell, hell, hell, hell! When the hell are you getting up, b . . . !"

She leapt out of bed, roused by a sense of obedience, the passive obedience of a woman who had been beaten black and blue, a woman who still remembered that particular voice, even after four years had passed, and who would always obey it!

"I'm here, Patin," she said. "What do you want?"

But Patin did not reply.

Terrified, she looked all around her, then checked everywhere—in the wardrobes, in the fireplace, under the bed—finding no one, then collapsed into a chair almost mad with fear, convinced that Patin's soul was there, right next to her, just his spirit, and that it had come back to torment her.

Suddenly, she remembered the attic, and that you could get into it by climbing up a ladder on the outside of the house. He surely must have hidden there to catch her unawares. He must have been held captive by savages on some faraway shore, unable to escape until now, and he had come back, more evil than ever. She had no doubts at all, not after hearing his voice.

"That you up there, Patin?" she asked, looking up toward the roof.

Patin did not reply.

So she went outside, with such fear in her heart that she was shaking, and climbed up the ladder, opened the window, peered in, saw nothing, went inside, looked some more and still found nothing.

She sat down on a bale of hay and started to cry, but while she was sobbing, overwhelmed by some heartbreaking, horrific supernatural fear, she heard Patin's voice saying things, from below, from inside her bedroom. He sounded less angry, calmer as he spoke:

"Filthy weather!—Such strong winds!—Filthy weather!—I ain't eaten, damn it!"

She shouted down through the ceiling:

"I'm here, Patin; I'll make you some soup. Don't get mad. I'm comin'."

And she ran downstairs.

There was no one in her room.

She felt as if she might faint, as if Death itself had touched her, and she was about to run away and get help from her neighbors when the voice shouted into her ear:

"I ain't eaten, damn it!"

And the parrot stared at her from his cage with a wide-eyed, sly, evil expression.

And she looked back at him, terrified.

"Ah!" she whispered. "It's you!"

The parrot shook his head and kept talking:

"Just you wait, wait, wait . . . I'll teach you to be a layabout!"

What ran through her mind? She felt, she understood, that it really was him, the dead man, who had come back, hidden in the feathers of this beast to continue torturing her; he was going to swear at her all day long, just as he had in the past, and bite her, and shout out curses to bring the neighbors rushing in, to make them laugh. So she lunged toward the cage, opened it and grabbed the bird; it fought back, tearing at her skin with its beak and claws. But she held onto it with both hands, using all her strength, and throwing herself down on the ground, she rolled on top of it with the fury of a woman possessed, crushed it, turned it into a limp little green lump that didn't move or speak: it just lay there. Then she wrapped it up, using a dishtowel as a shroud, and went out, barefoot, in her nightgown. She walked across the quayside, washed over by the sea's low waves, and shaking open the cloth, she threw the tiny dead thing in the water; it looked like a little tuft of grass. Then she went home, fell onto her knees in front of the empty cage, and sobbing, distraught at what she had done, begged God's forgiveness, as if she had just committed some terrible crime.

WHO CAN KNOW?

❧

I

MY GOD! MY GOD! SO I AM FINALLY GOING TO WRITE DOWN WHAT has happened to me! But can I? Dare I? It is so strange, so inexplicable, so incomprehensible, so unbelievable!

If I weren't sure of what I'd seen, sure there has been no fault in my reasoning, no errors in my findings, no loopholes in all my disciplined observations, I would think I was nothing more than a simple lunatic, at the mercy of bizarre hallucinations. After all, who can know?

Now I am in a mental institution; but I came here of my own free will, out of prudence, out of fear! Only one person knows what happened to me: the doctor here. I am going to write it down. Do I even really know why? To be rid of it, for I feel it within me like an unbearable nightmare.

Here is my story:

I have always been a solitary soul, a dreamer, a kind of lone philosopher, well meaning, needing little to be happy, bearing no bitterness toward men and no grudge against Heaven. I have always lived alone, continually alone, due to a kind of irritation aroused in me by the presence of other people. How can this be explained? I don't know. I don't refuse to socialize, to chat, to have dinner with friends, but as soon as I feel I have been around them for any length of time, even my closest friends begin to bore me, tire me, annoy me, and I experience an ever-increasing, insistent desire to have them go away, or for me to leave, to be alone.

This desire is more than a need, it is an overwhelming necessity. And if

I continued to find myself in the company of those people, if I were forced not just to keep hearing their conversations but listen to them as well, something terrible would surely happen to me. What exactly? Ah! Who can know? Perhaps I would simply just faint? Yes, probably!

I like being alone so much that I can't even stand having anyone else sleeping under my roof; I cannot live in Paris because I constantly feel as if I'm about to die whenever I'm there. I feel I am dying morally, and my body and nervous system suffer because of the immense crowds swarming everywhere, living all around me, even when they are asleep. When other people are asleep it pains me even more than when they speak. And I can never get any rest when I know, when I can sense, there are other people behind the wall whose lives are just as broken off, suspended by these regular lapses of reason.

Why am I like this? Who can know? The reason is perhaps quite simple: I grow very tired of anything that doesn't happen within me. And there are many others like me.

There are two categories of people on this earth: those who need others, are entertained, kept busy, calmed down by others, and who are exhausted, worn out, destroyed by solitude, feeling the way they would if they had to climb a mighty glacier or walk across a desert, and the others, who, on the contrary, are worn out, bored, irritated and pained by other people, while solitude calms them, bathes them in peace through the freedom and imagination of their minds.

All in all, this is a normal psychological phenomenon. The first type of person is made to be extroverted, the others to be introverted. My own attention span for anything outside myself is short and quickly exhausted, and as soon as I can stand no more, an intolerable sense of uneasiness runs through my whole body and mind.

The result of this has been that I became attached, became greatly attached, to inanimate objects, objects that take on the same importance as people to me, and so my house became, had become, a world in which I lived an active but solitary life, surrounded by objects, furniture, curios, that were as familiar and pleasing to my eye as people's faces. I'd furnished my home gradually, decorated it, and it was where I felt content,

satisfied, as happy as if I were in the arms of a loving woman whose familiar caresses had become the calm, sweet thing I needed most.

I had the house built in a beautiful garden that cut it off from the roads,
and near the edge of a city where I could have, when necessary, the pos-
sibility of mingling with other people, since I did feel that need every now
and then. All my servants slept in quarters quite a distance away, at the
back of the vegetable garden, surrounded by a high wall. And the darkness of night over the silence of my isolated, hidden home, completely
enclosed by the leaves of the tall trees, was so peaceful, so good, that
every night I would put off going to bed for hours in order to savor it for
longer.

That day, there had been a performance of *Sigurd*[1] in the town theater.
It was the first time I'd seen this wonderful, magical story and heard its
music; it gave me much pleasure.

I was walking home, feeling lighthearted, my head full of melodic
music and beautiful visions. It was dark, very dark, so dark that I could
barely make out the wide road in front of me and I nearly stumbled into a
ditch on several occasions. It was about a half a mile from the city limits to
my home, maybe a little more, perhaps a twenty-minute walk if you don't
hurry. It was one o'clock in the morning, either one o'clock or one-thirty.
The sky brightened up a little in front of me and I could see the crescent
moon, the sad final stage of the crescent moon. The first crescent moon,
the one that appears at four or five o'clock in the evening, is bright, cheerful, tinged with silver, but the one you see after midnight is reddish, somber, troublesome, the true crescent of the Witches' Sabbath. Anyone who
is awake late at night must have noticed this. The first quarter, even if it is
as slim as can be, casts a joyful little light that delights the heart and casts
clear shadows on the ground. The final crescent barely gives off a dying
light, so lifeless that it hardly highlights any shadows at all.

I could make out the dark shape of my garden in the distance, and I
don't know why, but I felt somewhat uncomfortable at the idea of going

---

1   An acclaimed opera by Ernest Reyer, first performed in Paris in 1885, five years before
this story was written.

through it. I walked more slowly. It was very mild out. The high cluster of trees made me think of a tomb in which my house was buried.

I opened my gate and went down the long path lined with sycamore trees that led to the house. They formed a high archway like a tall tunnel through impenetrable clumps of trees and winding around the lawns full of flowerbeds, oval forms with indistinct shapes beneath the fading shadows.

As I approached the house, a strange feeling of uneasiness spread through me. I stopped. There was not a single sound. Not the slightest wind through the leaves. "What's wrong with me?" I thought. I've been coming home like this for ten years without feeling the least bit anxious. I wasn't afraid. I'm never afraid at night. Seeing a man, some prowler or thief, would have filled me with rage, and I would have attacked him without a second thought. I did have a weapon, though. I had my revolver. But I wouldn't touch it, for I wanted to overcome this feeling of dread that was growing within me.

What was it? A premonition? The mysterious premonition that takes over your senses when you are on the brink of experiencing the inexplicable? Perhaps . . . Who can know?

The closer I got, the more I felt myself shaking, and when I was in front of the wall, near the closed shutters, I knew I would have to wait a few moments before opening the door and going inside my spacious house. So I sat down on a bench under my living room windows. I stayed there, feeling rather unnerved, my head leaning against the wall, staring into the leafy darkness. For the first few moments, I noticed nothing out of the ordinary around me. My ears were humming, but that often happens. Sometimes I think I can hear trains passing, bells ringing, a crowd of people walking by.

The humming soon became more distinct, more precise, more recognizable. I was wrong. I wasn't hearing the usual humming of blood rushing through my veins but a unique yet very vague sound that was definitely coming from inside my house.

I could hear it through the wall, a continuous sound, more like something moving than a noise, the muted movement of a great many things, as if someone had lifted up all my furniture, put it down and was slowly dragging it along.

Oh! For a long time after, I still doubted what I heard. But I pressed my ear against the shutter to better listen this strange commotion in my house, and I remained convinced, certain, that something abnormal and incomprehensible was happening inside. I was not afraid, but I was—how can I express it?—I was so surprised that I was scared to death. I didn't load my revolver—I could tell there was no need to. I waited.

I waited for a long time, unable to make a decision of any kind; my mind was clear but I was incredibly nervous. I stood there, waiting, persistently listening to the sound that grew louder and every now and again became powerfully intense, as if it were groaning with impatience, with anger, in mysterious turmoil.

Then, suddenly, ashamed of my cowardice, I grabbed my bunch of keys, chose the one I needed, forced it into the lock, turned it twice, and pushing open the door with all my might, I slammed it against the wall inside.

It sounded as if a rifle had been fired, and then, from the top to the bottom of my house, this explosion was followed by a thunderous uproar. It was so unexpected, so horrible, so deafening that I took a few steps back and pulled my revolver out of its holster, even though I could sense it was pointless.

I waited some more, but not for long. I could now make out the extraordinary sound of footsteps on my staircase, on the parquet floors, over the rugs, footsteps not made by shoes, by people's shoes, but by crutches, wooden crutches and metal crutches that vibrate like cymbals. Then, suddenly, I saw an armchair, the large armchair from my study, shuffling out onto the doorstep. It went out into the garden. Others followed: chairs from my living room, then small sofas dragged along like crocodiles on their short legs, then all of my chairs, leaping about like goats, and little footstools scurrying along like rabbits.

I was so afraid! I slipped into a clump of trees where I remained, crouching down, staring at this endless parade of my furniture—for everything rushed past, one thing after the other, quickly or slowly, depending on its size and weight. My piano, my grand piano, flew by with the speed of a galloping horse with the echo of music in its flanks; the smallest objects slid across the sandy ground like ants—brushes, fine glassware, cups— and the moonlight cast a phosphorescent glow on them, so they looked like glowworms. Fabrics crept along, spreading out like the tentacles on an octopus. My desk appeared, a precious antique from the previous century that contained all the letters I had received, my entire romantic past, a former love affair which had caused me so much suffering! And there were photographs inside as well.

Suddenly, I was no longer afraid. I leapt at the desk and grabbed it as you would a thief, the way you might catch hold of a woman who was trying to run away, but it was moving so fast that it simply couldn't be stopped, and despite my efforts, despite my anger, I could not even slow it down. As I desperately fought this horrifying force, I was thrown to the ground in the struggle. Then it rolled me around, dragged me along the sandy ground, and the furniture that followed was starting to walk over me, trampling my legs and bruising them. Then, after I let go, the rest of the furniture charged over my body like cavalry attacking a fallen soldier.

Mad with terror, I finally managed to pull myself away from the wide pathway and hide in the trees again. I watched everything disappear, the tiniest things, the smallest objects, the least valuable, things I didn't even remember had belonged to me.

Then, in the distance, I heard an incredibly loud banging of doors slamming shut in my house that now echoed as if it were empty. Doors banged from the top to bottom of the building, even the front door slammed shut, the last to close, the door I had foolishly opened myself so I could get away.

I fled, running toward the village, and only calmed down when I met some people in the street who were out late. I went and rang the bell at a hotel where the people knew me. I had brushed the dust off my clothing and explained how I had lost all my keys, including the key to the kitchen garden where all my servants slept in an isolated house, inside the outer wall that protected my fruit and vegetables from thieves.

I covered myself up to the neck in the bed I was given. But I couldn't sleep, so I listened to my heart pounding and waited for dawn. I had asked that my servants be told where I was as soon as it was light, and my valet knocked at my door at seven o'clock in the morning.

He looked completely distressed.

"Something terrible happened last night, Monsieur," he said.

"What was it?"

"All your furniture was stolen, Monsieur, everything, everything, right down to the smallest items."

This piece of news pleased me. Why? Who can know? I was in complete control of myself, certain I could hide my true feelings, never saying a word to anyone about what I had seen; I could keep it hidden, bury it in my mind like some terrible secret.

"Well, the same people must have stolen my keys," I replied. "You must go and tell the police at once. I'll get up and meet you there shortly."

The investigation lasted five months. Nothing was ever found, not the smallest stolen item, nor was there the slightest trace of the thieves. Heavens! Imagine if I had said something about what I knew . . . If I had told them . . . they would have locked me up, me, not the thieves but the man who had witnessed such a thing.

Oh! I knew how to keep silent. But I didn't refurnish my house. It was quite pointless. It would have happened again. I didn't ever want to go back there. I never saw it again.

I came to Paris, to a hotel, and I consulted doctors about my nervous condition, as it worried me a great deal ever since that hideous night.

They suggested that I travel. I took their advice.

II

I BEGAN WITH A TRIP TO ITALY. THE SUN DID ME GOOD. FOR SIX months, I wandered from Genoa to Venice, from Venice to Florence, from Florence to Rome, from Rome to Naples. Then I explored Sicily, a wonderful place thanks to its landscape and monuments, relics left by the Greeks and Normans. I went to Africa, peacefully crossing the calm, golden desert where camels, gazelles and nomadic Arabs wander past, where, under the clear, light sky no haunting thoughts float around you, not in the daytime, not at night.

I returned to France through Marseille, and despite the city's liveliness, the light in Provence was less brilliant, which saddened me. When I got back to this continent, I had the strange feeling I was a sick man who thinks he's been cured but who still experiences some slight pain, a warning that the source of his illness has not disappeared.

Then I returned to Paris. By the end of the month, I was bored. It was autumn, and I wanted to take a short trip to Normandy before winter, as I'd never been there.

I started in Rouen, of course, and for a week, I wandered through this medieval city feeling entertained, delighted, enthusiastic in this surprising museum of extraordinary Gothic monuments.

One afternoon, around four o'clock, as I was following an amazing street along a river as black as ink called the "Eau de Robec," giving all my attention to the unusual ancient architecture of the houses, I was suddenly distracted by the sight of a series of secondhand shops set all in a row.

Ah! They had chosen this spot well, these sordid dealers of things from the past, in this eerie alleyway, along this sinister flowing water, beneath the pointed slate and tile roofs where old weathervanes still creak!

Deep inside these dark shops, you could see piles of carved chests, earthenware from Rouen, Nevers, Moustiers, statues, some in oak, others painted, figures of Christ, the Virgin Mary and the saints, church ornaments, liturgical vestments, even sacred vessels and an old tabernacle in gilded wood from which the Sacred Host had been removed. Oh! The strange cellars in these tall houses, in these large houses, were completely full, from top to bottom, full of objects of all kinds that seemed to no longer exist, objects that had outlived their original owners, their centuries, their eras, their styles, in order to be bought, as curiosities, by successive generations.

My fondness for curios was reawakened in this neighborhood of antique sellers. I went from shop to shop, taking two great strides to leap across the bridges made of four planks of rotting wood placed over the nauseating flow of water from the Eau de Robec.

Heaven have mercy! What a shock! I could see one of my most beautiful wardrobes at the side of an archway stuffed full of various objects; it looked like the entrance to the catacombs of a cemetery of antique furniture. I walked closer to it, trembling from head to foot, trembling so much that I didn't dare touch it. I stretched out my hand, then hesitated. It really was mine, though: a unique Louis XIII wardrobe, recognizable by anyone who had ever seen it even once. Quickly glancing a little further away, toward the back of the room, which was even darker, I spotted three of my armchairs upholstered in petit point tapestry, then, even further away, my two Henri II tables, so rare that people used to come from Paris just to see them.

Imagine, just imagine my state of mind!

And I walked closer, suffering, rigid with emotion, but I walked closer, for I am brave. I moved closer, like a Knight of the Dark Ages entering a witches' den. With every step I took, I saw everything that had once belonged to me, my chandeliers, my books, my paintings, my clothing, my weapons, everything, everything except my desk full of letters; that was nowhere to be seen.

I walked through the shop, then downstairs to dark rooms only to go back upstairs again. I was alone. I called out; no one answered. I was alone; there was no one else in this enormous house with as many twists and turns as a labyrinth.

Night fell, and I had to sit down on one of my chairs, for I did not want to leave. Every now and again, I shouted, "Hello, hello! Anybody there?"

I had been there for more than an hour when I heard footsteps, soft, slow footsteps, coming from somewhere, I couldn't tell where. I nearly ran off, but I drew myself up to my full height and called out once more, then I saw a light in the next room.

"Who's there?" said a voice.

"A buyer," I replied.

"It's very late to be coming to antique shops," he said.

"I've been waiting for you for more than an hour," I replied.

"You can come back tomorrow."

"I will have left Rouen by tomorrow."

I didn't dare go any closer, and he wasn't coming to me. I could see his light shining on a tapestry with two angels flying above the dead on a battlefield. It, too, belonged to me.

"Well!" I said. "Are you coming?"

"You come to me," he replied.

I stood up and walked toward him.

In the middle of the large room was a very small man, very small and very fat, as fat as a freak, a hideous freak.

He had a short beard, dotted with sparse, yellowish hairs, and not a hair on his head! Not a single hair? He held his candle up to see me, and his skull looked like a small moon in this vast room stuffed with old furniture. His face was wrinkled and puffed up, his eyes barely visible.

I bargained with him to buy three chairs that were mine, and paid a great deal of money for them. I paid for them right then and there, giving him only my room number at the hotel. They were to be delivered the next morning before nine o'clock.

Then I left. He walked me to the door and was very polite.

I headed straight for the police headquarters and told the Captain about the theft of my furniture and what I had just discovered.

He immediately sent a telegram for information to the Public Prosecutor's Office that had dealt with the matter and asked me if I would wait for their reply. An hour later, he got his answer, which completely vindicated me.

"I'm going to arrest that man and question him immediately," he said, "for he might have become suspicious and gotten rid of your belongings. If you go and have supper and come back in two hours, I'll have him here and will question him again in front of you."

"Very gladly, Monsieur. I thank you from the bottom of my heart."

I went and dined at my hotel, with a much better appetite than I thought I would have. I felt rather satisfied. They would get him.

Two hours later, I went back to the police station where the Captain was waiting for me.

"Well, Monsieur," he said as soon as he saw me, "we haven't been able to locate your man. My detectives couldn't arrest him."

Ah! I felt myself weakening.

"But . . . you found his house all right?" I asked.

"Absolutely. It has been put under surveillance and will be watched until he returns. As for him, though, he's disappeared."

"Disappeared?"

"Disappeared. He normally spends every evening at his neighbor's place; she's an antiques dealer too, an odd old witch, the widow Bidoin. She didn't see him tonight and couldn't give us any information. We'll have to wait until tomorrow."

I left. Ah! How sinister, troubling and haunted the streets of Rouen seemed!

I slept very badly and had nightmares every time I fell asleep.

The next day, not wishing to appear too anxious, I waited until ten o'clock before going to the police station.

The merchant had not come back. His shop remained closed.

"I've taken care of all the necessary formalities," the Captain said. "The Public Prosecutor's Office is aware of what's happened; we will go to the shop together and open it up, and you can point out all the things that are yours."

We were driven there. Some policemen stood in front of the shop with a locksmith; it had been opened.

When I went inside, I saw none of the furniture, nothing that had been in my house, nothing at all, not my wardrobe, not my armchairs, not my tables, while the day before, I hadn't been able to turn around without seeing something of mine.

The Captain, surprised, looked at me suspiciously at first.

"My God, Monsieur," I said, "the disappearance of my furniture coincides strangely with the disappearance of the merchant."

He smiled. "How true! You shouldn't have bought and paid for your things yesterday. That must have aroused his suspicions."

"But what is completely incomprehensible," I continued, "is that all the space taken up by my things is now filled with other furniture."

"Oh!" the Captain replied, "he had all night, and accomplices, no doubt. This house must adjoin the neighbors' place. Don't worry about anything, Monsieur, I'm going to stay on top of this case. This crook won't evade us for long since we're watching his hideaway."

. . . .

Ah! My heart, my heart, my poor heart, how fast and hard I felt it beat!

. . . .

I stayed in Rouen for two weeks. The man never returned. Good heavens! Good heavens! Who could possibly stop that man or catch him off guard?

On the morning of the following day, I received a strange letter from my gardener, who had been looking after my empty, pillaged house. This is what it said:

"Dear Monsieur,

I am pleased to inform you that last night something happened that no one can understand, not us and not even the police. All the furniture was back, all of it, without exception, right down to the smallest items. The house is now exactly as it was just before everything was stolen. It's enough to drive anyone mad! It happened between Friday night and Saturday morning. The paths are ripped apart as if everything had been dragged from the gate to the house. It was the same the day it all disappeared.

We await Monsieur's arrival.

Your very humble servant,
Philippe Raudin

Ah! No! No! No! I will not go back there!

I took the letter to the Captain of Police in Rouen.

"It's a very clever move, taking back all your things," he said. "We'll lie low. We'll get him, one of these days."

· ·

But they didn't get him. No. They didn't get him, and I'm afraid of him now, as if he were a ferocious beast let loose to attack me.

Impossible to find! He is impossible to find, that monster with the moon-shaped head! They'll never catch him. He'll never go back to his place. What does he care? I'm the only one who might find him, and I don't want to.

I don't want to! I don't want to! I don't want to!

And what if he does come back, what if he goes back to his shop? Who could prove that my furniture was ever there? It's my word against his; and I can tell my story is already starting to look suspicious.

Ah, no! I couldn't live like this any more. And I couldn't keep what I saw a secret. I couldn't continue living like everyone else with the fear that something similar might happen again.

I came to see the doctor who runs this hospital and I told him everything.

After questioning me for a long time, he asked:

"Would you agree to stay here for a while, Monsieur?"

"Very gladly."

"Are you wealthy?"

"Yes, Monsieur."

"Would you prefer to stay in private quarters, isolated?"

"Yes, Monsieur."

"Would you like to have your friends visit?"

"No, Monsieur, no, no one. That man from Rouen might dare to follow me here, to take revenge."

And so for three months I have been alone, alone, all alone. I feel calm, more or less. I have only one fear . . . What if that antiques dealer went mad . . . what if they brought him to this mental hospital . . . Even prisons are not always safe.

A NIGHTMARE[1]

I LOVE THE NIGHT PASSIONATELY. I LOVE IT THE WAY YOU LOVE your country or your mistress, with an invincible, deep, instinctive kind of love. I love it with all my senses, my eyes that can see it, my sense of smell that breathes it in, my ears that can hear its silence, with my whole body caressed by its shadows. The larks sing in the sunshine, in the blue sky, the warm air, the gentle breeze of bright mornings. The owl flies at night, a shadowy shape crossing the dark skies, and, rejoicing, intoxicated by the infinite blackness, he lets out his resonant, sinister cry.

Daytime bores and tires me. It is harsh and noisy. I get up with difficulty, dress wearily, go out reluctantly, and every step, movement, gesture, word, and thought exhausts me as if I were trying to free myself from some crushing burden.

But when the sun sets, my body is filled with overwhelming joy. I awaken, become alert. The darker it gets, the more I feel myself becoming someone else, someone younger, stronger, more attentive, happier. I watch the great, soft shadows grow darker as they descend from the sky: they drown the city, like an intangible and impenetrable wave, hiding, obliterating, destroying colors and shapes; they surround houses and people and monuments with their feathery-light touch.

Then I feel the desire to cry out with pleasure like an owl, to run over

---

1   This is the subtitle of the story; the original title is *La Nuit* (*Night*).

the rooftops like a cat; and an impetuous, invincible desire sends fire rushing through my veins.

I go out, I walk, sometimes in the somber outskirts of the town, sometimes in the woods just outside Paris, where I can hear my sisters, the
animals, and my brothers, the poachers, rushing about.

Whatever you love passionately ends up killing you. How can I explain
what is happening to me? How can I make you understand that I might
even be able to explain it? I don't know, I don't know any more, I just
know what happened. Here it is.

So yesterday—was it really yesterday?—yes, of course, unless it was
before then, a different day, a different month, a different year—I don't
know. Yet it must have been yesterday, since it is not yet daylight, the sun
has not yet risen. But how long does night last? How long? Who can say?
Who could ever know?

YESTERDAY, I WENT OUT after dinner, as I do every evening. The
weather was very lovely, very mild, very warm. As I walked toward the
boulevards, I looked above my head at the dark river full of stars, a backdrop to the rooftops on the winding street, a moving stream of stars that
undulated as if it were a real river.

Everything was bright in the light air, from the planets to the lamp-
posts.[2] So many fires burned high above and in the city that even the shadows looked lit up. Luminous evenings are more joyful than bright sunny
days.

On the wide avenue, the cafés were brightly lit and people were laughing, walking by, drinking. I went into the theater for a few minutes. Which
theater? I don't recall. It was so light inside that I was saddened, and I went
outside again feeling my heart heavier because of the shock of that brutal
light on the gilt balcony, the artificial sparkling of the enormous crystal
chandelier, the blazing footlights, the melancholy of this unnatural, raw

---

2   At the time de Maupassant was writing, the street lamps were lit by gas.

brightness. I walked along the Champs-Elysées where the *cafés-concerts*[3] looked like houses on fire amid the trees. The chestnut trees swathed in a yellowish light seemed covered in phosphorescent paint. And the electric globes—pale, dazzling moons, lunar eggs fallen from the sky, monstrous, pulsating pearls—made the strings of colored lights and the fine streams of filthy, vile gas grow pale beneath their regal, mysterious, pearly light.

I stopped under the Arc de Triomphe to gaze down the wide boulevard, the long, attractive avenue all ablaze that led to Paris between two rows of fire. And the stars!

The stars above, the mysterious stars randomly scattered toward infinity where they form strange shapes that make us wish and dream so very much.

I went into the Bois de Boulogne and stayed there for a long, long time. A peculiar shiver had rushed through me, a surprising, powerful emotion, an intense euphoria that bordered on madness.

I walked for a very long time. Then I turned back.

What time was it when I walked back under the Arc de Triomphe? I don't know. The city was asleep, and the clouds—great dark clouds— were spreading slowly across the sky.

For the first time, I felt that something new, something strange was about to happen. It seemed as if it had suddenly turned cold, as if the air was denser, as if the night, my beloved night, weighed heavily on my heart. The wide avenue was deserted. Only two policemen were walking where the horse-drawn carriages[4] were lined up, and, on the street, barely lit by the gaslights that seemed to be dying out, a row of carts full of vegetables headed toward Les Halles.[5] They drove slowly, laden with carrots, turnips and cabbages. The drivers dozed, invisible, while the horses fell into step, following the carriage in front, making no noise on the cobblestones. As they passed in front of each streetlight, the carrots

---

3   These cafés had singers who entertained the clients.

4   *Fiacres* in French.

5   The central market in Paris (it was moved to the outskirts in 1971). Wagons arrived all night long with fresh produce and the cafés stayed open serving hot onion soup and white wine to the drivers.

lit up bright red, the turnips gleamed white, the cabbages glowed green, and the carriages passed by, one after the other, red carriages, fiery red, carriages as white as silver, as green as emeralds. I followed them, then turned down the Rue Royale and went back along the wide boulevards. No one in sight, no more bright cafés, only a few people who had stayed out very late hurried past. I had never seen Paris so dead, so deserted. I looked at my watch. It was two o'clock.

Something forced me to keep going, a need to keep walking. So I walked as far as the Place de la Bastille. Once there, I realized I had never seen such a dark night, for I couldn't even make out the Colonne de Juillet;[6] even its golden statue was invisible in the impenetrable darkness. A canopy of clouds, as thick as infinity, engulfed the stars and seemed to weigh down on the earth, as if to blot it out.

I headed back. There was not a soul in sight. At the Place du Château-d'Eau, however, a drunkard nearly bumped into me, then disappeared. For some time, I could hear his uneven, echoing footsteps.

I kept walking. At the top of the Faubourg Montmartre, a horse-drawn carriage passed by, heading toward the Seine. I called out. The driver didn't reply. A woman was wandering around near the Rue Drouot: "Monsieur, listen, please." I rushed ahead to avoid her outstretched hand. Then nothing more. In front of Le Vaudeville, a ragman was rummaging in the gutter. His little lantern flickered at the water's edge. "You there, what time is it?" I asked him.

"You think I know!" he grumbled. "I ain't got a watch."

I suddenly noticed that the gaslights had gone out. I know they are turned off early, before daybreak at this time of year, to save money; but it was a long time until dawn, a very long time!

"Let's go to Les Halles," I thought. "There should be people around there at least."

I set off, but it was so dark I couldn't see where I was going. I walked

---

6   This monument commemorates the 1830 Revolution, the fall of Charles X and the commencement of the "July Monarchy" of Louis-Philippe.

slowly, the way you do in the woods, counting the streets I passed to recognize them.

In front of the Crédit Lyonnais bank, a dog growled. I turned down the Rue de Grammont and got lost; I wandered around, then recognized La Bourse[7] and the iron gates that surround it. All of Paris was asleep, in a deep, terrifying sleep. Yet in the distance I heard a carriage, just one carriage, perhaps the one that had passed me a little while ago. I tried to find it, heading toward the sound of its wheels through the dark, empty streets, so very dark, as dark as death.

I got lost again. Where was I? What madness to turn off the gaslights so early! Not a single passerby, not one person out late, no one wandering around, not even the meowing of a cat on the prowl. Nothing.

Where were the policemen? "I'll call out," I said to myself, "and they'll come." I cried out. No one replied.

I shouted louder. My voice faded away, weak, without an echo, stifled, obliterated by the night, by this impenetrable night.

I screamed: "Help! Help! Help me!"

My despairing cry went unanswered. What time was it now? I took out my watch but I had no matches. I listened to the watch's faint *tick-tock* with a strange, unfamiliar feeling of joy. It seemed to be alive. I felt less alone. It was so mysterious! I started walking again, like a blind man, feeling my way along the walls with my cane, and constantly looking upward toward the sky, hoping that day would finally break; but the sky was black, utterly black, even darker than the city.

What time could it be? I felt as if I had been walking forever; my legs were giving way beneath me; I was panting and starving half to death.

I decided to ring the first door I came to. I pressed the brass doorbell and I could hear it reverberate through the house; it echoed strangely, as if this quivering sound was the only thing inside.

I waited, no one replied, no one opened the door. I rang the bell again; I waited some more—nothing!

I was afraid! I ran to the next house, and twenty times in a row, I rang

---

7   The French stock market.

the doorbell in the dark entrance where the concierge must be sleeping in his room. But he didn't wake up, so I went further down the street, knocking with the brass rings and pressing the bells with all my strength, banging at the doors with my feet, my cane and my fists, but they remained obstinately closed.

And suddenly, I realized I had reached Les Halles. It was deserted, not a sound, not a carriage, not a soul, no vegetables, not a bunch of flowers.

The entire place was empty, still, abandoned, dead!

Terror ran through me—horrifying. What was happening? Oh, my God! What was happening?

I walked away. What time was it? What time? Who could tell me the time? Not a single sound from the clocktowers or the monuments. "I'll open the glass cover of my watch," I thought, "and feel for the hands with my fingers." I took out my watch . . . it wasn't working . . . it had stopped . . . There was nothing now, nothing, not the slightest movement in the whole city, not a sliver of light, not the faintest echo of a sound through the air. Nothing! Nothing! Not even the distant sound of the carriage— simply nothing!

I was at the quayside; an icy chill rose from the river.

Was the Seine still flowing?

I wanted to know, I found the steps and went down . . . I couldn't hear the water bubbling beneath the arches of the bridge . . . More steps . . . then sand . . . sludge . . . the water . . . I put my arm in . . . the river was still flowing . . . flowing . . . cold . . . cold . . . so cold . . . almost freezing . . . almost dried up . . . almost dead.

And I truly felt that I would never have the strength to pull myself away again . . . and that I would die right there . . . of hunger—of exhaustion—of the cold . . . I too would die.

LE HORLA[1]

May 8

WHAT A WONDERFUL DAY! I SPENT THE ENTIRE MORNING STRETCHED
out on the grass in front of my house, under an enormous plane tree that
completely covers it, shades it and hides it from view. I like this region, and
I like living here because this is where my roots are, the fine, deep roots
that tie a man to the land where his ancestors were born and died, roots that
tie him to how he thinks and what he likes to eat, to tradition as well as
food, to the local dialect, the unique intonation of the farmers when they
speak, the smell of the earth, the villages and even the air itself.

I love the house where I grew up. I can see the Seine from my windows; it flows along the edge of my garden, behind the road, nearly up to
my house: the wide, long Seine that stretches from Rouen to Le Havre,
full of passing boats.

To the left, in the distance, lies Rouen, that sprawling city of blue slate
roofs beneath countless tall Gothic steeples, both delicate and solid, in
the shadow of the cathedral's iron spire. These steeples are full of bells
that ring out in the clear blue light on beautiful mornings, sending me the
soft metallic hum of their distant bronze songs that are swept along by
the wind, sometimes louder, sometimes softer, depending on whether the
bells are starting to peel or are fading away.

How beautiful it was this morning!

---

1 In French, this invented word for a supernatural being sounds identical to *hors-là*,
which means "something beyond, not of this world."

At about eleven o'clock, a long convoy of ships passed by my gates: they were pulled along by a tugboat that was as fat as a fly and groaned with the effort, spewing out thick smoke.

After two English schooners, whose red flags fluttered against the sky, came a superb Brazilian three-master, all white, wonderfully clean and shiny. This ship filled me with such pleasure that I saluted it, I don't really know why.

May 12

I'VE HAD A SLIGHT FEVER FOR THE PAST FEW DAYS; I DON'T FEEL well, or rather, I feel somewhat sad.

Where do these mysterious influences come from that can transform our happiness into discouragement and our confidence into distress? It's as if the air, the invisible air, is full of unknowable Forces, mysterious Forces that close in around us. I wake up full of cheerfulness, with a song in my heart—Why?—I walk down to the water's edge and suddenly, after a short stroll, I come back home in despair, as if some misfortune lies in wait for me in my house—Why?—Has a chill wind swept over my body, setting my nerves on edge and filling my soul with gloom? Has the shape of the clouds, or the colors of the day, the colors of objects, so changeable, flowed past my eyes and unsettled my mind? How can we know? Everything that surrounds us, everything we look at without really seeing, everything we brush against without knowing what it is, everything we touch without actually feeling it, everything we encounter without recognizing it, do all these things have an inexplicable, surprising, immediate effect on us, on our physical being, and through our bodies, affect our thoughts, even our very hearts?

How profound is this mystery of the Invisible! We can never know its depths with our inadequate senses, our eyes that do not know how to truly perceive what is too small, or too big, or too close, or too distant, or the beings that inhabit the stars or a drop of water . . . with our ears that deceive us, for they carry vibrations through the air as sonorous notes. They are fairies that accomplish the miracle of transforming movement into sound and through this metamorphosis, bring music to life, making the silent turbulence of nature sing out . . . our sense of smell, weaker than a dog's . . . our sense of taste that can barely determine the age of a bottle of wine!

Ah! If only we had more organs that could accomplish other miracles for us: then we could discover so many things that are all around us!

May 16

I AM NOT WELL; THERE IS NO DOUBT ABOUT IT! I FELT SO GOOD last month! I have a fever, a horrible fever, or rather, a feverish nervousness that is making my soul suffer as much as my body! I have a continual, terrifying sense of impending danger, a feeling of apprehension, as if something terrible is about to happen, or that death is drawing closer, a premonition which is surely an expectation of some evil as yet unknown, taking root in my body and my blood.

May 18

I HAVE JUST COME FROM SEEING MY DOCTOR FOR I COULDN'T SLEEP any more. He found my pulse racing, my pupils dilated, my nerves on edge, but with no alarming symptoms. I have to take showers and drink potassium bromide.

May 25

NO CHANGE AT ALL! MY CONDITION IS TRULY STRANGE. AS EVENING approaches, an incomprehensible anxiety rushes through me, as if the night is hiding some terrible danger it has in store for me. I eat dinner quickly, then I try to read; but I don't understand the words; I can barely make out the letters. So I pace back and forth through my living room, oppressed by a vague, compelling fear, the fear of sleep and the fear of my bed.

I go up to my bedroom at around ten o'clock. As soon as I am inside, I double-lock the door and secure the bolts; I am afraid . . . but of what? . . . I was never frightened of anything until now . . . I open my wardrobes,

I look under my bed; I listen . . . I listen . . . For what? . . . Is it not strange that a simple feeling of unease, perhaps a minor circulation problem, the irritation of nerve endings, a bit of congestion, a very slight disturbance in the very imperfect and delicate functioning of our living organism can make the most cheerful of men morose and transform the bravest into cowards? Then I get into bed and wait for sleep to come as one waits for the executioner. I wait in terror for it to come; and my heart pounds, and my legs shake; and my entire body is trembling beneath the warm sheets, until the moment when I suddenly fall into a deep sleep, the way a man would fall if he were trying to drown himself in deep, stagnant waters. I cannot feel it coming, as I did in the past, this treacherous sleep that hides close by, lies in wait to grab hold of my head, to close my eyes, to send me into dark oblivion.

I sleep—for a long time—two or three hours—then a dream—no—a nightmare seizes hold of me. I can sense quite well that I am in bed and asleep . . . I can sense it and I know it . . . and I also sense that someone is coming closer, watching me, touching me, getting into my bed, kneeling on my chest, grabbing me by the throat and strangling me . . . strangling me . . . with all his strength.

I struggle, I try to fight, held back by this atrocious powerlessness that paralyzes us in our dreams; I want to cry out—and cannot—I want to move—and cannot; I am panting, in anguish, I try with all my might to turn over, to throw off this being that is crushing me, suffocating me—and I cannot!

And suddenly, I wake up, terror-stricken, covered in sweat. I light a candle. I am alone.

After this attack, which happens again and again, every night, I finally go calmly to sleep and do not wake until dawn.

June 2

MY CONDITION IS GETTING WORSE. WHAT CAN BE WRONG WITH ME? The bromide has no effect at all; the showers do nothing to help. This afternoon, to tire my body out—even though it is already so weary—I went for a walk in the Roumare woods. At first I thought that the fresh air, so sweet and calm, full of the scent of grass and leaves, would pour new blood into my veins, new energy into my heart. I crossed a wide hunting ground, then headed toward the little village of La Bouille, taking a narrow path lined by two armies of trees that were unbelievably tall, forming a thick, very dark green roof between myself and the sky.

A shiver suddenly ran through me, not a cold shiver, but a strange shiver of anguish.

I walked more quickly, anxious at being alone in this wood, frightened for no reason, absurdly frightened, by my utter solitude. Suddenly, I felt as if I were being followed, that someone was right behind me, close by, so close that he could touch me.

I turned sharply around. I was alone. All I could see behind me was the wide road, empty, long, frighteningly empty; and on the other side it was just the same: it stretched out and was lost in the distance, terrifying.

I closed my eyes. Why? And I started spinning around on my heel, very quickly, like a top. I nearly fell; I opened my eyes again; the trees were swaying; the ground wobbled; I had to sit down. Then, ah! I no longer knew which way I had come! It was strange! Strange! So strange! I had no idea at all. I headed for the road to my right and was back on the avenue that had led me to the middle of the woods.

June 3

LAST NIGHT WAS HORRIBLE. I WILL GO AWAY FOR A FEW WEEKS. A little trip will no doubt cure me.

July 2

I'M BACK AT HOME. I AM CURED. I HAD A WONDERFUL TRIP. I VISited Mont Saint-Michel, where I'd never been.

What a sight it is when you arrive, as I did, at Avranches, toward the end of the day! The town stands on a hill, and I was taken to the public gardens, at the far end of the city. I cried out in astonishment. An endless bay stretched out before me, as far as the eye could see, set between two remote coasts lost in the distant mist. And in the middle of this golden bay, beneath a clear, shimmering sky, a dark, pointed, strange mount rises up from the sand. The sun had just set, and on the horizon, still ablaze, you could make out the silhouette of this incredible rock that bears an incredible monument at its summit.

As soon as day broke, I headed toward it. The sea was at low tide, as it had been the night before, and as I got closer, I could see the astonishing abbey rising in front of me. After walking for a few hours, I reached the mass of stone that supports the small village dominated by the great church. Having crossed the short, narrow street, I entered the splendid Gothic temple built here on earth to worship God, sprawling like a city, full of low rooms that are dwarfed by the vaults, and high galleries supported by slender columns. I entered this gigantic granite gem of architecture, light as lace, covered with towers and svelte little steeples with spiral staircases, all linked by delicately carved arches, and its strange heads of chimeras, devils, fantastic beasts and enormous flowers rise up toward the blue heavens by day and the black firmament by night.

When I reached the top, I said to the monk who accompanied me: "Father, how happy you must be here!"

"There's a lot of wind here, Monsieur," he replied. Then we started to chat while watching the tide rise; it ran over the sand, enclosing it in steel armor.

And the monk told me stories, all the old stories that happened in this place, and legends, all the legends.

One of them struck me forcibly. The people in this area, the ones who live on the top of the hill, claim that they hear voices at night, coming from the beach, sometimes they hear goats bleating, one with a strong voice, the other making a faint sound. The unbelievers say it is only the sea gulls squawking, which sometimes sounds like bleating and sometimes like someone wailing; but the fishermen who stay out late swear they have met someone wandering around the sand dunes, between high and low tide, around the little village so isolated from the rest of the world: an old shepherd whose face is always hidden by his coat and who is followed closely behind by a billy goat with the face of a man and a nanny goat with the face of a woman, both with long white hair and talking continually, arguing in an strange language, then suddenly stopping their shouting in order to bleat with all their might.

"Do you believe this?" I asked the monk.

"I don't know," he murmured.

"If beings other than us existed on this earth," I continued, "why have we not known about them for so long? Why haven't either of us—not you, not I—ever seen them?"

"Do we ever see a hundred thousandth of what actually exists?" he replied. "Take the wind, for example, which is the greatest force of nature: it knocks men over, tears down buildings, uproots trees, lifts the sea to form mountains of water, destroys cliffs and forces ships onto the reefs; the wind kills, it whistles, it groans and howls, but have you ever seen it? Could you ever see it? And yet, it exists."

I said nothing in reply to this simple reasoning. This monk was either a wise man or a fool. I couldn't actually tell; but I kept silent. What he had been saying, I had often thought myself.

July 3

I SLEPT BADLY; THERE IS SURELY SOME CONTAGIOUS FEVER GOING around, for my coach driver seems to have the same disease. When I got back home last night, I noticed how terribly pale he looked.

"What's wrong with you, Jean?" I asked.

"I just can't sleep any more, Monsieur; my nights are ruining my days. Ever since Monsieur left, I feel as if I'm under some kind of spell."

The other servants seem fine, though, but I am very frightened that I will become ill again myself.

July 4

IT IS DEFINITELY BACK. MY OLD NIGHTMARES HAVE RETURNED. Last night, I felt someone crouching over me who placed his mouth against mine and was sucking the life out of me. Yes, he was drawing the life from between my lips like some sort of leech. Then he got up, sated, and I . . . I woke up, so battered, broken, overwhelmed, that I couldn't even move. If this continues a few more days, I will certainly go away again.

July 5

AM I GOING MAD? WHAT HAPPENED LAST NIGHT, WHAT I SAW, IS SO strange that I feel I'm going mad when I think about it!

I had locked my door, as I do every night now; then, as I was thirsty, I drank half a glass of water; I happened to notice that my decanter was full, right up to the crystal stopper.

I went to bed and fell into one of my terrifying sleeps, and woke up after about two hours with a jolt that was even more frightening.

Imagine a man who is asleep, who is being murdered and who wakes up with a knife in his chest; he is gasping for breath, covered in blood, unable to breathe, about to die and doesn't understand why—that was my dream.

After finally calming myself down, I was thirsty again; I lit a candle and went over to the table where I'd left the decanter of water. I picked it up to pour some into my glass; nothing came out—It was empty! Completely empty! At first, I just couldn't understand; then, suddenly, I had a feeling that was so horrifying that I had to sit down, or rather that I needed to collapse into a chair! I sprang up to look around the room! Then I sat down again and looked at the empty decanter, overwhelmed with astonishment and terror! I stared at it wide-eyed, trying to understand. My hands were shaking! So someone had drunk all the water? But who? Me? It had to be me, didn't it? It could only have been me, couldn't it? So I must be a sleepwalker; without knowing it, I was living this mysterious double life which makes us wonder if there are two people who inhabit us, or if some stranger, unknowable and invisible, is awakened at times, when our soul is deadened, our body captive, obeying this other being the way they usually obey us, even more than they obey us.

Ah! Who could understand my hideous anguish? Who could understand the emotion of a man who is of sound mind, wide-awake, completely rational and who stares in terror at an empty glass decanter from which a bit of water had disappeared while he was asleep! I remained there until daybreak, not daring to go back to bed.

July 6

I AM GOING MAD. SOMEONE DRANK ALL THE WATER IN MY decanter again last night—or rather, I drank it!

But was it me? Was it me? Who else could it be? Who? Oh, my God! Am I going mad? Who can save me?

July 10

I HAVE JUST CARRIED OUT SOME UNUSUAL EXPERIMENTS.

I am definitely insane! Even so!

On July 6, before going to bed, I put some wine, milk, water, bread and strawberries on my table.

Someone drank—I drank—all the water and a little milk. The wine, bread and strawberries remained untouched.

On July 7, I repeated the experiment; same result.

On July 8, I left no water or milk. Nothing was touched.

Finally, on July 9, I only put the water and milk on the table, taking care to wrap the decanters in white muslin and tie string around the stoppers. Then I put some graphite on my lips, my beard and my hands and I went to bed.

Invincible sleep seized hold of me, followed soon afterwards by my horrifying awakening. I had not stirred; even my sheets had no traces of black. I rushed toward the table. The muslin surrounding the bottles was spotless. I untied the strings, my heart beating hard out of fear. All the water was gone! Someone had drunk all the milk! Ah, my God! . . .

I am leaving for Paris right away.

July 12

PARIS. I HAD REALLY GONE MAD THESE PAST FEW DAYS! MY UNSET-
tled imagination must be toying with me, unless I truly am a sleepwalker,
or have been subject to one of those influences claimed, though unex-
plained until now, that are called suggestions. In any case, my panic was
bordering on insanity, and twenty-four hours in Paris were enough to
recover my equilibrium.

Yesterday, after doing some shopping and visiting friends, who filled
my entire being with new vitality, I ended my evening at the Théâtre-
Français. They were performing a play by Alexandre Dumas the younger,[2]
and this vibrant, powerful spirit managed to cure me. Solitude is surely
dangerous to active minds. We must have thinking men and conversation
around us. When we are alone for a long time, we fill the void with ghosts.

I walked along the boulevards to go back to my hotel, feeling very
cheerful. As I rubbed shoulders with the crowd, I thought, not without some irony, about my terrors, my assumptions of a week ago, how I
believed, yes, I actually believed that an invisible being was living under
my roof. How weak our minds are, and how quickly they panic and are
led astray the minute one small, incomprehensible fact assails us!

Instead of reaching a conclusion with the simple words: "I don't understand because the reason escapes me," we immediately imagine terrifying
mysteries and supernatural forces.

July 14

BASTILLE DAY. I STROLLED DOWN THE STREETS. THE FIRECRACK-
ers and flags amused me as if I were a child. And yet it is quite ridiculous
to be happy on a specific date designated by a government law. People are

---

2   Alexandre Dumas *fils* (1824–1895) the playwright and novelist, was a contemporary
of Maupassant. His most famous novel, *La Dame aux camélias* (*The Lady of the Camellias*)
(1848), became a play in 1852.

a foolish herd, sometimes stupidly patient, sometimes revolting fiercely. When they are told: "Have a good time," they have a good time. When they are told: "You must go to war with our neighbor," they go to war. When they are told: "Vote for the Emperor," they vote for the Emperor. Then when they are told: "Vote for the Republic," they vote for the Republic.

Their leaders are also fools; but instead of obeying men, they obey principles—principles that can only be inane, fruitless and false precisely because they are principles, that is to say, ideas that are deemed to be unchanging and definitive in this world in which no one is certain of anything, because enlightenment is an illusion, great events are an illusion.

July 16

YESTERDAY, I SAW THINGS THAT TROUBLED ME GREATLY.

I was having dinner at Mme Sablé's house; she is my cousin and her husband is Commander of the 76th Regiment of Chasseurs[3] in Limoges. I found myself in the company of two young women, one of whom is married to a doctor, Dr. Parent, who specializes in nervous conditions and extraordinary symptoms that are currently the subject of experiments with hypnotism and the influence of suggestion.

He recounted at length the extraordinary results obtained by English scientists and some doctors from the medical school in Nancy.

The facts he put forward seemed so strange to me that I immediately said I did not believe them.

"We are on the verge of discovering one of the important secrets of nature," he stated, "I mean one of the most important secrets on this earth; for nature certainly holds other important secrets, beyond this world, in the firmament. Ever since man was able to speak and write down his thoughts, he has felt the invisible presence of some impenetrable mystery that his crude, imperfect senses cannot grasp; and, through the effort of his intelligence, he has tried to compensate for the powerlessness of his senses. When man's intelligence was still in a rudimentary state,

---

3   Infantrymen.

being haunted by invisible phenomena took on forms that were frightening in the most ordinary of ways. These led to the birth of popular belief in the supernatural, legends of wandering spirits, fairies, gnomes, ghosts, I would even go so far as to say the legend of God, for our ideas about a master creator, from whatever religion we are taught them, are truly the most mediocre, the most stupid, the most unacceptable ideas to emerge from the human mind that is afraid of such creatures. Nothing is truer than what Voltaire once said: 'God made man in his own image, but man truly returned the favor.'

"But for more than half a century now, we seem to sense something new. Mesmer and others have taken us down a surprising path, and we have had truly astonishing results, especially in the past four or five years."

My cousin, also quite skeptical, smiled. "Shall I try to hypnotize you, Madame?" Dr. Parent asked.

"Yes, willingly."

She sat down in an armchair and he began staring at her and hypnotizing her. Suddenly, I . . . I felt nervous, my heart was pounding and my throat constricted. I watched as Mme Sablé's eyes started feeling heavy, her mouth become tense, her chest started to heave.

Ten minutes later, she was asleep.

"Go and stand behind her," the doctor told me.

So I sat down behind her. He placed a visitor's card in her hand.

"This is a mirror," he said. "What do you see reflected in it?"

"I see my cousin," she replied.

"What is he doing?"

"He is twisting his moustache."

"And now?"

"He is taking a photograph out of his pocket."

"Whose photograph is it?"

"His."

It was true! And the photograph had just been delivered to me at my hotel that very evening.

"What does he look like in this picture?"

"He is standing up and holding a hat in his hand."

And so she could see in the card, in this piece of white card, as if she were looking in a mirror.

"Enough! Enough!" the young women said, terrified. "That's enough!"

But the doctor gave an order: "You will get up tomorrow morning at eight o'clock; then you will go to see your cousin at his hotel and you will beg him to lend you five thousand francs that your husband has asked you to give him when he leaves on his next trip."

Then he woke her up.

On the way back to my hotel, I thought about this strange séance and was overwhelmed with doubt, not about the absolute good faith of my cousin—that was above suspicion, as I had known her since we were children and she was like a sister to me—but about the possible hoax perpetrated by the doctor.

Perhaps he was hiding a mirror in his hand that he showed to the hypnotized young woman at the same time as his calling card? Professional magicians do other such extraordinary things.

I went home to bed.

The next morning, around eight-thirty, I was awakened by my valet.

"Mme Sablé is here," he said, "and she is asking to see you right away, Monsieur."

I dressed quickly and went out to greet her.

She was sitting down and looked very upset indeed; her eyes were lowered, and without raising her veil, she said:

"My dear cousin, I have a great favor to ask of you."

"What favor is that, my dear?"

"It troubles me greatly to ask you and yet I must. I need, I am in dire need, of five thousand francs."

"Is that so? You really are?"

"Yes, yes, or rather, my husband is, and he has asked me to find the money."

I was so astonished that I muttered my reply. I wondered if she had actually not plotted with Dr. Parent to trick me, if it were nothing more than an elaborate joke prepared in advance and well played out.

But when I looked at her closely, all my doubts disappeared. Making this request was so painful to her that she was trembling with anguish, and I realized she was trying to hide her sobs.

I knew she was extremely wealthy so I continued:

"What! Your husband doesn't have five thousand francs of his own! Come now, just think about it. Are you sure that he sent you to ask me for the money?"

She hesitated for a moment as if she were making a great effort to remember something.

"Yes . . . yes," she replied, "I'm quite sure."

"Did he write to you?"

She hesitated again and thought about it. I could guess how difficult it was for her to think it through. She didn't know. All she knew was that she was supposed to borrow five thousand francs from me for her husband. And so she actually lied.

"Yes, he wrote to me."

"When was that? You didn't mention anything about it at all last night."

"I got his letter this morning."

"Can you show it to me?"

"No . . . no . . . no . . . It contains personal things . . . it's too personal . . . I've . . . I've burnt it."

"So has your husband been running up debts?"

She hesitated once more, then murmured:

"I don't know."

"It's just that I don't have five thousand francs to lend you at this time, my dear cousin," I said quickly.

She let out a cry of anguish.

"Oh! Oh! I beg of you, find the money for me, I'm begging you . . ."

She was getting very upset, clasping her hands together as if she were praying to me! I could hear the tone of her voice change; she was crying and stammering, obsessed, overwhelmed by the irresistible order she had received.

"Oh! Oh! I'm begging you . . .if you only knew how much I'm suffer-ing . . . I must have the money today."

I took pity on her.

"You will have it this afternoon, I promise."

"Oh! Thank you! Thank you! You are so kind."

"Do you remember what happened last night?" I asked.

"Yes."

"Do you remember that Dr. Parent hypnotized you?"

"Yes."

"Well! He ordered you to come and borrow five thousand francs from me this morning, and you are obeying his command."

She thought for a few seconds.

"But it's my husband who is asking me for the money," she replied.

I tried to convince her for an hour, but without success.

When she left, I hurried to the doctor's house. He was about to go out; he listened to what I had to say and smiled.

"Do you believe in it now?" he asked.

"Yes, I have to."

"Let's go and see your cousin."

She was already half-asleep on a chaise longue, overcome with exhaustion.

The doctor took her pulse, looked at her for a time with one hand raised toward her eyes; she gradually closed them, unable to fight his spellbind-ing force.

"Your husband no longer needs the five thousand francs," he said, once she was asleep. "You will forget that you asked your cousin to bor-row the money, and if he mentions it to you, you won't understand what he is talking about."

Then he woke her up. I took my wallet out of my pocket.

"Here you are, my dear cousin, here is the money you asked for this morning."

She was so surprised that I didn't dare insist. Instead, I tried to help her to remember, but she hotly denied it, thought I was teasing her and, in the end, nearly got angry.

And there you have it! I just got home and this experience upset me so much that I couldn't eat my breakfast.

July 19

MANY PEOPLE I TOLD THIS STORY TO MADE FUN OF ME. I NO LON-ger know what to think. The wise man says: Perhaps?

July 21

I WENT TO BOUGIVAL FOR DINNER, THEN SPENT THE EVENING AT the dance the boatmen held. Undoubtedly, everything depends on where you are, and the atmosphere. Believing in the supernatural on Ile de la Grenouillière would be the height of folly . . . but at the top of Mont Saint-Michel? . . . or in the Indies? We are intensely influenced by everything that surrounds us. I will go home next week.

July 30

I'VE BEEN HOME SINCE YESTERDAY. EVERYTHING IS FINE.

August 2

NOTHING NEW; THE WEATHER IS SUBLIME. I SPEND MY DAYS watching the Seine flow by.

August 4

THE SERVANTS ARE QUARRELING. THEY CLAIM THAT GLASSES IN the cupboards are being broken during the night. The valet accuses the cook, the cook accuses the laundress, who in turn accuses the other two. Who is responsible? Who on earth can tell?

August 6

THIS TIME, I AM NOT MAD. I SAW IT . . . I SAW IT . . . I SAW IT! I CAN no longer have any doubts. I saw it! I am still frozen to the bone . . . frightened to my very core . . . I saw it with my own eyes!

I was walking through my rose garden, at two o'clock, in bright sunlight . . . in the path where the first roses of autumn are beginning to blossom.

When I stopped to look at a *géant des batailles*[4] that had three magnificent flowers, I saw, I distinctly saw, right next to me, the stem of one of these roses bend and then break off—as if some invisible hand had twisted it and picked it from the bush! Then the flower rose in the air, making an arch, as if an arm had raised it to its mouth, and it remained suspended in the clear air, all alone, motionless, a terrifying red patch close to my eyes.

Frantic, I lunged forward to grab it! There was nothing there; it had disappeared. Then I was stricken by fierce anger toward myself, for it is not acceptable for a logical, serious man to have such hallucinations.

But was it really a hallucination? I turned around to look for the stem and immediately found it on the rosebush, freshly broken off, between the two other roses that remained on the branch.

So I went back home, my soul in turmoil. For now, I am certain, as certain as day follows night, that an invisible being is living at my side, a being that drinks milk and water, who can touch things, pick them up and move them, is endowed with physical characteristics that we are quite incapable of seeing, and who lives, as I do, under my roof . . .

August 7

I SLEPT PEACEFULLY. HE DRANK SOME WATER FROM MY DECANTER but did not wake me.

I wonder if I am mad. While I was walking along the riverbank in the sunshine today, I began to have doubts about my sanity, not vague doubts like the ones I've had up until now, but precise, absolute doubts. I have known madmen; some of them remained intelligent, lucid, even perceptive

---

4 A type of rosebush.

about everything in life, except in one way. They talked about everything with clarity, finesse, insight, and suddenly their thoughts would hurtle against the stumbling block of their madness, break up into little pieces, scattering and foundering in a terrifying, raging ocean, full of soaring waves, layers of fog and squalls—the ocean that is called "insanity."

Of course, I would believe myself to be mad, absolutely mad, except for the fact that I was perfectly aware, conscious of my condition, for I probed it and analyzed it with complete lucidity. In short, I was, therefore, simply a logical man who was suffering from hallucinations. Some unknown disorder must have taken hold of my brain, one of those disorders that the physiologists of today attempt to record and define; and this disorder must have left a great crevice in my mind, in the logic and order of my thoughts. Similar phenomena take place in dreams, providing us with the most unbelievably bizarre scenarios, without being in the least surprised, because the mechanism that verifies and controls us is asleep, while our imagination is awake and at work. Perhaps one of the imperceptible ivories on my brain's keyboard no longer works? After an accident, some men cannot remember people's names or certain verbs or figures or simply dates. The location of all the areas of thought has been defined in our time. So why should it be surprising that my ability to control certain unreal hallucinations has gone dead in me at present!

I thought about all these things as I walked along the water's edge. The sun made the river sparkle, the countryside look delightful, filling my eyes with a love of life, for the swallows, whose agility is a joy to behold, a love of the reeds along the riverbank, whose rustling sound brings me happiness.

And yet, little by little, an inexplicable feeling of anxiety ran through me. Some force, or so it seemed, some supernatural force was taking over my body, stopping me, preventing me from going further, forcing me to go back. I felt a painful, oppressive need to go back home, like the feeling you get when you have left a sick person you love in the house and you get a premonition that they are getting worse.

And so, in spite of myself, I went back home, certain that I would find a letter or telegram that contained bad news waiting for me there. There was nothing; and I remained more surprised and more anxious than if I had had some new eerie vision.

August 8

I HAD A HORRIBLE NIGHT. HE IS NO LONGER MAKING HIS PRESENCE known but I can feel him near me, spying on me, watching me, entering my body, taking over; and he is even more formidable when he hides himself this way than when he makes his constant, invisible presence known through supernatural phenomena.

And yet, I managed to sleep.

August 9

NOTHING, BUT I'M AFRAID.

August 10

NOTHING; BUT WHAT WILL HAPPEN TOMORROW?

August 11

STILL NOTHING; I CAN NO LONGER STAY AT HOME WITH THIS FEAR and these thoughts that have invaded my soul; I am going away.

August 12

TEN O'CLOCK AT NIGHT—ALL DAY I HAVE WANTED TO LEAVE; BUT I couldn't. I wanted to accomplish this act of freedom, so easy, so simple— to leave—to get into my carriage and go to Rouen—but I couldn't. Why?

August 13

WHEN SUFFERING FROM CERTAIN ILLNESSES, THE INNER WORK- ings of the physical human body seem to be broken, every type of energy becomes dissipated, all the muscles slack, the bones as soft as flesh and the flesh as liquid as water. I experience this feeling in my soul in a strange, depressing way. I have no more strength, no more courage, no more control over myself, none at all, not even the power to accomplish an act of will. I no longer have a will; someone has taken over my will, and I obey.

August 14

ALL IS LOST! SOMEONE HAS POSSESSED ME AND IS CONTROLLING me! Someone is commanding my every action, every movement, every thought. I no longer count for anything: I am nothing more than an enslaved spectator, terrified by everything I do. I want to go out. I cannot. He does not want me to, and so I remain overwhelmed, trembling in my armchair where he keeps me seated. I only wish to rise, to stand up, so I can believe I am still my own master. I cannot! I am riveted to my chair; and my chair grips the floor so strongly that no power in this world could release us.

Then, suddenly, I must, I must, I must go to the back of my garden to pick strawberries and eat them. And so I go. I pick strawberries and eat them! Oh my God! My God! Is there a God? If there is, save me, free me! Help me! Forgive me! Take pity on me! Have mercy on me! Save me! Oh! Such suffering! Such torture! Such horror!

August 15

THIS IS SURELY HOW MY POOR COUSIN WAS POSSESSED AND CON-trolled when she came to borrow five thousand francs from me. She was yielding to some strange will that had entered her, like another soul, like another parasitic, dominating soul. Is the world coming to an end?

But the thing that controls me, what is it, this invisible being? This unknowable creature from a supernatural race who wanders through my soul?

So invisible life forms exist! Well, then, why haven't they shown them-selves in such a concrete way since the beginnings of the world, as they have shown themselves to me? I have never read anything that is like what is happening in my home. Oh! If only I could leave, go away, flee and never return. I would be saved then. But I cannot.

August 16

I MANAGED TO ESCAPE TODAY FOR TWO HOURS, LIKE A PRISONER who, by chance, finds the door of his cell unlocked. I felt completely free suddenly and that he was far away. I ordered my carriage to be quickly prepared and I went to Rouen. Oh! What a joy to be able to tell someone: "Drive to Rouen" and have him obey!

I had him stop at a library and asked if I might borrow Dr. Hermann Herestauss's famous treatise on the unknown inhabitants of the ancient and modern world.

Then, just as I got back into my carriage and wanted to say: "Take me to the station!" I shouted—I didn't say it, I actually shouted—in such a loud voice that passersby turned around: "Take me back home." And I fell back against the seat of my carriage, mad and overcome with anguish. He had found me and taken control of me again.

August 17

WHAT A NIGHT! WHAT A NIGHT! AND YET IT SEEMS I SHOULD BE rejoicing. I read until one o'clock in the morning! Hermann Herestauss, Doctor of Philosophy and Theogony, wrote a history of the instances of all the invisible beings who exist alongside man or who are dreamed by us. He describes their origins, their worlds, their powers. But none of them resembles the one who is haunting me. You could say that ever since man was able to think, he could sense and fear some unknown creature, stronger than himself, his successor in this world; and feeling him nearby, yet unable to understand the nature of this master, in his terror he created all the fantastical race of supernatural beings, vague ghosts born of fear.

Having read until one o'clock in the morning, I sat down next to my window to feel the cool, calm wind against my face and refresh my mind in the darkness.

It felt so good; it was warm outside! How I would have enjoyed such a night in the past!

No moon. The stars glistened and shimmered far away in the dark sky. Who inhabits those worlds? What spirits, essences, animals, plants are living there, in the beyond? If there are thinking life forms in these distant universes, how much more do they know than we do? How much more are they capable of than us? What do they see that we have no knowledge of whatsoever? One day, as they are traveling through space, one of them will land on Earth in order to conquer it, just as in the past the Normans crossed the sea to enslave races of men who were weaker than them.

We are all so handicapped, so helpless, so ignorant, so unimportant on this speck of mud that spins around in a drop of water.

I fell asleep in the cool evening air while wondering about such things.

After sleeping for about forty minutes, I opened my eyes without moving a muscle, awakened by some strange, inexplicable, confused feeling. At first I saw nothing, then, suddenly, it seemed that a page of the book I had left open on my table had just turned over by itself. No gust of wind had entered through my window. I was surprised and waited. After about four minutes, I saw, I saw—yes, I saw with my own eyes—another page rise and fall down onto the one before it, as if some hand had been leafing through it. My armchair was empty, at least it looked empty; but I realized that he was there: he was sitting in my chair and reading. I leapt up in a rage, like a wild animal intent on ripping his master to shreds; I crossed my room to grab hold of him, pin him down, and kill him! . . . But before I could get there, my armchair tumbled backwards as if someone was running away from me . . . my table shook, my lamp wobbled and went out, and my window closed as if some evil-doer had been discovered and ran off into the night, slamming the door behind him.

So he had run away; he was afraid, afraid of me: *he* was afraid of *me!*

Well, then . . . that means that . . . tomorrow . . . or the day after . . . or some day, I could grab hold of him and crush him into the ground! Don't dogs sometimes bite and kill their masters?

August 18

I THOUGHT ABOUT IT ALL DAY LONG. OH, YES! I'LL OBEY HIM, FOL-
low his whims, fulfill all his desires, make myself humble, submissive,
cowardly. He is the stronger. But the day will come when . . .

August 19

I KNOW . . . I UNDERSTAND . . . I KNOW EVERYTHING! I HAVE JUST
read this in the *Revue du Monde Scientifique*:[5]

> A rather curious piece of news has been brought to our attention
> from Rio de Janeiro. A form of madness, an epidemic of hysteria
> comparable to the contagious madness that swept through Europe
> in the Middle Ages is currently rife in the province of São Paolo.
> Its terrified inhabitants are leaving their homes, deserting their vil-
> lages, abandoning their fields, claiming they are being followed,
> possessed, controlled like human cattle by invisible beings whose
> presence can be sensed, a kind of race of vampires who feed off
> their lives while they sleep, and who drink water and milk without
> appearing to touch any other type of food.
>
> Professor Don Pedro Henriquez, accompanied by several
> medical scientists, went to the province of São Paolo in order to
> study the origins and manifestations of this surprising madness on
> site, and to suggest what measures the Emperor should best take to
> return his demented people to a rational state of mind.

Ah! Ah! I remember it now: I remember that beautiful Brazilian three-
master that passed beneath my windows while gliding up the Seine. It was
last May 8. I thought it so superb, so white, so cheerful! The Being was
on it, coming from there, from São Paolo where its race was born! And he

---

5 *International Scientific Journal*, a fictional journal.

saw me! He saw my house that was also white; and he jumped off the boat onto the riverbank. Oh, my God!

Now I know, I can sense it. The rule of mankind is over.

He has come. He who is the embodiment of all the primeval terrors of innocent people in this world, He who is exorcised by anxious priests, He who is summoned by witches on dark nights but has not yet appeared, He whom the fleeting masters of this world fear in every monstrous or graceful form: gnomes, spirits, genies, fairies, elves. After the crude ideas of primitive terror, shrewder men have understood Him more clearly. Mesmer had imagined Him, and for the past ten years, doctors have already imagined and detailed the nature of His power even before He used it. They experimented with this new Lord's weapon: the domination of a mysterious will over a human soul that had been enslaved. They called it casting a spell, hypnotism, the power of suggestion . . . what can I know of it? I have watched them amuse themselves with this horrible force like foolish children! How wretched we are! How ill-fated is man! He has come, the . . . the—what does He call Himself?—the . . . I feel as if He is shouting out His name to me and I cannot hear it . . . the . . . yes . . . He is shouting it . . . I am listening but I cannot . . . say it again . . . Le Horla . . . Now I've heard it . . . Le Horla . . . that is who He is . . . Le Horla has come!

Ah! The vulture ate the dove; the wolf devoured the lamb; the lion killed the buffalo with its sharp horns; man killed the lion with his arrow, with his sword, with his gunpowder; but Le Horla will make of man what we have made of horses and cattle: will we belong to Him, become His servant and His food, solely by the power of His will. How wretched we are!

And yet, sometimes an animal revolts and kills whoever has tamed it . . . I too want to . . . I could . . . but first I must know Him, touch him, see Him! Scientists say that an animal's eye is different from ours and sees things differently . . . And my own eyes cannot make out this stranger who oppresses me.

Why? Oh! Now I remember the words of the monk at Mont Saint-Michel: "Do we ever see a hundred thousandth of what actually exists? Take the wind, for example, which is the greatest force of nature: it knocks men over, tears down buildings, uproots trees, lifts the sea to form mountains of water, destroys cliffs and forces ships onto the reefs; the wind kills, it whistles, it groans and howls, but have you ever seen it? Could you ever see it? And yet, it exists."

And I went on musing: my eyes are so weak, so imperfect, that when solid objects are as transparent as glass, I cannot even make them out! . . . It's as if a two-way mirror is blocking my path, throwing me around like a bird that gets into the room and crashes into the window, breaking his neck. Do a thousand other things trick him or make him lose his way? So there is nothing surprising about the fact that a bird cannot see a new object when light shines through it.

A new being! Why not? He was bound to come! Why would we be the final race? We cannot make Him out, just like all the others that came before us. It is because His nature is more perfect, His body more delicate and more subtle than ours, because ours is so weak, so awkwardly conceived, burdened with organs that are always tired, always straining as if they were overly complex; we live like plants and animals, existing, with great difficulty, on air, vegetation and meat, a bestial organism prone to illness, deformity, decay; we are short of breath, unstable, naïve and strange, ingeniously but badly designed, with a delicate yet crude construction, a rough sketch of a being with the potential to become intelligent and magnificent.

There are so few of us, so very few species in this world, from the oyster up to man. Why not yet another type of being once the time span has passed that separates the successive evolution of the various species?

Why not one more? Why not other trees and enormous flowers as well, flowers that are dazzling and spread their perfume across entire regions? Why not other elements apart from fire, air, earth and water?—There are only four of them, only four, these elements that nourish our living beings! What a shame! Why not forty, four hundred, four thousand! How feeble, petty and pitiful everything is! Given reluctantly, created quickly, crudely made! Ah! The elephant, the hippopotamus, such grace! The camel, such elegance!

But what about the butterfly, a flower that can fly, you might say. I dream of one that would be as big as a hundred universes, with wings whose shape, beauty, color and movement I cannot even begin to describe. But I can picture it . . . it goes from star to star, cooling them and filling the air with a light, rhythmic breeze as it passes! . . . And the people who live in those distant lands watch it go by, ecstatic with delight.

. . . .

What is wrong with me? It's Him, Him, Le Horla who is haunting me, making me think of such mad things! He is inside me. He is taking over my soul. I will kill Him!

August 19

I WILL KILL HIM! I HAVE SEEN HIM! YESTERDAY, I SAT DOWN AT MY table and pretended to be writing with great concentration. I knew very well that He would come and hover around me, quite close to me, so close that I might be able to touch Him, grab hold of Him. And then , . . then, I will have the strength of a desperate man: I will use my hands, my knees, my chest, my head, my teeth to strangle Him, crush Him, bite Him, tear Him apart.

And feeling every part of my body ready to pounce, I waited for Him.

I had lit my two lamps and the eight candles on my mantelpiece, as if I might be able to see Him in the bright light.

Opposite me was my bed, an old oak four-poster bed; to my right was the fireplace; to the left, I had carefully closed my door, after leaving it open for a long time, in order to draw Him in; behind me was a very tall wardrobe with a mirror that I used every day to shave and dress, where it was my habit to gaze at myself, from head to toe, every time I walked by it.

And so, I pretended to be writing, in order to trick Him, for He was also spying on me; and suddenly, I felt, I was certain, that He was reading over my shoulder, that He was there, almost touching my ear.

I sprang up, my fists clenched, and turned around so quickly that I nearly fell over. And then? . . . It was as bright as day inside the room and yet I did not see my reflection in the mirror! . . . It was empty, bright, deep, full of light! But my reflection was not there . . . and I was standing right opposite it!

I could see the clear glass from top to bottom. And I stared at it wild-eyed. I didn't dare take a step forward; I didn't dare make a move, and yet I could sense that He was there—He was there but He would escape my clutches once more, He whose invisible body had devoured my reflection.

I was so very afraid! Then suddenly, I gradually began to see myself in a mist, deep inside the mirror, in a fog as if through a layer of water; and it seemed as if this water glided from side to side, slowly, making my image clearer with every moment that passed. It was like the end of an eclipse. The thing that was hiding me did not appear to have any clearly defined shape, but a sort of opaque transparency that gradually grew more and more visible.

I could finally see myself clearly, just as I did every day when I looked at myself in that mirror.

I had seen Him! I could still feel the terror of that moment that made me continue to tremble.

August 20

HOW CAN I KILL HIM? I CAN'T EVEN GET HOLD OF HIM? POISON? But He will see me mix it with the water. And besides, will our poisons have any effect on his invisible body? No . . . no . . . of course they won't . . . So what can I do? What can I do?

August 21

I HAD AN IRONSMITH COME FROM ROUEN AND COMMISSIONED HIM to make me some iron shutters, the kind that certain private houses have in Paris, on the ground floor, out of fear they may be robbed. He will also make me a door of the same material. I came across as a coward but I couldn't care less!

. . . .

September 10

ROUEN, CONTINENTAL HOTEL. IT'S DONE . . . IT'S DONE . . . BUT IS he dead? My mind is in a spin over what I saw.

Yesterday, after the ironsmith had set the shutters and door in place, I left everything open until midnight, even though it was starting to get cold.

Suddenly, I sensed that He was there, and a feeling of joy, of mad joy ran through me. I got up slowly and paced back and forth for a long time, so He wouldn't guess anything. Then I casually took off my boots and put on my slippers.

Then I closed the iron shutters and walking calmly toward the door, I double-locked it. I then walked back over to the window, padlocked the shutter and put the key in my pocket.

Suddenly, I realized that He was becoming agitated close by me, that it was His turn to be afraid. He was commanding me to open the door for Him and I nearly gave in. But I didn't give in; leaning against the door, I opened it just a crack, just enough for me—and me alone—to get out. I slowly stepped backwards, and as I am very tall, my head nearly touched the top of the doorway. I was sure that He was unable to escape and I locked Him inside, alone, all alone, completely alone! What joy I felt! I had Him! Then I ran downstairs. I took the two lamps from my sitting room and spilled the oil over the carpet, over the furniture, over everything. Then I set it on fire and ran outside, after having double-locked the large front door.

Then I went and hid at the back of my garden, in a clump of bay trees. How long it took, how very long! Everything was dark, silent, still; not a breath of air, not a single star, mountains of clouds that you couldn't see but that weighed so heavily, so very heavily, on my soul.

I watched my house and waited. How long it took! I thought the fire had already gone out by itself, or that it had been put out by Him, when one of the large windows on the ground floor shattered under the force of the fire, and a flame, a great red and yellow flame, long, languid, climbed straight up the white walls, surrounding them right up to the roof. Light shimmered against the trees, the branches, in the leaves, and a shiver of fear ran through me! Birds woke up; a dog began to howl; it felt as if day were breaking! Two other windows shattered at that very moment and I could see that my entire house had been reduced to a terrifying inferno. But then a woman's cry, a horrible, shrill, heartrending cry was heard through the still night, and two garrets opened! I had forgotten about my servants! I could see their terrified faces as they waved their arms about! . . .

And so, frantic with horror, I started running toward the village shouting: "Help! Help! Fire! Fire!" I came across some people who were already on their way there and I went back with them to see what had happened.

By now, the house was nothing more than a magnificent but horrible funeral pyre, an enormous pyre that was lighting up the earth and burning men to death, the place where He was burning, He as well, my prisoner, the New Being, the new master, Le Horla!

Suddenly, the entire roof collapsed between the walls and a volcano of flames spurted up toward the sky. I could see the fireball through all the open windows of the house and I thought that He was in there, inside that furnace, dead . . .

Dead? Perhaps? . . . But what about His body? His body that light passed through . . . was it not impossible to destroy it in ways that kill our bodies?

What if He weren't dead? . . . Perhaps only time had an effect on this Terrifying, Invisible Being. Why would He have a transparent body, an unknowable body, a body made of pure Essence if He had to fear pain, wounds, illnesses, untimely death just as we did?

Untimely death? All human horror springs from this idea! After man, Le Horla. After we who could die on any day, at any hour, at any moment, through any accident, after us has come the Being who need not die until it is His time, at exactly the right day, hour, minute, because He has reached the end of His existence!

No . . . no . . . there is no doubt, no shadow of a doubt . . . He is not dead . . . And so . . . so . . . it is up to me; I will have to kill myself! . . .

GUY DE MAUPASSANT

A Chronology*

1850 AUGUST 5: birth of Henri René Albert Guy de Maupassant, the first child of Gustave de Maupassant and Laure Le Poittevin.

1851–54 The Maupassants live in several different places in Normandy before moving into the Château de Grainville-Ymauville near Le Havre. This remains his home for the first ten years of his life.

1856 Birth of Guy's brother, Hervé.

1861 His parents experience marital problems. Guy's father remains in Paris. Laure and her two sons move to Etretat.

1862 Legal separation of Guy's parents, although divorce was not legalized until 1884.

1863–68 Guy is expelled from a Catholic school in Yvetot for his disrespectful attitude toward religion, then sent as a boarder to the Lycée Impérial in Rouen. He gets to know Louis Bouilhet, the writer, city librarian, and close friend of Gustave Flaubert. Both men encourage and advise him in his writing, initially of poetry.

---

* Reproduced with the kind permission of Professor Robert Lethbridge.

1869   The death of Louis Bouilhet leaves Flaubert as his mentor. Guy enrolls as a law student in Paris.

1870   JULY 15: France declares war on Germany, the start of the Franco-Prussian War. Maupassant is drafted and works in the military administration in Rouen.

   SEPTEMBER: the French are defeated at Sedan. Maupassant joins the army's retreat to Le Havre.

1871   JANUARY 28: Armistice signed. A few months later, Guy leaves the army to continue his law studies.

1872   Applies unsuccessfully to join the Ministry for the Navy as a civil servant, but is offered an unpaid position pending a vacancy. He becomes a frequent weekend visitor to Argenteuil, on the Seine, enjoying boating and entertaining women.

1873   Finally appointed to a position at the Ministry.

1875   FEBRUARY: his first short story, *La Main d'écorché* (*The Skinned Hand*), is published under the pseudonym Joseph Prunier, and some poetry under another pseudonym: Guy de Valmont.

1876   Maupassant becomes increasingly involved in Parisian literary life with Flaubert, Mallarmé, Zola, Daudet, Huysmans, Edmond de Goncourt, Turgenev, and others. His first critical article on Flaubert is published.

1877   Maupassant becomes aware of having contracted syphilis (probably in 1875) and suffers from hair loss, headaches, eye problems, and stomach pains.

1880   Publication of the collection *Les Soirées de Médan*, including *Boule de suif*.

   MAY 8: Flaubert dies suddenly.

1881   Publication of *La Maison Tellier* (*The House of Tellier*), the first of Maupassant's many collections of short stories.

1883   *Une Vie* published; Maupassant also produces some sixty short stories.

1884   Starts work on *Bel-Ami*, his second novel, while another fifty short stories are published this year.

1885   *Bel-Ami* published. For the first time, critics recognize Maupassant as a major writer.

1886   Maupassant works on the definitive version of *Le Horla*.

1887   *Mont-Oriol* published. He spends the summer working on *Pierre et Jean*. Goes to Antibes in September, much concerned by signs of his brother's mental illness. At the end of the year, Guy takes Hervé to spend a month in an asylum near Paris.

1888   Publication of *Pierre et Jean*, his fourth novel, and *Sur l'eau* (*On the Water*), his second travel book.

1889   Publication of *Fort comme la mort* (*Strong as Death*), his fifth novel.

          AUGUST: he arranges for his brother to be committed to an asylum near Lyon.

          NOVEMBER 13: death of Hervé, Maupassant at his bedside.

1890   Publication of *La Vie errante* (*The Life of a Wanderer*), his third travel book. His final completed novel, *Notre cœur* (*Our Heart*), is published.

          Maupassant's long-standing health problems have now become increasingly acute.

1891   Contemporaries note the writer's obvious physical and mental disintegration, while he desperately ranges through a succession of doctors, thermal spas, and medical treatments.

1892   After visiting his mother on New Year's Day, Maupassant
         returns to his home in Cannes and slits his throat, either
         intentionally or in a state of delirium. A week later, he is taken
         (straitjacketed) to Paris and interned in Dr. Blanche's clinic.
         He has clearly gone insane. Modern medical opinion leaves
         little doubt that the symptoms of the diagnosed "general
         paralysis" are those of the tertiary stage of syphilis.

1893   JULY 6: death of Maupassant, at age forty-two.

ABOUT THE AUTHOR

Born in Normandy, Guy de Maupassant (1850–1893) and his younger brother, Hervé, were raised by their mother, Laure Le Poittevin, after she and his father separated in 1861. After being expelled from a Catholic school for his disrespectful attitude toward religion, Guy was sent to a boarding school in Rouen. There he met the writer Louis Bouilhet, a close friend of Gustave Flaubert. Both writers mentored Maupassant, and Flaubert, already at the height of his fame when the young Maupassant met him, would have the greatest influence on his writing.

In 1869, Maupassant enrolled as a law student in Paris, but a year later, at the start of the Franco-Prussian War, he was drafted to work in the military administration in Rouen. After a brutal French defeat at the Battle of Sedan, Maupassant witnessed the army's retreat to Le Havre firsthand. The stories in "Tales of War," this volume's second section, reflect Maupassant's own feelings about the German victors, and ultimately contributed to his profound view of the absurdity of war and the essential bleakness of the human condition.

After France's humiliating defeat in 1871, Maupassant left the army to continue his law studies and was appointed to a position at the Ministry for the Navy. However, thanks to the intercession of Flaubert, he became increasingly involved in Parisian literary life, meeting some of the most important writers of his day: Mallarmé, Zola, Daudet, Huysmans, Edmond de Goncourt, as well as many others. His first critical article on Flaubert was published in 1876, followed by a collection of stories, *Les Soirées de Médan*, which included *Boule de suif*, one of his best-known novellas. Critics finally recognized Maupassant as a major writer in 1885 with the publication of his novel *Bel-Ami*. During his brief career, Maupassant was extremely prolific, writing over 300 short stories and six novels, many of them relating to madness and the macabre, themes that are explored in this volume's third section, "Tales of the Supernatural." Largely written near the end of his short life, these stories are thought to be influenced by his own debilitating struggle with mental illness in the last decade of his life.

Maupassant suffered from the symptoms of advanced syphilis, including a decline into madness that led him to attempt suicide on New Year's Day in 1892. A week later, he was interned in Dr. Blanche's clinic in Paris. He died there the following year at the age of 42.

ABOUT THE TRANSLATOR

Sandra Smith was born and raised in New York City. As an undergraduate, she spent one year studying at the Sorbonne and fell in love with Paris. Immediately after finishing her B.A., she was accepted to do a Master's Degree at New York University, in conjunction with the Sorbonne, and so lived in Paris for another year. She then moved to England, where she began teaching 20th-Century French Literature, Modern French Drama and Translation at Cambridge University.

Sandra Smith is the translator of all twelve novels by Irène Némirovsky available in English, as well as a new translation of Camus's *L'Etranger* (*The Outsider*, Penguin UK, 2012).

Smith's translation of Némirovsky's *Suite Française* won the French-American Foundation and Florence Gould Foundation Translation Prize for fiction, as well as the PEN Book-of-the-Month Club Translation Prize, the first time that one book has ever won both prizes in the same year. *Suite Française* also won the Independent British Booksellers Book of the Year prize and was voted Book of the Year by *The Times of London*.

Smith's translation of *The Necklace and Other Stories* by Guy de Maupassant was inspired by her belief that Maupassant was a master of the short story genre who should be discovered by English-speaking readers.

After ten years as a Fellow of Robinson College, Cambridge, Smith has returned to the United States and now lives in New York.

TRANSLATOR'S ACKNOWLEDGMENTS

My sincere gratitude for their advice and encouragement goes to my editor, Robert Weil, Professor Robert Lethbridge, Patricia Freestone, Philippe Savary, my husband Peter and son Harrison, and my colleagues at Robinson College, Cambridge.